SAUL *and* PATSY

Also by Charles Baxter

SAUL *and* PATSY

Charles Baxter

Pantheon Books, New York

All rights reserved under International and Pan-American Copyright Conventions. Published in the United States by Pantheon Books, a division of Random House, Inc., New York, and simultaneously in Canada by Random House of Canada Limited, Toronto.

Pantheon Books and colophon are registered trademarks of Random House, Inc.

Grateful acknowledgment is made to W. W. Norton & Company, Inc., for permission to reprint "Saul and Patsy Are Pregnant" from *A Relative Stranger* by Charles Baxter. Copyright © 1990 by Charles Baxter. Reprinted by permission of W. W. Norton & Company, Inc.

Portions of this work have been previously published as: "Saul and Patsy Are Getting Comfortable in Michigan" in *Through the Safety Net: Stories* (Vintage Books, 1985); "Saul and Patsy Are in Labor" in *Believers* (Pantheon Books, 1997).

Library of Congress-in-Publication Data
Baxter, Charles, 1947–
    Saul and Patsy / Charles Baxter.
        p.   cm.
    ISBN 0-375-41029-5
    1. High school teachers—Fiction.   2. Married people—Fiction.
  3. Michigan—Fiction.   I. Title.

PS3552.A854S28 2003   813'.54—dc21   2003042027

www.pantheonbooks.com

Book design by Johanna S. Roebas

Printed in the United States of America
First Edition

9 8 7 6 5 4 3 2 1

For Lewis Baxter and John Thayer Baxter

I very much wanted to manage in that first movement without using trombones, and tried to. . . .

But . . . I must confess to you that I am a profoundly melancholy man, that black wings flap incessantly above us . . . no—I must have my trombones.

—JOHANNES BRAHMS,
in a letter to Vincenz Lachner

Michigan seems like a dream to me now.

—PAUL SIMON, *"America"*

Part One

One

About a year after they had rented the farmhouse with loose brown aluminum siding on Whitefeather Road, Saul began glaring out the west window after dinner into the unappeasable darkness that pressed against the glass, as if he were angry at the flat uncultivated farmland for being farmland instead of glass and cement. "No sane Jew," he said, "ever lived on a dirt road." Patsy reminded him of Poland, Russia, and the nineteenth century. Then she pointed down at the Scrabble board and told him to play. To spite her, he spelled out "axiom" over a triple-word score, for forty-two points. "That was totally different," Saul said, shaking his head. "Completely different. That was when everyone but the landowners lived on dirt roads. It was a democracy of dirt roads, the nineteenth century." Patsy was clutching her bottle of root beer with one hand and arranging the letters on her slate with the other. Her legs were crossed in the chair, and the bottle was positioned against the instep of her right foot. She looked up at him and smiled. He couldn't help it. He smiled back. She was so beautiful, she could make him copy her gestures without his meaning to.

"We're not landowners either," she said. "We're renters. Oh, I forgot to tell you. I had to go into the basement this afternoon for a screwdriver, and I noticed that there's a mouse in the trap downstairs."

"Is it dead?"

"Oh, sure." She nodded. "It looks *quite* dead. You know—smashed back, slightly open mouth, and bulging eyes. I'll spare you the full description. You'll see the whole scene soon enough when you go down there—I didn't want to throw it out myself."

"I did the dishes," Saul complained, sitting up, running his fingers through his hair.

"I *could* throw the mouse out," Patsy said, leaning back, taking a swig and giving him another obliging smile. "I can now, and I could have then." She straightened her leg and placed her foot against his ankle, and she raised her eyebrows as an ironic courtesy. "But the truth is, those little critters give me the whimwhams, and I'd rather not. I'd rather you did it, Saul. Just, you know, as a favor to me. You do it, my man, and there might be something in it for you."

"What? What would be in it for me?"

"The trick in negotiations," she said, "is not to make promises too soon. Why don't you just do it as a favor to me? A sort of little gratuitous act of kindness? One of them guys?"

He stood up, shaking the letters on the Scrabble board, and clomped in his white socks to the kitchen, where the flashlight was stuck to the refrigerator with a magnet that was so weak that the flashlight kept sliding down to the floor, though it was only halfway there now. "I didn't say you had to do it *instantly*," Patsy shouted. "This very minute. You could wait until the game is over."

"Well, if you didn't want it thrown out now, you shouldn't have mentioned it. Besides, I can't concentrate," Saul said, half to himself as he flicked the flashlight off and on, "thinking about that dead mouse." The batteries were so low that the light from the bulb was foggy and brown. He opened the door to the basement, fanning stale air, and stared down the steps into the darkness that smelled of must and heating oil. He didn't like the basement. At night, in bed, he thought he heard crying from down there, ancestral accusations. "You'll do anything to beat me at Scrabble," Saul said aloud to himself. "This is gamesmanship, honey. Don't tell me otherwise."

He snapped on the wall switch, and the shadows of the steps saw-toothed themselves in front of him. "I *really* don't like this," he said, walking down the stairs, a sliver from the banister leaping into the heel of his hand. "This is not my idea of a good time." He heard Patsy say something consoling and inaudible.

On his left were the wooden shelves once meant for storing preserves. On these shelves, mason jars, empty and gathering dust, now lined up unevenly. Saul and Patsy's landlord, Mr. Munger, a retired farmer and unsuccessful freelance preacher who had a fitful temper, had thrown their lids together into an angry heap on a lower shelf. The washtubs were on Saul's right, and in front of him, four feet away, was the sprung mousetrap. The mouse had been pressed flat by the trap, and its tiny yellow incisors were showing at the sides of its mouth, just as Patsy had said.

He loved her, but she could be manipulative when it came to getting him to do household chores that she didn't want to do. Maybe, out of his sight, she was exchanging her letter tiles.

Saul grunted, loosened the spring, and picked up the mouse by the tail, which felt like cold rubber. His fingers brushed against the animal's downy fur, soft as milkweed pods. Being, on a miniature scale, had once been inhabited there. With his other hand he held the flashlight. He heard other mice scratching in the basement corners. Why kill mice if there were always going to be more of them? After climbing the stairs and opening the back door, he set the flashlight down: the cool air and the darkness made his flesh prickle. Still holding the tiny pilgrim, he took four steps into the backyard. Feeling a scant moment of desolation, nothing more than a breeze of feeling, he threw the mouse toward the field, its body arcing over the tiny figure on the horizon of a distant radio transmitting tower, one pulsing red light at its tip. Saul took a deep breath. The blankness of the midwestern landscape excited him. There was a sensual loneliness here that belonged to him now, that was truly his. He thought that fate had perhaps turned him into one of those characters in Russian literature abandoned to haphazard fortune and solitude on the steppes.

Nothing out there seemed friendly except the lights on the horizon, and they were too far away to be of any help.

He walked into the living room, where Patsy was wrapped in a blanket. "Good news and bad news," Saul said, tilting his head. "The good news is that I threw out the mouse. The bad news is that it, she, was pregnant. Maybe that's good news. You decide. By the way, I see that you've wrapped yourself in a blanket. Now why is that? Too cold in here?"

She had dimmed the light, turning the three-way bulb to its lowest wattage. She wasn't sitting in the chair anymore. She was lying on the sofa, the root beer nowhere in sight. With a grand gesture she parted the blanket: she had taken off her clothes except for her underwear, and just above her breasts she had placed six Scrabble letters:

HI
SAUL

"Nine points," he said, settling himself down next to her, breathing in her odor, a clear celery-like smell, although tonight it seemed to be mixed with ether. He picked the letters off her skin with his teeth and one by one gently spat them down onto the rug.

"I guess it's good news," Patsy said, "that we don't have all those baby mice in a mouse nursery down there." She kissed him.

"Um," Saul said. "This was what was in it for me?"

"Plain old married love," Patsy said, helping him take his jeans off. Then she lifted up her pelvis as he removed her underwear. "Plain old married love is only what it is."

He moved down next to her as she unbuttoned his shirt. He said, "Sometimes I think you'll go to any length to avoid losing in Scrabble. I think it's a character weakness on your part. Neurotic rigidity. David Shapiro talks about this in his book on neurotic styles. Check it out. It's a loser's trick. I spelled out 'axiom' and you saw the end of your possibilities."

"It's not a trick," she said, absentmindedly stroking his thighs, while he pointed his index finger and pretended to write with it across her breasts and then down across her abdomen. "Hey," she said, "what're you writing with that finger?"

"'I love Patsy,'" he said. "I'm not writing it, I'm *printing* it."

6

"Why?"

"Make it more readable."

" 'I love Patsy,' " she said. "Seventeen points."

"Sixteen. And it depends where it's placed."

"A V is worth four." His eyes were closed. With one hand he was caressing her right breast, and with the other he wrote other words with imaginative lettering across her hips. "I don't remember making love in this room before. Especially not with the shades up." She stretched to kiss his face and to tease her tongue briefly into his mouth. Then she trailed her finger across his back. "I can do that, too." She traced the letters with her finger just under his shoulders.

"That was an I," Saul said.

"Yes."

" 'I love Saul'?" he asked. "Is that what you're writing?"

"You're so conceited. So self-centered."

"The curtains are parted," he said. "The neighbors will see."

"We don't have neighbors. This is the rural middle of American nowhere. Always has been."

"People will drive by on Whitefeather Road and see us having sex on the sofa." He waited. "They might be shocked."

"We're married," she said.

He laughed. "You're wicked, Patsy."

"You keep using old adjectives," she said, sliding her hands up the sides of his chest. "Old blah-blah adjectives that no one uses anymore. That's a habit you should swear off. *Let* those people watch us. They might learn something." She slithered down to kiss the scar on his knee, then moved up. "The only thing I mind about sex," she said after another minute, "and I've said this before, is that it cuts down on the small talk."

"We talk a lot," Saul said, positioning himself next to her and finally entering her. He grunted, then said, "I think we talk more than most people. No, I'm sure of it. We've always jabbered. Most people don't talk this much, men especially." He was making genial moves inside her. "Of course, it's hard to tell. I mean, who does surveys?"

"Oh, Saul," she said. "You know, I'm glad I know you. Out here in the wilds a girl needs a pal, she really does. You're my pal, Saul. You are. I love you."

"It's true," he said. "We're buddies. Bosom buddies." He kissed a breast. On an impulse, he twisted slightly so that he could reach over to the card table behind him and scoop up a handful of Scrabble letters from the playing board.

"Aren't you too cute. What're you doing?" she asked.

"I'm going to baptize you," he said, slowly dropping the tiled letters on her face and shoulders and breasts. "I'm going to baptize you in The Word."

"God," she said, as a P and an E fell into her hair, "to think that I wanted to distract you with a mouse caught in a trap."

Saul had been hired eighteen months earlier to teach American history, journalism, and speech in the Five Oaks High School. In its general appearance and in its particulars, however, Five Oaks, Michigan, was not what he and Patsy had had in mind. They had planned to settle down in Boston, or, in the worst-case scenario, the north side of Chicago, a good place for a young married couple. They had been working at office jobs in Evanston at the time after graduating from Northwestern, and one day, driving home along the lake, Saul seemed to have a seizure of frustration. He began to shout about the supervision and the random surveillance, how he couldn't breathe or open his office window. "Budget projections for a bus company," he said, "is no longer meaningful work, and it turns out that it never *was*." He rambled on about getting certified for secondary school because he needed to contribute to what he called "the great project of undoing the dumbness that's been done."

"Saul," Patsy said, sitting on the passenger side and working at a week-old Sunday crossword, "you're underlining your words again."

"This country is falling into the hands of the *rich* and *stupid*," Saul grumbled, underlining his words while waving his right hand in an all-purpose gesture at the windshield. "The plutocrats are taking over and keeping everybody ignorant about how things are. The conspiracy of the inane starts in the schools, but it gets big results in business. Everywhere I've looked lately I've seen a cynic in a position of *tremendous responsibility.* We're being undermined by rich cynics and common people who have been, forcibly, made stupid. This has got to stop. I've got to be a teacher. It's a political necessity. At least for a few years.'"

"There's *lots* of stupidity out there, Saul," Patsy said, glancing up at a stoplight. "A big supply. You think you're going to clear it away? That's your plan?" She waited. "The light just turned green. Pay attention to the road, please." She smiled. "'Drive, he said.'" She reached out and touched him on the cheek. "'For christ's sake, look out where you're going.'"

"Don't quote Creeley at me. I'm the big man for the job," Saul said. "This country needs me."

"Well, of course." She scratched her hair. "Write an editorial, why don't you? Nine letters for 'acidic.' First letter is V and the fourth one is R."

"'Vitriolic,'" Saul said. "And you could get certified, too. Or you could insinuate yourself into a bureaucracy and reorganize it. You're so lovable, everybody just does what you ask them to do, without thinking. Boston is full of deadwood. God knows, you can reorganize deadwood. It's been proved." He waited. "You could do whatever you wanted to, if we moved out of here. What *do* you want to do, Patsy?"

"Finger-exercise composer," Patsy said. "Six letters, last letter Y and first letter C."

"Czerny."

"Boston, huh?" She gazed at the sky. "It's sort of hard to get teaching jobs there, isn't it? Oh, and, by the way, what am I going to do if you start teaching? I don't want to teach."

"That's what I was just asking you. You're not listening to me. What do you want to do?" Patsy had had half-a-dozen majors before she settled for a double major in dance-performance and English.

"I don't know," she said. "I don't know what I want to do." She studied the sky. "I'd like to go work in a bank, actually." Another pause. "In the mortgage department."

The statement was so unlike her, Saul smiled. One of her dry, shifty, ironical asides whose subtext you had to go in search of. Then he realized that perhaps she meant it, and he studied her face for aspersions, but Patsy, who was vehement about privacy issues, did not give herself away.

Saul had found, in his landlord's shed, a ladder that was long enough to get him up to the roof of the house on Whitefeather Road. He'd been exploring Mr. Munger's shed while Patsy was out getting groceries, and when she returned, he was sitting on the south peak with his legs dangling over the edge. Patsy put the grocery bags down on the driveway. "I won't scream," she said. "But I do have some questions."

"Good," he said.

"Saul, be truthful. Why are you sitting on the roof of our house?"

"Thinking," he shouted. "Looking at the horizon." He smiled down at her. "At the view. You are so beautiful. You're the only beautiful sight here to see."

"Thanks, but there's no view," she said. "Including me. I'm not a view. Nothing to see except what's here. You need hills for variety, and we don't have that."

"Well, I was just hoping for a little variety—you know, a *break*. Maybe a show of some sort. I thought maybe I'd see *something*. An incline, a knoll, a mound would all have been fine. I'm not asking for an alp."

"Well, you won't get one. You won't get one of any of them. No hills, honey. Remember? We agreed. No hills out here. Just drainage ditches. Come down from the roof, Saul, before you fall and kill yourself."

"Patsy," he asked, "how'd we end up here?"

"Times were hard," she said, quoting the Wizard of Oz, "so we took the job." She watched him. "That is, *you* took the job. Remember? It was the stupid crusade. *Against* stupidity, I mean. It was all your idea. I came along for the ride." She gazed at him with a deliberately cool expression. "First I come along for the ride, and then you do."

"Oh, right. Look at this," he said despairingly, pointing at the land around their house. "You know, I think we made a terrible mistake, but I'm not blaming anybody. Including myself. All I see up here is dirt roads and farmers reading *The Protocols of the Learned Elders of Zion*."

"Saul," she said, "they watch television now. They listen to police scanners. Also, it's too early in your stay here for paranoia. They don't have opinions about Jews, least of all you. Please come down. I've got to take those groceries in, and I could use your help. And please don't break your neck. I'd have to supply more of the backbone for both of us."

"It's not Boston," he said, edging toward the ladder. "And it's not Chicago. It's not Omaha. It's this other thing. My brother warned me about this, and even my *mother* warned me. It's this place smack out in the middle of nowhere, and now it has us in its grip." One of the shingles loosened and slid to the gutter. The ladder trembled as he began to make his way down. "It's scary up there, honey. It's a view for adults. Not for kids. Kids couldn't handle it." He looked straight into her eyes.

"I hope—" she said, pausing.

"That you don't go nuts out here? Me too. Me too."

"Why should I go nuts?" she asked. "I like it here. Would you please help me with those groceries?"

Rung by rung he lowered himself and took the remaining grocery bags out of the car in a double embrace. He kept his eyes on Patsy as she carried her two bags toward the back door before propping them against the wall in order to free one hand to turn the doorknob. The house was never locked; there was no one to lock it against. Saul admired her physical agility as she went inside, and in any case rarely found fault with her. He loved his wife profoundly; it had become the theme to his life, his antidote to everything else. Sometimes, just watching her carrying in the groceries or making dinner, he thought his heart would break out of sheer happiness in her presence. He believed that nothing else in his life would equal his love for Patsy. Still, he thought she was being a little smug about how much she liked it here. She could be snobby about her populism.

Their nearest neighbor, Mrs. O'Neill, looked so much like Thelma Ritter in *Rear Window* that Saul and Patsy smirked at each other when she introduced herself at their door one Friday afternoon, peering inside as she asked them for a bottle of molasses that she might borrow for a batch of her cookies. Mrs. O'Neill's curiosity about them was greedy but harmless, Saul thought. It was curiosity bred out of loneliness. As soon as Patsy found the bottle, Mrs. O'Neill invited them over to sample the cookies she had already made, and those that she would make with the molasses she was borrowing. Saul couldn't decide whether Mrs. O'Neill's nosiness was part of the community's nosiness, or whether she was just nosy for herself alone. When Saul and Patsy pulled into her driveway, her garage door began to go up, even though Mrs. O'Neill had arrived before they had and her car was already inside. An iron coach-and-horse weathervane stood on an iron stalk atop the garage's cupola. Mrs. O'Neill stood near the geranium-surrounded flagpole, holding on to a push-button signal box, her eyes squinched.

"I'm garage-poor," she said, pressing the button again to make the door go down. "But I never could resist a toy." She offered the garage-door opener to Saul, who pressed the button. The door began to open again. "I said to myself, well, I need the gadget because I'm a single lady out here—the safety feature—but even that doesn't explain the curtains." Mrs. O'Neill's garage had windows at the sides, with lace curtains. "I spent hours on those curtains. Imagine!" She gave out a self-deprecatory little laugh. "Curtains for a garage!"

"A good garage is important," Patsy said, and immediately Saul smiled.

"That's exactly it," Mrs. O'Neill said, picking a bug off Patsy's shoulder. "I'll tell you what it was, since you'll discover it soon enough. A project. I needed a project. Making curtains kept me awake during the daylight hours. Now you, Saul, you trot inside that garage and look at that gizmo in case you want to build one yourself, while Patsy and I go inside and have a few moments of girl-talk in the kitchen."

Mrs. O'Neill grabbed Patsy's arm and pulled her toward the back door of the house.

Saul walked in a lackadaisical fashion toward Mrs. O'Neill's sheltered and curtained Buick, feeling that, as an adult, he need not follow instructions from a character like her. At least, he did not need to follow them to the letter. A steady wind from the unplowed fields to the south blew into the garage. The interior smelled of raw lumber and fresh paint, along with the fainter but more dense odor of overheated electrical wiring. Saul looked up—as instructed—at Mrs. O'Neill's new garage-door opener. Unmechanical to a fault, he was unable to guess what structural-dynamic principles were involved in lifting a garage door up a set of tracks. With his head tilted back, he saw the company name on the side of the motor. He felt suddenly dizzy. He inhaled quickly and leaned his arm against Mrs. O'Neill's car. He glanced out through the door and saw his own car, and then, beyond it, the horizon line of the Saginaw Valley, the semi-skyline of Five Oaks over there in the distance, and gold-brown topsoil whipped and scattered in spirals. He sat down on the bumper and put his head in his hands.

What was he doing here? What was he doing anywhere?

From the house came the sound of singing: Mrs. O'Neill's voice— Patsy didn't sing—a choir-loft soprano, a thin Irish upper register, without resonance or depth but as piercing as a factory whistle. Saul listened, the skin on the back of his neck slowly beginning to prickle. *"Mi chiamano Mimi,"* she was singing, *"il perchè non so. Sola, mi fo il pranzo da me stesa."* She sang half the aria, the sound careening out of the house and dispersing in the yard. Saul felt his own mouth opening. A bird fluttered into the garage, changed course in an instant, and flew out, alighting at the top of Mrs. O'Neill's flagpole. Saul wanted the garage door shut. He pressed the button. When he opened the door a minute later, Patsy was standing in front of it on the driveway, a plate of cookies in her hand.

"Aren't you funny," she said.

"She sings." They looked at each other. "Where is she?"

"Yes, she sings. Still in the house. I noticed she had some opera records, and she said that she and her late lamented husband Earl used to listen to the Texaco broadcasts. She sings in church, as you can imagine."

"Yeah, I guessed."

"Anyway, she has all these records and CDs and she managed to learn some of the words. That was a demo she gave me. Want some of these cookies?"

"Of course. Dumb question." He reached out and grabbed four off the plate. "I eat cookies while I'm deciding whether I'm going to eat any cookies."

"She had some uncertainties about you."

"About me? Uncertainties?"

"That's why she wanted you to inspect her garage."

"Oh."

"She thought it was safe to ask me. Woman to woman."

"What sort of questions did she have?"

"Oh, friendly questions, I think, or at least you could assume they were friendly."

"Such as?"

"Does Saul eat cookies? Or is that against his religion?"

"Do Jews eat cookies."

"That's right. 'Does he go to a temple?' 'Does he mind living here among us?' She asked if we were rich. She asked if I was one of you." Patsy bit into a cookie and wiped the sweat off her forehead with the back of her hand.

"What'd you tell her?"

"I said I was once an Episcopalian, sort of, but now I was your wife."

"And what did she say to that?"

"She said she was glad that you liked cookies."

"There she is."

Patsy turned around as Mrs. O'Neill leaned out of the back door to wave them both inside. "I won't sing anymore," she shouted. "You two lovebirds can come in now. It's safe."

Through the summer they visited Mrs. O'Neill every two weeks for Sunday-afternoon picnics in the shade of her maple tree. Patsy found a Tuesday-Thursday-Saturday job as a bank teller, a job that required very little training. They played Scrabble and Jeopardy, Trivial Pursuit and chess, and they listened to all their records and CDs at least twice. Patsy suggested that they travel north to explore the Upper Peninsula, but Saul said that travel was dangerous in those locales. When Patsy asked what dangers he was possibly talking about, he said that of course the Department of Natural Resources had kept the problem under wraps but that he, Saul, knew . . . things. She could not budge him. He just didn't want to go anywhere.

They had an oddball marriage, and they both knew it. Their love for each other had created a magic circle around themselves that outsiders could not penetrate. No one who had ever met them knew what made the two of them tick; the whole arrangement looked mildly fraudulent, a Hallmark Card sort of thing. Saul's mother, Delia, had had an unremarkable marriage and as a still-youthful widow could be gamely witty on the subject of matrimony. Her opinion was that marriage was a practical economic arrangement demanded by the raising of children. In her view, Saul was a fanatical husband, close to unpresentable when he was around Patsy. He should recognize this devotedness of his as a social problem. People who stay in that kind of love once they're married are a burden to others, Saul's mother intimated. They should learn to tone themselves down. They don't mean to show off, but the show-offing happens anyway with the gestures and the endearments and the icky glances. In this regard, Saul and Patsy also perplexed their other relatives and friends, who sometimes wanted to know their secret and at other times just wanted to get away from them, quickly.

Because he loved Patsy so much, Saul was constantly disappointed with the rest of the world. It didn't measure up. Having moved to Five Oaks, mingling with the Cossacks, Saul could feel his disappointment beginning to fester. Why couldn't the world be more like Patsy? The rest of the world—especially where they had found themselves, here in the Midwest—presented itself as both bland and coarse. Intelligence and attention were wasted on it, he thought. It occurred to him sometimes that Patsy did not want to be loved the way he was loving her, that he was bedeviling her, but he did his best to put that thought out of his mind.

With all the time they had before school began, Saul and Patsy made love frequently as an antidote to their boredom, Patsy having decided that they should try it in every room in the house. One afternoon late in the month they spread out a blanket in the backyard, out of sight of the road, and worked up what Saul called love sweat. Patsy claimed she had never made love outdoors before and said she liked it, it was like going to the midway at the state fair, except for the grass on her bare back—they had crawled away from the blanket. She worried about ants, for which she had a repugnance. She said she liked looking into the sky and thought it would be neat to gaze at a cloud while coming. They waited for the perfect cloud, and then Saul watched her as she came. True to her word, she kept her eyes wide open, focused, on the distance.

Two

Saul having his hair cut: Five Oaks's north-side barbershop contained four chairs, a black-and-white television set on a wheeled table, a set of old magazines, and one barber with a permanently downcast expression. An antique barber pole twirled listlessly outside the front door. The barbershop looked more like a bookie joint than a genuine barbershop. When Saul sat down in the chair, the barber, whose name was Harold, tucked his cover cloth under Saul's collar and whistled between his teeth. "Don't see hair like yours much around here," he said. "It's almost kinky, wouldn't you say?" The barber looked young but acted old.

Saul said yes, it was almost kinky, and what he basically wanted was a trim.

The barber set to work, sneaking looks at *Days of Our Lives*, which appeared in a pointillist quilt of snow and interference on the television set. Saul closed his eyes but opened them five minutes later, feeling the barber's hand resting peacefully on his shoulder, the scissors motionless in his hair. "Say," Saul said, nudging the barber's stomach with his elbow. "Are we awake here? Harold? Hello?"

The barber inhaled, exhaled, snorted, and said sure, of course he was awake. The scissors started up again, their tips scraping Saul's scalp. "Could be I did doze off there a minute," the barber said. "But it's only the third . . . no, fourth time I've ever done that in this particular shop. I can sleep standing up, you see. Learned it in the army. Like a horse. The truth is, I have my troubles. I have woman trouble. It keeps me up part of the night, thinking about it. The soaps usually keep me awake. Are you from around here? We don't see hair like yours too much in this town. It's hard to cut."

"We just moved here," Saul said, to explain.

"From New York City, I'll bet," the barber, Harold, said. "They see hair like yours a lot in New York City, I hear." He shook his head, as if to shake off his dreams. "But I imagine they have insomnia there, too. By the way, do you ever play basketball?"

Once classes at the high school had started, Saul's route took him down Whitefeather Road for two miles before he turned left onto County Road E. On County Road E he pressed the car's cruise-control button and removed his foot from the accelerator for the six-mile straightaway. There were no curves to the road; there never had been. With his foot off the accelerator, he ate his breakfast of Patsy's muffins washed down with low-caffeine cola while he shaved with his electric razor and listened to the car's tape deck, his early-morning music friend, Thelonious Monk, whose attitude toward daylight was offhand, smart, and antirural.

Three miles down County Road E and half a mile before it intersected with Bailey–Fraser Road was the morning's bad news, standing on two legs on an average of three days a week. This bad news wore a hat and a jacket, sported gray socks and thick glasses—on some days he looked like the barber's brother—and he stared at Saul with a mean, hateful expression.

The first few times Saul passed him, he waved. Saul didn't expect a counterwave, and he didn't get it. Like a sentry, the man stood glaring, an unwobbling pivot, his arms down at his sides. At last, in October, Saul slowed down on a Tuesday, and on the next day he stopped. Saul leaned out and said, "You want to say hello? Here's your opportunity. The name's Saul. Howdy."

His greeting was returned with a blank look. Slowly, carefully, Saul lifted the finger to him and then hit the accelerator.

Saul to Patsy at dinner: "There's this ghoul standing in his yard every morning giving me the Big Stare, and he's got this hat *nailed* to his skull, and what I think is, he's on to me, the schmuck hates Jews. Have I mentioned him? I have? He wants me out. One of these days he's going to hoist a rifle and get me between the eyes."

"You're paranoid." They were in the dining room and had been listening to Nielsen's *Four Temperaments* Symphony, the anger movement. Choler spilled out of the speakers. It was not dinner music but an antidote to the rest of the day. Nielsen or Mingus, that was the choice.

"I've got a right to be paranoid," Saul said angrily. "History encourages it. Plus, the man hates me. And for no reason: he doesn't know me. I bet he's a colonel in a Minuteman cadre. Or some militia or other. I'm going to get the Jewish Defense League on his case. They'll blow him out of his yard straight into Lake Huron."

Patsy stood up. "I'll call Mrs. O'Neill."

"You'd better not." Saul looked alarmed. "What if she's part of this conspiracy? She'd tip the rest of them off."

Patsy shrugged. In five minutes she was back.

"Well?" While they ate, they had also been playing Scrabble, and when she was out of the room, Saul had traded two of his bad letters for better ones.

"Mrs. O'Neill says his name is Bart Connell."

"A rabid anti-Semite."

"Not exactly. He has Alzheimer's. He lives with his daughter. They don't let him stray out of the yard—we're talking category-three dementia, living on his own private planet. He used to wander off onto the road. He flew bombing missions during the Second World War. Then he worked as a mechanic at a Ford dealership. Could fix anything. Now he can't, quote, figure out how to put a key to a keyhole. Shame on you, Saul. He's a plain good man with all his mind gone."

Saul sulked.

"And put those two letters back," she said. "I saw what you did."

. . .

Saul's students were younger than he remembered students were supposed to be for high school. Some were intelligent; others were not. How Saul performed in class didn't seem to make that much difference one way or another. Those who were stupid stayed stupid, stubbornly. Some he inspired with an interest in American history, or with writing, or public speech. The work was hard, the preparations for his classes longer and more grueling than he had expected, the grading onerous, and the rewards only occasional, and he found himself now and then losing his train of thought from the effect of so many youthful eyes watching him, all those students wondering what he would do next. In the back of his classroom, the losers—those with learning deficiencies and antisocial habits—fell asleep or chewed gum or laughed inappropriately or wrote their illiterate little notes. Saul felt he should do something about them, and one of these days he would think of what that *something* would be. The mean-spirited, learning-disabled lost souls: he would attend to them sooner or later.

The Five Oaks School District was close to bankruptcy, and in his classrooms the fluorescent lights flickered or burned out and were not replaced. There was always a shortage of chalk, and the windows leaked. The district had pink-slipped its remedial-reading teacher the previous year.

In the teachers' lounge, the talk was of their children, or health insurance, or places to go on vacation in July, or what had been on television the night before, or gossip. Sometimes Saul joined in. He often thought he was observing them and himself from a distance.

Now and then in his classrooms he watched, with sympathy and irritation, the boys and girls falling in love with each other.

One weekend evening in the late fall, an old blues guitarist whose music both Saul and Patsy liked was advertised as playing on the following Saturday night at Holbein College. The campus was on the other side of Five Oaks, about twenty minutes away. He would be performing in an auditorium in the campus student center, the ad said, and the event was open to the public, with tickets on sale at the door. The next weekend, Saul and Patsy dressed in the most drab-and-ratty clothes they still owned, to disguise themselves as postadolescent but preadult, and drove over to the campus one hour early, hoping that the concert hadn't been sold out.

They parked in a visitors' parking lot and walked hand in hand to the front entrance. It was a mild, cool evening with a hint of rain in the distance. Students called to each other and tossed Frisbees on the lawns. In the student union, undergraduates in the latest complicated fashions, with faces fitted out with contemporary distastes and forms of earnestness, walked past them in the foyer, paying no attention to them, transfixed with themselves alone. They were beautiful but wanted to be admired for their *minds,* of all things. Saul stopped to inhale.

"God," he said. "I miss it. I miss being on a campus. I miss not being an adult, quite yet. I miss being twenty. I miss that stink."

Patsy studied him. "Yeah," she said, "you do have that nostalgia thing going on. Come on, Saul. Enough about you. I'm hungry. Let's get me a bag of potato chips." After buying the tickets—the concert was far from being sold out, the blues having little purchase here at Holbein College— they walked down the student union hallway to an alcove where some vending machines stood. On one of the vending machines, the dispenser of individually bagged snack foods, someone had taped a warning sign:

OUT OF

ORDURE

"God, I miss it," Saul said. "Cleverness. Verbal agility. I wonder if a French major put that up," Saul said. *"Et pourtant vous serez semblable à cette ordure—"*

"For Christ's sake, Saul," Patsy said, giving him a peeved look. "I know the poem." She softened quickly. "You used to recite it to me, remember? To freak me out with Baudelaire?"

"Yeah, I was just being nostalgic. Just as you say." They stood there and watched the students parading by, accessorized with their preoccupations, and Saul glanced over at Patsy and saw instantly that she had outgrown the glamour of youth, the metallic sheen of immaturity and total enraptured self-mindedness. She had been glad to get out into the world where she lived now; he had not. Involuntarily, he put his hand over his heart.

All through the concert he noticed from his wife's stillness and concentration that, in fact, he understood the blues much better than she did. The old black guy up on the stage, with his gray hair and pressed pants and shoes spotted with flecks of mud, sang and played his heart out. Saul didn't have to think about the music to get it; for him, no effort at translation was necessary.

Also, he was beginning to suffer from insomnia, just like Harold, the barber. During the day while teaching his classes, he would feel drowsy, but when his head fell onto the pillow, he would sleep for an hour and then wake with the sensation that a movie-premiere arc-light was shining in his face. Along his legs and his chest there fluttered a distinct feeling of insects. This sensation made Saul want to jump out of his skin, leave his body behind like an ill-fitting pair of pajamas. At these times, still in his cocoon-body, he lay there thinking that the meaning of a serious career and of adulthood generally had escaped him. In the middle of the night, life did not seem to be the trifling joke he once thought it might be, nor were its problems merely academic ones. Devils lurked. At such times he would take Patsy, awake or asleep, into his arms. He wanted to admit that he had made a terrible mistake and that they were suffering the consequences of his misjudgments.

After all, his brother, Howie, the entrepreneur, was on the West Coast, making West Coast money in various start-ups, fledgling technology and software projects of which Saul understood nothing. Howie was younger than Saul and already a millionaire, or so he claimed. Saul's impression was that West Coast businesses were like West Coast football: you threw the ball up into the air and sort of expected someone to catch it, and usually someone did. Howie did not hesitate to call now and then to announce his various successes in vague incomprehensible detail. Then Saul's mother, Delia, would call to talk about Howie's successes to Saul, repeating the vague incomprehensible details at greater length and fuller incomprehensibility. Being an older brother whose idealism had resulted in a high school teaching job—this made Saul feel, during his bouts of insomnia at three in the morning, in his rented house, with midwestern farmland outside, as if he had been bested, outdone and undone. Sounds came up from the basement. Dream hounds bayed. Never again would he and his wife live in the fully human world. He had brought his wife out to this godforsaken place. The trouble with Patsy was that she said she liked it fine in Five Oaks. She could be sanctimonious about her adaptability. All he could do was hold on to her and wait for the hours to pass.

If anything should happen to her, he thought, he would surely die.

He climbed to the roof of the house to correct quizzes and tests. Staring out over the fields, he felt his attention disperse into the landscape, floating gradually into the topsoil, like pollen. Then he would look down and underline a sentence fragment in green ink.

Saul's mother, Delia, had lost her husband, Saul's father, Norman, to a premature heart attack some years ago, when Howie had been eight years old and Saul ten. In a traffic jam outside Baltimore, Norman Bernstein had died quietly and submissively inside his Buick, his head slumped over the wheel, his car clogging the already clogged arterial-highway. Thinking of this, Saul sometimes imagined his father's coronary thrombosis producing a traffic thrombosis, blocking the flow of vehicles for hours. His self-effacing father would have hated his own death for its public-nuisance value. He would have preferred to die in a private manner that would have bothered no one.

As for Delia, Saul's mother had had a wild youth, Saul had understood from one or two family friends who had reported that she had been a real "firecracker," but he also inferred from her indifferent manner of talking about her husband that the marriage had been a convenience of sorts, a way of starting a family with a reliable man, a means of avoiding loneliness; and his father's death, while certainly a shock, had not

plunged her into mind-numbing grief. She had traded passion for relia-
bility, and when a reliable man dies, he leaves behind a sufficiently huge
sum of life-insurance money to take care of everybody, and Saul's father
had done exactly that. Saul missed his dull, sweet, and reliable father the
way a child misses a favorite dog, but every time he tried to speak to his
mother (who was still, after all, in her mid-forties) about his dad, she listened carefully but did not participate in his sorrow, perhaps on principle.

Musing about his mother, Saul recognized that she missed high school
(not college, as he did) and the grand passions more than she missed her
husband, who had been, in romance, a utility player. There was still an
out-of-control quality to her emotions, an uncapped heat coming from
her furnace heart that Saul was afraid of, both for her and himself. In her
marriage, his mother had been undermatched. She was ready for a wonderful midlife crisis, and Saul was bracing himself for it.

Whenever she called, she disparaged the Midwest, and Saul's career
choice, though she was careful never to criticize Patsy, or Saul and Patsy's
unseemly love for each other. She would praise, incomprehensibly, Saul's
brother, and always refer to Howie's good looks and his parade of girlfriends—Saul suspected his brother had boyfriends as well—and his
income. It was as if Saul and Patsy's marriage, with its crazy love, was an
error in taste or judgment; it lacked the interesting variety to be found in
Howie's succession of bedmates. It lacked anecdotal value. If Saul would
only return to Baltimore, his mother intimated, perhaps she could set
him straight.

"Ma," he said. "We're staying here." Any suggestion from his mother,
no matter how sensible, had to be rejected, simply because it came from
her.

"Staying? Staying for what? For how long?"

"For as long as it takes."

"As long as what takes? Honey, you'll never have a normal life as long
as you live there."

"What's normal? Explain that to me."

"Ah, now you're setting one of your traps. I know your tricks. You
want me to say restaurants and concerts and good movies and book-
stores, but I won't."

"They have some of those things here."

"I didn't say it!" She waited. "Think of Howie's wonderful life, out there in San Francisco. I worry about you, living on that dirt road. I don't like dirt roads. I don't like the people who live on them—"

"—You've never known anybody who lived on a dirt road, except those people, the Friedkins, who lived in that sixty-thousand-square-foot house out in that suburb where they—"

"—Let me finish. I'm not talking about the Friedkins. I'm talking about you. Earning such a lousy salary. Don't think I don't admire your wonderful idealism. Everyone in the family admires your wonderful idealism, Saul, you know that. But it's like you've fallen into a . . . *cave.*"

"Like a bear," Saul said, thoughtfully. "A bear in a cave. Now, that could be true."

"So move out. Find an urban cave this time."

"Don't want to. I'm starting to like it here."

"What's to like? Dirt? Fields? Sheep?"

"They don't have sheep here. No, I'll tell you what there is to like about it, which you would discover if you ever came to visit."

"What?"

"The indifference. Ma, I never lived with indifference before."

"Indifference?" she roared, and jingled her bracelets. He could smell her perfume over the phone. "You value indifference? Have you gone crazy?"

"You never gave me a moment of it. You never left me alone." Saul felt himself getting angry. "You were always *kissing* me." Actually, now that he thought about it, the kissing had occurred *before* his father died. After his father died, she stopped with the kissing. Some psychic economy had gone to work on her. He was careful not to say that his father had always been the recipient of Delia's genial and friendly indifference. She wasn't cold, just cool to *him.* Even as a boy, Saul knew that his father was not a passionate man, that his thermostat was set lower than his mother's—even Saul as a boy could see that his parents' marriage lacked something. Nevertheless, Saul's father had managed to thrive on his wife's indifference, until he died; in death he had finally achieved a greater indifference than hers.

"Indifference is a terrible thing, kiddo," Delia was saying. "Awful. Cold. Cold at the heart."

"How would you know? You've never lived with it," Saul said, knowing that he was saying the-thing-which-was-not. "Imagine people not caring that much what you do. Imagine people *leaving you alone.*"

"You're describing a nightmare."

"Now you're guessing. When did people ever leave you alone? When did they ever leave *me* alone? Never. That's when."

"Saulie, let's not fight." She sighed dramatically. "Furthermore, if you're baiting me to talk about Norman, I won't. Maybe you should move to another city. If only you were in Detroit. You have relatives in Detroit."

"Exactly what Harold says. You been talking to him?"

"Who's Harold?"

"He's my barber. He says people look like me in Detroit. Or New York, I forget which."

"Last time I talked to Patsy," Saul's mother said, changing the subject, "a couple of weeks back, she said you'd joined a bowling league." Delia waited. "You, bowling? Jews don't bowl."

"Another eleventh commandment!" Saul protested. "Besides, what do you know about Jews?"

"I'm Jewish. That's all I have to know about it. And I know you're Jewish, and you're trying to aggravate me."

Saul felt his breathing passages getting clogged. He gasped for air. "Ma," he said, "you're giving me asthma. Let's not discuss this."

"Have you been to a doctor?" He replied with silence. "For your breathing, go to a doctor. Honey," she said, "what am I going to say to my friends about you?"

"You can say Saul and Patsy are getting comfortable in Michigan."

"All right, Saul. I give up. You want me to say that, that's what I'll say. Pour your life down the drain, if that's your ambition. I accept it." She sighed, a two-note sigh. "But let me tell you something, my friend. It's not a normal life you're leading out there."

"Okay, Ma. I'll bite. What kind of a life is it?"

"It's *nothing,* and that's my last word on the subject. You're living in nothingness. It'll eat you up. As anyone with a brain in his head would tell you. But I won't interfere. Maybe nothingness suits you."

"Oh, I thrive on it. It is my mother's milk."

There was a long pause.

"All right, *be* sarcastic," she said. "I can tell we aren't making progress. Goodbye, honey. I'll call again in two weeks." She made artificial and insincere kissing noises on the mouthpiece.

"Bye, Ma." Saul hung up the telephone in the kitchen and walked into the living room, where Patsy was watching the Sunday-afternoon movie, *From Here to Eternity*. "Take off your clothes," he said. "We're going to mess around."

She kept her eyes on the screen. "Not now. I don't want to right now. At least not until this scene is over." She glanced up at him. "Did the Marschallin call, sweetheart? You must've just talked to her."

Saul waited impatiently until the movie was over.

In the April tournament held at the Aqua Bowl, Saul scored 201, 194, and 132, and at the party afterward at Mad Dog Bettermine's summer house on the Tittebawasee River, he was exultant. Everyone had been told to bring a favorite CD to the party, and Saul, in an ironic mood that then gave way to earnestness, had brought Etta James singing Billie Holiday.

Mad Dog taught shop class and coached the wrestling team. No one had ever seen him button a collar around his own neck. For the party, his statuesque girlfriend Karla had prepared two huge casseroles, one with tuna and the other with chicken, and in the back room Mad Dog was busy rolling joints packed with the most powerful Colombian—grown, Mad Dog claimed, in the wet upper altitudes—that money could buy. Around the room on bookshelves were Mad Dog's Lionel trains, including a complete model of the *Twentieth Century Limited* with baggage car, lounge, Pullman sleepers, diner, coaches, and engines. The track had been laid on top of a little red carpet. Sitting on a blue beanbag chair, Saul asked, his voice thickening with smoke, why Mad Dog didn't run his trains on a layout but had set them up on a bookshelf display instead.

"These trains," Mad Dog announced, "are too *good* to run." He inhaled and inhaled and inhaled. "They're classics," he gasped. He slipped his fingers inside his shirt and started to scratch.

Saul nodded. He was wearing his bowling shirt with his name patch sewed on in front. In the next room, also thick with smoke, Patsy was dancing with Toby Finch, a fat man, as his name suggested, who taught social studies. On the other side of the room various people were tossing money on the floor as an incentive to someone to run down to the Tittebawasee River and jump into it. The money would be collected whether the daredevil wore clothes or not.

An hour later, Saul's Etta James CD was playing, and Saul himself was standing upright in the middle of the living room, a bottle of Chablis in one hand, a cigarette in the other (he was not a smoker, but he was smoking—Saul insisted he could not be identified by the acts he occasionally performed). He was singing loudly, an unpracticed baritone. There was some muted applause and encouragement as Mad Dog appeared at one side of the room with another joint, and Toby appeared at the other, his clothes soaking wet. He was demanding cash.

"You needed a witness!" Mad Dog said. "For all we know, you went out there and wet yourself down with a garden hose."

"It's not connected," Toby said. "I tried it."

"Well, you got wet once," Saul said. "Get wet again. What's the difference? We'll watch you this time."

"Yeah," Mad Dog said. "That's right. We'll watch you jump in."

The entire party left the house and stumbled down the hillside steps, Mad Dog shushing them, until they reached the river. Half of them stood in a clump on Mad Dog's dock, while the rest gathered in the weeds and high grass just behind a small patch of sand. Toby was standing at the end of the dock, complaining of friends who doubted one's word, friends who had not taken his measure as a man and as vice-president of the Five Oaks teachers' union.

As he talked, Patsy nudged Saul in the ribs. "What about the current?" she whispered. "What about the current in the damn river?"

Saul offered the bottle of Chablis to Patsy. She shook her head. "I asked you about the current."

Just as Toby jumped in, Saul said, "If he can survive the cold, he can survive the current." Upon hitting the water, Toby's bulk threw up a splash in all directions, wetting down those spectators on the dock. Patsy felt several drops of water in her eyes, and as she wiped them away, she said, "Where is he? Where's Toby?"

"He's there." Saul pointed. "Look."

Toby stood waist deep in the Tittebawasee River, bowing to a broken round of applause. The lower buttons of his shirt had loosened, and the rolls of fat around his midsection glowed porcelain white in the darkness. Someone threw him a dollar bill, which floated in front of him and then began drifting downstream.

"I was worried," Patsy said, turning back toward the hillside. "I thought he might drown or something."

Back in the house, someone had put on a band called The School of Velocity, and then someone else played Magnetic Fields. There was an argument about what time it was. Toby was stuffing his soaked trousers with dollar bills scattered on the floor near the kitchen, and then Saul was demonstrating how to do the tango with Patsy, and as they time-stepped across the living room, they knocked over an ashtray. People were applauding and laughing; someone—Mad Dog said it was Karla—was throwing up in the bathroom, and then the CD player was playing a rap artist, Dr. Dogg E.

Then it was two o'clock, and Saul and Patsy were at the door, Patsy's hand on Mad Dog's shoulder.

"Mad Dog," Patsy said, "you are one hundred and seventy pounds of brain death."

Mad Dog held up his index finger. "One hundred seventy-five pounds." He laughed. "Don't knock brain death until you've tried it."

"I've tried it," Saul said, searching the darkness for their car. "And I *love* it. Thanks, buddy. Tell Karla thanks, when she's cooled down. Great hot dish. Great party. See you Monday."

The two of them staggered off toward the unappeasable dark. Mud stuck to the soles of their shoes. At the car, Saul fiddled with his keys, trying to get at least one of them into the door lock. "You know, Patsy," he said, "I do love this place sometimes. I love these people."

"I know," Patsy said, leaning against the car, waiting for him, her eyes already closed. "I know."

And then they were in the car, strapped in, and the car was heading south on State Highway 14, and Patsy was asleep beside Saul. Saul leaned back and pressed the cruise-control button. He did not even realize that he was shutting his eyes. How drowsy he suddenly felt! It was the effect of the insomnia. It turned waking life into a dream. He was dreaming of Patsy, sleeping within arm's reach: Patsy, whom he loved all the way down to the root. If anything happened to her, he would surely die. He thought of his mother. Then he was dreaming of Mrs. O'Neill, carrying a gigantic plate of chocolate chip cookies. And Bart Connell and the barber, Harold, asleep on their feet. Then he thought of an aging African-American man with a goatee playing the guitar and singing the blues on an otherwise empty stage, in a single spotlight, to a sparse, unbluesy audience at Holbein College. He loved that man, the blues and the dignity. The two red taillights of Saul and Patsy's car went around a corner that wasn't there; then one of them moved up directly above the other. It came down again hard, on the wrong side, and began blinking.

Three

A smell of spilled gasoline: when Saul opened his eyes, he was still strapped in behind his lap-and-shoulder belt, but the car he sat in was upside down and in a field of some sort. The car's headlights illuminated a sky of dirt, and, in the distance, a tree growing downward from that same sky. Perhaps he had awakened out of sleep into another dream. "Patsy?" he said, turning with difficulty toward his wife strapped in on the passenger side, her hair hanging down from her scalp, but, from Saul's perspective, standing up. She was still sleeping; she was always a sound sleeper; she could sleep upside down and was doing so now. The car's radio was playing Ray Charles's "Unchain My Heart," and Saul said aloud, "You know, I've always liked that song." His voice was thick from beer, Chablis—whatever they had had to drink—and cigarettes, and he knew from the smell of the beer that this was no dream because he had never been able to imagine concrete details like that. No: he had fallen asleep at the wheel, driven off the road, and rolled the car. Here he was now, awake but unsober. At least this road was remote and unpatrolled. A thought passed through him in an unpleasant slow-motion way that the car was upended and that the ignition was still on. He switched it off and felt intelligent for three seconds until the lap belt began to hurt him and he felt stupid again. No ignition, no Ray Charles. His mind,

31

which had eased itself into oblivion for Mad Dog's party, returned to a sort of homeroom anxiety, as it moved slowly down a dark narrow alleyway cluttered with alcohol, fatigue, and the first onset of shock. Probably the car would blow up, and the only satisfaction his mother would receive from this accident would come years from now, when she would tell people, at the point when they were all through reminiscing about Saul, "I *told* him not to drink. I told him about drinking and driving. But he never listened to me. Never."

"Patsy." He reached out and gave her a little shake.

"What?" She opened her eyes.

"Wake up. I rolled the car. Patsy, we've got to get out of here."

"Why, Saul?" She looked at him with displeasure.

"Because we have to. Patsy, we're not at home. We're in the car. And we're upside down. Come on, honey, wake up. Please. This is serious."

"I *am* awake." She blinked, twisted her head, then looked calm. Her opal earring glittered in the light of the dashboard. The earring made Saul think of stability and a possible future life, if only he would normalize himself. Patsy smiled. Saul thought that this smile had something to do with guardian angels who, judging from the evidence, flew invisibly around her head, beaming down benevolence. "Well, Saul," she said, turning to look at him carefully, "are you all right?"

"Yes, yes, I'm not hurt at all."

"Good. Well. Neither am I, I don't think." She reached tentatively toward the ceiling. "This isn't fun. Did *you* do this, Saul?"

"Yes, I did. How do we get out of here?"

"Let's see," she said, speaking calmly, in her usual tone. "What I think you do is, you release your seat belt, stick your arms straight up, then lower yourself slowly so you don't break your neck. Then you crawl out the window, the higher one. That would be yours."

"Okay." He held his arm up, then unfastened the clasp and felt himself dropping onto the car's ceiling. He pulled himself toward the side window. When he was outside, he leaned over, back in, and extended his hand to Patsy to help her out.

As she emerged through the window, she was smiling. Disasters didn't appear to have the power to alienate her from life. "Haven't you ever rolled a car before, Saul? I have. Or one of my boyfriends did, years ago." She was breathing rapidly. She dragged herself out, dusted her jeans, and strolled a few feet beyond the car's tire tracks in the mud, as if nothing much had happened. "Beautiful night," she said. "Look at those stars." For a moment he thought she was dissociating.

"Jeez, Patsy," Saul said, jumping down close to where she stood, "this is no time for being cosmic." Then he gazed up. She was right: the sky was pillowed with stars. She took his hand.

"Are you really okay?" she asked. "My God, feel that. You're shaking like a leaf. You must be in shock." She wrapped her arms around him and held him fast for half a minute. "There," she said, "now that's better." She studied him. "You're still drunk. What a mess you are."

"We're not kids anymore," Saul said. "We can't get drunk all the time at parties and roll cars. We'll get killed. We could have died."

"But we didn't."

"We *could* have."

"All right. Yes. I know. You can die in your sleep. You can die watching television." She observed him in the dark, as if she were spying on him. "I wish I had been driving. It's so warm, a spring night, I think I would have been singing along to the radio to stay awake. 'Unchain My Heart'—I would have been singing along to Ray Charles and I would have stayed awake and we'd be home by now." She leaned over. "Smell the soil? It's loamy. You know, Saul, you should turn the car's headlights off. Save the battery."

"Patsy, the car is *wrecked*! Look at it."

"Don't be silly." She studied the car with equanimity, one hand raised to her face, the other hand cradling her elbow. Patsy's equanimity was otherworldly and constant. The combination of her beauty and her persistent unexplainable interest in Saul was puzzling to him. "Saul, that car is fine. We might be driving it tomorrow. The roof will have a dent, that's all. The car turned over softly and slowly. It's hardly hurt. What we have to do now is get to a house and call someone to help us. We could walk across this field, or we could just take the road back to Mad Dog's. I'm sure they're still going strong."

"Patsy, I can't think. My brain has seized up."

"Well," she said, taking his hand, "I happen to like these stars, and that looks like a nice field, and I'd rather stay away from Highway 14 this time of night, what with the drunks on the road and all." She gave him a tug on his sleeve, and he almost fell. "There you are," she said. "Come on."

As Saul walked across the field, hearing the slurp of his shoes in the spring mud, he saw the red blinking light of a radio tower in the distance, the only remotely friendly sight anywhere beneath the horizon. Just when he thought he had been accepted among these Midwesterners, not just as a Jew but as himself, his car had turned over. Oblivion had almost swallowed him, as his mother had predicted it might. That he was here at all was a sign, he thought, that his life was disordered after all, abandoned to chaos among rural Gentiles, connoisseurs of rifles, violence, and piety. He smelled manure nearby, and somewhere behind him he thought he heard the predatory wingbeat of a bat or an owl. First the Gentiles, then the Gnostics.

He had thought he was a missionary, bringing education and the higher enlightenments to rural, benighted adolescents, but somehow the conversion had gone the other way, and now here he was, acting like them: going to parties, getting drunk, falling asleep, rolling his car. It was the sort of accident Christians had. He felt obscurely that he had given up personal complexity and become simple in the midwestern style, like those girls who worked at the drugstore arranging greeting cards. They were so straightforward that two seconds before they did anything, like give change, you could see every gesture coming. He was becoming like that. As a personality, Saul had once prided himself on being interesting, almost Byzantine, a challenge to any therapist. But having joined the school bowling league, he couldn't seem to concentrate on Schopenhauer on those days when, at odds and ashamed of himself, he took the battered Signet Classic of *The World as Will and Idea* down from the shelf and glowered at the indecipherable lines he had highlighted with yellow Magic Marker in college. When he did understand, the philosopher seemed no longer profound, but merely a disappointed idealist with an ungainly prose style.

"Saul?"

"What?"

"I've been talking to you. Did you hear me?"

"Guess not. I was lost in thought." He stumbled against a bush. He couldn't see much, and he reached out for Patsy's hand. "I was thinking about girls in drugstores and Schopenhauer and the reasons why we ever came to this place."

"Jesus. I wish to Christ that you would listen to me sometimes. If you had been listening to me, you wouldn't have stumbled into that bush. That's what I was warning you about."

"Thanks. Where are we?"

"We're going down into this little gully, and when we get up on the other side, we'll be right near that farmhouse. What's the matter?"

He turned around and saw, across the field, the headlights of his car shining on the upturned dirt; he saw the Chevy's four tires facing the air; and he thought of his new jovial recklessness and of how he had almost killed himself and his wife. He said nothing because he was beginning to feel soul-sick, a state of spiritual dizziness, and also because he had forgotten to turn off the headlights. He was possessed by disequilibrium. He felt the urge to giggle, and was horrified by himself. He had a sudden marionette feeling.

"Saul! You're drifting off again. What is it this time?"

"Puppets."

"Puppets?"

"Yeah. You know—the way they don't have a center of gravity. Uh, Kleist . . . What I mean is. The way they look . . ."

"Watch out for that stump."

He saw it in time to avoid it. "Patsy, how do you live in the world? This is a serious question."

"Stop it, Saul. You've been to a party. You're tired. Don't get metaphysical on me. Please. It's two in the morning. You live in the world by knocking on the door of that farmhouse, that's what you do. You ring the doorbell."

They walked up past a shed whose flaking red door was hanging open, and they crossed the pitted driveway onto a small front yard with an evenly mowed lawn. A tire swing, pendulating slowly, hung down from a tree branch. Saul couldn't see much of the house in the dark, but as they crossed the driveway, kicking a few stones, they heard the bark of a dog from inside the house, a low bark from a big dog: a farm dog with a name like Trixie.

"Anti-Semites," Saul said.

"Just ring the bell."

After a moment, the porch light went on, yellow, probably a bug light, Saul thought; and then under the oddly colored glare a very young woman appeared, pale blond hair and skin, very pretty, but under the effect of the bulb looking a bit jaundiced. With her fists she was rubbing her eyes with sleepiness. She wore a bathrobe decorated with huge blue flowers. Saul and Patsy explained themselves and their predicament— Saul was sure he had seen this young woman before—and she invited them in to use the phone. When they entered, the dog—old, with a gray muzzle—growled from under the living-room table but did not bother to get up. After Patsy and the woman, whose name was Anne, began talking, it developed that they had met before in the bank where Patsy worked as a teller. They leaned toward each other. Their voices quickly rose in the transfiguration of friendliness as they disappeared into the kitchen. They seemed suddenly chipper and cheery to Saul, as if a new party had started. He had the impression that women enjoyed being friendly, whereas for men it was an effort. At least it was an effort for *him*. He heard Patsy dialing a number on an old rotary phone, laughing and whispering as she did so.

He was left alone in the living room. Having nothing else to do, he looked around: high ceilings and elaborate wainscoting, lamps, table, rug, dog, calendar, the usual crucifix on the wall above the TV. There was something about the room that bothered him, and it took a moment before he knew what it was. It felt like a museum of earlier American feelings. Not a single ironic sentence had ever been spoken here. Everything in the room was sincere, everything except himself. In the midst of all this midwestern earnestness, he was the one thing wrong. What was he doing here? What was he doing anywhere? He was accustomed to asking himself such questions.

Mad Dog's party now seemed to be months, or years, ago.

"Mr. Bernstein?"

Saul turned around and saw the man of the house, who at first glance still seemed to be a boy, standing at the bottom of the stairs. He had his arms crossed, and he wore a sleepy but alert look on his face. He had on boxer shorts and a T-shirt, and Saul recognized, underneath the brown hair and the beard, a student from last year, Emory . . . something. Emory McPhee. That was it. A good-looking, solid kid. He had married this woman, Anne, last year, both of them barely eighteen years old, and moved out to this place. That was it. That was who they were. He had heard that Emory had become a housepainter.

"Emory," Saul said. The boy was stocky—he had played varsity football starting in his sophomore year—and he looked at Saul now with sleepy inquisitiveness. "Emory, my wife and I have had an accident, over there, on the other side of your field."

"What kind of accident, Mr. Bernstein? Are you okay?"

"We drove off the road." Saul waited, his hands in his pockets. Then he said the rest of it. "The car turned over on us. But I think we're all right."

"Wow," Emory said. "You're lucky you weren't hurt. That's amazing. Good thing it wasn't worse."

"Well, yes, but the car was going slow." Saul always sounded stupid to himself late at night. The boy's bland, blue-eyed gaze stayed on him now, not moving, genial but inquisitorial, and Saul thought of all the people who had hated school, never liked even a minute of it except maybe the sports, and maintained a low-level suspicion of teachers for the rest of their lives. They voted down school-bond issues. They didn't even like to buy pencils.

"How'd you go off the road?"

"I fell asleep, Emory. We'd been to a party at Mr. Bettermine's and I fell asleep at the wheel. Never happened to me before."

"Wow," Emory said again, but slowly this time, with no real surprise or inflection in his voice. He shrugged his shoulders, then bent down as if he were doing calisthenics. Saul knew that his own breath smelled of beer, so there was no point in going into that. "Do you want a cup of coffee?

I'd offer you a beer, but we don't have it." *Besides, you've already had one too many.*

Saul tried to smile, an effort. "I don't think so, Emory. Not tonight." He looked down at the floor, at his socks—he had taken off his muddy shoes—and saw an ashtray filled with cigarette butts. "But I would like a cigarette, if you could spare one."

"Sure." The boy reached down and offered the pack in Saul's direction. "Didn't know you smoked. Didn't know you had any vices at all." He smiled. "Until now."

They exchanged a look. "I'm like everybody else," Saul said. "Sometimes the right thing just gets loose from me and I don't do it." He picked up a book of matches. He would have to watch his sentences: that one hadn't made any sense. On the outside of the matchbook was an advertisement.

SECRETS
OF THE
UNIVERSE
*** see inside ***

Saul put the matchbook into his pocket after lighting up.

"Were you drunk?" the boy asked suddenly.

"No, I don't think so."

"Teachers shouldn't drink," Emory said. "That's my belief."

"Well, maybe not."

Saul inhaled from the cigarette, and Emory came closer toward him and sat down on the floor. He gave off the smell of turpentine, and he had two or three tiny flecks of white paint in his hair close to his ear. He rubbed at his boy's beard again. "Do you remember me from school?"

Saul leaned back. He tried to think. "Sure, of course I do. You sat in the back and you played with a ballpoint pen. You used to sketch the other kids in the class. Once when we were doing the First World War, you said it didn't make any sense no matter how much you read about it. I remember your report on the League of Nations. You stared out the window a lot. You sat near Annie in my class, and you passed notes to her."

38

"I didn't think you'd notice that much about me. Or remember." Emory whistled toward the dog, who thumped her tail and waddled over toward Emory's lap. "I wasn't very good. I thought it was a waste of time, no offense. I wanted to get married, that's all. I wanted to get married to Anne, and I wanted to be outside, not stuck inside, doing something, making a living, earning money. The thing is, I'm different now." He stood up, as if he were about to demonstrate how different he had become or had thought of something important to say.

"How are you different?"

"I'm real happy," Emory said, looking toward the kitchen. "I bet you don't believe that. I bet you think: Here's this kid and his wife and baby, out here, ignorant as a couple of plain pigs, and how could they be happy? But it's weird. You can't tell about anything." He was looking away from Saul. "Schools tell you that people like me aren't supposed to be happy or . . . what's that word you used in class all the time? 'Fulfilled'? Yeah, that's it." He sneered at Saul so quickly that it was like a flashbulb popping. "We're not supposed to be that. But we're doing okay. But then I'm not trying to tell you anything."

"I know, Emory. I know that." Saul raised his hand to his scalp and touched his bald spot.

"Hell," Emory said, apparently building up steam, "you could work all your life to be as happy as Anne and me, and you might not do it. People . . . they try to be happy. They work at it. But it doesn't always take." He laughed. "I shouldn't be talking to you this way, Mr. Bernstein, and I wouldn't be, except it's the middle of the night, and I'm saying stuff. You know, I respected you. But now here you are, in my living room, and I remember the grades you gave me, all those D's, like you thought I'd never do anything in life except fail. But you can't hurt me now because I'm not in school anymore. So I apologize. See, I apologize for messing up in school and I forgive you for flunking me out."

Emory held out his hand, and Saul stood up and took it, thinking that he might be making a mistake.

"You shouldn't flunk people out of school," Emory said, "if you're going to get drunk and roll cars."

Saul held on to Emory's hand and tried to grip hard and diligently in return. "I didn't get drunk, Emory. I fell asleep. And you didn't *flunk* out. You *dropped* out."

Emory released his hand. "Well, I don't care," he said. "I was sleeping when you came to our door. I don't go to parties anymore because I have to get up and work. I sleep because I'm married and working. I can't see anything outside of that."

Saul suddenly wanted Patsy back in this room, so that they could go. Who the hell did this boy think he was, anyway?

"Well, none of this is nothing," Emory said at last. "I don't blame you for anything at all. Maybe you did me a favor. I had to do something in my life, so I rented this farm. I'm reading up on horticulture." He pronounced the word carefully and proudly. "You want to sleep on the floor, you can, or on the sofa there. And there's a spare bed upstairs, you want it."

"Sorry about the bother," Saul said.

"No trouble."

"I appreciate it."

"Forget it." Emory patted the dog.

"But thanks."

"Sure."

The two men looked at each other for a moment, and Saul had one of his momentary envy-shocks: he looked at this man, this boy—he couldn't decide which he was—his hair standing up, and he thought: Whatever else he is, this kid is real. Emory was living in the real. Saul felt himself floating up out of the unreal and rapidly sinking back into it, the lagoon of self-consciousness and irony.

In a kind of desperation, Saul looked at the wall, where someone had hung a picture of a horse with a woman beside it, drawn in pencil, and framed in a cheap dime-store frame. The woman was probably Anne. She looked approximately like her. "Nice picture."

"I drew it."

"You have real talent, Emory," Saul said, insincerely examining the details. "You could be an artist."

"I *am* an artist," Emory said, staring at his old teacher. He picked at a scab on his calf. He turned his back to Saul. "I could draw from when I was a kid." A baby's cry came from upstairs. Emory looked at the ceiling, then exhaled.

"What kind of horse is that?" Saul asked, in what he vowed silently would be his final effort at politeness this evening. "Is that any kind of horse in particular?"

Emory was going back up the stairs. Then he faced Saul. "Every horse is some horse in particular, Mr. Bernstein. There aren't any horses in general. You can sleep there on the sofa if you want to. Good night."

"Good night."

Whatever had happened to the God of the Old Testament, Saul wondered, looking at Emory's crucifix, the God that had chosen Israel above the other nations? Why had He allowed this scene to take place and why had He allowed Emory McPhee, this dropout, to make him feel like a putz? The Red Sea had not parted for Saul in a long time, in any sense; he felt he had about as much clout with God as, perhaps, a sparrow did. The whole evening had been a joke at Saul's expense. He heard God laughing, a sound like surf on rocks.

When Patsy and Anne came out of the kitchen, announcing that an all-night towing service was on its way and would probably have the car turned over and running in about half an hour, Saul smiled as if everything would be exactly as fine as they claimed. Anne and Patsy were laughing. The flowers on Anne's bathrobe were laughing. God was, even now, laughing and enjoying the joke. Feeling like a zombie, and not laughing himself, but wearing the smile of the classically undead, Saul hooked his hand into Patsy's and went back outside. Some nights, he knew, had a way of not ending. This would be one.

"How was Emory?" Patsy asked.

"Emory? Oh, Emory was fine," Saul told her.

On the days following, Saul began to be obsessed with happiness, an unhealthy obsession, he knew, but he couldn't get rid of it. On some days he could not get out of bed to go to work without groaning and reaching for his hair, as if to drag himself up bodily for the working day.

Prior to his accident and his meeting with Emory McPhee, Saul had managed to forget about happiness, a state that had once bothered him for its general inaccessibility. Now he believed that, compared to others, he was, *except for his marriage,* actually and truly unhappy, especially since his mind insisted on thinking about the problem, poring over it, ragging him on and on. It was like the discontent of adolescence, the discontent with situations, but this was larger, the discontent with being itself, a psychic itch with nowhere to scratch. This was like Schopenhauer arriving at the door with a big suitcase, settling down for a long stay in the brain.

Patsy wasn't ordinary for many reasons, but also because she loved Saul. Nevertheless, she was happy, like a character in Chekhov who can't help but proclaim a satisfaction with life every few minutes. She did want a better job, and, in some sense, a different life. Early in the summer he stole glances at her as she turned the pansies over in their pots, tamping them out and planting them in the flower beds near the front walk. Blue sky, aggressive sun. She was squatting down in her shorts, wearing one of Saul's old flannel shirts flecked with dirt and the sleeves rolled up to the elbows. Her hair fell backward down her shoulders. From the front window he watched her and studied her hands, those slender fingers doing their work. Helplessly, his eyes took in the clothed outlines of his wife. He was hers. That was that. She liked being a woman. She liked it in a way that, Saul now knew, he himself did not like being a man. There was the guilt, for one thing, for the manly hobbies of war and the thoroughgoing destruction of the earth. Patriarchy, carnage, rape, pleasurable bloodletting, fanatic greed, and bloodsport: Saul would admit a gender responsibility for all these if anyone asked him to acknowledge it, though no one ever did.

Patsy wiped her forehead with the back of her hand, saw Saul, and waved at him, turning her head slightly, tilting it, as she did whenever she caught sight of him. She smiled, a smile he had gladly given his life away for, a look of radiant intelligence. She was into the real, too; she didn't ponder it, she just planted flowers, if that was what she wanted to do. Beyond her was the driveway and their Chevrolet with its bashed-in roof. Her smile faded. It always did when she noticed him studying her.

Saul turned from the window—it was Saturday morning—and tried to think for a moment of what to do next. Taking a Detroit Tigers cap off the front-hall hat rack, he went outside and with great care put it, from behind and unannounced, on Patsy's head. "Save you from sunburn," he said when she turned around and looked at him. "Save you from heat-stroke."

"I want a motorcycle," Patsy said. "I've been thinking about it. We don't need another car, but I do want a motorcycle. I always have. Women can ride motorcycles, Saul, don't deny it. Oh, and another thing." She dropped one hand into the dirt and balanced herself on it. "This morning I was trying to think of where the Cayuse Indians lived, and I couldn't remember, and we don't have an encyclopedia to check. We need that." She put her hand over her eyes, to shade them. "Saul, why are you looking like that? Are you in a state?"

"No, I'm not in a state."

"Yes, you are. Damn it, I have to break out sometimes. I've just *got* to. I'll die here otherwise. A motorcycle would do wonders for *both* of us, Saul. A small one, not one of those hogs. Do you like my petunias? Should I have some purple over there? Maybe this is too much red and white. What would you think of some dianthus right there?" She pointed with her trowel. "Or maybe some sweet william?"

"Sure, sure." He didn't know what either variety looked like. Flowers seemed so irrelevant to everything.

"Where *did* the Cayuse Indians live, Saul?"

"Oregon, I think."

"What do you think about a motorcycle? For little trips into town. For those small occasions when I have to get away from you."

"Sounds okay to me. But they aren't exactly safe, you know. People get killed on motorcycles."

"Those people aren't careful. I'll be careful. I'll wear a helmet. I just want to do it. Imagine a girl—me—on one of those machines. Makes you feel good, doesn't it? A motorcycle girl in Michigan. The car's silly for small trips. Besides, I want to visit my friends in town."

It was true: Patsy already had many friends around Five Oaks, friends that Saul didn't have. She could be vain about it, her ability to adapt to anything—after all, she was married to *him*. Now she stood up, dropped her trowel, and put her weight on Saul's shoes and leaned herself into him. The visor of her cap bumped into his forehead. But she embraced him for only a moment. There wouldn't be any big, long love thing, not just now. "Want to help, Saul? Give me a hand putting the rest of these flowers in?"

"Not right now, Patsy, I don't think so."

"What's the matter? You're looking peckish."

"Peckish? I don't know."

"You *are* in a state."

"I guess I might be."

"What is it this time? Our recent brush with death? The McPhees? My incredible impatience about getting another job?"

"What about the McPhees?" he asked. She had probably guessed.

"Well, they were so cute, the two of them. So sweet. And so young, too. Plus their baby. And I know you, Saul, and I know what you thought. You thought: What have these two got that I don't have?"

She *had* guessed. She usually did. It was unfair. He stepped backward. "Yes," he said, "you're right. What *do* they have? And why don't I have it? I'm happy with *you*, but I—"

"Jesus. You can't be like them because you can't, Saul. You fret. That's your hobby. It's how you stay occupied. You've heard about spots? About how a person can't change them? Well, I *like* your spots. I like how you're a professional worrier. And you always know about things like the Cayuse Indians. I'm not like that. And I don't want to be married to somebody like me. I'd put myself to sleep. But you're perfect. You're an early-warning system. You bark and growl at life. You're my dog. You do see that, don't you?"

"Yes." He nodded.

After he had kissed her and returned to the house, he took the matchbook he had pocketed at the McPhees' up to his study. At his desk, with a pair of scissors, he cut off the flap of the matches, filled in his name and address, and wrote a check for six dollars to the Wisdom Foundation, located at a post office box number in Cincinnati, Ohio. Just to make sure, he enclosed a letter.

Dear Sirs,

Enclosed please find a check for six dollars for your SECRETS OF THE UNIVERSE. Also included is my name and address, written on the back of this book of matches. You will also find them typed at the bottom of this letter. Thank you. I look forward, very much, to reading the secrets.

Sincerely,
Saul Bernstein

He examined the letter, wondering if the last sentence might sound too skeptical, too . . . something. But he decided to leave it there. He took the letter, carefully stamped—he put commemorative stamps on all his important mail—out to the mailbox and lifted the little red flag.

He thought: I am no longer a serious person. My great-grandfather read the Torah, my grandfather read Spinoza and Heine and books on immunology, and here I am, writing off for this.

On his trips into town, Saul began to take the long route past the McPhees' house, slowing down when he was close to their yard. Each time that he found himself within a mile of their farm, he felt his stomach knotting up in anxiety and sick curiosity. He recognized himself twisting in the coils of something like envy, yet not envy exactly, but a more biblical emotion, harder to define, like covetousness. Driving past in the evenings, he occasionally saw them outside, Emory mowing or clipping, their baby strapped on his back, Anne up on a ladder doing something to the windows, or out in the garden like Patsy, planting. They could have been anybody, except that, for Saul, they gave off a disturbing aura of unreflective happiness, which meant that they could have been anybody except Saul.

The road was sufficiently far away from their house and from the shed flaking with paint so that they wouldn't see him. His car was just another car unless you looked closely and saw the dented roof and Saul inside it. But on a particular Friday, in early June, several hours after work, he drove past their property and spied Emory in the front yard, in the gold twilight, pushing his wife, sitting in the swing. Emory, the ex–football player, had on his face a solemnly contented expression. The baby blithered in a stroller close by. His wife was in a white T-shirt and jeans, and Emory himself wore jeans but no shirt. She was probably proud of her breasts and he was probably proud of his shoulders. Anne held on to the ropes of the swing. Her hair flew up as she rose, and Saul, who took this all in in a few seconds, could hear her cries of delight from his car. Taking his surreptitious glances, he almost drove off the road again. Of course they were children, he knew that, but their youth wasn't the problem as such. No: they gave off a terrible steady-state glow. They had the blank moronic shimmer of angels. They were glistering. It was intolerable.

They lived smack in the middle of reality and never gave it a minute's thought. They'd never felt like actors. They'd never been sick with knowingness. The long tunnel of their thoughts had never swallowed them. They'd never had sleepless nights, the urgent, wordless, unexplainable wrestling matches with the shadowy bands of soul-thieves. They were just a couple of Midwesterners.

Goddamn it, Saul thought. Everybody gets to be happy except me. Saul heard Anne's cries. The sun was sweating all over his forehead. He felt faint and Jewish, as usual. He turned on the radio. It happened to be tuned to a religion station, and some choir was singing "When Jesus Wept."

"It's your play, Saul."

"I know, I know."

"What's the matter? You got some bad letters?"

"Duh. The worst. The worst letters I've ever had."

46

"You always say that. You whine and complain. You're such a whiner, Saul, you even whine in bed. You were complaining that time just before you spelled out 'axiom' over that triple word score and got all those points last year. You do this *act* when we play Scrabble and then you always beat me." Patsy was sitting cross-legged in her chair, as she liked to do, with a root beer bottle positioned against her instep, as she arranged and rearranged the letters on her slate.

Saul examined the board. The only word he could think of spelling out was "paint," but the word made him think of Emory McPhee. The hand of fate again, playing tricks on him. Glancing down at the words on the board, he thought he saw that same hand at work, spelling out some invisible story.

Saul always treated Scrabble boards as if they were fortune-telling equipment, with the order of the words creating a narrative. Patsy had started with "moon," and he had added "beam" onto it. When she hung a "mild" from the moonbeam, he spiced it up with "lust," but she had responded to his interest in sex with "murky," hanging the word from that same moonbeam. "Mild" and "murky" came close to how he felt. His mother, Delia, had said so on the phone yesterday. "Saul, darling," she had said, "you're sounding rather *dark* and *mysterious* lately. What's gotten into you?" He had not told her about the accident.

"I'm okay, Ma," he had said. "I'm just working some things through."

"You're leaving Five Oaks?" she had asked hopefully.

"No, Ma," he had said. "This town suits me."

"All that mud, Saul," she had said, dubious as always about the soil and people who made large claims for it. "All those farms," she added vaguely. "The slush. The snow. The *fur*."

"Saul," Patsy said. "Wake up." She shook him. "You're wool-gathering."

"Just thinking about my mother," he said. He looked up at Patsy. "What are all those deer doing on our Scrabble board?" he asked. "Give me a swig of your root beer."

"No," she said, before she handed it to him. He appreciated the golden color of the fine hairs on her arm in the lamplight. "Sweetheart, I think I saw some, as a matter of fact," she said. "I thought I saw, what would you call it, a herd of deer, far in back, beyond the property line, a few nights ago. If you ever go back up to the roof, honey, give a look around. You might see them."

"Right, right." He couldn't put all five of his letters for "paint" on the Scrabble board. He removed the T. Pain. He held the four letters for pain in his hand, and he added them to the final T in "lust."

"Funny how 'pain' and 'lust' give you 'paint,'" Patsy said. "Sort of makes me think of the McPhees and the heady smell of turpentine."

They glanced at each other, and he tried to smile. A fly was buzzing around the bulb in the lampshade. He was thinking of Patsy's new expensive blue motorcycle out back, shiny and powerful and dangerous to ride. The salesman had said it could go from zero to fifty in less than six seconds. The hand of fate was ready to give him a good slapping around. It had announced itself. Saul felt a groan coming on. He looked at Patsy with helpless love.

"Oh, Saul," she said. "Honey. *Shit.* You always get this way during these games. You always do." He saw her smiling in the reflection of his love for her. "You're so cute," she said, with a tone of patience that might soon run out.

At ten minutes past three o'clock, he rose out of bed to get a glass of water. When he looked out the back window, he saw them: just about where Patsy said they would be, far in the distance beyond the property line—a herd of deer silently passing. He ran downstairs in his underwear and went out through the unlocked back door as quietly as he could. He stood in the yard in the June night, the crickets sounding, the moon dimly outlined behind a thin cloud in the shape of a scimitar. In this gauzy light, the deer, about eight of them, distant animal forms, walked across his neighbor's field into a stand of woods. He found himself transfixed with the mystery and beauty of it. Hunting animals suddenly made no sense to him. He went back to bed. "I saw the deer," he said. He didn't know if Patsy was asleep. During the summer she wore Saul's T-shirts to bed, and that was all. Like a Crusader portrayed in marble on a coffin lid, Patsy slept on her back with her feet crossed at the ankle; it gave the impression that she had returned from seeing the Holy Land.

Two days later, the letter containing the secrets of the universe came from the Wisdom Foundation in Cincinnati. Saul sat down on the front stoop and tore the letter open. It was six pages long and had been printed out by a computer, with Saul's name inserted here and there.

Dear **Mr. Bernstein,**

Nothing is settled. Everything is still possible. Your thoughts are both yours and someone else's. Sometimes we say hello to the world and then goodbye, but that is not the end and we say hello again. God is love, **Mr. Bernstein,** denying it only makes us unhappy. Riches are mere appearances. **Our thoughts are more real than hammers and nails.** We can make others believe us, **Mr. Bernstein,** if the truth is in us. Buddha and Jesus the Christ and Mohammed agreed about just about everything. Causing pain to others only prolongs our own pain. A free and open heart is the best thing. Live simply. Don't pretend to know something you don't have a clue about. You may feel as if you are headed toward some terrible fate, **Mr. Bernstein,** but that may not come to pass. You can avoid it. **Throw your bad thoughts into the mental**

49

wastebasket. There is a right way and a wrong way to dispose of bad thoughts. Everything about the universe worth knowing is known. What is not known about the universe is not worth knowing. Follow these steps. Remember that trees will always be with us, mice will always be with us, mosquitoes will always be with us. Therefore, avoid mental cleanliness. Never start a sentence with the words "What if everybody . . ."

It went on for several more pages. Saul liked the letter. It sounded like his other grandfather, Isaac, the pious atheist, an exuberant man much given to laughter at appropriate and inappropriate moments, who offered advice as he passed out candy bars and halvah to his grandchildren. This letter from the Wisdom Foundation was signed by someone named Giovanni d'Amato.

Saul looked up. For a moment the terrifying banality of the landscape seemed to dissolve into geometrical patterns of color and light. Taken by surprise, he felt the habitual weight on his heart lifting as if by pulleys, or, better yet, birds of the spirit sent by direct mail from Giovanni d'Amato. He decided to test this happiness and got into the dented car.

He drove toward the McPhees'. The dust on the dirt road whirled up behind him. He thought he would be able to stand their middle-American happiness. Besides, Emory was probably working. No: it was Saturday. They would both be home. He would just drive by, and that would be that. So what if they were happy, these dropouts from school? He was happy, too. He would test his temporary happiness against theirs.

The trees rushed past the car in a kind of chaotic blur.

He pressed down on the accelerator. A solitary cloud, wandering and thick with moisture, straying overhead but not blocking the sun, let down a minute's worth of vagrant rainbowed shower on Saul's car. The water droplets, growing larger, bounced on the car's hood. He turned on the wipers, causing the dust to streak in protractor curves. The rain made Saul's car smell like a nursery of newborn vegetation. He felt the car drive over something. He hoped it wasn't an animal, one of those anonymous rodents that squealed and died and disappeared.

Ahead and to the left was the McPhees'.

It looked like something out of an American genre painting, the kind of second-rate canvas hidden in the back of most museums near the elevators. Happiness lived in such houses, where people like Saul had never been permitted. In the bright standing sunshine its Midwestern Gothic acute angles pointed straight up toward heaven, a place where there had been a land rush for centuries and all the stakes had been claimed. Standing there in the bright theatrical sun—the rain had gone off on its way—the house seemed to know something, to be an answer ending with an exclamation point.

Saul crept past the front driveway. His window was open, and, except for the engine, there was no sound, no dog barking. And no sign, either, of Anne or Emory or their baby, at least out here. Nothing on the front porch, nothing in the yard. He *could* stop and say hello. That was permitted. He could thank them for the help they had given him two months before. He hadn't yet done that. Emory's pickup was in the driveway, so they were at home. *Happy people don't go much of anywhere anyway,* Saul thought, backing his car up and parking halfway in on the driveway.

When he reached the backyard, Saul saw a flash of white, on legs, bounding at the far distances of the McPhees' field into the woods. From this distance it looked like nothing he knew, a trick of the eye. Turning, he saw Anne McPhee sitting in a lawn chair, reading the morning paper, a glass of lemonade nearby, their baby in the playpen in the shade of the house, and Emory, some distance away in a hammock, reading the sports section. Both of them were holding up their newspapers so that their view of him was blocked.

Quietly he crossed their back lawn, then stood in the middle, between them. Emory turned the pages of his paper, then put it down and closed his eyes. Anne went on reading. Saul stood quietly. Only the baby saw him. Saul reached down and picked out of the lawn a sprig of grass. Anne McPhee coughed. The baby was rattling one of its crib toys.

He waited another moment and then walked back to his car. Anne and Emory had not seen him. He felt like a prowler, a spy from God. He also felt now what he had once felt only metaphorically: that he was invisible.

When he was almost home, he remembered, or thought he remembered, that Anne McPhee had been sunning herself and had not been wearing a blouse or a bra. Or was he now imagining this? He couldn't be sure.

Patsy nudged him in the middle of the night. "I know what it is," she said.

"What?"

"What's bothering you."

He waited. "What? What is it?"

"You're like men. You're a man and you're like them. You want to be everything. You want to have endless endless potential. But then you grow up. In spite of yourself. And you're one thing. Your body is, anyway. It's trapped in *this* life. You have to say goodbye to the dreams of everything." She waited. "You don't want to do that one little bit, do you?"

"Dreams of everything."

"Yes." She rolled over so that she could look at him in the dark. "Don't pretend that you don't understand. You want to be a whole roomful of people, Saul. That's kid stuff." She let her head drop so that her hair brushed against him.

"What about you?"

"What about me? I'm not a problem the way you're a problem. I don't want to be anything else," she said sleepily, beginning to rub his back. "I do want a better job at the bank, I'll tell you that. But I sure as hell don't have to be a great person. I just want to do a little of this and a little of that as long as I can make some serious money." She waited. "You know. To get by. For that trip to Finland."

"What's wrong with ambitions?" he asked. "You could be great at something."

Her hand moved into his hair, tickling him. "Being great is too tiring, Saul, and it's boring. Look at the great ambition people. They're wrecking the earth, aren't they. They're leaving it in bits and scraps. Look at the Lord of Misrule, our current president." She concentrated on him in the dark. "Saul," she said.

"Your diaphragm's not on."

"I know."

"But."

"So?"

"Well, what if?"

"What if? You'd be a father, that's what if." She had turned him so that she was right up against him, her breasts pressing him, challenging him.

"No," he said. He drew back. "Not yet. Let me figure this out on my own. There'd be no future."

"For the baby?"

"No. For me." He waited, trying to figure out how to say this. "I'd have to be one person forever. Does that make sense?"

"From you, it does." She pulled herself slightly away from him. They rearranged themselves.

The following Saturday he drove into Five Oaks for a haircut. When his hair was so long that it made the back of his neck itch, he went to Harold, the barber, and had it trimmed back. Saul liked Harold and his pensive mannerisms, even though Harold was a pale Lutheran, and a terrible barber. Harold made up for it with his occasional affability, and he happened to be in the same bowling league with Saul and sometimes played basketball at the same times that Saul did. Many of the men in Five Oaks looked slightly peculiar and asymmetrical, thanks to Harold. The last time Saul had come in, Harold had been deep in a conversation with a woman who was accusing him of things; Saul couldn't tell exactly what Harold was being accused of, but it sounded like a lover's quarrel, and Saul liked that. Anyone else's troubles diminished his own.

By coincidence, the same woman was back again in the barbershop with her son, whose hair Harold was cutting when Saul passed by the ancient barber pole before he rang the bell over the door as he entered. To pass the time and achieve a moment's invisibility, he picked up a newspaper from the next chair over and read the morning's headlines.

53

SHOTS FIRED AT HOLBEIN REACTOR
Iraqi Terrorists Suspected

Somebody was always shooting at something. Shielded by his paper, Saul heard the woman whispering instructions to Harold, and Harold's faint, exasperated "Louise, I can do this." Saul pretended to read the article. The shots, it turned out, had been harmless. Even though there had been no damage, some sort of investigation was going on. Saul thought Iraqis could do better than this.

There was more whispering, which Saul tried not to hear. After the woman had paid for her son's haircut and left, Saul sat himself down in Harold's chair.

"Hey, Saul," Harold said, covering him with the white cloth. "You always come in when she does. How do you do that?"

"Beats me. Her name Louise?"

"That's right. The usual trim, Saul?"

"The usual. Torture by Mr. Harold of Paris. Harold, this time try to keep it the same length on both sides, okay?"

"I try, Saul. It's just that your hair's so curly."

"Right, right." Saul saw his reflection in the mirror and closed his eyes as a reflex. He felt like asking Harold, the Lutheran, a moral question. "Harold," he said, "do you ever wonder where your thoughts come from? I mean, do we own our thoughts, or do they come from somewhere else, or what? For example, you can't always control your thoughts or your impulses, can you? So, whose thoughts are those, anyway, the ones you can't control? And another thing. Are you happy? Be honest."

The scissors stopped clipping. "Gosh, Saul, are you okay? What drugs have you been taking lately?"

"No drugs. Just tell me: Are your thoughts always yours? That's what I need to know."

The barber looked into the mirror opposite them. Saul saw Harold's plain features. "All right," Harold said. "I'll answer your question." Then, with what Saul took to be great sadness, the barber said, "I don't have many thoughts. And when I do, they're all mine."

"Okay," Saul said. "I'm sorry. I was just asking." He tried to slump down in his chair, but the barber said, "Sit up straight, Saul." Saul did.

Days later, Saul is asleep. He knows this. He knows he is asleep next to Patsy. He knows it is night, that cradle of dreams, but Earth's mad lovelorn companion, the moon, is shining stainless-steel beams across the bed, and Saul is dreaming of being in a car that cannot stop rolling over, an endless flip of metal, and this time Patsy is not belted in, and something horrible must be happening to her, judging from the blur of her head. She is being hurt terribly thanks to the way he has driven the car, the mad way, the un-American way, and now she is walking across a bridge made of moonlight, and she falls. The door, Saul's door, is being kept open for Elijah, but Elijah does not come in. How will we recognize him? Saul's mind is not in Saul's head; it is above him, above his yarmulke, above his prayer shawl, his tallis. When was Saul ever Orthodox? Only in dreams. Patsy is hurt, she lies in a ditch, *and he has done this damage to her.* Deer and doubt mix with the milky roar of mild lust on the Scrabble board. And here behind the barber chair is Giovanni d'Amato, sage of Cincinnati, saying, "You shouldn't flunk people out of school if you're going to get drunk and roll cars." The sage is using his scissors to cut away Saul's clothes. Saul the child is speaking to Saul the grown-up: "You'll never figure it out," and when Saul the adult asks, "What?" the child says, "Adulthood. Any of it." And then he says, "Saul, you're pregnant."

Saul woke and looked over at Patsy, still asleep. He groaned audibly with relief that she hadn't been hurt. What an annoying dream. He had never even owned a tallis or known anyone who had one. His parents had been relentlessly secular. After putting on his shirt, jeans, and boots, he went downstairs, and, after taking the keys off the kitchen table, he went outside.

The motorcycle felt quiet and powerful underneath him as he accelerated down Whitefeather Road. He had ridden a motorcycle briefly in college—until a small embarrassing accident—and the process all came back to him now. This one, Patsy's new machine, painted pink and blue, 250 cc's, was easy to shift, and the machine gave him the impression that he was floating, or, better yet, was flowing down the archways of dark, stunted Michigan trees. His eyes watered, and bugs hit him in the face as he speeded up. He felt the rear wheel slip on the dirt. He didn't know what he was doing out here and he didn't care. He had no helmet. He was illegal.

He turned left onto Highway 14, and then County Road H, also dirt, and he downshifted, feeling the tight, close gears meshing, and he let the clutch out, slowing him down. On the road the cycle's headlight was like a cone leading him forward, away from himself, toward a possibility more inviting and dangerous. In the grip of spiritual longing, a person goes anywhere, traveling over the speed limit. The night was warm, but none of the summer stars was visible. Behind the clouds the stars were even now rushing away in the infinity of expanding space. Saul felt like an astral body himself. He too would rush away into emptiness. In the green light of the speedometer he saw that he was doing a respectable fifty. Up ahead the wintry white eyes of a possum glanced toward him before the animal waddled into the high grass near the road. Saul wanted to be lost but knew he could not be. He knew exactly where he was: fields, forest, fields. He knew each one, and he knew whom they belonged to, he had been here that long.

And of course he knew where he was going: he was headed toward the McPhees', that damnable house of happiness, that castle of light, where everyone, man, woman, and child, would be sleeping soundly, the sleep of the happy and just and thoughtless. Saul felt blank, gripped by obsession, simultaneously vacant and full of shame.

He looked at his watch. It was past midnight. Their house would be dark.

But it was not. On the road beyond their driveway, Saul slowed down and then shut off the engine, holding on tightly to the handlebars as he stared like the prowler he was, toward the second-floor windows, from which sounds emerged. From where he was spying, Saul could see Anne sitting in a rocking chair by the window with their baby. The baby was crying, screaming. Saul could hear it from the road. And in the background, back and forth, Saul could see Emory McPhee pacing, the all-night walk of the helpless father. An infant with colic, a rocking mother, a pacing father, screams of infant misery, and now the two of them, Anne and Emory, beginning to shout at each other over what to do.

Saul turned his motorcycle around, pushed it down the road, then started the engine. He felt better. He could have gone to their front door and welcomed them as the official greeter of ordinary disharmony. *I was always as real as they were,* Saul thought. *I always was.*

On the left, the broken fences bordering the farmland quavered up and down and seemed to start bouncing, visually, as he accelerated. The lines on the telephone poles jumped nervously as he passed them until they had the rapid and nervous movements of pens on graph paper making an erratic heartbeat. Rain—he hadn't known it was going to rain, no one had told him—began falling, getting into his eyes and dropping with cold precision on the backs of his hands. He felt the cloth of his shirt getting soaked and sticking to his shoulders. The rain was persistent and serious. He felt the tires of Patsy's motorcycle slipping on the mud, nudging the rear end of the bike off, slightly, thoughtfully, toward the left side. Then the road joined up with the highway, where the traction improved, but the rain was falling more heavily now, soaking him so he could hardly see. He came to a bridge, slowed the bike, and huddled in its shelter for a moment, until the rain seemed to let up, and he set out again. Accelerate, clutch, shift. He wanted to get home to Patsy. He wanted to dry his hair and get into bed next to her. He couldn't think of anything else he wanted.

A few hundred feet from his own driveway, he looked through the rain, only a drizzle now, and he saw, looking back at him, their eyes lit by his headlamp, the deer he had seen before, closer now, crossing his yard. But this time, there was another, a last deer, one he hadn't seen before, behind the others, slightly smaller, as if reduced somehow. It was an albino. In the darkness and rain it moved in a haze of whiteness. Seeing it, Saul thought: Oh my God, I'm about to die. The deer had stopped, momentarily frozen in the light. The albino's eyes—it was a doe—were pink, and its fur was as white as linen. The animal flicked its tail, nervously hypnotized. Its terrible pink eyes, blank as neutron stars, stared at him. Saul turned off the engine and the headlight. Now in the dark two brown deer bounded toward the west, but the albino stood still, staring in Saul's direction, a purposeful stare. He gripped the handlebars so hard that his forearms began to knot into a cramp. The animal was a sign of some kind, he was sure. Only a fool would think otherwise. He felt a moment of dread pass through his body as the deer now turned her eyes away from his and began to walk off into the night. He saw her disappear behind a maple tree in his backyard, but he couldn't follow her beyond that. He was trembling now. Shivering spasms began at his wet shoulders and passed down into his chest toward his legs. The dread he had felt before was turning rapidly into pure spiritual fright. Alternating waves of chill and heat rushed up and down his body. He remembered to get off the road. He pushed the motorcycle into the garage, kicking down its stand. He crossed the yard and reached the back door. The rain picked up again and sprayed into him as the wind carried it. In his mind's eye he saw the deer looking back at him. He had been judged, and the judgment was that he, Saul, was only and always himself, now and onward into infinity. His boots were wet. They stank of wet leather. Outside the back door on the lawn he took the boots off, then his wet shirt and his jeans. It occurred to him to stand there naked. With no clothes on he stood in the rain and the dark before he fell to his knees. He wasn't praying. He didn't know what he was doing. Something was filling him up. It felt like the spirit, but the spirit of what, he didn't know. He lay down on the grass. One sob tore through him, and then it was over.

He felt like getting up and running out into the field in back of the house, but he knew he couldn't break through the wall of his self-consciousness enough to do that. In the rain, which no longer felt cold, he sensed that he was entering a condition that had nothing to do with happiness because it was so far beyond it. All he was sure about was that he was empty before and now was filled, filled with both fullness and emptiness. These emotions didn't quite make sense, but he didn't care. The emptiness was sweet. He could live with it. He hurried into the house and dried off his hair in the dark downstairs bathroom. Quickly he toweled himself down and then rushed up the stairs. There was a secret, after all. In fact there were probably a lot of secrets, but there was one he now knew.

He entered their bedroom. Rain fingernailed against the window glass. Patsy lay in bed in almost complete darkness, wearing one of Saul's T-shirts. Her arms were up above her head. He could see that she was watching him.

"Where were you?"

"I went out for a ride on your motorcycle. I couldn't sleep."

"Saul, it's *raining*. Why are you naked?"

"It's raining now. Not when I started."

"Why are you standing there? You don't have any clothes on."

"I saw something. I can't tell you. I think I'm not supposed to tell you what I saw. It was an animal. It was a private animal. Patsy, I took off my clothes and lay down on the lawn in the rain, and it didn't feel weird, it felt like just what I should do."

"Saul, what is this about? I need some idea right now."

"I'm not sure."

"Try. Try to say."

"I think I'm pregnant."

"What does that mean?"

"I think it means that whoever I am, I'm not alone with myself."

"I don't understand that."

"I know."

"Come to bed, Saul. Get in under the sheet."

He climbed in and put his leg over hers.

"I can't quite get used to you," she said. "You're quite a mess of metaphors, Saul, you know that."

"Yes."

"A man being pregnant." She put her hand familiarly on his thigh. "I wonder what that portends."

"It's a feeling, Patsy. It's a secret. Men have secrets, too."

"I never said they didn't. They love secrets. They have lodges and secret societies and stuff. They have the CIA."

"Can we make love now, right this minute? Because I love you. I love you like crazy."

"I love you, too, Saul. What if you make *me* pregnant? It could happen. What if I get knocked up? Is it all right now?"

"Yeah. What's the problem?"

"What will we say, for example?"

"We'll say, 'Saul and Patsy are pregnant.'"

"Oh, sure we will."

"Okay, we won't say it." He had thrown the sheet back and was kissing her on the side of her knees.

"Are you crying? Your face is wet."

"Yes."

"But you're being so jokey."

"That's how I handle it."

"Why are you crying?"

"Because . . ." He wanted to get this right. "Because there are signs and wonders. What can I tell you? It's all a feeling. In the morning I'll deny I said this."

"So like a man." She was kissing him now, but she stopped, as if thinking about his recent sentences. "You *want* to make me pregnant, too, don't you?"

"Yes."

"You're not afraid? Of diapers, exhaustion, sullenness? Fatigue, indifference, hostility, silence, boredom, quarrels, rage, infidelity?"

"No."

"You're a brave man. I'll give you credit for that. One more little ambassador from the present to the future. That's what you want."

"Sort of." He moved up and took her fingers one by one into his mouth and bit them tenderly. Patsy had started to hum. She was humming "Unchain My Heart." Then she opened her mouth and sang quietly, "Unchain my heart, and set me free."

"I'll try, Patsy."

"Yes." A moment later, she said, "This won't solve anything."

"I know." He felt as though he heard someone wailing softly in the next room. Still he continued. "Patsy," he said, "the window. We should stand by the window."

"Why?"

"To try it." He disentangled himself from her, stood, and brought her over to the window. He opened it so that the droplets of rain blew in over them. "Now," he said. There was a bit of lightning, and he lifted her. She held on, arms clasped behind his neck. He felt as though a thousand eyes, but not human eyes, were looking in on them with tender indifference. They were and were not interested. They would and would not care. Finally they would turn away, as they tended to turn away from all human things, in time. Saul felt Patsy tremble, a slight shivering along her back, a rising in tension before release. More rain came in, spattering lightly on his arm. He felt Patsy's mouth passing by his hair, recently cut by Harold. She was panting in time with his own breathing, and for a split second he understood it all. He understood everything, the secret to the universe. Then, after an instant, he lost it. Having lost the secret, forgotten it, he felt the usual onset of the ordinary, of everything else, with Patsy around him, the two of them in their own familiar rhythms. He would not admit to anyone that he had known the secret of the universe for a split second. That part of his life was hidden away and would always be, the part that makes a person draw in the breath quickly in surprise and stare at the curtains in the morning upon awakening.

Four

Saul, Patsy thought, was like one of those pastries you couldn't get enough of at first—you'd gorge on them. And then, it seemed, once you'd had enough of them, you wanted to get rid of that addiction, but you couldn't, there was no way to stop. You were always going to have those jelly doughnuts in your life because you had once craved them. Slowly but surely, they would put weight on you.

Mornings, on her way down to the mortgage department at the bank, where she had become—at last—an assistant loan officer (she admitted to herself, and to no one else, that she liked to be around places where money was—it even had a smell to it she liked), she would pass by school-bus stops and nursery schools. Sometimes, on lunch breaks, she would park the car near the curbs and watch the little people, three- and four-year-olds, holding hands or holding on to delicate ropes to keep them all together as they progressed down the sidewalks. She loved seeing children lined up in their school clothes and backpacks, waiting for the bus. They yelled at each other. They fell into the dirt and mud. They were beautiful.

A week after her baby was due, she would drive around on her lunch hour just looking for children, hoping her labor would start out of sympathy. And on a Tuesday, as she sat parked across the street from a playground, watching a softball game, her water broke. On the way to the hospital that evening, she remembered to thank the moon, which had been shining in the daytime sky above the playing field, though it was invisible by nightfall, having gone on its lunatic way.

The labor room: between contractions and the blips of the fetal monitor, she was dimly aware of Saul. He had donned his green hospital scrubs. They hadn't let him wear his Detroit Tigers baseball cap (too unsanitary), but he was holding her hand and his eyes were anxious with nervous energy as he sat at her bedside. He thought he was coaching her. But he kept miscounting the breaths, and she had to correct him.

After two hours of that, she was moved into the huge circular incandescence of the delivery room. She felt as if she were about to expel her entire body outward in a floorflood. With her hair soaked with sweat and sticking to the back of her neck, she could feel the unsteady universe sputtering out for an instant into two flattened dimensions. Everything she saw was painted on a flat surface in front of her, and she felt herself screaming self-consciously, as if she were screaming performatively when she was both screaming and doing something else, the serious work. Then she swore—she had learned to swear like a man from her father, who was only eloquent when he cursed—and she loosened her hand from Saul's—his touch maddened her—and swore again. She looked at Saul with a deep hatred. He had gotten her into this mess, and now he was dumbly watching her trying to get herself out. Terrible, unforgivable words, slightly out of her control, came out of her mouth directed toward Saul. Wrath, bitterness, and then some screeching. The seconds blew themselves up into hours, with time seizing up, thickening and slowing as if the river of it had turned to offal, ordure, and slush.

"Okay, here's the head. One last push, please."

Patsy backstroked through the pain. Then the baby presented herself in a mess of blood and fleshy wrappings. After the cord was cut, Patsy heard her husband say from a great distance, "She's beautiful. Uh, Patsy, you didn't *really* mean those things you said about me, did you? When you were screaming? Those curses?" Oh, the hell with Saul. *Where was her baby?* They were giving her an Apgar test. Typical of Saul, Patsy thought, as she began to recover herself, to worry about what somebody was saying about him at the moment of his daughter's birth. I see that you're having a baby—but what about *me?* Enough about you—you're just giving birth. Anyway, Saul always stole scenes. It was in his nature.

"Where's my baby?"

"Here," the nurse said. The world had rematerialized and accordioned out into three dimensions again. The baby fit perfectly into the crook of Patsy's arm, and she was, Patsy thought, perfect in every respect, beautiful beyond thought. She touched her delicate chin. How strange it was to have a daughter so new that she didn't have a name! It was the beginning of the world for her, before the invention of language. And she looked like Patsy's grandmother Ella, lovable and ancient and irritable, a fan of murder mysteries and a smoker of cigarettes, who picked wild strawberries and fed them to her dogs. But, no: she wasn't Grandmother Ella, she was herself. The nurse's smile and her daughter's impatient expression made a sunspot near Patsy's heart, and the huge overhead delivery-room light went out, like a sigh.

Someone took Patsy's hand, the other hand, the one not cradling the baby. Who else but Saul, unsteady but upright, wanting some part of her? Cold sweat dripped down his forehead. He kissed Patsy through his face mask, a sterile forgiving kiss, feeling of paper that landed on her cheek, and he informed her that they were parents now. He touched his daughter on her forehead, a blessing. As he said it, his eyes expressed excitement and terror. He would be one of those men unready for fatherhood but full of intermittent, wild, undirected enthusiasm for it. "Hi, Mom," he said. He apologized for worrying about Patsy's opinion of him, and Patsy apologized for what she had said about Saul during her labor. Releasing her hand from Saul's, Patsy raised it and caressed his face. "Oh, don't worry," the nurse said, apparently referring to Patsy's verbal abusiveness, and from behind him, she patted Saul on the back, as if he had been some sort of good dog, a retriever.

. . .

They named their daughter Mary Esther Carlson-Bernstein, a string of words that Patsy thought awkward and ungainly but, once she had said it and attached it to her daughter, somehow fine.

But Saul didn't seem so pleased with it. While making dinner a week later, one of his improvised stir-fries that made use of fresh ingredients to combine with and camouflage the leftovers, Saul said that he had been having second thoughts: Mary Esther, he said, was burdened with a lot of name, maybe too much Christianity and Judaism mixed in there for comfort. "Whose comfort?" Patsy asked, from her chair in the kitchen, wondering about how Saul was managing. Standing in front of the stove, listening selectively, Saul ignored the question. Possibly another name would be better, he went on, uninterruptable. Jayne, maybe, or Liz. Direct, futuristic American monosyllables. Bottom-line names. Or maybe they could combine the M of Mary and the E of Esther to make Emmy.

As he muttered and chopped carrots and broccoli before dropping the bamboo shoots and water chestnuts and some other unidentifiables into the pan, Patsy could see that he was so tired that he was only half-awake. His monologue wasn't meant to make any sense; it was meant to fill time, to get his thoughts out of his head and into the room, and then into Patsy's head. He spoke words the way a ventilator blew out air. Of course he didn't plan on renaming his daughter after naming her the first time; he said only crazy people did that, loading down their children with aliases. His socks didn't match, his jeans were beltless, and his hair had gone back to wildness, sprigs and sections hanging down over his eyes, his ears, his neck. He was a mess. Still quite handsome, though, in his way, and very lovable, though he tired you out, being the way he was.

The night before, between feedings—feedings for the baby, not for Saul, who had become, in a way that Patsy couldn't quite pinpoint, slightly more baby-like himself—Saul had confessed that he didn't know if he could manage it, *it* being the long haul of fatherhood. But that had just been Saul-talk. Right now, Mary Esther was sleeping upstairs. Fingering the pages of her magazine, Patsy leaned back in the alcove, still in her bathrobe, watching her husband prepare dinner. She liked watching him. She breathed in and out, her lungs as dependable in their way as her husband. She was still sore everywhere and took pleasure in not moving; she liked staying put and watching the ceiling or the cars outside on the road, or the spectacle of Saul, cooking. Long stretches of bland ordinariness staged anywhere in the house soothed her. Ordinary life seemed to be full of a previously hidden grace as long as she didn't have to get up very far to meet it. She had already done that by giving birth to Mary Esther. You couldn't get much closer to life than that. Feeling her breasts engorged, still feeling familiar pains all over herself in her most private places, she wondered what she had done with the breast pump and when the diaper guy would deliver the new batch.

Bending down toward the pan, stolid and dutiful and husbandly, Saul sniffed, added some peanut oil, stirred again, and after a minute he ladled out dinner onto Patsy's plate. The food gave off a damp tropical aroma. Then with that habit he had of reading her thoughts and rewording them—a habit that amazed Patsy and irritated her in equal measures—he turned toward her and said, "You left the breast pump upstairs." And then: "Hey, you think I'm sleepwalking. But I'm not. I'm conscious. I only *look* like a zombie." He smiled at her with a full-fledged zombie smile, the right side of his mouth going up, the undead left side staying right where it was. "You smell of ether," he said, unkindly.

If he can read my thoughts, she thought, where's my privacy? But there wasn't any privacy anyway, not when you gave birth in front of strangers and brought out a breast anytime the baby wanted it.

For the last nine months, Saul had glimpsed the albino deer, always at a distance, on the fringes of the property that he and Patsy rented. After work or on weekends, he had walked across the unfarmed fields up to the next property line, marked by rusting fence posts, or, past the fields, into the neighboring woods of silver maple and scrub oak, hoping to get a sight of the animal and to find out why it was pestering him. It had only revealed itself, however, when he had not been looking for it, and it had this out-of-the-corner-of-the-eye trick that made Saul feel as if the deer had a project of some sort, like converting him to Catholicism or explaining fatherhood to him. Once it had stood grazing near a stump and was visible until he looked directly at it. Then it disappeared with one instantaneous leap into the underbrush. Here, there, gone. It gave him the shivers, this hallucinatory beast with pink eyes and white fur.

Out on his walks, or while jogging, searching the ground for clues, Saul went into emotional reveries, which Patsy had characterized as manic-depressive fits, a phrase that Saul hated. He missed the old pre-therapeutic words like "sorrow" and "exuberance" and "forbearance." Just now he was a bit short of forbearance. What was he doing out here taking these walks? The sky lately was habitually overcast, like a patient in need of therapy. There were no hills worth mentioning. You couldn't eat the berries that grew here because if you did, you would sicken. The streams and creeks hardly flowed at all because the ground was so flat that the water became indecisive. Yes, semirural Michigan (things were changing: there was a new outlet mall two miles away, they had paved Whitefeather Road and were beginning to put up stoplights, and condos were being built in a hurry) was a blank slate, but he felt right at home in it, just like that freak of nature, that deer. Maybe everywhere was a blank slate. And now he had a daughter, right here, to care for. A daughter! The fungal smell of wood rot in the culverts strengthened him, he believed, made him a better man, perhaps a better father, or at least made him think of words that nobody used anymore, such as "rue."

Clouds, mud, wind. Joy and woe, mad happiness and rue lived side by side in Saul with very few emotions in between. Even his gloom was thick with lyric intensity, like a brass band playing a funeral march all day and having a good time doing it. No longer a figure in a Russian novel, he imagined all winter that he lived stranded in an ink drawing by a Chinese artist who lived in the Midwest. He himself was the suggested figure in the lower-right-hand corner. Colors—the bright happy colors—were for elsewhere, for those suspicious characters who comported themselves in California or Florida, who couldn't face up to cloudy days, who required sports cars and perpetual sunlight and suntans to get through the day.

Wearing his Northwestern University gym clothes, he liked to jog after work alongside the drainage ditch, where he could watch a microwave transmission tower being constructed two miles away. He heard noises of construction, the distant sounds of heavy machinery. From a spidery oak tree, a crow cawed, announcing rain. Near the highway on a Sunday morning two weeks after Mary Esther was born, he had spotted a soiled Ben Franklin half-dollar next to a tossed-away beer can and picked it up. It had been his lucky day. But all the days were lucky, recently. He reminded himself to give thanks to somebody or something. He would start with Patsy.

He made his way back to the house, mud chuckling underneath his boots, Ben Franklin in his pocket, the first fifty cents of Mary Esther's college fund. He had a secret he had not told Patsy, though she probably knew it: he did not think that he had any clue to being a parent. Not one. His father had died before he might have shown him the fatherhood tricks—all Saul could remember was his father making scrambled eggs for the family on Saturday mornings. Saul's mother, Delia, had not tried to find a substitute for the boys once their father was gone. Perhaps Saul would fail at fatherhood and they would take his daughter away from him on grounds of parental incompetency. He did not love being a parent, though he loved his daughter with a newfound intensity close to hysteria. To him, fatherhood was one long unrevisable bourgeois script full of long-expected plot turns and predictable blow-ups in the third act, but that was the script he had been handed, and now he was in the play.

Love, rage, and tenderness disabled him in the chairs in which he sat, miming calm, holding Mary Esther. What was the matter with him? He loved his daughter. It was himself he had a problem with. He just didn't know what the problem was, although his therapist in Chicago had once told him that he suffered from "pointless remorse" and "inappropriate longings." His typical despairs were beginning to look like luxuries to him. He could be a despair junkie and a virtuoso of fretfulness but probably not anymore, not with a daughter around. Somehow he would have to discard his friends, the long-term discontents, those houses of metaphysical yearnings where he had once made his home. Probably he couldn't go over to Holbein College anymore on weekends and pretend to be a student. He came in and thanked Patsy with a kiss. But that night, when Patsy was fast asleep, Saul knelt on the landing and beat his fists on the stairs, but softly, so as not to awaken anybody.

On the morning when Mary Esther was celebrating her birthday—she was four weeks old—they sat at the breakfast table with the sun, in a rare appearance, blazing in through the east window and reflecting off the butter knife. With one hand, Patsy fed herself corn flakes. With the other hand she held Mary Esther, who was nursing. Patsy was also glancing down at the morning paper on the table and was talking to Saul about his upcoming birthday, what color shirt to get him. She chewed her corn flakes thoughtfully and only reacted when Mary Esther sucked too hard. It hurt, and it showed on Patsy's face. A deep brown, she said. You'd look good in that. It'd show off your eyes.

Listening, Saul watched them both, rattled by the domestic sensuality of their pairing, and his spirit shook with wild, bruised, jealous love. He felt pointless and redundant, a citizen of the tiny principality of irony. His heart, that trapped bird, flapped in its cage. Patsy's breast belonged to him, he thought, not to Mary Esther, even though she could make better use of it than he could. He was ashamed of being jealous of his baby daughter, and he squirmed in his chair as he finished his oatmeal. Actually, he realized, Patsy's breast belonged to Patsy. Behind Patsy the kitchen spice rack displayed its orderly contents. Everything in the house was orderly, thanks to Patsy, everything except Saul. A delivery truck rumbled by on Whitefeather Road. He felt specifically his shallow and approximate condition. In broad daylight, night enfolded him.

He went off to work feeling superfluous and ecstatic and horny, his body glowing with its fatherly confusions.

That semester, Saul had been pulled from one section of American history and had been reassigned to remedial English for learning-disabled students in the high school. "Anyone can teach English," his principal, Zoltan Kabeláč, liked to say. "It's our mother tongue." Zoltan, speaking for the school, had claimed that the economic times being what they were, the district could not afford a full-time specialist in remedial education, and because Saul had been a persistent advocate of the rights of the learning-disabled at school meetings and elsewhere, and because, he suspected, Zoltan Kabeláč did not like him, he had been assigned a group of seven kids in remedial writing, and they all met in a converted storage room at the back of the school at eight-thirty, following the second bell.

Five of them were pleasant and sweet-tempered and bewildered (by life, by Saul, by most of what happened to them day after day, the confusing pageant of getting dressed, taking the bus, and telling time), but two of them appeared to hate the class and, very convincingly, Saul himself, their hatred occasionally focused to a fine point on him. They sat, these two, as far away from him as possible, near the back wall close to the brooms, whispering to each other and smiling with energetic young-adolescent malevolence at him. Saul had tried everything with them— jokes, praise, discipline—but nothing had worked to increase the boys' interest in reading or to lower their scorn for education, and he had arrived at a state of strong, steady uneasiness, a feeling that soon they would try to enact some awfulness upon him, a terrible dangerous prank. He could feel it coming.

He thought of the two boys, Gordy Himmelman and Bob Pawlak, as the Child Cossacks. They belonged in Central Asia somewhere. However, interesting hatred could arise anywhere. Gordy apparently had no parents, just an aunt. His mother had died in a house fire, and his father had gone west and stayed there and had gradually disappeared. No one knew where he was; he had not been heard from in years. Gordy lived with his aunt in a manufactured home on the north side of town. Marly Albertson, the school social worker assigned to Gordy, said the situation out there at Brenda Bagley's house—Brenda Bagley was Gordy's aunt— was like a museum of creepiness and warned him not to ask about it if he didn't want to know. Saul had met Brenda once. She had an unattractiveness so painful to look upon that you felt guilty of rubbernecking if you glanced at her twice. When she came in for a conference, her facial complexion looked scaly, and she sat down with the slow elaborate courtesy of working people out of their element in a classroom, the unease of the uninvited. She gave the appearance of knowing that she was not wanted anywhere she happened to be. She had said almost nothing for the fifteen minutes during which Saul described Gordy's failings. She appeared to be broken down by hard work—she was a waitress at the Fleetwood—

and she nodded dumbly at everything Saul told her, as if his desolate words were no more than what she had expected, wounds on top of wounds.

Saul had driven by Gordy's home a couple of times and had seen a desperate barking dog chained to a stake in the front yard. Often Gordy came to school wearing a T-shirt spotted with blood. His boots were scuffed from objects he had kicked or that had simply fallen haplessly into his path. On his face were two rashes, one from acne, the other from blankness. Girls avoided him. His eyes, on those occasions when they met Saul's, were cold and lunar. If you were dying on the side of the road in a rainstorm, Saul thought, Gordy's eyes would pass over you and continue on, after you died, to the next interesting sight.

Sometimes Gordy would begin to stare at Saul at the beginning of class and not stop until the class was finally over. The contours of Gordy's fixation were unknowable, Saul had decided.

Politically and socially and ideologically, Saul had once felt pity and compassion and generosity toward the wretched of the earth. He still did, when he considered them as a class, and only when they appeared as individuals did they sometimes alarm him. He suspected that Gordy hated him in a final, visceral manner, above or below argument.

Gordy's friend Bob Pawlak was a dog-killer and a cat-killer, he claimed. He shot them with his 410, he said. Perhaps it was just talk. In a moment of intimacy he had bragged to Saul about killing cats, and his laughter, describing how he went about it, was not quite under control. His smile was the meanest one Saul had ever seen on an ex-child, a smile also visible on the face of Bob's father, Bob Pawlak, Sr., who once came in, unbelievably, for a parent conference. About his boy, Bob Sr. agreed that Bob Jr. was a hell-raiser, but, then, so was he. He shook his dismayed and proud parental head, decorated with gin blossoms.

Saul could hardly stand to look at Gordy and Bob. But Gordy was not afraid to look at Saul. As was his habit, he stared and stared. There were no windows in the room where he taught them, and no fan, and after half an hour of everyone's mingled breathing, the air in the room was foul enough to kill a canary.

Earlier in the week Saul had given the kids pictures clipped from magazines. They were supposed to write one-sentence stories to accompany each picture. For these high schoolers, the task would be a challenge. Now, before school started, his mind still on Patsy and Mary Esther, Saul began to read yesterday's sentences. Gordy and Bob had as usual not written anything. Gordy had torn his picture to bits, and Bob had shredded and eaten his. But the other students had made their brave attempts.

It is dangerous to dive into a pool of water without the nolige of the depth because if it is salow you could hit your head that might creat unconsheness and drowding.

Quite serprisingly the boy finds among the presents rapings which are now discarded a model air plan.

Two sentences, each one requiring ten minutes' work. Saul stared at them, word by word, feeling himself stumbling in a cognitive limp. What was the next lesson? Where did one start? The sentences were like glimpses into the shattered mind of God.

Like the hourse a cow is an animal and the human race feasts on its meat and diary which form the bulky hornd animal.

The cold blooded crecher the bird will lay an egg and in a piriod of time a new bird will brake out of it as a storm of burth.

Saul looked up from his desk at the sputtering overhead lights and the grimy acoustic tile. It was in the storm of birth—mouths of babes, etc.—that he himself was currently being tossed.

He looked down at the floor again and spotted a piece of paper with the words "your a kick" close to the wastebasket. Finally, a nice compliment! He tossed it away.

Saul's mother had been visiting. When Saul arrived at home, carrying the *Five Oaks News-Chronicle,* Delia met him at the door and gave him a kiss on the cheek, leaving lipstick and perfume on him, like a claim check. She had more scents than a cougar. This was the fourth day of a projected six-day visit. She had been cooking meals, helping out with the housework, and taking care of Mary Esther whenever Patsy flagged or needed to nap. Delia did not like the name "Mary Esther" and much preferred "Emmy." Whenever his mother called her grandchild "Emmy," Saul felt himself getting slowly but steadily irritated at his mother's assumption that he and Patsy were disqualified from naming their own daughter themselves, that they would do it incorrectly.

The house, which had once smelled of Saul and Patsy, and the sweet-sour loamy smells of parenting and babyhood, now smelled pungently of Delia's perfume, a fragrance with the power of an air-raid siren. What was the point? Why did a new grandmother have to wear so much perfume? Well, Saul thought, the question answers itself. His mother had given birth to him when she was twenty-one. She was now in her forties, and still, she thought, a player.

Delia was tall, with brilliant red hair, and restless. Bracelets rang noisily on her wrists, and she favored large clumpy necklaces of amber. She had long elegant fingers tipped with brilliant blood-red nail polish. She had a dominatrix side, he thought uncharitably. Saul, who liked Richard Strauss's operas and once played trombone in one of the Northwestern University student pit orchestras, sometimes referred to his mother as "the Marschallin" and thought that Eleanor Steber could do a good job of playing her. Moving around the house like a woman who meant business no matter what she was doing, she had missed her calling, Saul claimed in bed to Patsy. She should have been a full-time aristocrat running a palace, planning masked balls, arranging other people's affairs. She aspired to a certain level of domesticated depravity. Just watching her tired him out and gave him headaches. Always tanned and fit, she had a personal trainer at a health club in Bethesda, and Saul was always dismayed by how good-looking his mother was, how disconcertingly sexy. No middle-aged woman needed to be that beautiful, he thought, especially when the beauty is fading just enough to give it warmth, and that woman is your mother, and your father has died young, and your mother has gone on to have a succession of boyfriends, and . . . and . . .

His mother took his hand. He wondered if he had a streak of misogyny. Probably only in regard to his mother. Other women did not inspire it.

"Emmy was a little angel today," the Marschallin said, nodding toward the living room, where Mary Esther was sleeping in Patsy's arms. Patsy raised her face toward Saul. "How was work?" his mother asked, keeping her voice down. "How was school?"

The question made him feel like a child. Delia had that effect on him. Saul removed his hand from his mother's and pursed his lips in Patsy's direction. He took out a handkerchief to wipe off his mother's lipstick from his face. But he could feel its imprint there, worming its way through the skin toward his brain. "Work was fine. Someone left me a note. They said I was a kick."

"That's nice," Delia said dubiously. "A kick? In what sense?"

"In the sense that . . . oh, you know. A party. *That's a real kick.* Fun."

Very quietly, from her chair, Patsy said, "Nobody uses that word that way anymore." Having gathered her blond hair back in a ponytail, she gazed down at Mary Esther and touched the baby's own perfect feathery hair. Patsy's beauty was fuller and more human, Saul thought, than his mother's. It was actionable. You wanted to mate with her. His wife's beauty made him happy and crazy, and his mother's beauty just made him crazy, period. Maybe menopause would calm his mother down, but he doubted it.

"They don't? Sure they do," Saul said.

"Not in a learning-disabilities class, they don't." Patsy shook her head. "You can bet your bottom dollar that they don't use expressions like that."

"I agree with Patsy," Delia announced with a huge smile. "We have womanly solidarity here."

"Oh, I hope not," Saul grumbled, suddenly thirsty for a beer. He wanted to escape from the room and Delia's presence. There was too much femaleness around all of a sudden. He rushed to the refrigerator for a beer, then returned to the living room so that he could drink it from the bottle in front of his mother. He couldn't wait until she was gone and Patsy's relatives arrived. Her parents were sweet and generous and harmless, very fond of Saul. In contrast to his mother, they were not like wild animals in a zoo. He would trade his mother for his mother-in-law anytime. Saul's mother sat down close to Patsy and threw a large radiant scary smile in her son's direction.

"Your brother used to use that expression constantly," she said. "'Oh, that's a kick,' he'd say." She examined her fingernails. "Your brother loved kicks."

"Yes, he did," Saul said. "And he still does." He had not had a phone call or a letter from Howie in ages. It irked him, Howie's indifference to Patsy and himself and to Mary Esther's birth. What Howie did was give birth to money, money, and then more money. "Where *is* he? The last I heard he was rock climbing in Colorado or someplace."

"Your handsome brother?" Delia sat up, stretching her long legs wrapped in designer jeans. Then she straightened, somehow displaying herself further, unnecessarily. More of her perfume seemed to seep into the air. It was making Saul light-headed, like pepper-spray. "Howie hasn't called you? In how long? He promised me he would. Oh, he gave up the rock climbing for a few months. Got it out of his system, I guess. It's all information technology now. Well, he always did have a head for math. Didn't I tell you?" Delia looked at Saul as if his ignorance on this subject was his fault. "That friend of his, what's his name, Gerald Some-body, has got him working in computers and things, some start-up company making programs for instant balance-sheet assessments. Or something digital." Delia waved her hand abstractedly, conjuring up computers and whirring machinery. "High-speed information flow stuff. He *said* he'd call. Call *you*, I mean. I told him about Mary Esther. He seemed interested. I can't believe Howie hasn't called you to keep you informed."

"That's nice," Saul said. "'Interested' is nice." He took a swig of the beer. "I'm pleased about the 'interested' part."

"Don't be so ironical about your brother. He doesn't have all the feelings about things that you have. He's not so . . ." She searched for the word. "*Emotional*. He sails along on the surfaces. That's his gift. Besides, he's making a lot of money," Delia reported. "A *lot* of money, he says, almost by accident. Of course he's immature, but that's . . . I wish you wouldn't drink beer right out of the bottle, sweetheart. Not in the living room." Saul's mother made a distaste-expression. It reminded Saul of years of distaste-expressions, and he looked away, though it pleased him that she was annoyed.

On New Year's Eve, he would make a resolution about not being petty with his mother, but not until then.

Saul and his younger brother had never been close. In Saul's estimation, Howie's brains and his good looks (he was painfully handsome, everyone said, beautiful, a male version of Delia), and Howie's efforts to get some distance on their mother had made him simultaneously distant and arrogant, or distantly arrogant. In any case, he was hard to get close to, and his thoughts were often a mystery. Like many extraordinarily good-looking men, he never bothered saying very much. Other people were always trying to talk to him, to make the first move, desperate just to keep him around. Saul's brother had deep brown eyes, a perfectly symmetrical face with high cheekbones, curly black hair, and perfectly straight posture. His princely appearance was perfect in a way that Saul found unpleasant. People stared at him helplessly. He never shambled anywhere, never had a hair out of place, any clothes looked good on him, and as a result he was always being given special attentions.

Howie had once called Saul, during the period of Saul's life when Saul was driving a taxicab in Chicago, to report that two women had proposed marriage to him that very week. This was at Princeton, where Howie was a junior, majoring in math and computer science. Howie thought it was hilarious, all these propositions, all these women, and the men, too, who hung around him, and he thought that Saul would also be amused. Popularity was a stitch. He was a lucky guy, Howie was, starting with his looks and going on from there. In any particular room, if Howie had not slept with all of the women, it was just an oversight. Well, Howie played the part of the grasshopper, and Saul played the part of the ant. Except grasshoppers weren't also supposed to be smart and to make a lot of money. Winter was supposed to come in due course and kill them dead.

"Tell him to call me," Saul said. "Tell Howie to drop us a line and give us his address. Tell him we're alive and he's Uncle Howie now, and his niece would like a nice present from him."

"I certainly won't say *that*. Such a shame," Delia said mournfully, "that you two don't get along."

"Oh, they get along," Patsy said. "We just don't hear much from him. By the way," she said, sitting up, "who was that character in comic books who made money no matter what he did?" Patsy stood up and swayed back and forth for Mary Esther's sake. Saul noticed that Patsy had circles under her eyes, a recent detail—a fact—about her that had escaped him. His heart surged like a motor racing, revving up its RPMs, all for her sake. "Money fell out of trees for him. Some duck. Some relative of Donald Duck."

"Gladstone Gander," Saul said, suppressing a belch. On the subject of comic books, books generally, baseball, music, philosophy, and movies, Saul was Mr. Memory.

"Oh, let's go outside," Delia said, staring at Saul's beer bottle. "For just a moment. For a breath of air. All right, kids? What do you say? It's getting stuffy in here."

"It's your perfume, Mom," Saul said. "You're wearing a gallon of it."

"Not *quite* a gallon." She smiled. "More like a half-gallon." She stood up and strode briskly toward the back door, her bracelets and necklace jangling. Saul and Patsy heard the door slam behind her, and then her muffled voice, softly shouting, "It's *beautiful* out here!"

"It can't be beautiful," Saul said. "It's March." He looked at Patsy. "It's too cold to take the baby outside," he said softly. "What is she thinking?" His eyes scanned his wife's face. "When will we ever make love again, honey? Can you tell me that? I'm dying over here."

Just then he heard his mother scream, a subtle scream, half-private. For a moment he thought it was because he had propositioned his wife. Collecting himself, Saul rushed out past the kitchen into the mud room, out through the back porch with its snow shovel, sand bucket, and bag of salt, onto the wood steps that descended unevenly to the back lawn, covered here and there with patches of dirty snow.

The air had cleared itself of clouds and overcast, and the moon was back in the sky. Just to the side of the steps, the Marschallin stood in the moonlight, her red hair looking silver gray, just as if she had aged thirty years within the past minute. Then Saul realized it was only the effect of the moonlight, and he said, "Mom, it's just the moonlight. You're not *that* old."

She turned toward him, stricken. "What're you talking about? What *ever* on earth are you talking about, Saul? Look!"

She pointed one of her long fingers, decorated with its red nail polish that in the moonlight also looked gray, and he followed where she indicated to the middle of the field, where the albino deer walked with a slight stagger, an arrow sticking out of its back leg, seemingly blinded and wounded now by Saul's students, the pimply Cossacks. Still, the deer was alive, as it slowly faded back into the dark. Saul considered his options, all of them vague and transitory: he would have tried to run after it, that animal, somehow take its pain away, but for now he was not equipped with the necessary time and energy and speed for that particular kind of rescue.

Five

For the first two weeks after Mary Esther's birth, Saul and Patsy's neighbors and friends had called ahead, following country manners, before bringing over dishes of food. Day in and out, the food had accumulated on the kitchen counter and in the refrigerator: chicken-and-noodle casseroles and Jell-O salads and desserts, baked beans, and one poached salmon cooked by a fellow teacher at the school, a subscriber to *Gourmet* magazine and an avid watcher of the Food Network.

But Saul could be picky. "Well, it's certainly not Jew food," he had said after his friend Hugh Welch left. He picked up Hugh's donated honey-baked ham before he pretended to pass it, like a football, through the kitchen window. "This is pig meat."

"Don't complain," Patsy said. "You're doing all this for effect. You like ham as much as I do, and you're just going for cheap laughs." She took the ham out of his hand and tried to stuff it into the refrigerator, where there was no room for it. "And I like Hugh, besides."

"Listen, I'm fully assembled in America, but he's doing this as an ethnic insult, and I'm not being paranoid. At least I don't think so."

"Oh, right. Honey," she said, "calm down." She turned around and gave him a square smile, beautiful and radiant but not without analytic substance. "You're an imposter. I've seen you eat ham. Ham and sausage and bacon. You're just playing to the galleries. I suppose next you'll be keeping kosher. Besides," she said, "these are *gifts,* Saul. I'd really appreciate it if you were grateful to your friends, because they're my friends, too. Stop being a snob."

"Sometimes they're only your friends," he said.

She gave him a long look. "And sometimes they're only yours."

"Okay. You want to divide them? Which ones are yours?" he asked. "Which ones aren't? Let's divide them up, Patsy, your friends and my friends, and let's see who has more. The winner has more friends than the loser. The winner gets to go to the state fair for free."

He stood near the table, balancing on one leg.

"Honey," she said, "if you want to have a fight, we'll fight about something actual when you're ready to do that. And not until then. Actually, not a damn moment before that."

They had gazed at each other carefully, as if they were entering a new landscape of embittered matrimony, one they had only heard about but never seen until now.

Harold, Saul's barber, stared down into the crib and at Mary Esther while the meatloaf he had brought cooled under its tinfoil in the kitchen. With the gray March overcast behind her, Mrs. O'Neill, beaming fixedly on the front stoop with her expression of paralyzed charity, offered them a container of the ginger cookies that, despite her aging and memory loss, she could still remember how to make. She had packed the cookies inside a dusty uncleaned goldfish bowl. But she could still not remember the baby's name after Saul and Patsy had told her three times, and before she left, she said music from somewhere still went through her head, Puccini and Mozart, but she could not remember whether the hour of the day was morning or afternoon, and she was going to have to move herself into a place where there were nurses and people who helped you eat dinner and told you the time. She would not be able to sing arias from opera, once there; she was sure of that. Emory and Anne McPhee gave Patsy a gallon of homemade potato salad preserved in Tupperware; Anne was pregnant again, she said, and couldn't stay. Harry and Lucia Edmonds, who had worked with Patsy at the bank, brought over a pair of pink baby pajamas, complete with footies, that Lucia had bought at the new outlet mall. Gary Krochock, their neighbor and their insurance agent, also Jewish, dropped off a box of cigars. Mad Dog Bettermine, who had left his girlfriend at home because, he told Saul over the phone, he didn't want her to get any big ideas about babies and his own potential for fatherhood, grew unexpectedly abashed at the sight of Mary Esther. Having hauled a case of discount no-name beer onto the front porch, he stood quietly over the crib, wordless from baby-fear, staring at Mary Esther, and he could not move until Patsy picked up Mary Esther and Saul took Mad Dog by the arm and guided him out of the room.

Saul removed him to the small back den, gave him a cigar, and from there the two men retired to the back stoop, lighting up and drinking, belching smoke, somehow unable to make conversation. Mad Dog had an odd expression on his face. Saul would have liked to talk to him but didn't know how. He would have said that fatherhood was great, terrifying, too, of course, but you could handle the terror by imagining yourself having been invited to a large noisy and sloppy party where all the guests made uproar and messes—this was parenthood. Only he didn't quite believe it was as festive as all that.

But charity was everywhere. Saul had never seen anything like it. Saul's mother- and father-in-law, Susan and Dick Carlson, arrived after Saul's mother had left, and they slept in the living room, Susan on the sofa, Dick in a sleeping bag on the floor, during the three days of their visit. Patsy was their only child. During their time in the house, they cooked and cleaned and talked in whispers, like servants. In their quietness, Saul thought they compared favorably to his mother, but they were eerie in their placid and muted operations. They enjoyed companionable and friendly silences—as Delia did not—interrupted by the occasional and characteristic cry of "Here, let me do that." They said they loved the baby, and Patsy's mother held Mary Esther with great tenderness, kissing her on the forehead each time she lifted her up and cradled her in her arms and rocked her.

They were sweet to Saul in an airy and distant way, as if they liked the idea of him a bit more than the actuality, and they took great care to defer to him as long as they were in the house: Where were the spare lightbulbs, they would ask, instead of just looking for them. Saul noticed that they often gazed at his hands when they were speaking to him, as if he were about to break into sign language. They treated him like a lovable Martian—and seemed pleased with themselves for being able to love such a creature. "Just you relax," they often said to him.

After Patsy's parents departed, Saul could hardly remember that they had been present in the house at all, they removed the traces of themselves so thoroughly. They left no scent behind; they just vanished. His in-laws took an odd sort of pride, in a Protestant way he couldn't quite pinpoint, in being nearly invisible. They didn't want anyone to remember that they had ever been anywhere or had been sighted, like rare birds. Some sort of prideful modesty or humility on their part made them withdraw from the footlights in an effort at self-erasure, and it was rather starchy and New England of them. With their mild, quiet voices and their agreeable manner, they didn't try to assert claims of ownership over Patsy, as his mother certainly would have over him. He tried to remember their faces, Susan's hair graying in beautiful streaks and Dick's half-hearted smile, her reading glasses and his Rolex, but all he managed to keep in his head were bits and pieces of their appearance, as if they had evaporated somehow, keeping their souls unviolated and intact and completely private. That was their selfishness, if you wanted to think ill of them. They had no character that they would share. They were charitable with their actions but gave you nothing of themselves, and when they were gone, they were gone for good. All they left behind was a sterling silver teething cup with Mary Esther's name engraved on it.

The albino deer had vanished, too. He'd seen no trace of it for days, though he had gone looking for it.

Mary Esther lay in the rickety crib that Saul himself had assembled, following the confusing and contradictory instructions enclosed in the shipping box. Above the crib hung a mobile of cardboard stars and planets. Mary Esther slept and cried and gurgled while the mobile turned slowly in the small breezes caused by the visitors as they bent over the baby.

When Saul's brother Howie finally called, as Saul knew he would, he asked to speak to Mary Esther right away. "I gotta talk to her. Put her on," he said. Saul told Howie that the baby was only a baby and couldn't talk on the phone, but Howie argued and said that she certainly could. At a month old, she should start to learn how to use telecommunications. Saul brought the phone down to the baby's ear, and Howie said whatever he had to say while Mary Esther appeared to smile, and after a minute or so, Saul took the phone away from his daughter and raised it to his ear to speak to Howie himself, but whatever Howie had had to tell his niece was finished, and the phone line had gone dead.

Having a new baby was like having an affair or having committed a murder, Saul decided, as he patrolled the house: you couldn't really talk about it. People found it disagreeable whenever you started up about your new child; if they were single or childless, they thought you were boastful and self-centered, and if they had children of their own, they were politely bored by your stories. *Oh, yeah. Been there, done that,* they said—a phrase Saul had always hated. Women could talk to other young mothers about their children, but men could not. There seemed to be a rule about this. Men could boast about their children but not discuss the intricacies of child care, though perhaps this was all changing. The birth of his daughter felt like the biggest event that had ever happened to him, and he had no one to talk to about it except Patsy, and even she, he thought, was getting bored with him, his husbanding of her. *To husband:* a dreary transitive verb meaning "to conserve, to save."

One night when Mary Esther was eight weeks old and the smell of early spring was pouring into the room from the purple lilacs in the driveway, Patsy awakened and found herself alone in bed. Checking the clock, she saw that it was three-thirty. Saul had to be up for work in three hours. From downstairs she heard very faintly the sound of groans and music. The groans weren't Saul's. She knew his groans very well. There was always a touch of irony to them. These were different. She put on her bathrobe.

In the living room, sitting in his usual overstuffed chair and wearing his blue jeans and T-shirt, Saul was watching a porn film on the TV, the

VCR whirring quietly. His head was propped against his arm as if he were listening attentively to a lecture. He glanced up at Patsy, flashed her a guilty wave with his left hand, then returned his gaze to the movie. On the TV screen, a man and a woman were having showy sex in a curiously grim manner inside a stalled freight elevator. They behaved as if they were under orders. Then Patsy realized that, of course, they *were* under orders, which was at least one reason why their lovemaking looked so odd.

"What's this, Saul?"

"Video I rented."

"Where'd you get it?"

"The store."

Moans had been dubbed onto the soundtrack, but they did not match the actors' expressions. The man and the woman did not look at each other. For some reason a green ceramic poodle sat in the opposite corner of the freight elevator. "Not very classy, Saul."

"Well, no. Why do you suppose Howie didn't want to talk to me? He didn't stay on the line. He congratulated me and then said he wanted to speak to the baby. I don't get it. There's a lot I don't get these days."

"Maybe he's jealous. Of our having a daughter."

The woman on the TV set wheezled.

"I doubt it. He's making all the money, but he doesn't come to visit and he doesn't send us a present. It's strange . . . I miss him. I miss everybody. Look at that, Patsy. She hasn't taken her shoes off. That's pretty strange. They're having sex in the freight elevator and her shoes are still on. I guess the boys in the audience don't like feet."

Patsy studied the TV screen. Unexpected sadness located her and settled in like a headache. She rested her eyes on the Matisse poster above Saul's chair: naked people dancing in a ring. In this room the human body was excessively represented, and for a moment Patsy had the feeling that everything in life was probably too much, there was just too much to face down. Eventually you were done in by the altogether.

"Saul," she said, "you need more friends. People to talk to. Don't turn into a sitcom sort of guy, one of those typical Americans. I'd hate that."

"Don't I know it." He waited. "I need a purpose, as long as you're at it."

"Come upstairs."

"In a minute, my love, after this part."

"I don't like to look at them. My idea of good porno is something else. I guess I don't even like you looking at them, these two."

"It's hell, isn't it?"

She touched his shoulder. "This is sort of furtive. Not that I'm a prude or anything."

"Oh, you can see it too, if you want. I'm not hiding it. I still have my jeans on. No jerking off or anything like that. I'm an impartial observer. I'm *disinterested*. See? I even know the proper definition of that often mis-used word." He gave her a flat smile.

"Why are you doing this, Saul? How come you're watching this?"

"Because I wanted to. Didn't you read the training manual on me? I do this after my daughter is born. Besides, I wanted a real movie and I got this instead. I was in the video place and I went past the musicals and the action thrillers into the sad, private room where all the X's were. There I was—me—full of curiosity."

"Curiosity? About what?"

"Well, we, you and I, used to have fun. We used to get hot. So this . . . anyway, it's like nostalgia, you know? Nostalgia for something. It's like going into a museum where the exhibits are happy, and behind glass, and you watch the happiness, your nose on the glass, and it isn't yours, so you watch more of it."

"This isn't *happiness* you're watching. Jesus, Saul, that's a big soul error. And furthermore, this isn't like you. Doesn't it make you feel like shit or something?"

He sat in his chair, thinking. Then he said, "Oh sure, it does. Very shit-like." He clicked off the TV set, stood up, and put his arms around Patsy, and they embraced for what seemed to Patsy a long time. Behind Saul on the living-room bookshelf were volumes of history and literature—Saul's collection of Dashiell Hammett and Samuel Eliot Morison and several volumes of the Loeb Classical Library—and the Scrabble game on the top shelf. They had not played the game for months. "Don't leave me alone back here," Patsy said. "Don't leave me alone, okay?"

"I loved you, Patsy," he told her, and she shivered at the past tense of the verb. It felt like a decision on his part, a conscious act. It felt like the first step of a trial separation. "You know that. Always have."

"Not what I'm talking about."

"I know."

"It's just that you don't get everything now," she said. "I don't give it all to you. Mary Esther gets some of it. You need to diversify."

They stood for a few moments longer, swaying slightly together. They were physically intimate, but it felt to Patsy as if their souls were miles apart, hers in Guatemala and Saul's in Greenland.

Two nights later, Saul finished diapering Mary Esther and then walked into the upstairs hallway toward the bathroom. He brushed against Patsy, who was heading downstairs. Under the ceiling lights her eyes were shadowed with fatigue. They did not speak, and for ten seconds she was a stranger to him. He could not remember why he had ever married her, and he could not remember having desire for her. She was a young, wearied mother, and she looked temporarily used up. For half a minute, he breathed in the pure air of despondency. After shaking for a moment, he tried to regain his balance in the hallway in front of the open bathroom door, angry and frightened, feeling his wounds opening but bleeding inward rather than outward.

When Saul entered his classroom the next day, Gordy and Bob greeted his arrival with rattled throat noises, sociopathic gargling. On their foreheads they had written MAD IN THE USA, in pencil. "Mad," or "made" misspelled? Saul didn't ask. Seated in their broken desks and only vaguely attentive, the other students fidgeted and smiled politely, picking at their frayed clothes uniformly one or two sizes too small.

"Today," Saul said, "we're going to pretend that we're young again. I don't mean a year or two younger, I mean *much* younger. We're going to think about what babies would say if they could talk."

He reached into his jacket pocket for his seven duplicate photographs of Mary Esther, in which she leaned against the back of the sofa, her stuffed gnome in her lap.

"This is my daughter," Saul said, passing the photographs out. "Mary Esther." The four girls in the classroom made peculiar cooing sounds. The boys reacted with squirming nervous laughter, except for Gordy and Bob, who had suddenly turned to stone. "Babies want to say things, right? Except they can't, not yet. What would she say if she could talk? Write it out on a sheet of paper. Give her some words."

Saul knew he was testing the Cossacks. He was screwing up their heads with parental love that they themselves had never sampled. For Gordy Himmelman, the idea of an actual father would be the mystery beyond all mysteries. It would make him crazy, and that might be interesting. At the back of the room, Gordy, in all his bewilderment, studied the photograph. His face expressed the staring-nothing with which he was on intimate terms. All his feelings were bricked up; and nothing escaped from him.

His was the zombie point of view.

Nevertheless, he bent down over his desk, pencil in hand.

At the end of the hour, Saul collected the papers, and his students shuffled out into the hallway. Saul had noticed that poor readers did not lift their feet off the floor. You could hear them coming down the hallway from the slide and scrape and squeal of their shoes.

He searched for Gordy Himmelman's paper. Here it was, mad in America, several lines of scrawled writing.

They thro me up in to the air. Peopl come in when I screem and thro me up in to the air. They stik my face up. They never cacht me.

The next lines were heavily erased.

her + try it out . You ink

Saul held up the paper to read the illegible words, and he saw the word "kick" again, next to the word "lidel."

His head randomly swimming, Saul held the photographs of his daughter, the little kike thoughtfully misspelled by Gordon Himmelman, before bringing the photos to his chest absentmindedly. From the hallway he heard the sound of lively braying laughter.

That night, Saul, fortified with Mad Dog's no-brand beer, read the want ads, deeply interested. The want ads were full of trash and leavings, employment opportunities (most of them at Five Oaks's largest employer, WaldChem, where every job was lethal), and the promise of new lives amid the advertised wreckage of the old. He read the personals like a scholar, checking for verbal nuance. Sitting in his overstuffed chair, he had been scanning the columns when his eye stopped on a singular item.

BEEHIVES FOR SALE—MUST SELL. SHELLS, FRAMES, EXTRACTOR. ALSO INCL. SMOKER AND PROTECTIVE HAT TOOLS AND FACE COVERING. GOOD CONDITION. ANY OFFER CONSIDERED. EAGER TO DEAL. $$$ POTENTIAL. CALL AFTER 7 PM. 890-7236.

Saul took Mary Esther out of her pendulum chair and held her as he walked around the house, thick with plans and vision. In the vision, he stood proudly in front of Patsy, holding a jar of honey. Sunlight slithered through its glass and transformed the room itself into pure gold. Sweetness was everywhere. Honey would make all the desires right again between them. The peaceable kingdom would return, and the arrows would fly backward away from their targets and find themselves on the string of the bow as the bow itself was unstrung and put away into its case. Gordy Himmelman, meanwhile, would have erased himself from the planet. He would have caused himself in a feat of Flash Gordon–like magic to dematerialize. In this dream, whose colors resembled those of the porn film, Patsy accepted Saul's gift. She couldn't stop smiling at him. She tore off her clothes, his too. She poured the honey over Saul.

It was one of his better daydreams. Gazing at the newspapers and magazines piling up next to the TV set and VCR, as he held and burped Mary Esther, Saul found himself shaking with a kind of excitement. Irony, his constant lifelong faithful sidekick, was asleep, or on vacation, and in its heady absence Saul began to reimagine himself as a moneymaker, a beekeeper, a man Patsy could not stop herself from loving. *Rescue me*, he thought, not sure if the words were his or Patsy's or just came from that great old Motown song.

He did not accuse Gordy of anti-Semitism, or of anything else. He ignored him, as he ignored Bob Pawlak. At the end of the school year they would all go away and drain down into the earth and the dirt and swill they came from and become one with the stones and the all-embracing sewage. A new principle: Some things you can't help; some things you can't save, and you're better off not trying.

On a fine warm day in April, Saul drove out to the north side of town, where he bought the wooden frames and the other equipment from a laconic man named Gunderson. Gunderson wore overalls and boots. Using the flat of his hand, he rubbed the top of his bald head with a farmer's gesture of suspicion as he examined Saul's white shirt, pressed pants, funky two-day growth of beard, and brown leather shoes. "Don't wear black clothes around these fellas," Gunderson said, meaning the bees. "Bees hate black. Just hate it. Don't know why, but they do." Saul paid him in cash, and Gunderson counted the money after Saul handed it over, wetting his thumb to turn the bills.

With Mad Dog's pickup, Saul brought it all back to Whitefeather Road. He stored his purchases behind the garage. He took out books on beekeeping from the public library and studied their instructions with care. He made notes on a yellow tablet and calculated hive placement. The bees needed direct sunlight, and water nearby. By phone he bought a colony of bees complete with a queen from an apiary in South Carolina, using his credit card number. He did not think he was being hysterical, though the possibility had occurred to him.

When the bee box arrived at the main post office, he received an angry call from the assistant postal manager telling him to come down and pick up this damn humming thing.

As it turned out, the bees liked Saul. They were more predictable than his students, and they worked harder. He was calm and slow around them and talked to them when he removed them from the shipping box and introduced them into the shells and frames, following the instructions he had learned by heart. The hives and frames sat unsteadily on the platform he had laid down on bricks near two fence posts on the edge of the property. But the structure was, he thought, steady enough for bees. He gorged them on sugar syrup, sprinkling it over them before letting them free, shaking them into the frames. Some of them settled on his gloved hands and were so drowsy that, when he pushed them off, they waterfalled into the hive. When the queen and the other bees were enclosed, he replaced the frames inside the shell, being careful to put a feeder with sugar water nearby, outside the shell.

The books had warned him about the loud buzzing sound of angry bees, but for the first few days Saul never heard it. Something about Saul seemed to keep the bees occupied and unirritated. He was stung twice, once on the wrist and once on the back of the neck, but the pain was pointed and directed and so focused that he could manage it. It was unfocused pain that he couldn't stand.

Out at the back of the property, a quarter-mile away from the house, the hives and the bees wouldn't bother anyone, he thought. "Just don't bring them in here," Patsy told him, glancing through one of his apiary books. "Not that they'd come. I just want them and me to have a little distance between us, is all." She smiled with uncertainty. "Bees, Saul? *Honey?* You are quite an amazing literalist."

"I am? I thought they were metaphors."

"Literal metaphors," she corrected him. "Just don't buy a herd of cows. We can get milk at the store."

And then one night, balancing his checkbook at his desk, with Mary Esther half-asleep in the crook of his left arm, Saul felt a moment of calm peacefulness, the rarest of all his emotions, and he remembered for that instant exactly what it was like to be in that blessed condition. He hadn't felt that way for at least eighteen months. Under his desk lamp, with his daughter drooling on his Northwestern University sweatshirt, he sat forward, waiting. A presence made itself felt behind him. When he turned around, he saw Patsy in worn jeans and a T-shirt watching him from the doorway. Her arms were folded, and her breasts were outlined perfectly beneath the cloth. No bra, God save us, he thought, no bra, her nipples visible like the floodlights of heaven across the river. She was holding on her face a tentative expression of sly playfulness. She would be able to do the erotic thing, but it might sometimes be an effort, but she was there again, and she was ready. Saul could see her working at it. He would have to help her out. He would have to pitch in. She couldn't do this by herself because . . . because she didn't feel like it.

"Well, aren't you something?" he said. "Kind of sleek-looking."

"Aren't I something? Yes, I am. Just look at me."

"Come here, babe," he said.

"'Babe'? We don't have to do endearments. How about if you come over here?"

"No, you first. I gotta put the baby down. I've got the baby here."

"Ah, yes. Saul and the baby." She came into the room, her bare feet whisking against the wood floor, and she put her arms around him so that the baby wasn't also embraced, and she pressed herself against him strategically and stealthily.

"Put Mary Esther into her crib," she whispered. She clicked off the desk lamp.

As they made love, Saul thought of the bees, of procreation, and citizenship. Already, he thought, those insects—*Apis mellifera*—were proving to be a kind of solution.

Spring moved into summer, and in the distance the outlet mall was completed, with a new cineplex going up nearby, and the microwave tower constructed. Saul bought a new computer. Just before school ended, he told his students about the bees and the hives. Pride escaped from his face, radiating it; he could feel it bathing his students with its unwholesome glow. When he explained how honey was extracted from the frames, he glanced at Gordy Himmelman and saw a look of what he took to be dumb animal malice directed back at him. What was the big deal? Saul wondered before he turned away. The kid hated Saul anyway. A bit more hatred would be salt on top of salt.

One night in early June, Patsy was headed upstairs, looking for the Snugli, which she thought she had forgotten in Mary Esther's room, when she heard Saul's voice coming from behind the door. She stopped on the landing, her hand on the banister. At first she thought he might be singing to the baby, but, no, Saul was not singing. He was sitting in there—well, he was probably sitting, Saul didn't like to stand when he spoke—talking to his daughter, and Patsy heard him finishing a sentence: ". . . was never very happy."

Patsy moved closer to the door.

"Who explains?" Saul was saying, apparently to his daughter. "No one does."

Saul went on talking to Mary Esther, filling her in on his mother and several other mysterious phenomena. What did he think he was doing, discussing this ephemera with an infant? "I should sing you a song," he announced, interrupting his train of thought. "That's what parents do. It's in all the books. Maybe I'll do Zorastro's aria. Or 'Pigeons on the Grass, Alas.' You might like that."

To get away from Saul's sitcom vocalizing, Patsy retreated to the window for a breath of air. Looking out, she saw someone standing on the front lawn, bathed in moonlight, staring in the direction of the house. He was thin and ugly and scruffy, and he looked a bit like a shadowy clod, but a dangerous shadowy clod, and the hairs on the back of her neck stood up.

"Saul," she said. Then, more loudly, "Saul, there's someone out on the lawn."

He joined her at the window. "I can't see him," he said. "Oh, yeah, there." He shouted, "Hello? Can I help you?"

The boy turned around. He got on a bike and raced away down the driveway and onto Whitefeather Road.

Saul did not move, his hands planted on the windowsill. "Well, I'll be damned. It's Gordy Himmelman," he groaned. "That little bastard has come onto our property. I'm getting on the phone."

"Saul, why'd he come *here*? What'd you do to him?" She held her arms against her chest. "What does he have against us?"

"I was his teacher. And we're Jewish," Saul said. "And to top it all off, we're parents. He never had any. I showed those kids the baby pictures and he had a psychotic break. Big mistake. He's not *used* to being psychotic. Somebody must have found Gordy in a barrel of brine. He was not of woman born." He tried to smile. "I'm kidding, sort of."

"Do you think he'll be back?" she asked.

"Oh, yes." Saul wiped his forehead. "They always come back, those kind. And I'll be ready when he does."

It had been a spring and summer of violent weather, and Saul had been reading the Old Testament again, looking for clues. On Thursday, around four in the afternoon, he had finished mowing the front lawn and was sitting on the porch, drinking the last, the final, bottle of Mad Dog's no-brand beer when he looked to the west and felt a sudden cooling of the air, a shunting of atmosphere from higher to lower. Just above the horizon a mass of clouds began boiling. Clouds that looked like breasts and hand tools—he couldn't help thinking the way he thought—advanced over him, with other clouds hanging down, pendulous. The wind picked up.

"Patsy," he called. "Hey, Patsy."

Something calamitous was happening in the atmosphere. In a moment a voice could easily emerge from the whirlwind. The pressure was dropping so fast that Saul could feel it in his elbows and knees.

"Patsy!" he shouted.

From upstairs he heard her calling back: "What, Saul?"

"Go to the basement," he said. "Close the upstairs window and take Mary Esther down there. Take a flashlight. Something's coming. We're going to get a huge storm."

Rushing through the house, Saul closed windows and switched off lights, and when he returned to the front door to close it, he saw the tall and emaciated apparition of his student Gordy Himmelman out in the yard, standing fixedly like an emanation from the dirt and stone of the fields. He had returned. Toward Saul he aimed his vacant stare. Flies buzzed around his head. Saul, who could not stop thinking even in moments of critical emergency, was struck into stillness by Gordy's presence, his authoritative malevolence—or whatever it was—standing there in the just-mown grass. For the first time the thought entered Saul's mind

95

that *he* was responsible for Gordy somehow, that he had had a small but important part in his creation, that he had been the minor lab-coated assistant in Dr. Frankenstein's laboratory, attaching the wires behind the Tesla coils. But they'd all collaborated: the volatile ambitious sky and the forlorn backwardness of the fields had together given rise to this human disaster, who, even as Saul watched, yelled toward the house, "Hey, Mr. Bernstein. It's a storm." Or maybe he said, "I'm a storm." Saul didn't quite hear. Then the boy said, "Go take a look at your bees, shitbird." In slow motion, he smiled.

Feeling like a commando, Saul, in whom necessity had created the illusion of speed, caught up to Gordy, who was pumping away on his broken and rusted bicycle, and pulled him off. He threw and kicked the junk Schwinn into the ditch. In the rain that had just started, Saul grabbed Gordy by the shoulders and shook him back and forth. He pressed his thumbs hard enough to bruise. Gordy, violently stinking, smelled of neglect and seepage, and Saul nearly gagged. But he could not stop shaking him; it was like the release of a terrible pressure, a shaking cure. Violence was a sort of joy after all. But he himself was shaking, too. With violent, rapid, horizontal jerking motions, the boy's head was whipped. His face was level with Saul's. They were the same height.

Saul wanted to see his eyes. But the eyes were as empty as mirrors.

"Hey, stop it," Gordy said. "It hurts. You're hurting. You're hurting him."

"Hurting who?" Saul asked. Thunder rolled toward him. He saw himself reflected in Gordy Himmelman's eyes, a tiny figure backed by lightning. *Who, me?*

"Stop it, don't hurt him." Patsy's voice, repeating Gordy's words, snaked into his ear, and he felt her hand on his arm, restraining him. She was there, out in the rain, less frightened of the rain than she was of Saul. The boy had started to sag, seeing the two of them there, his scarecrow arms raised to protect himself, having assumed, probably, that he was about to be killed. There he squatted, the child of attention deficit, at Saul's feet.

"Stay there," Saul mumbled. "Stay right there." Through the rain he began walking, then running, toward his bees.

. . .

The storm, empty of content, tucked itself toward the east and was being replaced—one patch of firmament after another—by one of those insincere midwestern blue skies.

Mary Esther began to cry and wail as Patsy jogged toward Saul. Gordy Himmelman followed along behind her.

When she was within a hundred feet of Saul's beehives, Patsy saw that the frames had been knocked over, scattered. Saul lay, face down, where they once stood. He was touching his tongue to the earth momentarily, for a taste.

When he rose, he saw Patsy. "All the bees swarmed," he said. "They've left. They're gone."

She held Mary Esther tightly and examined Saul's face. "How come they didn't attack him? Didn't they sting him?"

"Who knows?" Saul spread his arms. "They just didn't."

Gordy Himmelman watched them from a hundred yards away, and with his empty gaze he made Patsy think of the albino deer, the one with the arrow in it—half blind, wandering these fields day after day without direction.

"Look," Saul said, pointed at Mary Esther, who had stopped crying when she saw her father. "Her shoe is untied." He wiped his face with his sleeve and shook off the dirt from his jeans. Approaching Patsy, he gave off a smell of soil and honey and sweat. Distracted, he tied Mary Esther's shoe.

His hair soaked with rain, he glanced at Patsy, who, with some difficulty, was keeping her mouth shut. What she loved intermittently about Saul was the vagary of feeling that focused itself into the tiniest actions of human attention, like the tying of this pink shoe. Better to keep her emotions a secret than to talk about them all the time, she thought. It would generate more energy that way. It was a variety of discouraged love that she felt, not the plain unvarnished kind. He finished the knot and kissed them both. Dirt and honey were on his lips, and they came off on Patsy's.

At a distance of a hundred yards, the boy, Gordy, watched all this, and from her vantage point Patsy saw the boy's empty expression, those mortuary eyes. She felt certain that he would stick around. They would have

97

to give him something, some form of tribute, because, like it or not, he was following them back, their faithful zombie, made, or mad, in America. She heard his shoes shuffling on the driveway.

Well, maybe we *are* missionaries, Patsy thought, as she stumbled and Saul held her up. We're the missionaries they left behind when they took all the religion away. But missionaries for what? On the front porch of the house she could see the empty bottle of Saul's no-brand beer still standing on the lip of the ledge, and she could see the porch swing slowly rock back and forth, as if someone were still sitting there, waiting for them.

Six

Later that night, several hours after Gordy had left, Saul returned to the toppled wreckage of his beehives. In the damp and still unappeaseable darkness, he carried the frames two at a time into the shed at the back of the yard. His hand-crank extractor was stored in the corner, and he dropped the frames into the barrel one by one, each making a hollow clank. A few of the bees still clung to them, and Saul did his best to shoo them out, but they were angry with him—he could hear it, a distinctly irritated insect murmur—and after being stung several times, he let them stay. He would deal with them later. He didn't know what to do with the honey on the frames. It would just remain there for now. He felt selfish and proprietary. He didn't want it himself, but he didn't want anyone else to get it, either. Milk and honey, the various rewards, all out of his hands. In the corner, a mouse scurried behind a pine board, its paws making fingernail-skittering sounds, and outside, very distantly, came the hooting of an owl. He let the stillness of the evening absorb him, travel through him, like the onset of sleep.

When he was finished, he sat down in the doorway of the shed, caught his breath, and smelled the air off the fields, the generously muddy odor following summer rain on dry soil. Overhead, the familiar stars slipped further and further away.

. . .

Several days later, dressed in his jeans and his T-shirt, Saul was standing at the kitchen counter drinking a glass of grapefruit juice and checking Patsy's dusty African violets on the sill. When he glanced out the kitchen window, he saw Gordy Himmelman planted on the lawn, staring up into the sky impatiently, as if waiting for a hot-air balloon to snatch him up and rescue him. His hands were knitted together. The boy always seemed to be gazing skyward or earthward. He rarely could look out at his own level, at the human scene; Saul had never seen his gaze pointed in that direction, where his prospects seemed to be as dim as he was.

In any case, he was back.

The previous week, the night of the storm, Saul had instructed Gordy to go home and never to return, though he had said it without the necessary anger to make the correct frightening impression. Gordy had seldom listened to him, anyway, in class or out. He had given Saul one of his several blank expressions, like that of someone waiting for a translation. On Gordy, blankness had a certain eloquence. The boy was profoundly blank. Nevertheless, after following Saul around for a few minutes, doglike, he had mounted his rusting bicycle, nodded once, and disappeared down the road as twilight came on and the setting sun bathed him in a misleading post-rainstorm rosy glow. Watching him pedal away, Saul had felt a distinct relief. He was tired of the ragtag unfortunate and the disengaged and the special-needs types who had clustered around him in classrooms and elsewhere, and he was glad to see Gordy bicycling out of his life. He had come to think of himself as an opportunist of misfortune, his own and others'. Somehow, without knowing how the process had been effected, he had taken advantage of the disadvantaged. Now that he had a child of his own, his compassion for other people's children felt all used up. He was finished with the unlucky and the disabled. No more charity in the service of narcissism. With the bees gone, redemption seemed—what? *Unworkable.* He was tired of the romance of failure, anyway.

But someone had failed to tell Gordy Himmelman that Saul was through with him, because here he was, loitering on the morning lawn, a sentry dressed in his uniform: soiled jeans and torn shirt. Saul put down his juice glass carefully in a cereal bowl near the kitchen sink and strolled outside to where Gordy was standing. Already the air was unsettled and feverish, though it had rained again in the middle of the night, another brief tantrum of a downpour, and the grass had a warm, damp prickliness, as if Saul were stepping on a horsehair doormat. It was a disagreeable sensation. In the trees the blue jays and crows flapped and screamed. The weather was getting so moody and violent these days: it was the warfare of heaven against earth, the opening of the seven seals.

"So," Saul said. "Hey, Gordy." Close up, his former student smelled of roasted pumpkin seeds and brine. He hadn't shaved, and his boy's scraggly indecisive peachfuzz facial hair mingled with his acne. He was wearing some sort of metal-and-leather apparatus around his neck, probably a dog collar, with a small broken soundless bell attached. He was chewing something—gum, Saul hoped.

"Hey, Mr. Bernstein." Gordy nodded at Saul, then looked away quickly, as if he were busy, occupied with many tasks.

"Can I help you with something?"

"Nope," Gordy said. "Not right now. Maybe later." Gordy waved. "See ya."

"Gordy, what're you doing here?"

There was a long silence, during which Gordy Himmelman studied Saul's feet. Finally he said, "I came here on my bike."

"I know that. I mean, what are you *doing* here?"

"Is this, like, a quiz?" Gordy shrugged and started to laugh, then stopped himself. "Hey, I don't mean to make no trouble. Ha ha ha ha ha. Not today anyways."

"No. Right. I'm just asking you why you came."

"It's a nice day. Can't I stand here?" Gordy smiled his odd square smile. He was now surveying the sky again. Once more the birds began their ritual screaming. Saul had the feeling that they were trying to tell him something important, in fact to convey an urgent message, in bird language. In addition, Saul could hear, behind him, Mary Esther's crying and Patsy's quiet, soothing, morning endearments.

"Yes, it *is* a nice day. I guess you can stand there, maybe for a minute. But did you come here to talk to me? Or apologize?" Hearing that word, whose meaning he could not possibly have known, the boy seemed to startle. "Gordy, *why did you knock down my beehives?*"

For his trouble, Saul got one of Gordy's sudden deadpan expressions. For a half-second it occurred to Saul that the boy might be lovestruck. Then Gordy said, "A hawk just went by, looked like. That thing you said, I couldn't help it. It was like an idea I had. Me and Bob. Only Bob wasn't there."

"Well, you . . . you hate me, right? And didn't you kill that deer?"

"Well, I dunno. Naw. It's not like that." He looked away. He looked at the sky. Nothing up there but sky. Wherever Gordy went, he created a cognitive fog, even in broad daylight.

"You don't *know*? Okay. Then what are you doing here?"

"You mean right now?" He gave Saul a goofy how-dumb-do-you-think-I-am expression. "I'm talkin' to you."

"Yes. Of course. Certainly. But what I'm asking you is, why did you get on your bicycle and come over here? I really don't get it. I'm missing something. You . . . I thought you hated me. Don't you? You and Bob Pawlak? I thought you couldn't stand the sight of me. You called me a shitbird. That's what you said. A *shitbird*. I don't even know what a shitbird *is*. And then there were the hives. You ruined them. You owe me for them," Saul said irritably.

"That was only *in school*. And the rest was just talk. Anyway I never said nothing about hating, not in that way. 'Cause *it's you who hate me*. I can *tell*. Is that your car over there?" With his thumb, Gordy gestured toward Saul's Chevy. He had been avoiding eye contact. The body shop had made the car look like new after Saul had rolled it all those many months ago.

"Yes." Saul sighed. "Yes, it is." He pointed a finger at the boy. "Gordy, if you can't explain to me what you're doing here, I'm going to have to ask you to leave."

"Okay." The boy nodded. "Okay." How hard it was to argue with someone when that person didn't listen to you! Or did listen, but didn't act on it. It was like being married.

"Gordy, please go home. You're trespassing. You have to get off my property right now."

"Okay." He did not move. "What year is it?" He motioned again at the car with his thumb.

"The car?" Saul felt flustered. "It's two years old."

"Still shiny, though. You wash it in soapsuds?"

"That's not the point."

Gordy grinned at Saul, the grin of the torturer. Some sort of discoloration had applied itself down through the years to the boy's teeth. They were rotting in a premature manner. "You must of just washed it, for it to look that clean. You must be proud of it."

"Hey, Gordy," Saul said. "I have a great idea. Let's go for a ride. What d'you say? Let's go for a ride in my car."

"Where?"

"Oh, who cares. Let's just go for a ride."

"Know what this is?" Gordy reached in under the back of his trousers and pulled out a small shiny handgun, a revolver of some sort, one of the common ones, maybe a .22-caliber. He held it in his palm for Saul's inspection. He grinned. Saul backed up two steps. He felt prickles on his skin and a sudden animal heat. He wanted to shout aloud at Patsy, to hide herself and Mary Esther. But silence for now might be better, less crisis-making.

"Well, it looks a lot like a gun," Saul said quietly. Behind him, Mary Esther's crying had ceased as suddenly as if a conductor had cued it to stop. Calm. *Be calm.* Saul thought that Patsy must be nursing the baby in the rocking chair upstairs, and he was counting the number of steps to the house and calculating how long it would take him to get there: about twenty-four running strides, approximately fifty seconds, much more time than the little metal duck in the shooting gallery had in its perilous journey from the right-hand side to the left. Saul imagined himself with a target painted on his chest, the same as the duck's. The rest of Saul's mind had gone haphazardly bare. He would protect his wife and child. But for now, he would not move. His entire life job was to stop this young man from creating harm. "What kind is it? Is it loaded?"

"That's right," Gordy said, suddenly serious. Then he gave himself a little squirrel-shake. "That's right, it's a gun. But, no, it ain't loaded." He raised it up to the sky and pulled the trigger again and again and again and again and again. After he lowered his arm, he looked directly at Saul. "You wouldn't like me if I came here with a loaded gun. But, hey. You can shoot the sky all you want, Mr. Bernstein. I just thought I'd show it to you. I thought you'd be interested. You want it? Want to shoot the sky?" His eyebrows went up. "You can pretend to aim at the sun—you know, shoot it out?" He smiled his discolored toothy smile. "Then the earth would go dark."

"No. Not now. Whose is it?" Saul asked. Somehow, as a survival trick, he felt he should keep Gordy talking. But the question seemed to flummox the boy. So Saul tried another question. "Why did you think I wanted to see it?"

" 'Cause everybody wants to see a gun," Gordy intoned with certainty. "Nobody *don't* want to see a gun. A thing can't get more important than a gun."

"I agree with you there," Saul said. Monitoring himself, he noticed how expert he was, how exemplary, at pretending to be calm, when in fact all he really felt was a certain variety of domesticated and internalized cancerous emotional riot. *Patsy. Mary Esther.* "Hey, Gordy, let's go for a ride in the car, okay?"

"Okay, I guess. Don't you need shoes?"

"Oh, I don't think so," Saul said. "I can drive barefoot. I've done it before."

"You sure have a lot of hair on your arms," Gordy said. "Hairiest man I ever saw. Is that Jew hair?"

"Sure is. Gordy, how about if we get into the car now, right this minute?"

"I was just askin'," Gordy said, as patient as a turtle. "Okay, let's do that."

Gordy pocketed the gun, picked up the rusty bicycle at his feet, and sauntered toward the car. He loaded the bike into the backseat, where it dripped rust over the upholstery. After Saul got in and twisted the key, challenging the car to start, they drove out onto Whitefeather Road. Down the road, three-quarters of a mile away, the old town dump was being filled in. They were going to put a housing development there.

Where would the rats go? It was a problem. You couldn't shoot them all. Even the rats needed somewhere to stay.

Within another mile of the landfill, the farmland quickly morphed into cement and asphalt parking lots outside the Wolverine Outlet Mall and the Happy Village CinePlex 25 and the Bruckner Buick-Honda MotorMart, dominated by the grinning giant white plasticene Bruckner polar bear, an attention-getting device two stories high with its pawful of green plastic cash, an offering to passing motorists, and, floating above the bear but still tethered to it, the Bruckner MotorMart blimp—really just an outsized helium balloon—unmoving in the infernal morning heat. On clear days, the blimp, floating above the trees, was visible from Saul and Patsy's bedroom window, although both Saul and Patsy tried to avoid looking at it. Now, behind the wheel, with Gordy next to him viewing the sights, the gun pocketed somewhere, Saul felt richly overloaded with anger and bad nerves, but at least he had Gordy in the car, far enough away from the house and from Patsy and Mary Esther so that the kid could do them no harm. He switched on the air conditioner, then remembered that the compressor wasn't working. The Chevy was a lemon, but Saul was too fatalistic to do anything about its various debilities; and, besides, he identified with the car and its failings. Any car he owned would eventually fall to pieces, simply because he owned it.

It was so hot the sky was almost more white than blue. The sun had some real anger behind it today, a distinctive solar rage.

After opening the window, he saw up ahead a group of middle school girls standing out on the side of the road, waving their arms toward a side drive and holding up signs that said FREE CARWASH! He knew those girls: it was a money-making scheme for the ninth grade, the pretty ones, the Eloi, standing out on the road to attract attention, while the homely ones, the Morlocks, washed the cars and begged for gratuities. It all felt posthumous to him, this morning spectacle, as if Gordy had loaded the pistol and shot him and Saul was driving toward the afterlife, which would be about fifteen miles out of town in a strip mall bordering a dairy farm.

"Look at them," Gordy said. "Dumb girls. They just spit on the cars they wash."

At least the gun wasn't loaded. Two of the girls watched him drive past, with Gordy on the passenger side. They waved with feigned cheerfulness until they saw Gordy, when their expressions were downgraded to surprise and alarm.

Thinking of the gun, Saul considered the prospects following his death. His chances weren't good. There would be no harps in the afterlife, but instead long moralistic debriefing sessions in classrooms, during which he would have to explain himself and his quirks at length to some querulous Christian saint wearing sandals and a business suit and holding a clipboard. It would be like a substance-abuse clinic, with slogans and checklists and chores and trivial corrections, and a big sign over the main gate: WE WON, YOU LOST. There would be no unconditional forgiveness. Everything would be on a contingency basis. God's anger would have to be placated with sacrificial offerings, starting with Saul's irony, which Saul would have to throw away on the eternal spiritual fire, along with his skepticism and his interest in baseball and his Charlie Parker LPs. It would all have to go. The population of souls in Saul's afterlife would have smiles on their faces, evangelical tent-show grins. Angels would be displaying their navel-less midriffs and grooming their wings with giant pearl combs. They would be dabbing their feet in the river of light. Saul didn't want to die because the possibility of his having to join the God cult, following the expiration of his body, unnerved him. Perhaps they'd toss him in Limbo, a place full of cubicles and malfunctioning coffeemakers intended to break everyone of the caffeine habit, and of every other habit, for that matter. He would have to take lessons in sanctity and sincerity. There would be odious piety. There would be sensitivity training. They'd start calling him "Paul" instead of "Saul" and he wouldn't be able to stand it. In Limbo, though, he'd have plenty of company: almost all of the Jews would be there, analyzing the situation. And, then, Patsy would appear on the scene, eventually. She would know how to handle whatever came up.

Unless Heaven happened to be run by Arabs. Perhaps Allah was actually in charge. If so, Saul's goose was cooked.

"Hey," Gordy said. "You're driving to my house. Can I turn on the radio?"

"The FM doesn't work. Only the AM."

"Hey," Gordy said, "this is a real shitty car." He squirmed in his seat. "Looks ain't everything. How come you never fix any of it?"

"How come you knocked down my beehives?"

"How come when I ask you a question, you ask me a question?"

"Who wants to know?" Saul asked. Gordy slouched down and put his hand over his face. They drove on in silence.

Saul had motored past Gordy Himmelman's house on Strewwelpeter Street many times before, so he knew where it was, in a low-rent neighborhood of dying and spindly oak trees behind the parking lot of the new WaldChem processing plant, where as their new sideline they made genetically engineered dehydrated fruit, and when he got to where Gordy lived, some woman was outside smoking a cigarette and hammering at the broken wooden steps leading up to the front door. She wasn't Gordy's mother—it was Brenda Bagley, Gordy's aunt, the waitress who worked in the Fleetwood. She was wearing a faded cotton housedress and sneakers, and when she stood up, she looked like an undersea creature.

Her face was disfigured by years of hard work and stupendous ugliness: her hair hung around her pockmarked cheeks like seaweed around a clam. Her hooded eyes were fatigued and suspicious and sullen; nothing done by human beings could surprise or please her. Behind where she was standing, the house, a white prefab with corrugated steel sides—the kind of house sought out by tornadoes—rested somewhat precariously on concrete blocks, a huge spiderweb satellite TV dish planted next to it on the lawn.

Brenda Bagley watched as Gordy pulled his bicycle out of the back of Saul's car. Gordy wheeled the bike across the street, and Saul started to wave just before he saw Gordy's aunt, whose voice was muffled, lift her left hand, the one with the cigarette, across her forehead. After another exchange—Saul couldn't hear what they were saying—she reversed her grip on the hammer and hit Gordy twice in the face, hard, with the hammer's wooden handle. She did it so fast, Saul could hardly see her hand moving. She did it like a virtuoso, practiced and instinctual. She did it with considerable force. She hauled back and brought her hand down in a familiar swift arc.

Gordy cried out. Then he fell to his knees and put his hands to his head at the scalp just above the ear. The woman reached back again with the hammer and then seemed to think better of striking the boy a third time. She leaned down, withdrew the gun from Gordy's back pocket, and lumbered into the house with it. When she came out again, Gordy was making his way up to his feet, and the woman began to shout at him, and Gordy shouted back. They did it casually, as if they were used to the dailiness of violent quarreling.

Saul steered the Chevy over to the shoulder of the road, killed the engine, and hurriedly got out. He jogged across the street and approached the woman, who had by now returned to her work. Gordy was bleeding, a small rivulet of blood trickling down from a bruise near his left ear across his cheek, and he was wiping it with his dirty hand. More blood came oozing out from his scalp, soaking his hair. Then his cursing stopped. As Saul neared them, both the woman and Gordy stared at him, the woman still hammering as she stared, though Gordy had retreated backward toward the house, against which he leaned, holding the side of his bleeding head. Saul had no idea what he himself would say. He hadn't been invited to this particular gathering. But there was always something to say if you could only think of it.

"Hello," Saul said.

"You're the teacher," the woman said. From inside the home came the sound of a TV set singing and selling. Straightening up, she reached into the pocket of her dress, pulled out an unfiltered cigarette, and lit it. "The reading teacher. I remember you. We met. I sure heard enough about you from him. He says you don't like him."

"Saul Bernstein," he said. "Yes, that's right. I'm Gordy's teacher. You and I have had a conference about him." He paused, thinking about his role in all this. "Ms. Bagley, I was always available for more conferences if you wanted to talk to me. Anyway, he bicycled over to my house this morning, and so I just brought him back."

"Oh, uh-huh," the woman said. "Well, like I say, I've heard about you lately. Gordy's been talking about you, now and then." Saul waited for secondhand praise, but it did not come.

"I couldn't help but notice. What did you hit him for just now?" Saul asked, nodding in Gordy's direction. He felt it was best not to ask her how, as the boy's aunt, she figured she had hitting rights over Gordy. He didn't know how to do this sort of interview. He didn't know how to talk to her.

"He needed hitting," Brenda Bagley said, relying, like one of Tolstoy's peasants, on simplicity and truth. "He can be a bad boy when he gets an idea into his head. Straw that broke the camel's back and all that, with me being the camel, y'know." She smiled briefly at Saul, not a camel but a lobster smile, all teeth and skull. It was horrifying. "I mean, do *you* think he should be carrying a gun around?"

"I would never hit a child," Saul told her.

"Oh, you wouldn't? That's interesting. What I heard was, you shook him so hard last week, his head just about come off, and his teeth out of his head. He had a headache afterwards."

"Gordy was on my property. He had knocked my beehives over," Saul said, in explanation, and his forehead broke out in a sweat. "He'd been prowling and trespassing." It sounded lame to him even as he said the words. His inadequacy in argumentation startled him.

"Could have been the storm did it. We had terrible winds around here, flung things all over the yard, as you can see." Saul didn't dare take his eyes off her. She had some sort of birthmark on her neck, a discoloration in the shape of a tiny football, and the smoke from her cigarette, when she exhaled, surrounded her head like an insulating aura. It was as if her head was smoldering, a peat bog of a head. She tossed the cigarette off into the bushes. "He came over to your house this morning again? Well, he was supposed to stay here," she said.

"That's why you hit him?"

"Nope. I hit him because he took my gun with him, stole it out of the house, and headed up on his bicycle to where you live. And even if it wasn't loaded, which it wasn't, it scared the death out of me just now that he had done that, that he would *think* of doing that. He's got a thick skull, Gordy has. You have to hit him pretty hard to make a single thing register on him."

"All he wanted to do was show me the gun. That's really all it was," Saul said, not certain that it was the whole truth, or that he should bother to excuse this inexcusable boy. "Well," Saul said, "I guess I had better be going."

"That's a good idea." She nodded. "I like your explanation for it, that he wanted to show you that gun. Well, you can think what you like. I certainly won't stop you. I'd invite you in for coffee, but you're not wearing shoes," the woman said, pointing at Saul's bare feet. She scowled at his appearance.

"Should we talk again about this? We need to talk about Gordy's future."

"That's a good one," the woman said, starting to laugh. She reached into her mouth and picked a shred of tobacco off her tongue. "His future." She laughed with feeling. "Well, I got work to do here, so if you'll excuse me," she said, and leaned down to finish the job she had started.

When Saul got back to the house, his barber-friend, Harold, was sitting in the kitchen with Patsy, the two of them drinking coffee, Mary Esther fussing in Patsy's arms. Harold had come over to steal Saul away to play basketball for an hour; he was dressed in his T-shirt, shorts, and expensive name-brand athletic shoes. Mad Dog and Karla would join them— Karla was a better player than Mad Dog anyway. It was a Saturday-morning ritual. Harold stared at Saul. "What happened to you?" he asked. "You look all messed up."

Patsy stared at him, too. Saul realized that he must be a sight. "Honey, where'd you go?" she asked, as she lightly bounced Mary Esther twice. "You were out here in the kitchen, and then you were gone, and you didn't leave a note or anything. I was a little worried." Her hair filigreed back from her forehead. There was a tiny stain on her blouse from her lactation. Her beauty tore through him like an electric shock, and he felt himself stirring. For a moment, he didn't even want Harold looking at her. At that moment, she handed the baby to Harold.

Recovering himself, Saul explained about Gordy, about the gun, and the hammer handle to the head. "Funny that she broke the skin," Harold observed. "Usually you just get a lump raised with a hammer handle." Both Patsy and Saul examined Harold in the moment that followed, and

Harold shrugged. When Saul mentioned Gordy Himmelman's gun, Patsy inhaled so suddenly that the baby started to wail. Harold passed the baby back to Saul.

"We have to report this to somebody," she said.

"Report what? To whom? And for what? Possessing a concealed weapon? Trespassing? You can hit your kid all you want in this country. It's fully legal," Saul said, bouncing Mary Esther until she quieted. "People do it just to get their excess energy out. Anyway, it wasn't loaded, and this whole state is sympathetic to concealed weapons."

"Oh, you don't want to get mixed up with Brenda Bagley, anyway, that whole crew," Harold said, scratching himself and standing up to provide a certain inflection to his sentences. As he stood and stretched, he said, "That woman you saw is Gordy's aunt, as you know. Gordy was the son of common-law Mrs. Himmelman number one, that woman's sister, that woman you talked to being Brenda, and as for the man of the house, he's been gone for a couple of years. I knew him—now *there* was a piece of work. Rufus, his name was, and dumb as a box of rocks, but he did always have girlfriends, and he liked to hurt people. She—Brenda—got custody of the boy, I don't know, a year ago, at least, long after Rufus disappeared into the depths of Wyoming. It's complicated. It's always complicated with people like that."

"What happened to her? To Gordy's mother?" Patsy asked.

"Lois? Oh, she died in a house fire." Harold shrugged again, but there was something behind the shrug, some anger or resentment, and a shake of the head. "They smoke cigarettes twenty-four hours a day, preferably in bed, they drink like fish, they pass out with their cigarettes burning, and bingo, you've got yourself a house ablaze, people screaming and what have you."

"How do you know all this?" Saul asked.

"Saul, I wasn't always as you see me now," Harold said. "And I was in school here with those people." He bent down to stretch, touching his toes. "I'm a townie. I dated some of those women, when we were small." He waited. "I knew her. I knew the first wife. I knew the one who died in the fire. I *dated* her." Harold's face took on a quick passing melancholy.

"You dated her?" Mary Esther grabbed at Saul's fingers, making intricate tiny fists.

"Yeah, I dated her before Rufus appeared on the scene. Rufus overcame Lois with his charm. He's got two other brothers, one named Cash, and the other Kerry. Cash and Kerry—both of them are in prison. The kid, Gordy, wasn't killed in the fire because he was being baby-sat with the aunt at the time, this Brenda you had your encounter with today. Where Rufus was during that fire, that's never been completely established, and I don't like to talk about this, so can we play basketball now?" He glanced down at Saul's feet. "Want to put on some shoes?"

"It's too hot to play basketball," Patsy said. "Are you two guys nuts?"

"Could be," Harold informed her. "Get some shoes on." Once Saul was out of the room, Harold turned conspiratorially toward Patsy and, after twisting his head from side to side to loosen the muscles, said in a smilingly hopeful, daydreaming tone, "I'm going to *school* his ass. Saul can't play in the heat."

Patsy watched them go. Men were such bluffers. It was all a bluff. With relief, after the baby's brief outburst, Patsy opened her blouse and her nursing bra. As she nursed, Mary Esther lifted her tiny, perfect hands so that the palms faced outward onto Patsy's breast, and it occurred to Patsy that in adults, this same gesture was one of adoration and astonished happiness.

Her nipples were still sore, but the soreness was occasionally pleasing to her. She felt as if her entire body was being used in the way for which it was designed. She had kept this thought to herself. The apocalyptic sun flung itself through the window onto the linoleum floor as Mary Esther shifted in her arms, and Patsy leaned back, hot and tired but happy, though she could feel a spell of weeping coming on, more or less out of nowhere. Mary Esther had been eating well and was past her first siege of colic. She was growing a fine five-month-old baby. What was there to weep about? But there was no logic to crying sometimes; it was simply a visitation. When Patsy turned around, she performed a small inventory of the kitchen: the toaster, the polished white blender, the array of cooking utensils hanging to the side of the stove—spatula, serving spoon, potato masher. She loved to stake her claims by listing humble domestic objects to herself, and doing an inventory calmed her down whenever the tears appeared. Here was the dish drainer, there was the phone, and next to it the small yellow pad of paper for messages, with the blue plastic mechanical pencil nearby. The kitchen utensils liked her and accepted her. She gazed at her daughter, who had fallen asleep, though her lips were still moving, small contractions like kisses.

African violets, refrigerator magnets, photo of Mary Esther, jar for sugar, jar for rice, cookbook, unwashed eggbeater left out on the counter.

But she was tired of renting. She thought they should own a home of their own. Single people and couples came through her office, arranging home loans, and lately they had made her sick with envy.

She wanted another child. Somehow her tears were mixed up with this particular desire. There was a boy out there who wanted to be born. His name was already Theo. Patsy had noticed Saul gazing at her with desire a few minutes ago, and that look had pleased her.

With the softest of all possible motions, she hoisted Mary Esther onto her shoulder, carried her upstairs, and put her into her crib, kissing her on the forehead lightly, because it was so hot. Mary Esther called forth kisses. You kissed her without thinking, the way you breathed in air. Patsy touched her own forehead, gauging the depth of her sweat. Though she liked to sweat, the heat was beginning to get to her. Clothes were an irritation wherever they touched her in this heat, and so, automatically, she took her shoes off in the bedroom and left her blouse unbuttoned. Her wedding ring was an irritant against her skin, but it was who she was, as intimate as her own thoughts. As a dancer, Patsy practiced objectivity about bodies. Before the era of Mary Esther, whenever the warm weather arrived, she and Saul had walked around the house naked whenever they could, creating opportunistic situations for lovemaking, but that had ended. You couldn't do that in front of a toddler: trauma and bitterness for decades, years of therapy, would result. Still, she would miss it. She would miss her animal-self, the beating of her heart, the feeling of her body, wholly body, fluttering its sleeves, walking through space, through the rooms, all the air on her skin, small eddies and bouquets of air. The pride of it, the power and certainty.

She made the bed and straightened up the baby's things in the nursery. She collected some of the dirty laundry from the floor, first in her closet and then in Saul's. Lifting one of his undershirts, she smelled him on it, that scent of vinegar and intelligent anxiety and friendliness. She carried the laundry down to the basement and dropped all the underwear into the washing machine. She could have done her tasks in pitch darkness— she knew where everything was—but on second thought, she flipped the light switch. Then she reached down to the dehumidifier.

She hardly felt anything, really nothing more than a solid blow of electrical current through her body, like a punch after anesthetic, but, as impersonal as it was, it held her for a moment before it threw her to the floor. Her first thought was, "*My baby*. Mary Esther. Don't let me be dead." Lying on the basement floor on her back, she saw the branching water pipes, and she heard the water gurgling through them. She saw the floorboards above her, the beams, the inconsequential slats.

She had been hit, she thought, by a small panel truck. A rusty urban truck, the size of a dog kennel, doing its hardscrabble tasks. But what was a truck doing in their basement? Near the laundry tubs? She would have to tell someone about the panel truck in the basement. But that was delirium, that thought—the afterburn of electricity scattering from her bare feet through her arm and then up into her brain. She put her hand to her eyes. The coldness of the basement floor against her back was, second by second, more than she could endure. Why hadn't Saul ever fixed the damn humidifier? He simply hadn't. She pushed herself upright and placed her feet, one after the other, on the waiting dirty stairs. They creaked. Wanting to get her blouse buttoned before she passed out or Saul and Harold returned, she made her way through the hallway into the kitchen and then up to the second floor, and she leaned down to pick up the remaining laundry in the bedroom, and when a second fit of dizziness took her, she dropped slowly, in extended slow motion, like a special effect, to a sitting position on the rug. Outside, a bird was singing, roaring hallucinating chirps, a terrible noise, music through saturated cotton.

After propping herself up, Patsy dazedly took off her blouse and put on a T-shirt, the clothes feeling like dream-stuff to her, dream-clothes on her suddenly clammy skin. Very tentatively, she stood up, grasping the windowsill for balance. She was okay. Rather quickly, she felt fine. She knew that it was eighteen minutes after one o'clock without looking at her watch. The electric shock had done that to her. She would never need a watch again in her life. She would always know what time it was. She went into Mary Esther's room; with the shades drawn, even in this heat, the baby was still sleeping soundly, making tiny baby-snores. When she looked outside through the dusty glass, she saw the Bruckner Buick balloon above the treetops, and, on the front lawn, sitting next to his bicycle, Gordy Himmelman, holding the side of his broken head. Was she hallucinating again? No, he was back. Now he was always back.

Through the thick blanket of heat, she navigated her way out to where Gordy Himmelman was sitting. She didn't think he had brought his gun this time. Where the bruises were, he had swelled up. He looked like a cartoon of a man with a toothache, or a boxer after eight rounds. As she approached him, she couldn't think of what to say or what to do. So she just stood there in front of him.

"Don't nobody around here ever wear shoes?" Gordy Himmelman asked, not looking up.

Patsy looked down at her feet. "Guess not." Then she added, "It's summertime."

He nodded in agreement. "Okay," he said pleasantly, pounding the grass with his fist. You *could* convince him with logic.

"Hi," she replied. She sat down on the lawn next to him. She noticed that he gave off a powerful smell of rotting sugar beets, or vegetables left forgotten in the back of the refrigerator. "I was in the basement," she said. "Just now. There's a bad dehumidifier down there, it's not grounded or something, and the electric shock . . . I was . . . it threw me to the floor. I didn't know electricity could do that. I was almost . . ." She couldn't think of the word. It was nineteen minutes past one. Now it was twenty minutes past one.

"Yeah?"

"I was almost . . ."

"Killed?"

"Yes. No. Killed with electricity. But there's a word . . ."

"Electric-chaired."

"No, that's not the word." She thought she would faint again, so she put her head between her knees. The blood rushed to her brain. "*Electrocuted*. I finally remembered it. Gordy, what are you doing here?"

"Dude." He shook his head with exasperation. "Everybody keeps asking me that. Can't I have some company?"

"So what else is happening, besides you?" Patsy asked, interested suddenly in all aspects of life. "You didn't bring that gun again, did you?"

"She hid it. Hey, I saw a rat on my way over here," he said. "Crossing the road in broad daylight. That's what's new. Homeless, on account of they filled in the dump. It was looking sickly. You ever see a rat dancing in broad daylight?"

No, she never had. They sat out on the lawn for another five minutes, saying nothing, Gordy pulling up little bits of grass, the two of them making small adjustments on the lawn so that they would stay in the shade, until Saul and Harold returned, both of them soaked in sweat and smelling like dogs, and Saul loaded Gordy and his bicycle back into the car and drove him home again, this time without incident. By that time, it was twelve minutes after two.

Seven

During the fall and winter, Mary Esther, whom they often called Emmy now, grew so rapidly and easily that her parents could not always believe their good fortune in having such a child. She was a mild, sweet-tempered baby, given to smiles and careful listening with her eyes wide open and her head slightly tilted in concentration. She only seemed to cry when there was something specific she wanted—food, or a diaper change, or sleep. Her screaming always appeared to have a rational purpose. She did not cry—as Delia informed Saul that he had done—for no particular reason, or for the pleasure of sheer temperamental discharge. When Emmy was eight months old, in November, her verbal sounds already seemed to be on the verge of becoming words, and she looked at her parents with such intelligence and full comprehension that at certain times Saul felt his privacy violated. Through some means that he could not imagine, his daughter had already acquired—he was certain of this—an ability to read his mind.

The house with loose brown aluminum siding was now too small for the three of them. Saul and Patsy were getting in one another's way. That physical congestion had been a pleasure when they were first married, but now it was not. And the problem with mice in the basement was no longer a pretext for comedy. Besides, they did not want to be renters anymore to a landlord like Mr. Munger, the unsuccessful Pentecostal evangelist whose raptures, it was said, were unconvincing. To make ends meet, he worked as an electrician. He had come to fix the ungrounded humidifier and talked without conviction about Jesus.

During the time that they had been in Five Oaks, the farm fields near their house had been purchased by a developer from Ann Arbor, and on all sides of their rental property, apartments and condos and housing projects were springing up in fields where cows had once grazed and soybeans had been planted. Mr. Munger had not yet sold his property to the developers, but it was just a matter of time before he did. After a week of indecision, Saul and Patsy finally purchased a house on Whitefeather Road two miles closer to downtown than their rental house had been. A two-story economy-sized colonial on a good-sized lot in a development called The Uplands, the house had large front and back yards and a shady tree in front, and with some contributions from Patsy's parents for the down payment, they had calculated that they could afford it, though just barely. Patsy found it curious, or mortifying, that she, a loan officer at the bank, had had to apply for a loan in exactly the way everyone else did.

They moved in in October. Saul took two personal days off from teaching American history to help Patsy unpack their earthly possessions—the furniture, the kitchen utensils, the posters, the board games, including the Scrabble set—and arrange the house. Patsy herself had taken two days' leave from the bank branch where she now worked. Emmy's room on the second floor looked north, where, in the distance, the Wolverine Outlet Mall was still visible, as was the Bruckner Buick plasticene polar bear, which their daughter also loved to see from the car. In the mornings, she would stand up in her crib and gaze out the window at the Bruckner Buick blimp balloon, which was usually observable on clear days to the east of the outlet mall.

After her first word, "Wzzat," and her second word, "Mama," her next word was "Dadda." Her seventh or eighth word was "Gordy."

Gordy had continued to show up intermittently on Saul and Patsy's front lawn when they still lived in the rented house with loose brown aluminum siding. At first they were alarmed at his arrivals and would try to get him to go home. After four or five visits, however, they began to get used to him. Sometimes they gave him odd jobs to do, which he would either try to perform or not, depending on his mood and skills. A few times they paid him, and he looked at the money they handed to him with disbelief and incomprehension. He never thanked them or expressed any gratitude.

They had both given up trying to discover the purpose of his visits. After asking him what he wanted or what they could do for him and receiving no comprehensible answer, they didn't persist. Saul called Brenda Bagley, and if she happened to be at home, she would tell him to send Gordy back if he was being a pest. He wasn't a pest, exactly, but you couldn't ask him anymore why he was there, because the question had become metaphysical. It was like trying to ask a dog why it followed you around.

Once they moved to their new house in The Uplands, however, they thought they were finally rid of him. It wasn't as if they had moved in order to ditch him, but they were sure that the new location would put an end to his visits.

Yet somehow Gordy, who had dropped out of high school by this time, found out where they had moved to, and one Saturday morning in November, there he was again, standing under the large tree, the linden, that the developers had spared in their yard. In his characteristic way, Gordy was staring at the house, then at the sky, then at the ground, then at the house again. Their local acned Bartleby. He hadn't come on his bicycle; The Uplands happened to be on the Five Oaks city busline route. Saul thought of calling the police to complain of Gordy as a trespasser, and then he imagined being laughed at for his complaint. He would have to take action himself.

He strolled out to the front yard. "You found us," he said.

Gordy nodded.

"How did you manage to do that?" Saul inquired.

"I seen your car in the driveway," Gordy informed him. "That white Chevy. That I rode in." Saul went back into the house and left Gordy outside. He was not about to invite him in, what with the new floors, and the carpeting, and the carefully placed furniture. He wasn't about to ask him to *do* anything.

At times Patsy would rise in the morning and walk into the nursery, only to find Mary Esther standing in her crib and, with a rapt expression, gazing through the window at the young man on the autumn lawn. Was he shivering? Patsy thought that they *should* call the police and have Gordy arrested for trespassing and stalking and harassment and just for making a general nuisance of himself—Gordy's visits bothered and upset her—but Saul disagreed, saying that if they ignored him, he would gradually go away, and besides, if they had him arrested, he would still eventually find his way back. What were they going to do, get a court injunction, or call Gordy's aunt again? No, Saul claimed, despite what he had once thought about Gordy—his mindlessness, his blank stares, the episode with the gun—he would cause them no trouble. Gordy meant them no harm, it seemed. He was just loitering without intent. It was an emotional thing with him. Sooner or later he would give it up.

Gradually they forgot about him even when he was there, the way you forget about your shadow. When they did remember to take notice of him, they would give him cookies, which he would sometimes eat.

As fall turned into winter, and Emmy gained weight and began to make herself crawl and achieved her first moves to an upright position, time seemed to pass more rapidly than Saul and Patsy had thought it would. Their jobs and their new house and their daughter took all their attention, and the presence of Gordy now and then on their front lawn gradually became an accepted part of their lives, a feature they recognized, anomalous though it was, as a given. Gordy Himmelman stood blankly on Saul and Patsy's lawn, wearing his raffish visored cap. When they were working in front, raking leaves, he would shadow them and sometimes, if he could, help them out. "Every couple has something freakish in their lives that they have to accept," Patsy said one evening at dinner, looking out at Gordy, standing there in the driveway as night fell and snow drifted slowly down. "He's ours."

Saul even began to think of Gordy as a sentry. On certain days he imagined Gordy as an unemployed bodyguard. At times, when winter's grip had loosened and the snows began to melt and the mud appeared, Saul would check the yard, and if Gordy was not there—Gordy, the faithful zombie, their own private security service, Sergeant Bartleby, the last creation of Dr. Frankenstein—Saul felt a strange furtive disappointment.

But it wasn't as if they were going to sanction this strange behavior. Gordy could stand out there facing the house—in the sunshine, or the rain, or the snow, or the mud—but they were not about to invite him in, or ask him again, or again, or again, why he was there. You didn't have conversations over extended periods of time with someone like Gordy Himmelman about motivations. He wasn't smart enough to have reasons for doing what he did. If he did have reasons, by now he would have revealed them. Or they would have appeared on his face: it would have taken on an expression of yearning, or resentment, or rage.

But his face, through the fall and then on through the winter, and then on to spring and early summer, remained as blank as ever. His eyes, as always, were distant and lunar. There was nothing to be done about him.

Eight

On Sunday mornings, if Mary Esther didn't stir, Saul and Patsy slept late. Usually Patsy awakened first. She would lie in bed watching the leaves of the linden shivering in the hot mottled summer air outside their bedroom window. Above her, hanging from the ceiling light fixture, a cardboard bird mobile turned slowly in the vestigial breezes. She gazed at it, vaguely admiring its equilibrium, its spiritless motion. Or she would examine Saul, wrestling with his angels as he muttered words that were all vowels—Hawaiian words, now that it was summertime and he was no longer dragging himself across the Arctic—and when she watched him and listened to his unintelligible garble, she tried to concentrate her attention on how it was she had married him, those steps of gradual womanly acknowledgment that had taken her toward him.

They had both been performers in those undergraduate days, Saul a musician and she a dancer, and they kept running into each other in the rehearsal halls.

She had *really* met him after a dance production of *The Unnamable*. She was one of the two dancers, and the production took place in a performance space with all of the seats on the north side. It was originally going to be staged in pitch dark—Patsy as a very young woman was interested in invisible performances—but the other dancer insisted on two black

123

lights and a single candle with a metallic shade. Patsy finally conceded the point. Offstage, a woman read excerpts from the Beckett text, and Patsy danced to it: preoccupied but nevertheless formal movements engaged in at extreme slow motion, right at the borderline of stasis. She had worked for weeks on nearly imperceptible body movements, stillness-dancing. It had been a challenge because such dancing excited her and quieted her at the same time, as yoga did. A fourth woman, a composer of aleatory sounds, though post-Cage in style, created amplified background audio using sand in Dixie Cups, and with rubber bands, Slinkies, and a watering can with ball bearings inside.

Patsy had wished to give the impression that if you took your eyes away from her for even a moment, she would not look the same the next time you saw her: her body under the influence of the spoken text had become illusionary, metamorphic, even metastatic: she aimed herself at the audience and opened her bare arms to them, replicating the gestures of a night-blooming cereus, or a youthful prostitute under a streetlight, or a cancer, or Eurydice.

All four women were after a certain tone: they wanted the production to be both impossibly brainy and also, and inevitably, so erotic as to risk accusations of obscenity. If it seemed unbearably pretentious, well, that was a risk they would take.

After the third performance—all the tickets were free because the Beckett estate wouldn't give them permission for the adaptation—Saul reintroduced himself to her outside the green room and began talking at great length about her performance. He had the piercing brown eyes of a repentant gangster, though he was gaunt in other respects, except for his thick peasant's hands. He was highly excited by the text ("self-incriminated language," he called it, "oxidizing in your ear") and the sounds ("lyrical aural insults, with no bottom to them"), but most of all, it seemed, he was excited by Patsy. "You were moving but *you* weren't moving," he said, "the *words* were moving your body," demonstrating that he had got it, that it hadn't slipped past him. "It was psychokinetic," he said, "and phonemic-kinetic," which was going a bit far. They were talking in the hallway, Patsy holding her knapsack, the hour was getting late, and then Saul blurted out, "I kept imagining what it would be like to be part-nered with you," and then he blushed under his beard, self-astonished. Patsy smiled. So it would be like this, from now on? The blurting of truth in the wee hours?

Coffee, dates, much talk (because it was Saul), the love attack—he had massaged her feet after her last performance, talking about Schopen-hauer as they reclined on her bed, still clothed. "I don't think Schopen-hauer is as pessimistic as people say he is, do you?" Saul asked. She had said she didn't know. Nor did she want to give him the impression that she would try to find out. She was not going to scamper after his preoccu-pations just because they were his.

Still, he had the most beautiful skin she had ever seen on a man, and a winsome smile.

One evening in the fall they had met at a campus coffee house, and as he was walking her back to her apartment, a soft rain began to fall. They were both wearing sandals, and they both ambled across the grass, grad-ually increasing their speed to a jog as they held hands. Patsy had looked over at Saul and saw her own sudden shocked, unprovoked joy on his face.

Then he had called her at two in the morning and played some Charlie Parker for her over the phone. In Saul, love took the form of desperation-to-share. He invited her over to his apartment, where he cooked dinner, played his trombone, and asked her to dance for him. Saul turned all the lights off, and Patsy danced by the light of the street-light, but there was no aleatoric, arranged sound, just the noise of the cars and the trucks passing by in the street, and so she danced to that, a dance for him, though resisting him as much as she could, a dance about that resistance, about the *refusals* of nakedness. They made love anyway when she was finished, Patsy still resisting him a little, all her movements initially sullen. She fucked him with sensual resentment; she let him know that she had her needs, too, that he could not apportion all the passions for himself.

She could not tell if he was able to appreciate or even to read the ways that she had made love to him at first, or to notice particularly how she did it, the way that a dancer like her performed sex, slyly, with touches of rhetoric, annoyance, always with an implicit audience watching the subtle errant moves, moves that were only half for herself, the other half for the purposes of visual expression, or even the denial of that need, any need, a statement of freedom: Look, I *can* play with this desire. And you can't, exactly.

Living together, movies, dinners, escalating comfort in each other's company, the unthinkability of not being together, the sense—where had this come from?—that they were setting up a small business together, and finally marriage. Soon, Saul could read all her gestures. That was both a triumph in human terms and a defeat in artistic ones. For consolation, she had someone with whom to discuss all aspects of life. Now here they were, in the Midwest, where *everybody's* gestures were immediately read-able. At these moments it no longer seemed inevitable that they should have met in the first place, that she should have ever loved him and finally married him. Arbitrary, the meeting, the love, all of it, a trick, after all, of the body she had trained and with which she now excited or soothed him. She might have loved anybody, but it had turned out to be this man, this Saul, a Scrabble player, a teacher. But there was no certainty of logic to it. He lay there now, the father of her daughter, his eyebrows twitching, his breath smelling of corn tassels. A man sleeping in bed in the morning is rarely a prize, it seemed to her at such moments. But she loved him, and her love puzzled her, as if Eros had played a prank on her and she wanted to unravel it. Because: if it had arrived as quickly and as haphaz-ardly as that, it could depart just as fast. It worried her, that their courtship had started with Saul being her audience. She knew she was beautiful as a performer. But as anything else? As a *wife*?

Being a wife stalled out the art. Being a mother put a stop to it. And now, she realized, there was some feature about Saul she didn't get—that she would never get.

"Oh, don't analyze," her friend Susan Palmer had once said. "Don't try to figure out why you love some guy. You'll only figure out that you *shouldn't*. In my experience, guys—well, the grown-up boys I've known—don't stand much scrutiny. They can barely stand up at all. You know what they're all about, under the microscope? They're all about their flaws, versus whatever else they've got. Their games."

"No, really," Patsy said. They were both working as tellers at the bank, and they were on their lunch break, in the back room, over sandwiches. There were no windows, and it felt very private in there. "It's the biggest thing that ever happened to me. But. It's a puzzle."

"*Jesus*, Patsy. A puzzle? If you've got a blessing, any blessing at all, just *count* it. Don't examine it. Are you crazy? Some of us don't even have what you have." Susan bit into her sandwich angrily, her eyes tearing up. Patsy didn't know what Susan was talking about: Susan was married, after all, to a nice guy, the assistant city manager of Five Oaks, a fellow named Wyatt. They had two children. Wyatt's mom was a little crazy, but so what? They lived model lives. Susan taught gymnastics to kids on weekends. She was beautiful, her gymnast figure still visible under her clothes. She had a trustworthy man sleeping next to her in bed each night. Still, Patsy had violated a rule: you never, ever brag to a coworker about loving your husband. It was bad manners, it was arrogant, and nobody's business, besides.

But now, two years later, thinking of what Susan had told her, Patsy realized that loving Saul was not, in fact, the biggest event that had ever happened to her. Mary Esther was. Mary Esther had pushed everything and everybody else off the map, and she had turned Saul into a father. It was Mary Esther she thought about, Mary Esther who commanded her repertoire of emotions. Saul, she had discovered, was the means for Mary Esther to come into the world. He was . . . the word came to her unpleasantly, an *expedient*. As if to recoil from this recognition, Patsy began to rub Saul's back. He slept naked during the summer, and she had just touched his back when the phone rang, downstairs, as if touching his skin had set off a bell elsewhere in the house.

In her nightgown, she ran down the stairs to get it before it woke anybody up, but she heard Mary Esther stirring and whimpering as she rose out of sleep. As soon as Patsy had picked up the phone, even before she heard the voice, she knew—the psychic insights of everyday life—that it was Saul's mother, Delia.

"Patsy." Delia's voice was regimental somehow, feminine-military, without being hard. Patsy didn't know how she did it. "I hope I didn't wake you up."

"No, no. *I* was up." Patsy heard Delia's toaster popping up in the background.

"Yes, I suppose. I mean, I suppose I shouldn't have called. It's—"

"Well, it's not *that* early." Without looking at her watch, Patsy knew it was eight thirty-nine.

"Well. Maybe it is in the Midwest. It's *always* earlier there. And it isn't just the time zones that cause that. In the Midwest it's always last week, compared to here. Is Saul still asleep?"

Patsy glanced up the stairs. Mary Esther was beginning to sing softly, and if she got louder, Saul would eventually arise, dazedly, go into the nursery, and change her. "Yes, I think so. He's still asleep."

"Good."

"Good?"

"Well, I need to talk to someone," Delia said. "And I was hoping I'd get you. This isn't the sort of information I should say to Saul. Or to Howie, either. Besides, I never know where Howie is. The last time I called him, I got him on his cell phone, and he was halfway up a mountain, climbing it. Excuse me, but I don't see the point of climbing a mountain. Why not buy a postcard? Or get someone else to climb it? Well, what can you do with a son like that?"

"I don't know," Patsy said automatically. "What can you do?" Then she realized belatedly that it was not a question she should parrot back to Delia.

"You can't do anything," Delia said obligingly. Then her voice dropped an octave. "Are you alone? Well, I mean, can you keep a secret?"

"Sure." Patsy looked down at her feet, at the polish flaking off her toenails.

"Don't tell Saul. It'll upset him. I just have to tell somebody, and it's obvious I can't tell my friends just now . . . well, it's not that you're *convenient*, Patsy, I'm not saying that. You know I love you, don't you? I got so lucky, having a daughter-in-law like you." Delia said these words distantly, and without inflection.

128

"Delia, what's going on?" Patsy felt herself clutching the phone tightly.

"Well, it's this way. You're young, you'll understand this, I *think*. I need to say this to somebody." Delia waited and took an audible breath. "I have a new boyfriend," she announced. "But I haven't told Saul, or anybody." Patsy waited for her to continue speaking, but she didn't, as if she had faltered momentarily. "Well, one friend, but that's it."

"Delia," Patsy said with whispered enthusiasm, "that's great! Congratulations. Who is it?"

"See, that's the thing."

Patsy waited. "The thing. Okay," she said.

"All right. He's quite young," Delia said. "He's younger than I am. Quite a bit younger. Actually, he's younger than you are. Actually, he's almost eighteen. But, no, the truth is that he's seventeen. I don't want to mislead you. He's seventeen." Her voice, in announcing this fact, was worldly and neutral, uninvolved in what it was saying.

"Isn't that illegal?"

"No, I don't think so. I think it's quite legal. Though I haven't checked. But here's the icing on my particular cake. He's the yard boy. His name is Jimmy. Jimmy the yard boy. What a cliché! I hired him to come over here to fix up the yard and to do some gardening, and he was unusually kind and considerate, absolutely not what I was expecting at all, of course, from a young man that age. You don't expect young men to be kind and considerate. Usually they're awful. And, I don't know, mostly as a joke, a nothing, I made a little play for him, and now . . . Patsy, you won't tell Saul, will you?"

"No, I won't tell Saul." Patsy considered this for a moment, what she would say next. After all, she was speaking to the Marschallin. The Marschallin had finally gotten her young man. "Is it a French novel or is it an American novel?"

"I don't follow you."

"Well, if it was an American novel, you'd have an affair with him, and you'd both feel soiled and degraded, and then he'd tell his parents, and his mother would file a suit against you, and somebody would be shot dead after a few months, you know, out of pure rage, and then there would be church-lady morals and a big mess to clean up with the litigation. If it was a French novel, though, you two would both have a perfectly good time, and he would be grateful to you and, you know, *tireless,* and you would teach him a thing or two about sex and the ways of love, and he'd remember you happily for a few years, have other girlfriends more his age who would all love him for his boldness and attentiveness and expertise, and then he'd get married and settle down."

"It's actually more like the French version," Delia said, a bit dryly. "So far."

"Well, good for you," Patsy said.

"But you know, in these matters, nothing is as simple as all that. I go through the house," Delia resumed, "muttering his name, and I think of his parents and whether they'll ever find out, and then I think, well, in a few weeks he'll start school again, and it'll be all over." She waited. "It *will* be over, and no harm will have come to anybody, as long as he doesn't tell anyone. He says he hasn't. And that's how it's supposed to work. But sometimes it's more complicated."

Delia stopped talking.

"Don't tell me you're pregnant," Patsy said. Mary Esther's cries upstairs were getting a bit louder now. Where was Saul?

"Oh, no, I'm not pregnant. I had my tubes tied a long time ago, and besides, I'm . . . no, it's not that, believe me."

"Well, what is it?" Patsy thought she knew what Delia would say, but she didn't want to anticipate it.

"See, the little complication is, I love him," Delia said, her voice still absolutely neutral, even a bit cold. "Just a little bit. Of course it's *completely* ridiculous. I mean, he's only a boy. This is like something middle-aged men do, with their proclivity for college girls. But I do love him. Patsy, he brings in little bouquets of flowers that he's picked. A boy does this! He brings them in for me, and we put them in water together. And you should see his smile. I don't think I've ever had a smile like that from a grown man. Men don't smile like that spontaneously. They forget how. He smiles at me and my insides just knot up, because he's so happy to see me." Delia's voice continued in its uninflected way.

"Count your blessings," Patsy instructed her mother-in-law, using the phrase she had just been thinking of. Delia was right, of course: Saul had forgotten how to smile, except to produce a result. "Does he love you?"

"Of course not. He's just a kid. And I'm just a middle-aged woman he . . . sometimes sleeps with. I'm a diversion. He doesn't know from love. But he's so devoted, and so sweet, and so kind—Patsy, he compliments me on my body, can you *believe* that?—and of course there's his skin, and *his* body, which is gorgeous, and his smile, that it doesn't matter that he doesn't love me, because he might as well love me, considering the way he treats me. Somehow I missed all this before, when I was an actual girl. Know what I mean? I thought when you were my age, you stopped doing foolishness like this. I thought women stopped falling in love, at least *comme ça.*"

"Well, I guess not."

There was a long pause, and Patsy could tell from the noises at the other end that Delia was blowing her nose, though tentatively. "Of course he has a little girlfriend, too."

"Of course."

"But he says that it isn't as good with her as with me." She waited. "Maybe he's being nice. It's his way, being nice. He'd say it even if he didn't mean it."

Patsy looked through the window and saw Gordy Himmelman sitting out on the front lawn. Like the proverbial bad penny, he kept turning up. What did he want *this* time? He had reappeared again, the poor zombie. He had been doing this for about a year now. It was his first anniversary. He was just sitting there, looking skyward. He wanted someone to pay attention to him. In this way, he was like everybody else.

"Delia, I don't think you have any rights in this matter. You can't be jealous. You just have a fling with him this summer and then let him go back to school in the fall."

"No, you're right, of course."

There was a pause of several seconds.

"What?" Patsy asked.

"Well, sometimes I go to bed and I think, *This seventeen-year-old is the love of my life.* Which is quite silly, but that's what I think. Don't tell Saul I said that. Saul's father was a good-enough man, all things considered. He was a hard worker. He worked himself to death. But a lover he wasn't. I was married to him, and still he never noticed me except sometimes over breakfast when I brought him his coffee. As a provider, of course, I can't complain about him."

"Delia, you shouldn't be romanticizing. Summer's going to be over, and you'll have to get your life back."

"I know," Delia sighed. Her voice was calm and unearthly. "I've had my French novel. So, how's the baby? How's little Emmy?"

Patsy crossed her legs at the ankles. She had been thinking of getting a tattoo, a tiny one, of a flower, on her left calf, but now that she was a mom, those thoughts were starting to seem senseless. Besides, tattoos were forms of expression for the inarticulate. She could always say what she meant. "Right now? She's just woken up. She's crying a little. Or maybe singing. She's really not a baby anymore. Not at fifteen months. I think Saul'll check on her in a minute." Patsy smiled into the phone. "Her first teeth are in, and she's still getting cranky. Of course, Saul is still a little jealous of her. He'll get over it."

"She's so adorable. And here I am, a grandmother. It's a strange thing to have happened to me, Patsy, it's a strange thing to have happened to a nice Jewish girl, being a grandmother. Well, I don't know about that 'nice.' I was a little wild in high school, you know. Privately. In public I was a nice girl. And then . . . I stopped being wild. And then I was respectable when I was married to Norman, right out of high school, and dutiful with him, before he died so young, and *then* I was a grandmother, and now I stand at the windows watching the shadows in the afternoon and waiting for the sound of Jimmy's pickup truck."

"So you've started again."

"Yes. I started again. But it's not so pleasing when a woman falls in love with a young man that much younger. It's not becoming in a grand-mother. People don't like it. And I can see why." She stopped and waited—Patsy thought—for the words to be carried to her, and back out again, in exactly the form she wanted. "You're right, you know. Once the summer's over, I'll give him up. And I will, I really will do that. A gift like that, it's best not to try to draw it out. You're right, it's a fling. And, after all, I've been addicted to things before." She said the last sentence with a weary inflection. "But not like this."

"Right."

"You won't tell Saul, will you? Promise?"

"No. I won't," Patsy said.

"Wish me luck."

"Good luck."

"Thank you. That was nice. I always wished I had a daughter, Patsy, but now I have you. And it's better having you than having a real daughter, because I would never have dared to tell her this. Goodbye, dear."

"Goodbye," Patsy said. She dropped the phone onto its cradle and sat for a moment waiting, trying to think of what Delia meant by that daughter statement. If she had had a *real* daughter, Delia had implied, she would have felt ashamed of herself and would never have confessed to having taken a lover, a boy still in high school, because . . . why? Because her daughter's opinion would have mattered to her, and Patsy's opinion didn't? Or because she wouldn't have wanted her daughter to think of her as an example? She tried to fight off the feeling that she was angry, and then she *was* angry, perspiring with anger, and not fighting it. A slight breeze blew in through the screen, and she closed her eyes to it.

She went back up the stairs and saw Saul standing in front of the window, bouncing Mary Esther and talking to her, long strings of Saul-talk. He had changed her diaper. When Patsy came into the doorway, Saul gave her a steady look. "Who was that? Was that my mother?"

"Yes," Patsy said. She liked watching her husband hold their daughter. She took pride in Saul's child-care skills, his intuitive leaps into infancy. Good husbands who were good lovers rarely made good fathers, too, and it was her impression that such men were exceptionally uncommon birds. Apparently Saul hadn't picked it up from his own father, but he had gotten it from somewhere. It made up for his other relentlessly irritating habits. "She just called to chat. You can call her back any time." Saul nodded. "Actually, that's not right," Patsy said. "I lied. That part about the chat. Your mother has taken a boyfriend," Patsy said, "an actual *boy*, this time—in high school." The words leapt out of her without her having been completely aware that she was saying them. Then they were gone, free of her, broadcast into the air.

Saul's face immediately broke into its constituent parts, one eyebrow going one way, the other eyebrow going another, the mouth drooping down here, rising there.

Patsy said, rushing ahead of herself, "The Marschallin didn't want me to tell you, and she said that if I had been her real daughter, she wouldn't have told me in the first place, but I guess I just broke my promise to her." *Jesus, listen to me,* Patsy thought.

Saul went on holding Mary Esther, bouncing her. The baby was hungry and was crying softly now, working up to some real noise. "You shouldn't have told me, Patsy," he said, with an odd, disarming calm. "I bet she told all of that to you in confidence."

"No kidding." She held her arms out. "Here. Give me the baby."

As he handed over Mary Esther, Saul appeared to be in a daze. "But you did. I wonder why. You broke a promise to her?" Patsy nodded, even though Saul wasn't looking at her. "Who is it, this lover?"

"The yard boy."

"The yard boy. Just like my mother to do that," Saul said, dispiritedly. Patsy perceived—odd that she hadn't noticed before—that Saul had no clothes on. She was so used to him by now that his nakedness made absolutely no impression on her except when he was amorous, or when she was. He pulled the window's curtain aside. The time was eight minutes after nine o'clock, she knew. "We should move to Berlin. *That'd* serve her right. There's Gordy, by the way."

Stepping up close to Saul at the window, Patsy lowered the straps of her nightgown and lifted Mary Esther, who at fifteen months was becoming quite heavy. She brought her daughter to her nipple and, as she did, registered how substantial her daughter was and how soon she would not be nursing her anymore. Really, she wasn't a baby now. All this breastfeeding would be over in no time at all. She would miss it, miss it like crazy, even with all the pain and soreness. But then there would be another baby, Theo. "What did you say?" she asked. "I was distracted." Mary Esther was sucking at her greedily.

"I said that Gordy is here." Patsy thought all at once that they shouldn't be standing naked at their bedroom window looking out at Gordy Himmelman. Just being visible in their own bedroom, they were inciting him to riot. But her anger, which had not died down from the phone call, kept her there in a frozen tableau with Saul: here was Sunday morning, a day—of all days—when young married couples could lie around naked, make love, feed the baby, read the paper, do anything they wanted to do, indoors or out, and there, on the front lawn, was Gordy Himmelman, their sentry, their guard dog, their zombie, their boy. With his little demands for attention, he was getting tiresome. What Patsy craved was her own attention, hers and Saul's and Emmy's, and she lifted her hand, as if to start a dance, a dance of please-go-away. "Sometimes I hate my mother," Saul said without warning.

Gordy Himmelman turned his gaze toward them. He stared for a long time at Saul and Patsy.

"You shouldn't hate your mother. She's only human. And by the way, we shouldn't be here, exposing ourselves to that ruffian on the lawn," Patsy said.

"What? What's his name?" Saul asked. "Her boyfriend."

"Oh, the boyfriend? His name's Jimmy," Patsy said, and at that point Gordy pulled out a gun from his back pocket, grinned momentarily, then opened his mouth, directed the barrel of the gun toward it, and then inside it, and fired. A flower-pattern of Gordy's blood and brains splashed against the tree trunk behind his head, and he fell backward.

The sound of the gun made the baby startle: her arms flew up to the sides of her face, and she pulled her mouth away from her mother's breast before looking up into her mother's eyes for an explanation. A trace of breast milk remained on her lower lip.

Part Two

That is what people are like in my district.
Always expecting the impossible from the doctor.

—Franz Kafka, "The Country Doctor"

Nine

The day had been beautiful with clear, dry air—though the sun was penetrating in a late-June sort of way—but now no wind or breeze blew through the yard while the various officials swarmed over the front lawn. The air felt still, or stillborn. Saul, in shock, thought that the patrol cars' flashing red lights gave the driveway the look of a movie set, or a television docudrama. Something, he wasn't sure what, didn't seem real about it. He himself felt less solid—unconcretized—than he had for years. Too much more de-realization, he thought, and he would fade right out.

The county medical examiner came to collect the body, and to pry into the bark of the tree for skull fragments. They took the gun out of Gordy's hand and placed it in an evidence bag. Then Gordy's body was loaded, one man reaching underneath the skinny shoulders and another at the ankles and feet in their scruffy, unlaced high-tops, onto a coroner's gurney. They covered all of it with a white sheet. Having loaded it—him—they took the body away to be examined in closer detail, for drugs in particular. They had explained all this. Three men sauntered toward Saul and Patsy for questions, two regular cops and one investigating detective, and Saul and Patsy offered them coffee that they declined to drink.

They had checked the scene for a suicide note, they said. But there was no evidence of one, and Saul told them it wasn't likely that such a note would ever show up. They asked why. Saul said that Gordy could barely write at all. A suicide note was pretty much beyond him.

Outside in the sunlight, and then in the kitchen for the sake of the shade, first Saul and then Patsy explained about Gordy's previous trips out to their houses, this one and the one they'd rented. Inexplicable, but with a vague, lost-in-space purpose. Saul explained about the remedial language-arts class, the anti-Semitic scrawlings, the beehives. Gordy didn't really know much of anything about Jews, Saul claimed. They were a convenience. It was like Israel for the Arabs, he said, briefly losing his cool. When Saul mentioned the notes, the cops became interested again. So he *could* write, after all. They had caught him in a contradiction. Had Saul saved them, these notes? No, he had not. One of the men went out with Saul to check the exact location where Gordy had been standing.

While they were gone, Mary Esther gazed from her mother's elbow at the two remaining men and then, once Saul returned, from her father's arms. She seemed interested in their hats and held out her hands as if to grab them by their wide brims.

The men from the sheriff's office were particularly intrigued with Gordy's obsessive fascination with Saul and Patsy's houses. Why had he stared at them? What had he wanted from them? Why this strange attention-deficit persistence? Had he threatened the family in any way?

No, not exactly. They claimed not to know why he kept coming out to see them, but that answer was unsatisfactory; it answered nothing. Finally Patsy said, "He was a slow student. He was in Saul's remedial class, of course, and he didn't do well. I think he wanted us to teach him how to read. He wanted us to pay attention to him. Or to teach him . . . how to do *something*."

Saul shook his head. "No. That's not it. It's more complicated. He was trying to get us to *adopt* him. He was like . . . ." Sitting at the kitchen table, his fingers knitted together, Saul was about to say that Gordy was like Dr. Victor Frankenstein's orphaned creature, made out of spare human parts, wandering around looking for love and wanting someone to notice him grunting and groaning, threatening to become a monster and then becoming an actual monster, but, strategically, he made himself go silent. After all, he himself had not known what to do with him. Finally he said, "He was like a lot of boys."

Then, to give them a story, if not *the* story, Saul told them about Gordy's visit from a year ago, when Gordy had waved the gun around in the front yard of their rented house and Saul had taken him and his bicycle and the gun back home. Gordy had been threatening, without actually threatening anything or anyone specifically, in detail. He had just wanted to be generically threatening, adolescent boy stuff, white rural gangsta midwestern skull-and-crossbones *Fear This* and *Don't Fuck With Me* sort of stuff. He was a messed-up kid; that was maybe the entire story. "He didn't think about things," Saul said. "He probably shot himself without thinking about it. Maybe he would've shot one of us without thinking about it. He had a weird kind of spontaneity."

They nodded, but their nodding did not indicate agreement. They wrote it all down. Then they went outside again, to confer.

Half an hour later, Gordy's aunt Brenda arrived. Saul and Patsy went outside to meet her. As she removed herself from her vehicle, a rusting Ford pickup, she expertly finger-flicked her cigarette out onto the lawn. She was still dressed in her waitress clothes, with a pink barrette in her hair, an application of lipstick and perfume, and—Saul was at first surprised, and then not surprised at all—she smiled automatically at the two cops standing near the front door of the house. She was accustomed to cops, Saul realized. For her, a waitress in a diner, cops were familiar and friendly customers, people she saw every day. But the smile was completely insincere—never had a face been built that conveyed less benevolence and good humor than this one. Her somber unattractiveness, her worn-down sorrowfulness, had no appeal.

She walked up first to Saul, who was standing by the tree where Gordy had shot himself. "Hi," she said. She shook his hand. Her face was a conglomeration of pockmarks and scars, perhaps the worst complexion he had ever seen on a woman. The perfume and the barrette and the lipstick did nothing to mitigate her appearance. They magnified the effect of helplessness. "Oh that boy. What a terrible situation here. That poor crazy clueless kid." She glanced around. She sobbed once. "What did they do with his body? I got to see it. This is such a waste," she said, the phrase coming out of her mouth tonelessly. She didn't seem surprised, despite her spasmodic grief—the zombie affect apparently ran in the family. It was the most peculiar response to a death that Saul had ever witnessed, though it occurred to him that it might be a form of working-class stoicism. If she had any grief, she would not give it away to the likes of Saul and Patsy.

Or what—he thought—what if she had been *expecting* this?

Any parent, any guardian would inevitably, Saul thought, be crying and making a scene. That was the standard expectation. But she seemed to be in steady though perhaps uncertain control of herself, standing there in her unattractive dignity. Saul wished he could think of some other category besides *ugliness* when he looked at her. But that word was inescapable with Brenda Bagley. She made you think about her looks the way a professional beauty would; she commanded your attention. Just being around her, you fell down a notch or two, you became less than you were, because you couldn't help but notice her shortcomings. Against Brenda's deficiencies, the gods themselves would have struggled in vain. He also wished he had some consolation to give her, but he did not. The correct words and phrases flew away from him, were gone. Calmly, still gazing down, inconsolable, she said, "Oh, my lord, I wish I knew where Gordy's father got himself to. He went out to Wyoming looking for work a couple years ago, and I haven't heard from him since, and here his son is gone for good and ever. And *he* doesn't even know. There's something else I don't get."

"What don't you get?" Saul asked.

"No TV."

"What?"

"Where's the TV reporters? Doesn't this count for something? A boy dying by his own hand? Just because it was a poor kid like Gordy don't mean you can't report it. It's like he counts for nothing. A pig runs away from the farmyard and they cover it on the news. A purse gets snatched and they cover it for a week. What about this? You've got a poor dropout being dead here by his own self-violence, and that ain't a story? Can you explain to me how come they aren't doing coverage?"

"Maybe they're busy." He shrugged. "They just aren't here yet," Saul told her. "Thank God. I don't know why. Do you want to see where it happened? Brenda, how did he get that gun?"

"No. Yes. Well, okay. Sure." She nodded her head, and Saul dutifully pointed down at the tree trunk where the blood was drying. "Right here then. How awful," Gordy's aunt said, reaching into her purse for another cigarette, which she lit up with a despairing shake of the head, followed by a stagy puff.

"He kept coming here," Saul said. "To this spot. He'd stand here like a sentry."

"I know that." She took a long despairing inhale from the cigarette, as if gasping for oxygen.

"He'd be out in the yard, hour after hour, staring at us, you know."

"Yes, he told me. He said he was over here." She paused to reflect. "The gun? You asked about the gun? He found it where I had hidden it."

"Did he ever tell you *why* he came over here?"

"No, he didn't," she said, rubbing her cheek. She made Saul think of a peeled tangerine. "I was just glad he wanted to do *something*. That he wanted to go somewhere. I couldn't look after him."

"He did it off and on for a whole year."

"Well, it gave him a place to go."

"A place to go?"

"Yes. I was at work, and he was old enough not to go to school—said he wasn't learning anything—and I couldn't think of anything to do with him, so, you know, he came over here. I guess he thought you cared about him and could maybe give him a place to be."

"We just got used to it," Saul said. "To *him*," he corrected himself.

"God-*damn*," Brenda suddenly erupted, a high keening wail. "I told and told him about guns, like I was in the NRA or something, and I sure damn well trained him to respect them. I just *whacked* it into him. You saw me trying to knock some sense into him. Made me feel *terrible*! If you didn't hit him, he wouldn't notice. 'Guns don't kill people,' I told him, 'people kill people.' This last time I hid that .22 so *no* one could find it, in a shoe box." She looked up, and her face took on a sudden fearful radiance. "No one. But then *he* did." The on-the-spot Channel Seven Mobile News van was speeding up the driveway, followed by Channel Three's news van. Maybe there would be a helicopter and skycam shots, and a direct-feed breaking-news story from the crime scene. Finally, the occasion felt like a movie premiere. Brenda touched her hair. The poor woman—what did she think she was doing, trying to get on television? Attract the talent scouts?

"Miss Bagley?" The police investigator, the detective—Saul was having trouble remembering his name, maybe because of the distraction of the weapons, and each time he saw one of them, the cop looked unfamiliar—took her aside for some questions and a statement and an identification. Saul overheard him asking her about a suicide note. They were certainly interested in suicide notes. Well, responsibility, after all. Cause and effect, after all. A villain, a fall guy. Saul suddenly wondered if maybe—just maybe—there might be one, might be a suicide note. Mentioning *him*. Barely readable, scrawled, but still scratchily specific. The Channel Seven reporter, whom Saul recognized as Traci McMahoney, hurried away from the mobile news van in a rather purposeful beeline toward him, followed by the camera and sound men. Involuntarily, he stood up straight and cleared his throat.

She was extraordinarily pretty, a small-town former beauty queen probably, with blond hair arranged in an expensive feathery style, startlingly blue eyes, and a strange expression of artificial concern. She was the visual antidote to Brenda Bagley. In spite of himself, Saul felt charged up, on the verge of a statement. Also in spite of himself, he gazed at her as she approached him. She had great legs with excellent calf definition. She worked out somewhere. They all did, now. Guiltily, he turned, looking for his wife. About ten feet away, Patsy had Mary Esther in hand, but Patsy was also checking on Saul. Mary Esther was sobbing quietly. Patsy's bangs were falling down over her sad eyes as she then hefted Mary Esther from one arm to the other. What was she being sad about? Gordy's death? That Saul had stared helplessly at the Channel Seven reporter? No. Saul had—they both knew it—a tendency to misstate himself in situations involving the stress of public speaking, so he flashed her his brimful-of-confidence expression; she did not seem immediately reassured.

The other news team, the one from Channel Three, had gone over to wait to interview Brenda until after the detective had finished with her, but this one, the Action News Team from Channel Seven, had stayed here. After Traci McMahoney had set herself up so that the house showed in the background, but before the videocam was rolling, she asked Saul if he'd be willing to answer a few questions on-camera. He nodded. She aimed herself at the lens, touched her hair, and then did her intro. Today, she said, *The Uplands has been a scene of tragedy,* in what appears to be a suicide by a Five Oaks man, Gordon Himmelman, who lived with his aunt on Strewwelpeter Street. The young man had shot himself in the front yard of one of his former teachers, Saul Bernstein. So far there was no explanation as to why he had taken the trouble to bike over to his teacher's house to shoot himself. No suicide note had yet been found.

Ah, Saul thought. So that settles that.

Traci McMahoney pivoted toward Saul. "You were his teacher."

"Yes."

"And in what subject?"

"Language arts." Saul looked at her and at the microphone, then at the sound guy. He felt something coming on, something wrong. "Last year. Not this academic year. *Last* academic year. He had dropped out."

"How were his grades?"

"His grades? It was a . . . remedial class."

"Oh. In that case, how well did you know the young man?"

"Pretty well. I don't know. How well does anybody know anyone?"

Traci McMahoney frowned. "Had he threatened you? Had he threatened anyone at school?"

"No. Not exactly. He had written those illegible notes of his. He once called me a shitbird."

Traci McMahoney moved the microphone away from her mouth. Quietly, confidentially, she said to Saul, "We can't put words like that on the air."

"I know," Saul said. "I was just telling you what he said." His eyebrow itched. He scratched it. "I thought I had just better tell the truth."

"Okay," she said, still conspiratorially, *sotto voce*. Then, resuming her professional voice, she said, "Had he seemed depressed to you?"

"Depressed? No. That wasn't like him. At least I don't think so."

"What about these notes you mentioned?"

"Oh, the notes? He wrote notes in class about how much he didn't like school. He once called me a kike, but he didn't really mean it. I don't even know where he found that word."

Traci McMahoney shifted her weight on her great legs, expressing impatience and dissatisfaction. She gave off a scent of some wonderful perfume redolent of the Elysian Fields. It made Saul think of Tahiti, where he had never been. Patsy never wore perfume; she had allergies. Brenda's perfume, by contrast, smelled like the perfume counter in a drugstore. Saul intuited that the interview was not going well, however, and that the fault was probably his. He would try to do better. He wanted to please Traci McMahoney.

"What were you doing when it happened?" she asked.

"I was standing in front of the bedroom window," Saul said, "listening to my wife tell me about my mother's affair with the yard boy."

"Oh, Jesus," Traci McMahoney said. She dropped the microphone again. "Can we start over? Let's start over. You don't need to go into details like that. It's distracting to the viewers. Let's start over. And let's try to stay on-message. This'll be the second take. This is all on tape anyway. We'll do some editing. Thank *God* this isn't an on-the-air breaking-news report."

Once again she did an introduction. Today, she said, *The Uplands has been a scene of tragedy,* in what appears to be a suicide by a Five Oaks boy, Gordon Himmelman. Boy, man. Which was he? This time they ran through the same questions one after the other, but Saul remembered not to mention his mother and not to say anything about shitbirds or kikes.

"Had he threatened anyone else?" she asked.

"Gordy? No. Well, I don't think so."

"Do you know where he got the gun?"

"From his aunt, I think. I believe she had hidden it, and he found it."

"Wouldn't you consider this a tragedy?"

"Sort of," Saul said.

"Could you expand on that?"

"Well, I don't think Gordy ever stopped to consider what he did. He just did things. He didn't think about what he was doing. He just did them, mindlessly. I don't know if you could call that a tragedy or not. It just happened. It was . . ." Saul struggled to find an adjective. "It was *tidal.*"

"Wouldn't you say it's a tragedy *every* time a young life is snuffed out?"

"Probably," Saul said. "Depends on what you mean by 'tragedy.'" Traci McMahoney frowned again. "If you mean a story of a great man brought low by circumstances related to his character, resulting in events that cause a purging of pity and fear, then no."

Her frown was growing permanent. "So what you're saying is, this is another meaningless tragedy, uh, story of violence among our young people."

"Oh, I wouldn't say it's *meaningless,*" Saul told her. "It's rare for something to be meaningless."

"Would you care to expand on that?"

"It's not meaningless if there are guns everywhere. If a weird unhappy kid can get a gun anytime he wants one, then it's not meaningless. It means that there are too many guns around."

Traci McMahoney smiled. "Too many guns?"

"This whole country is gun crazy," Saul said. "From the president on down."

"Well, you can save that for the Editorial Moment," Traci McMahoney said, grimacing. "On Sunday night just before sign-off. What about Gordon Himmelman?"

"What about him?"

"Do you feel that you failed him somehow? That the system failed him?"

"Failed him? Me? Who knows? But I doubt it."

"I mean, do you think you could have stopped him?"

"How?"

"Counseling. More one-on-one. Aggressive intervention. Mentoring."

"Boys like Gordy Himmelman don't usually take to counseling. Besides, I wasn't his parent. He *did* have this air of abandonment, I'll say that. He was like the creature set loose by Dr. Frankenstein." It had come right out of his mouth. He didn't mean to say it, but he had said it anyway. "You ignore them and they turn into monsters."

"A monster? No, I won't follow that up. I could, but I won't. Is there a chance that this wasn't a suicide? Could it have been an accident? Why did he come over to your house with a loaded gun?"

"It wasn't an accident," Saul said. "He had the gun barrel pointed inside his mouth. Maybe he wanted to impress us."

There was a long beat during which Traci McMahoney tried to think of a question. "So, in conclusion, why do you think he did it? Do you have an explanation for this terrible trage—,uh, event?"

"Yeah. Too many guns, too much television, not enough reading, a crazy violence-prone culture, and a kid, I mean an *okay* kid with lousy parenting, probably, or nonparenting, and he needed cognitive help, so you get this dumb bloodfest, this Americana suicide, right? I mean, is there really a big enigma? I don't see a big enigma here. Maybe the only big enigma is that he didn't wait to go charging into the school lunchroom next fall spraying bullets. Small favors, and all that. You've got to be careful not to sentimentalize when something like this happens."

"You feel strongly about this," Traci McMahoney said, in disbelief.

"Yes. I don't like sentimentality," Saul said.

"Okay." She lowered the microphone and nodded at the videocam guy, doing a quick gesture in front of her eyes and a nod indicating a cut. The cameraman lowered the videocam away from his eye before hoisting it backward onto his shoulder, and Saul could see that he was smirking. Then Traci McMahoney turned to Saul once again. "Well, *that* was mostly unusable. Look," she said, brilliantly smiling, "I agree with you about a lot of what you said, but you can't say those things on-camera. That's editorial-page. That's not front-page. We're doing front-page. This is a lead story. You *do* see the difference."

"Right."

"We're gonna have to do a lot of editing on that. Sorry. You're kind of a walking outtake."

"Okay. I was just trying to avoid the usual pieties."

"The usual pieties. Well, you succeeded. Let me make sure I have this right. You're Saul Bernstein." She wrote his name down in a tiny notebook. She licked her lips.

"Yes."

"Pronounced *'steen'* or *'stine'*?"

"For TV I don't care. *'Steen,'* usually."

"All right." She looked up at him, smelling of Tahiti, where he would never go. "You're very weird." She paused. "I shouldn't have said that. I apologize. Really. I apologize to you, profusely. Did I say that? Actually, no, in some sense, I *didn't* say that. We're agreed? All right? I didn't say that."

"All right," Saul said.

"Thank you for your interesting comments." She turned away. "Where's the aunt?" she asked. "Is the aunt free, yet?" The cameraman pointed toward Saul and Patsy's front door, where Brenda was waiting for them to interview her. She had a hand mirror out and was hopelessly fixing her seaweed hair. Everybody was working on the hair today. "Let's go," Traci McMahoney said, striding away. "Maybe we can get an aunt segment."

Saul looked up into the sky as Patsy approached him. He recognized what he was doing as one of Gordy's habits, staring up into the sky as if something of interest were located there. The day was extremely bright, still beautiful, perhaps, though the sun had disappeared, and no clouds were visible. The sky was like a heat radiator full of steam. "How did I do?" he asked her. Mary Esther was fussy and complaining in Patsy's arms, and Saul could tell from a pissy odor that her diaper needed changing. She handed Emmy to Saul.

"How did you do?" Patsy leaned back. Saul noticed immediately how much more human she was than Traci McMahoney. Less sexy but more human and more beautiful. Her integrity. Her love for him. Look at her eyes! There was genuine feeling there! "How did you *do*?" Now she leaned forward. "Honey. Listen to me. A boy killed himself in our yard this morning, and now, at eight minutes before five o'clock, you're asking me how you *did*? I should hit you. Or something. I don't mean for that woman and the way that you . . ."

She couldn't finish the sentence, because at that moment, which was also a future moment, and a past one as well—time had become indelibly confused somehow—Saul felt himself hit or nudged. Looking up at the upstairs window of his house, he saw (and didn't see) himself, and Patsy, the two of them naked there, with Mary Esther in Patsy's arms. He—the Saul of the here and now—was standing where Gordy had been, on the spot where the boy had stood. He did not break out into sobs. No, he wasn't even crying; no cathartic moment presented itself. After all, it had been a small death, and it was not, in any sense, a tragedy, as he had carefully noted. But it was still a death. And something precious to Saul—he couldn't even say what it was, and he prided himself on his occasional sensitivities—something precious to him felt, what was the word, *trashed*. And for that, and maybe even for Gordy Himmelman with a bullet hole at the back of his skull and his blood on the tree in the yard, his body carted away under a sheet, for all those things . . . what *was* the word, those things *unloved*, a boy who in a single moment hadn't wanted to live anymore, Saul felt suddenly like an accomplice, even though the expression on his face did not change, and Patsy leaned forward toward him, making an arc over their crying daughter, in common grief.

Ten

After the officers of the law had returned with their notebooks and clipboards to their patrol cars, and after the Action News vans had sped away to the next news site, and after the two reporters from the *Five Oaks News-Chronicle* had departed, taking the young staff photographer with the shaved head with them, and after the superintendent of schools, Floyd Vermilya, had called to schedule what he called a "strategy session" with Saul for the following week, maybe Tuesday, Saul and Patsy sat in their living room, wondering what would hit them next. They had taken the phone off the hook. Mary Esther toyed with her Busy Box in the playpen, and when she stood and whined (she could stand on her own now and would soon be in the toddler stage; her first words had already been said), Saul took her up to her bedroom. Patsy could hear him singing to her.

Patsy didn't want to be alone with Saul for the rest of the evening. She dreaded that prospect.

Hurriedly, she called Harold, Saul's friend, who said he would be over in a matter of minutes, with his wife, Agatha. After putting the phone down and consulting her address book, Patsy called her friend from the bank, in the loan office, Susan. She and Susan were both loan officers in different branches in town. Susan said yes, of course, she would drop everything. She said she didn't think she could bring her husband, Wyatt. Wyatt was working on the city budget. Then Patsy called Mad Dog Bettermine and the woman he lived with, Karla, and after they agreed to come, she invited another friend, Julie Dusenberg, an instructor in English at Holbein College whom Saul and Patsy had met at a day-care center in town. Julie was a single mom, and she said she'd be over in a jiffy as long as it was okay with them if she brought her daughter, Kate, with her, and as long as it was okay if she didn't stay until late. Patsy then called Laurie Welsh. Laurie couldn't come because of the kids—Hugh was gone, Laurie didn't say where, though Patsy guessed he was probably out drinking—but asked if there was anything else she could do. She had already heard about Gordy Himmelman's suicide. She wanted to *be there for her*. Before Patsy could say anything, Laurie said she'd bring some cooked chicken by tomorrow, would she be around at ten in the morning?

Still in a nervous rush, Patsy called two high school teachers, the Krolls, Rosanne and Hank. She called Gary Krochock, their funny and embittered divorced single neighbor and insurance agent. They all said that they would drop by. Then, like someone who has been on a binge, she stopped herself.

By the time Saul came back down the stairs, five of their friends were already sitting in the living room, waiting for him, and Patsy knew, just from the look on his face, that he understood why she had invited them, and understood why they were there.

Saul went into the kitchen to bring in the beer, but several of the guests had brought their own and had already opened theirs. When he came back out, the death party, such as it was, had ground to a standstill; an expressive air pocket of dead silence greeted him.

Everyone in Saul and Patsy's living room was oddly muted, mumbling. It's a desert in here, Patsy thought, as Saul handed out more beer to his friends. Gordy Himmelman had died storyless. Mad Dog and Karla and Saul had all taught him, but he had drifted invisibly, sullenly, into their classrooms and out again. Harold, the barber, had cut the boy's hair and had known Gordy's mother, once upon a time, but he had no stories about her son. No, he hadn't been a good athlete; no, he didn't have a good sense of humor; and, no, he wasn't especially kind or considerate. The one really memorable action he had performed in his life, the one thing that everybody would remember about him and say about him as long as they remembered him or talked about him was that he had shot himself.

Saul and Patsy told the story of how they had stood before the window when it had happened. They told the story of the reporter from Channel Seven, Traci McMahoney.

Julie Dusenberg, the English instructor, hoisting her sleepy daughter, Kate, to her left breast, said it was like a case study. The whole event was like a case study.

"A case study of what?" Frank Kroll asked.

"I don't know," Julie Dusenberg said dispiritedly. "A case study of something. Of our time," she said, finally, in desperation, "that you could *deconstruct.*"

"Well, it's already deconstructed," Gary Krochock said, from where he was stretched out on the floor. He was wearing a University of Oklahoma sweatshirt and was balancing his beer bottle on his stomach. "If it's in the morgue, it's completely deconstructed, if you want my opinion. It doesn't get more deconstructed than that. By the way, did you know that 'disarticulation' is a medical term? It means taking the body apart, limb by limb."

"Don't tell me that this is going to turn into a discussion of American youth," Mad Dog said, from his end of the sofa, peering with one eye into his empty beer bottle, "because if this turns into a discussion of American youth, I'm going home right now, no questions asked." He gave off a slight air of pre-drunkenness. "I don't want to hear about any of that."

"But the boy's *dead,*" Karla said to him. Karla, Saul noted, was the sexiest woman he had ever known who was not beautiful. She looked like a minor player in a porno movie. "Can't anyone say anything good about him?"

"No," Mad Dog said. "And I *knew* him." He sat there. "Wait a minute. I thought of something. He made good paper airplanes."

"But he's a human *soul*," Karla said, slapping him on the arm. "Where's your charity?"

"Where it belongs," Mad Dog said. "With you. With us."

"Poor kid, anyway," someone half-whispered. "Poor old kid, anyway."

Susan Palmer all at once spoke up. "I don't see why we have to feel bad. Patsy? You shouldn't be feeling all guilty and everything. He wasn't a charming orphan. He didn't have asthma. He didn't run away and then come home again, reformed like the prodigal whatever. He wrote semi-illiterate threatening notes, threatening our *friends,* and let's face it, he was a big stinking mess. He destroyed Saul's beehives, when you lived over there. It's lucky he didn't hurt Mary Esther. He came into their front yard and waved a gun around, and he sort of harassed them, and I agree, it's a trauma, but I don't see what obligation we have to be sentimental about some little *shit.*" She waited. "I'm sorry. I guess I got carried away."

A long silence followed, interrupted by the sounds of beer pouring into mouths. Mad Dog suppressed a belch. Someone—Patsy thought maybe it was Rosanne, who almost never spoke—said, "So what you're saying is, good riddance."

"Did I say that?" Susan Palmer asked. "No. I don't believe I said that."

Another air pocket of silence opened up. Finally, the insurance agent, Gary Krochock, said, "I've got to tell you guys about this dream I had last night. Since we're talking about the dead and everything. It was extremely weird. I pissed into Frank Sinatra's hat."

"You did what?" Saul asked.

"I pissed into Frank Sinatra's hat. We were in this big room, maybe it was a recording studio, which I don't know much about because I've never been in one, but I *know* there were microphones, and Sinatra is out of the room, but he's left his hat upside down on the floor. And because I had to take a pee, I pissed into it. I pissed into Frank Sinatra's hat."

"What did he say?"

"Frank? He didn't say anything. He was out of the room. But I got scared, and I woke up," Gary Krochock said. He was still stretched out on the floor. "I'm in big trouble now. I'm in a world of trouble."

"Frank Sinatra is dead," Patsy said. "You're beyond harm."

"No, but see, that's the difference. The Chairman of the Board is powerful even in death. That's why I'm telling you this. He has *not* lost his influence. He has friends here *and* there. He's going to be very, very angry that I pissed into his hat. I don't feel that I'm safe anymore. Frank Sinatra—well, there's someone you don't want to have for an enemy, especially in the afterlife."

"Take out a policy on yourself," Mad Dog suggested.

"Too late," the insurance agent said. "Preexisting condition."

"What time is it?" Julie Dusenberg asked. "I probably have to go."

"Two minutes before eleven," Patsy said without looking at her watch.

"Turn on the news," Agatha, Harold's wife, said. "Saul'll be on."

Harold reached down for the remote on the coffee table in front of him, pressed a button, and the TV sprang to appliance-life with a miscellany of hisses and crackles.

"Channel Seven," Saul said.

They watched an ad for Bruckner Buick, some sort of midsummer clearance sale on sedans and SUVs. Then they waited through an ad for a local house-and-garden store until at last the news, preceded by a brass fanfare, came on, with the tease headline, "Local boy dies in schoolteacher's front yard." Dennis Peterson, the local anchor for Channel Seven, appeared behind the news desk, his toupee a fraction of an inch off-center, and he gazed solemnly at the lens, the way he always did when he had a major story to report. "A shocking event in Five Oaks today," he began, in his baritone voice.

"He has a big ole head," Gary Krochock said, of Dennis Peterson. "He looks like a goddamn pedophile."

"Why can't they use complete sentences?" Saul asked. "Not even Tom Brokaw uses complete sentences anymore."

Everyone in Saul and Patsy's living room was watching the screen, Patsy noticed. Dennis Peterson continued. "A seventeen-year-old Five Oaks boy, Gordon Himmelman, died by his own hand this morning with a single gunshot to the head. The handgun used in the suicide belonged to the victim's aunt, and the young man had stolen it from her. The death occurred on Whitefeather Road, in the front yard of Five Oaks high school teacher Saul Bernstein. We do not yet know why the boy had bicycled to his teacher's house to end his life, and there are still conflicting

Charles Baxter

theories and many unanswered questions about this shocking event. We have a full report by Traci McMahoney."

"I *used* to teach in the high school," Saul said quickly. "I don't know what I do now."

"You should be making a tape of this," Harold muttered to Patsy. "You may need it."

"You think so?" Patsy asked.

"That's right, Denny," Traci McMahoney said. She was also seated at the news desk in the studio. Patsy noticed that she was wearing a different outfit from the one she was wearing earlier this afternoon. "Tonight," she said, "we have many more questions than answers about the tragic death of Five Oaks high schooler Gordon Himmelman."

There was a cut to an establishing shot of Saul and Patsy's brand-new house on Whitefeather Road, at The Uplands. Traci McMahoney's commentary continued in a voice-over as the screen presented more shots of the house, the lawn, and finally the tree, viewed from a back-angle so that the bloodstains didn't show. "The scene of the death was this quiet front yard in a residential area near the Wolverine Outlet Mall. The young man, Gordon Himmelman, lived with his aunt on Strewwelpeter Street. He was a troubled student, challenged academically in high school, currently a dropout, and a former member of the Cub Scouts. His mother had died several years ago in a house fire, and the boy, according to those who knew him, was known for his sense of humor and his pranks."

"What? Cub Scouts?" Saul asked the TV. *"Pranks?"*

"The boy's aunt, Brenda Bagley, filled us in on some details."

"Where's Saul?" Gary Krochock asked from the floor. "I want to see Saul."

The screen cut to a close-up of Gordy's aunt. She was smiling but the smile was stoic and unconvincing. "My nephew was a wonderful boy," she said. "Just wonderful. He didn't have a care in the world. He could get into scrapes, okay, but this is what he *was*, and what he *wasn't*, well, I don't know, because this thing doesn't make any sense, this tragedy that he *did*, to himself, with the gun he found that I had hidden, there's two and two. I can't put it together, two and two that just don't add up. It's still just two and two."

158

"Boy, is she ugly," Gary Krochock said. "A *poltroon*. She looks like someone slid into her face at second base. With cleats on."

"That's an awful thing to say," Julie Dusenberg said, turning around to look. "She's just scared."

"And what of Gordon Himmelman's teacher?" Traci McMahoney asked, on a voice-over again, with a medium shot on the tape of Saul looking perplexed, standing next to Patsy. "Saul Bern*steen*? When we asked him for some reaction, he seemed as baffled as the victim's aunt."

"Hey," Saul said. "I wasn't baffled."

Suddenly there was a close-up of Saul. People in Saul and Patsy's living room started to clap. The others shushed them. "I don't think Gordy ever stopped to consider what he did," Saul said onscreen into the microphone. "He just did things. He didn't think about what he was doing. He just did them."

The camera cut back to Traci McMahoney, and then to a shot of Garfield-Fraser Middle School, where the principal was being interviewed about school violence. "Where's the rest of me?" Saul cried.

"The police have searched for a suicide note but have so far turned up nothing to give them any insight to this terrible event," Traci McMahoney said. "So far, we have no clues as to why the armed boy bicycled over to his teacher's house, and we have no clues, either, concerning the motivations for his tragic suicide. The only person who had the answers to these questions cannot give us one. In an age of violence in our schools, there may in fact be no easy explanations. Those who are left grieving must still wonder over the causes tonight. Perhaps the only blessing is that this happened during the summer, during school vacation, so that Gordon Himmelman's school friends can have time before classes begin to mourn his loss. Reporting from Whitefeather Road, this is Traci McMahoney."

"That was totally insane," Harold said, shaking his head and looking away from the TV screen. "Jesus. That thing about summer vacation. What the fuck was *that* about?"

"Maybe it just slipped out," Saul said. Dennis Peterson had segued to another story about Derby Days in downtown Five Oaks, and then the phone started to ring.

"I thought you looked pretty good, Saul," Karla said. "You acquitted yourself very well." She clapped her hands several times in his direction, a form of applause. A few other people in the room also applauded. "Hear, hear," they said.

The party broke up half an hour later.

At two-fifteen, Saul was lying in bed with Patsy. "I can't sleep," he said.

"I know." She opened and shut her mouth quickly, realized that the nighttime epigram she was about to utter was not particularly clever, and was in the wrong key, besides.

They lay there together. It was a warm night, and they touched each other lightly, back to back.

"Do you feel it?" Saul asked. "He hasn't gone away."

"What do you mean?"

Saul looked up toward the ceiling in exasperation. "He's still here," he said. "Can't you tell?"

Yes, of course she could tell. Yes, indeed. He still was. It would take more than a bullet to put an end to him, but she would be careful not to say so.

Eleven

A day begins, sunny, the hint of a breeze, a relief from the stillness of the day before. The baby—really, her infancy is over, and the world is registering on her in complex patterns of light and sound—the baby is standing in her crib uttering greet-the-world noises, vocalizations. She practices her scat-singing. In the bedroom across the hall, her parents ponder the possibility of making love—the husband, who has not slept, staring at the ceiling, and the wife, who has slept very well indeed but who has a headache from a beer she drank just before she went to bed, studying the bedside clock, though she already knows the time. The encounter, if it happens, would be quick. This does not have to be said. No profound emotions would be exchanged, no virtuoso gestures; it would be like coughing: a relief for the moment, an analgesic against other urges and irritations. But after one or two tentative caresses on the arm, the back, the buttocks, they move away from each other. The spaces between them could be measured in millimeters, infinitesimal spaces expressing an inexpressible failure of desire. Neither one wants to hurt the other's feelings, and they both take great care to be physically tactful. Arising out of the drudgery of sleep, the wife (Patsy) is preoccupied with her dreams, her daughter in the next room, and a slight and casual indifference to her husband's body, an indifference that is new to her, and the husband (Saul) is preoccupied with death. He is, to use an antique word, heartsick. Morning sex will not cure it. Sex, today, would make it worse.

The measure of this particular marriage is that each one knows the other's thoughts. Day after day, the possibility of a private language between them is established and maintained. No private language, the wife thinks, no marriage.

The wife tosses aside the sheet and marches into the bathroom. She splashes water on her face. Then she brushes her teeth, enjoying the taste, like candied goo, of the toothpaste, a sunrise taste. After rinsing her mouth out and watching the water swirl down the drain that is beginning to be clogged with her husband's beard stubble, she searches in the medicine cabinet for the aspirin, pushing aside the antidepressants to get at it. She takes two caplets, then lowers her cupped hands to the running water. As she drinks the water, she notices that her toenails will soon need clipping. She looks at her face in the mirror and thinks of the word "haggard," because that is what she expected to be but is not. She looks pretty great, all things considered. Her eyes glow with intelligence and clarity, the dream-life and the headache fading out of them now that she is standing up. Her beauty—and she can recognize this—originates from her eyes. It flows out from there. The rest of her body is secondary, a problem in geometry, a dancer's problem.

Back in the bedroom, she stretches her clasped arms and twists her head back and forth to loosen the neck muscles. She lowers herself to the floor to perform her leg-raises, sit-ups, and more stretch exercises before she stands and walks over to the phone. She calls a special number at the bank to say she will not be coming in to work. Family emergency. Of course everyone at the bank will already know about Gordy Himmelman's death. In fact, the secretary to whom she speaks passes on her sympathies. Patsy hardly needs to call. After hanging up, she pads into the nursery to greet Mary Esther, nuzzle her, change her, and take her down to the kitchen for breakfast. Her daughter screech-sings happily when she first sees her mother.

As Patsy's mother used to say, following any event contaminated by sorrow, "Life goes on."

. . .

The husband hears his wife's light footsteps as she descends the stairs. Before he rises, he leans over to sniff her pillow to detect her mood. The smell on the pillow is businesslike, a female version of getting-on-with-things. How does he know this, how does he know he isn't imagining, right there on the borders of psychopathology, his wife's climates and thoughts? He shrugs to himself. He just does. He's married to her. Slowly he pushes the sheet aside and stands up. He lumbers with effort—he feels like a circus bear—past the dresser, festooned with framed pictures of his daughter, past the rickety wooden chair on which he throws his clothes at night. He ambles in front of the window, pushes aside the curtains, and raises the windowshade. He lingers there, idly rearranging his penis inside his pajamas as he looks out at the linden tree and the lawn.

From the kitchen he hears his wife and daughter making noises. The wife is weaning the daughter, a difficult process for both of them. Food is being spooned into the daughter's mouth, and this same food, projectile-spat, has appeared on the floor and the high chair. The husband at the window notices that his early-morning thoughts are in the passive voice. He is permitted to use the passive voice when he is sleepy.

The boy, Gordy Himmelman, is not there, outside, but he shoots himself anyway, randomly, airily, imaginatively, bringing himself back so that he can go away again. There he is, and isn't, now, pointing the gun into himself and firing. Insubstantial bits of brains and skull fly up against the bark of the linden tree. How calm it is. How it goes on, destruction, into its own afterlife. Still, this life, his own, Saul's, must be lived somehow. Saul shuffles into the bathroom for his shower, rubbing his eyes violently with the flat of his hand.

Under the cascading hot water, he cleans himself dutifully, dragging the washcloth layered with the antibacterial gold soap across his chest and arms and face, and at first his mind is pleasingly blank, until he thinks haphazardly, first of Gordy Himmelman, then of his mother and her teenaged boyfriend. He considers them as he washes his arms, doing his best to set up police crime-scene yellow tape around his imaginings, exiling them, forgetting them, ignoring them. It is like trying to ignore the enraged African elephant charging toward its victim. The unconscious never takes a vacation. Despite his regrets about the matter, his mother is a passionate woman. *Gordy Himmelman, his mother*—what choice does anyone have in the thoughts he is given to think? Still, he feels shame-soiled. He rinses himself off, pulls aside the shower curtain, and grabs a towel. This morning he will not bother to shave. Let the Saul-face be unfinished today.

In the kitchen, the phone is still off the hook, the hand-piece dangling down on its stretched coil wire from the wall-mounted phone to the floor. His daughter in her yellow-backed high chair with the teddy-bear headrest sits contentedly surrounded by the spatterings of breakfast, and she smiles when her father enters the room. "Hi, Princess," he says, kissing her on the top of her head. Her hair is so delicate and fine, smelling of stardust and spun gold, Saul feels a sensual pleasure touching his lips to it.

She is so extravagantly new. Half of her is from him. The other half is from his wife. But the half and half add up to something entirely original. The husband remembers to kiss his wife also on the top of her head. "Good morning, Patsy," he says to the woman he neglected to make love to half an hour earlier. For just a moment, he touches the tip of his tongue to her hair. She lifts her face to him, a smear of food on her cheek. "Oh, yes. Good morning, sweetheart," she replies. She gives off a faint scent of dry saltine crackers and milk. The smile she has for him is quick, as is the kiss she gives him. "I love you," she says, and after her husband tells her he loves her, he cleans her cheek with his index finger before sitting down at the table in front of the coffee cup she has placed there for him (cream, no sugar). Wearing a T-shirt and his pajama bottoms, he opens the paper. Perhaps it will be an ordinary day after all the extraordinariness of the previous day.

But, no: there on the goddamn fucking front page is a picture of his goddamn fucking front yard. In a separate column the editors have inserted a school picture of Gordy Himmelman, sporting a flattop. The boy looks dense and clueless and lunar and mean. He has the appearance of a convict-in-training. Leaning back in his chair, the husband considers the view out the kitchen window at this boy and the represented yard—his angle is different from that of the camera—and past it, to White-feather Road, when he notices that a car has slowed down so that its three occupants can point at the linden tree, where the blood is, though not on their side. The wife notes that her husband is observing some phenomenon or other, calculates the angle of his observation, and regards the scene outside the window. Gordy Himmelman, the deceased, stands vacantly out there. He is a little less dead this time than he was before.

"Gawkers," she says calmly.

"Rubberneckers," he says.

Patsy reaches out and grasps his hand. She caresses her husband's knuckles and says she's making some eggs for herself, would he like some, too? Scrambled? Yes, he would. She rises—she is still in her nightgown and slippers—and cracks four eggs into a frypan, adds some garlic powder, onion salt, some butter, a dash of milk, dash of Tabasco, paprika as it is dished up, a formula her husband likes and that she has learned from him. He prefers his scrambled eggs slightly runny, not . . . dried out. She wouldn't like eggs cooked this way if she weren't married to Saul. As she stands at the stove, her husband tells her that she is beautiful. He is good at this: he always compliments her spontaneously and with an air of sincerity and rarely with the hope of reward.

As she is mixing the ingredients in the frypan, before turning the burner on a low-medium heat, she says, "I wonder if there'll be a funeral," and her husband says, "I doubt it. He's not dead enough to bury."

It is fourteen minutes past eight.

At twenty-three minutes past ten, the wife finally puts the phone back on the hook, and within thirty seconds, it rings. She decides that she won't answer it, no matter who the caller might be. But her decisions have little to do with what she actually does. In any case, a ringing telephone can sometimes sound like a command or a scream following any domestic catastrophe. That is how it sounds now. Her husband is still in his pajamas, eating a midmorning bowl of cereal, Emmy on his shoulder asleep and drooling. When she answers the phone, their daughter startles into wakefulness. The caller is Patsy's friend Julie Dusenberg, asking if there's anything she can do. Food? Aid and comfort? She and Patsy talk for a while, and after the call ends and Patsy puts the receiver back down, the phone rings again, more insistently this time, louder, like a heavier knock on the door. This time, the caller is one of Saul's former students, Jeffrey Yonkey, wanting to say how sorry he is about the whole Gordy Himmelman thing. Patsy, surprised by the call, thanks him for his trouble, hangs up, and once again the phone starts to ring. The phone, today, is the other baby, crying and carrying on. There is nothing to do to quiet this baby except to talk softly to it.

Patsy picks up the receiver, and a voice says, "Hi, it's Gordy."

She waits to see whether the prankster has any other ideas of what to say or how to extend a cold and sadistic antic mischief using the voice of a day-old suicide, and because he doesn't, because he's a cruel and unimaginative juvenile, a long, slow, uneasy silence reigns until she delicately places her finger on the receiver hook, disconnecting him. Then she releases it. A faint dial tone hums into the air from the hanging phone. From the radio on the other side of the room, tuned to the local NPR affiliate, a waltz drifts absentmindedly into the air. What would it be? Ah, "The Merry Widow." Franz Lehar. Now the baby is wide awake, and Saul has finished his cereal.

"I don't like waltz music," Patsy says, shaking her head. "Too much butter. Too much cholesterol. It's just too . . . Viennese."

"Who was that?" he asks, nodding in the direction of the telephone. He has moved into the living room and is holding Mary Esther's arms up, so that she can practice her lurch-walking. She can stand on her own. So she is not a baby after all, but a toddler.

"Julie Dusenberg first. Then Jeffrey Yonkey. And then a crank caller," Patsy tells him. "You want some more coffee? Should I brew up a new pot?"

"What'd he want, the crank caller?" He half-turns toward her, gives her a look from a half-closed eye, playing the role of the inspector.

"He was a . . . crank. Cranks don't want anything," she says.

"They want your attention," Saul says. "What'd this one want?" He scoops his daughter up into his arms and twirls her around. The movement is festive, but the effect is one of great sadness.

"Some kid," Patsy tells him. "Said he was Gordy."

"More," Emmy seems to say, making her parents smile.

Saul, for some reason, doesn't seem particularly surprised. "Oh. Gordy. What'd *he* want?"

"*Saul,* I just told you." She takes a long sip of her tea. "It was a pretender. He didn't want anything. Said his name and then stopped. Oh." She straightens up and smiles. "He asked us how we were doing."

"That's not like him. Gordy always wanted something. He never bothered to ask us how we were doing. He was too sullen for that."

"Gordy's dead, honey. He shot himself. Remember? This was . . . what I told you. An imposter. Just a kid."

"Yup."

"Come on, Saul. Let's not get all creepy about this."

"*I'm* not. I'm not being creepy. Besides, I'm not the one who called." He gives her one of his odd housebroken smiles. These particular smiles always take the breath out of her. Nothing with Saul is unconditional when he is under stress; you always have to be slightly on your guard with him.

"It was just some kid," Patsy says. "Some kid-who-was-not-Gordy. One of your disgruntled students. You know," she says, "the woods are full of rural levity today."

"I didn't notice you laughing. Did you smile? Did you laugh?"

These are not friendly questions. They have a coldness that startles her. Maybe they should have made love after all. He feels her as she approaches him from behind, reaching around his chest, leaning her head against his back, standing there, just holding on, wanting him to anchor her. "Sometimes I think you're the last humanist," she mutters. "Sometimes I wonder how we'll ever get on with things with you around."

"Why do you say that?" He waits for a moment, then adds an endearment. "*Honey?*" There is a slight charge of irony, a sourness, to this, of love drained out of the endearment and bitterness poured in.

"Because," she says, "here's this kid. He's stupid. He's mean to you. He writes you terrible, illiterate notes. He doesn't like you. He knocks over your beehives. But he shows up here like a little thug with his handgun, and then you take him home. And then for months and months he hangs around our yard, staring at us like the boy outside the bakery window with his nose pressed against the glass. And finally he shoots himself for no particular reason except he's got his hands on a firearm again. So all day yesterday we try to explain what there's no explanation for. And there's nobody on the planet who'll grieve, Saul, except for you. So you try to do it. You really do make the effort. Credit where credit is due. For a worthless no-account illiterate ignorant anti-Semitic kid, you go the full charitable nine yards. The sadness, the remorse. That's why. Only the last humanist would do that. Everybody else, really, Saul, I'm not kidding, would be glad to see him gone. Well, not glad, but, you know."

"I don't know about the anti-Semitism part," Saul says. He stops what he is doing to rub his scalp. Mary Esther sits down abruptly, experimentally, on the floor. Patsy sits down next to the two of them. "He *was* human, Patsy, carbon-based just like ourselves, and he wasn't an anti-Semite, because that was too complicated for him. He was here, and then he was here, and then he was here again and again and again full of that negative energy of his, and now he's gone, but he's *still* here, and the thing is, they don't go away unless you grieve them." After turning around, he runs his hands tenderly through her hair. "And even then sometimes they don't. Oh, Patsy. You are so beautiful. I know I keep saying that, but it's true."

She smiles at his compliment as if he means it. He's only saying it, however, because they didn't make love and this is a reparation. "See, I don't think that's it," she tells him, still smiling. "This is where grieving shades over into the morbid."

"Morbid? Patsy," he says, "all this happened *yesterday*. He killed himself yesterday morning. God forgive us, we had a party last night. Morbid goes on and on. Morbid is for years. He hasn't even had twenty-four hours to be dead in. One day, is all I'm saying. Give me one day. He would have given us one day." Saul stops. He does not know what he meant by his last sentence.

"Okay, right. But you're treating him as if he was somebody, Saul. He wasn't."

"Oh, he wasn't?"

"Nope. He wasn't anybody much at all. It's just sentimental to say he was somebody. That's what we're talking about. That's what we've been talking about *all this time*. Sentimentality."

The word hangs in the air, radiating its contempt, Saul thinks, for himself. In order to protect himself, Saul thinks: The word despises me, but it got loose from Patsy, who could not have meant it.

After taking off her slippers, he begins to massage her feet. He has always had a thing for her feet, which are slender but strong. He addresses the Patsy he loves, not the Patsy who just used the word "sentimentality" against him. "Well, I think he was somebody. I don't know what kind of somebody he was, and I don't think anybody knew, but he was that, at least. On the list where it says 'Somebody,' Gordy Himmelman gets included."

"Saul," she says, leaning back and closing her eyes as he massages her, "wake up. We're in contemporary times now. And the kids they're making, Saul, I'm telling you, the kids they've got in the schools, they're not somebody anymore." Lowering her gaze, she gives him her perfectly reasonable smile and her voice-of-realism voice. Somebody around here, she thinks, has to save Saul from his errant compassion; it endangers their family.

"They're not?"

"No, honey, they aren't. I hate to say it, but it's true. They're facsimiles, these kids, American-made humanoids. All-American McHumans. Why d'you think they call them *zombies*? This is why the nations rage against us. This whole country has a robot-thing going with its kids. Jesus Christ, you're being mushy. These kids aren't *anybody*! If they were, they wouldn't call you on the phone or come into the front yard and then shoot themselves for no purpose at all in the world." She waits. "They'd have a reason."

"Well, if he wasn't anybody, Patsy, then it's perfectly all right for him to kill himself." He smiles winsomely, a counterattack smile to her previous smile.

"That's not what I'm saying," she says, her voice going metallic.

"*And* . . . if he's not human, it's all right for someone *else* to kill him. If he's nobody, then anybody can kill him, legally, you know? And all the nonhuman kids like him."

"Saul, you're deliberately misrepresenting me."

"And if these kids aren't human, then who is? Who gets a right to be human? The dopes? The droolers? The ones who slur their words and live under bridges with the bums and the trolls? The Gypsies? The Jews? The Arabs? The Mormons? Who gets to be human? Who gets to live? Show me the qualifications, Patsy, since you're such a goddamn expert on what it is to be human."

"All right, all right, all right," she says, shrugging, horrified by his sudden rage. "I see your point. Okay, okay."

"I'm going to take a nap," he says, but he stays right where he is, unmoving. "I'm tired."

At ten minutes past three o'clock in the afternoon, Saul is still in his pajamas. Patsy has never seen him stay in his pajamas all afternoon except when he . . . no, she has never seen it. Mary Esther is upstairs napping after having crawled all over her father, and Saul now has the parts of a broken cuckoo clock out on the floor. He pretends to repair the little bellows for the cuckoo's call. Perhaps he is actually repairing it. Mostly he just wool-gathers over there. He has the Brahms Clarinet Quintet on the audio system, always a bad sign—incipient, dangerous, and highly contagious lyrical melancholia, melancholy warbling its autumnal song as if that were the only song there ever was or could be, and Saul, her husband, singing right along with it, every scarily beautiful phrase, music like a virus, infecting the listener with lethal sadness.

And now Patsy hears a car coming up the driveway, and the phone ringing simultaneously. The phone, that teething baby, has been ringing whenever she places the receiver back on the hook. One friend after another, including Harold the barber, offering consolation and help. Out front, the car has stopped. Rushing past the spider plant, Patsy quickly answers the phone, to a voice that says, "Hi, Mrs. Bernstein? Is your Jew husband there?" before she hangs up. Then, quickly, she approaches the door, where Gordy's aunt, Brenda Bagley, has carried a large box from her car's trunk and dropped it on the front stoop.

"Ms. Bagley," Patsy says, shading her eyes against the afternoon sun.

"Well, hi there," Gordy's aunt says, tipping her head in what seems at first to be an ironic bow. But the bow isn't ironic; shyness or anxiety or sheer confusion propel it. Her face, pockmarked and roughened, has a cigarette with a long ash apparently growing out of the side of the mouth. Brenda Bagley projects, in all directions, an energetic look of savage desperation.

She puts her hand, now with the cigarette, to her forehead while she clears her throat, and the hot coal tip comes dangerously close to her hairline. The ash falls gracefully to the stoop. Patsy watches it fall. "I had to come over here. I've felt so bad, and I expect you have, too. Last night I couldn't sleep, of course. Poor worthless kid, how I miss him. You ever miss a poor worthless kid? I tried calling first but the lines were all busy. So I thought I'd just get in the car and drive past." She has tried to give her hair a few new curls, as if she knows she will be in the public eye. People will be judging her appearance. Her misapplied drugstore lipstick adds to the general overdetermined effect. She looks like a witch in a fairy tale with a poisoned candy house. Behind the house are frogs in a pen. Seeing Brenda Bagley's efforts to beautify herself, Patsy has to force back—what *are* these?—yes: tears. The pathos of Brenda's unattractiveness gives the woman an insidious power. Against her, Patsy feels all her defenses fading. *Ah,* Patsy thinks, *here is a real expert in unhappiness. Here is the tenured full professor of suffering.*

Patsy asks her if she'd like to come in. Please, Patsy adds. Gordy's aunt shakes her head, exhaling smoke as if her heart were a furnace. "No, I couldn't do that to you. Not invited, like I am. What awful times," she says. "I'm just so broken up, I don't know what to do with myself. Like I say, I'm not company for you or anyone. What I thought was, I should come over here with a gift, this gift box of his things that I gathered from his closet this morning. It's what I thought of last night, when I couldn't sleep."

"A box?"

"Right. I thought you and your husband would want some of the boy's clothing, your husband being Gordy's teacher and all, and considering what happened over here. Gordy had his feelings about you both. He just couldn't stay away. Never did tell me why." Something about her facial expression does not match what she is saying; her glance has become shrewd and inquisitorial, almost gleefully full of hatred. She is a woman who knows how to exploit her unattractiveness and unhappiness. She has all the considerable resources of the weak: the rags, the incompetence when dealing with catastrophe, the unendurable face, the incorrect tone, the addictions, the cluelessness, the echoing footsteps out of the ravaged town.

For a moment what Gordy's aunt has said does not register on Patsy at all. Then it does. "What feelings were those? And you mean to say," pointing at the box, "those are Gordy's *clothes*?"

"Not all the clothes he owned. Just some of them. That's what I'm telling you," Brenda says, repeating her confusing ironic bow, a failed gesture of respect, followed by a long inhale. Brenda's eyes are watering now, and the grief no longer seems to be feigned, though perhaps the tears simply follow the irritating effect of the smoke. Patsy wonders what her grief is based on, if that's what it is, and where she gets it from. How does a person mourn someone like Gordy Himmelman? Out of what tenderness could it possibly arise? You don't tear your hair and beat your breast after the demise of a kid like that. Do you? Some questions she does not dare to ask.

And now Saul in his pajamas appears behind Patsy, carrying the cuckoo clock bellows in his left hand. He squeezes it, and a cuckoo's call rises from his fingers. Life, Patsy thinks, is more dreamlike than any dream. "You're in your pajamas," Brenda says. "You sick?"

"Yes," Saul says without interest. "I am. You?"

"No, not me, not yet. Okay, I'll stay away from you. Right here is my distance. Well, like I was saying to your wife there, those're some of his clothes." She points down to the box, before she pulls up the top flap and reaches in. "A few of his shirts, and a couple pair of pants, and socks. I would like for you to have them." She lifts up a pair of blue jeans for display. Ash from her cigarette falls on them. "A remembrance gift." Dark stains decorate the jeans where the ash has not touched them.

"We can't take them," Saul says. "They're Gordy's."

"Not anymore, they ain't. Sure, you can take them. He was right about your size."

"No, I don't think so."

"Well, I'm certainly not taking them back," she says with sudden coldness. "You can do with them what you want, you and your wife, give them away to Goodwill if that's what you'd like to do, use them as rags. Don't even have to bring them into the house if you don't want to, leave 'em out here. *I just can't keep them around,*" she barks out, almost as a scream. "But," she then says, taking a deep breath as if to compose herself, "now that's taken care of, there's another thing I was having to ask you about, on a related matter. I haven't seen the boy's father in a couple years. Maybe you know. I tried him in Wyoming and then in Colorado. They never heard of him in either place. I've tried everywhere. Police have, too. Vanished from the face of the earth, Rufus has. God, that man was a pure worthless piece of worthlessness. Oh, well. There's the matter of the expense related to the cremation, and now I've got to take care of that by myself as the next of kin." She peers around Patsy toward Saul, in his pajamas. "And I just can't."

"I think I understand," Saul says. "You want some financial help." Patsy feels herself physically leaving this scene. She is not going to be here. Let Saul take care of it, she thinks, the money. Let him be the Last American Humanist. Let him exercise his compassion. That's his sideline. He's good at that. But she is not going to let him spend their money, including the portion that she herself has earned. Not here. Not now.

"Not in so many words," Gordy's aunt says, putting the soiled blue jeans back into the box, after carefully folding them. "What I'm asking is *whether* you can help out. A contribution. It's not like we can start a community-wide fund for him. People don't care for a suicide. That's not a cause they empty their pockets for."

"How much?" Saul asks, glancing at Patsy, who seems to be gazing off at the horizon, having somehow managed strategically to space out. She doesn't seem to be here anymore. No help from her, the professional loan officer. Not a dime for the dead boy's tribute.

"Whatever you can spare," Brenda half-whispers. "For the cremation. Or the box?"

"All right," he whispers back, in sympathy. "You take a check?"

"Whatever you can spare," Brenda repeats, her eyes filling with tears. "For that poor boy."

"Make sure it's your checkbook, honey," Patsy says, awakening. "Not the joint one."

"Whatever you can spare. For that poor boy," Patsy imitates late that night, in the living room. She needs to be callous. A bit of insensitivity allows her to breathe. She feels, and has for most of the afternoon, as if she had been fitted with a whalebone corset. She needs the relief of standoffishness from the harms that pity leaves on her spirit. "Good god, what a performance. And this is—"

"They're not even going to have a funeral, Patsy. They just need a box or something to bury Gordy in. That's all."

"Listen to me." They're both sitting on the floor, surrounded by a heap of soiled Gordy-clothing. There are clothes for warm and cold seasons. Flannel shirts, underwear, socks, jeans, corduroys—a mess of dirty stinking fraying fabrics. During the summer the boy had carried with him an odor of hay and old cheese. As the weather turned colder, his aromas mutated and became furry. The December-and-January Gordy had given off the scent of the dogs he probably slept with, and here were the clothes from those months, smelling as if they had come straight from the Humane Society.

She has raised her hand to his shoulder. It rests there a moment and then rises to his face. "You're not guilty of anything, sweetie. *You did nothing wrong.* And what happened yesterday here was shocking, and we have every right to be shocked. . . ."

"Oh, do you think so?" Saul asks. "I think that adults aren't shocked. They pretend to be shocked, but they aren't, not really. It's a pose."

"You weren't shocked? What would it have taken yesterday to shock you?"

"Something else. I wasn't *shocked*," Saul insists, running his hands through the pockets of Gordy Himmelman's trousers. "What were we expecting all those months, anyway? That he would eventually go away? We had gotten accustomed to him. No, yesterday I felt something else."

"Okay."

He searches her face before speaking. "Oh, I felt surprise, maybe, but that's different. Here's a dopey kid whose aunt has a gun and who stands and stands in our front yard without ever telling us what he wanted from us. And, by the way, why were *you* shocked? You're the person who worked up the conviction that he was not like us, a nonhuman. That's the height of sophistication, if you ask me, calling him a nonperson. That was really worldly of you. That was positively European."

"Okay, Saul," Patsy says. "Before we have a real fight, let me ask you a question. Between grief and indifference, what is there? There isn't anything. Show me the typical half-sob and maybe I'll sort of believe you."

"Actually, it's called sadness, Patsy. In English, that's the word they have available between grief and indifference. And someday I'll show you a half-sob. Just not now." He puts his hands inside another pair of the boy's pockets and removes some small torn bits of paper. "Hey, Patsy, you just don't feel it. Modest grief is not there for *you*. You're more a creature of black and white. What's this?"

The papers are nested, one inside the other, like puzzle parts. They seem to have been sections of a larger sheet of paper that has been ripped inexpertly. Saul puts them down on the floor in an attempt to reassemble them, five small pieces that together form a blue-lined page of school notebook paper, three punched holes on the left side. Outdoors, the wind starts up, and the lights flicker, but only for a moment. The papers tremble on the floor. They appear to be animated by the breathing of the world soul. Something is scrawled on them, and Saul bends down to make out the phrases, Gordy's modest scrawled leavings.

She did it
they toad the car
mad in america!!!!

"I taught him to write, so he could write this," Saul says. "I taught him language, so he could curse. I wonder what this 'she did it' business is all about." He turns the papers over and reassembles them. On the reverse side there are only four words.

no fear
exxxtrabila
tyemeszeemer

"Oh, right. No fear." Saul shrugs. "And 'exxxtrabila'—where d'you suppose he learned that word?"

The now-working cuckoo clock ticks from the wall. Patsy looks at the paper. "From the other polyglots, that's who. He watched a lot of TV. No real clues here, though," she says. "The kid didn't have a lick of sense."

"You know what I think?" Saul asks. His face takes on an animated stare. "I think the aunt was abusing him. That Brenda Bagley woman. That's what 'she did it' means. She was abusing him. So he shot himself. Mystery solved."

"Come *on*, Saul. Let's not do the abuse narrative." Just then, the phone rings. It is the twentieth call of the day, probably another kind friend offering help. Saul gets up to answer it.

"Hi," the voice says. "It's Gordy. How're you doin'?" The voice does not sound at all like Gordy but like a grown man imitating a boy.

"Just fine, Gordy," Saul replies. "And how're you?"

"You're lying," the voice says. "You're not fine at all."

"This isn't Gordy. Who am I talking to? Who is this?"

"Yes, it is. I just learned *German*. They teach all the dead buggers *German*. It's the universal language back here. You have to learn *German* in the afterlife. Didn't you know that? You can learn it here in a few hours." The voice laughs, with its bizarre inflections. "It's real easy learning *German* when you're dead because it's like a mind-thing that happens. It's like *boom,* and then you speak it. See, German solved all my problems." The speaker is laughing heartily. "You'll learn it, too, when you're dead. Which could be any time now."

Ah, Saul thinks, a militia guy, a trailer-park fascist.

"You know," Saul says, "it's late, my man, and I'm tired. It's been a long day, and I think I'll hang up on you now."

"Don't you hang up on me, you fucking Jew. With that boy's blood on your dirty Jew hands, you—"

"Wow," Saul says, putting the receiver down. "Wow, wow, wow." He stands for a moment, trying to find some object on which to rest his gaze. At last he sees Patsy and studies her. His hand is trembling with anger. "Maybe," he says, "we should get a gun ourselves."

"Shocked?" Patsy asks, gazing back at him.

Late that night Patsy discovers that she is alone in bed. When her legs sweep across the sheeted mattress, nothing meets them but cotton and air. Where is Saul this time? An unpleasant, ill-meaning summer wind blows against the house, causing the bedsheet to ruffle and the Chapstick to roll off Saul's dresser. On the wall, the photograph of Patsy's parents trembles in time to the rattles of the windowframes. Nothing in this house seems to be built solidly, to be able to withstand the onrushes of fate and wind, except Patsy. Saul has a tendency to be blown over, wherever he is. Where *is* he?

Walking down the hall past Mary Esther's room, she finds him hunched over in the spare bedroom. He is bent over his desk. Grit touches the bottoms of Patsy's bare feet. When she glances down, she sees that he is reading some story or other by Mishima.

"Come to bed, Saul," Patsy orders him. "Come to bed, my love."

She takes his hand with one of her hands and clicks off the desk lamp with the other. She draws him back to the bedroom. "No, wait a minute," she says. "Brush your teeth first. I want to make love to you after you've brushed your teeth. I like your mouth when it tastes of toothpaste."

Saul shuffles into the bathroom, and Patsy follows him, standing behind him with her head on his back as he raises the toothpaste tube, unscrews the cap, and covers the toothbrush with the candied goo, the morning-taste of it. She rubs the flat of her hands over his chest, one of her predictably effective arousal techniques, time-tested. Then she lowers her hand into his pajamas and takes hold of him, a familiar gesture, almost by rote, this preparatory ritual, their cure for the rest of the world. As he brushes his teeth, she feels him slowly becoming hard. The taming of passion into married ceremony has a sweet-and-sour taste for her, passion made manageable and harmless and almost comic, the forest fire reduced to the size of a Franklin stove. Whatever the great passions might be, they are not exemplified by married couples, who have nothing but their day-long familiarities and private languages and their ordinary love to bind them together. The wind outside continues to rattle the windowframes, and now the telephone is ringing again, senselessly. With Patsy's hand still holding on to him, Saul rinses his mouth out, puts the toothbrush away, and carefully screws the cap back onto the toothpaste tube. Then he turns around and kisses her, a kiss full of desperate friendliness and unsurprise, same old tongue, same old teeth. Saul is willfully half-smiling as he kisses Patsy. It is as if she has caught him in an affair, and now something about themselves as a couple has to be proved, or proved again.

She can almost always make him forget himself and remember her. She has been naked for him so often by now that nakedness has nearly lost its original meaning between the two of them. Sure enough, his mouth tastes of toothpaste. Sure enough, his mouth fits on hers in the usual way. The taste, on top of the Saul-taste, is amusingly discordant, like a bear that has been taught to ride a bicycle and use mouthwash, but the domesticity of it energizes her because he has tamed himself for her. He has renounced being someone else for being her husband, and that renunciation makes up for his anger and his sentimentality. So in addition to her usual nakedness, she will be more naked to him than usual, a disavowal to the indifference they both felt for each other this morning and which (she has kept this secret from him) has shadowed her all day like a bad, unforgettable, and prophetic dream of the death of love between them. This dreadful, sickly, mean-spirited day, one of the worst of her life—it has to be forgotten, it has to be purged.

She struggles tonight to demonstrate more desire than she actually feels just to cleanse the air, but in that struggle she achieves some measure of the craving she has not had access to for weeks. Pretending to have a missing emotion, sometimes you actually get it. A good actor can evoke the nonexistent. She wills herself to open herself to Saul in ways that feel new to her, and through the fog of his preoccupations, at last he notices: good God, what is she doing? Is she really doing *that*? Saul, for his part, can't quite believe how slithery and inviting and emotionally naked she is making herself. She is working a purgation, first on herself, and then on him, snaking her way over him and under him, doing a feverish humming thing for him until, as the windows continue to rattle from the stage-managed wind, at last they both come together within a few seconds of each other, and a minute or so later, still looking at the ceiling, Saul thinks: *Maybe we should get a dog, you know, we could use a dog,* and Patsy thinks: *That was it, that time, I'm going to be pregnant again, a boy, I just know it.*

Twelve

Gordy hadn't been suicidal. Still, he had committed suicide. The logic of this confounded everybody.

The superintendent of schools, Floyd Vermilya, called a meeting of faculty and concerned parents and family members one week after Gordy's death. The meeting was held in the high school auditorium on a Tuesday night. The season being summer, the hallways smelled of floor cleanser, and no one seemed to know how to get all the proper lights directed to the podium on the stage—Harry Bell, the custodial engineer, was on a fishing trip up north—with the result that Superintendent Vermilya, a pumpkin-faced overweight man with a buzzcut and slit-lens reading glasses perched at the tip of his nose, stood speaking to everyone in semidarkness, as did the psychiatric social worker who had been hired to consult and to give advice about the grieving process. The lights were shining on the rear of the auditorium stage, but the superintendent and the social worker by necessity stood in the front, and the effect was that of a poorly rehearsed show. They were probably kind people who meant well. The problem was, Saul thought, there was no grieving because the grief had no source or origin, as grief must. They were disposing of a boy whom nobody liked, who had already disposed of himself. Good intentions didn't mean much in a struggle with emptiness.

Patsy, carrying Mary Esther, estimated the crowd at about seventy, but no one except Saul seemed particularly sorrow-stricken, and Saul's mournfulness was freakish; it was not clearly understood by anyone, including Saul. Everyone else had shown up out of curiosity or dutifulness. Gordy Himmelman hadn't made much of an impression on any of his other teachers, Saul discovered, and when he had, the impressions were unfavorable. He had drifted, unloved and unsought, down the birth canal out of the womb, and then, in school, he had drifted from kindergarten onward and upward to the more challenging grades, where he had made his mark by a more accelerated drift toward failure, the boy being mostly friendless and frictionless, slipping and sliding toward his own death, and hostile to those who wanted to help him. Then he destroyed himself, and here, now, were the undestroyed, convening to talk.

After stepping up to the ill-lighted podium, the superintendent said that he had spoken to both of the Bernsteins, Saul and his wonderful wife, Patsy, who had witnessed this terrible event, and he had spoken to Gordy Himmelman's guardian and next of kin, his aunt, Brenda Bagley, who had owned the gun in question. The sheriff's office had investigated, and the medical examiner was doing an autopsy to check for a possible drug or alcohol component and to rule out any other possible contributing medical causes. Gordy's behavior *had* been observed to be erratic. The boy had been a behavioral problem, certainly, with a learning disability, but he was not particularly exceptional in this regard. So far no one, it appeared, was to blame. Besides, he was a dropout from school. "It was extremely fortunate," the superintendent said, underlining certain phrases by lowering his voice an octave, "that no one else was hurt." Then he stifled a yawn.

The collective judgment was that Gordy Himmelman had taken a tragic interest in guns. He had never been properly trained in their use. He played with guns to give himself a feeling of power—to compensate for his poor work at school and for his social failures. The suicide had certain aspects of an accident. Like other troubled youths, especially impulsive young men, Gordy Himmelman had, tragically—his voice once again dropped an octave—*taken the easy way out.* A life had been snuffed, like a candle's flame, but after the inquiries so far it appeared to have been nobody's fault, the superintendent had repeated. "Mistakes were made," he said, "but we cannot say who made them. Let's say that we all made them. And let's go on from there. We can't dwell forever in the past. The past," he said, "is a canceled check. We expect never to have another incident like this in Five Oaks. Therefore, we have invited Jane Henderson to help us out."

The psychiatric social worker, Jane Henderson, who had been brought in from Holbein College, carried her coffee cup to the podium. She was a brisk and efficient woman in her late thirties. Saul thought she had the hardened professionalism of a business consultant: the glaring half-smile, the chignon, the pitiless rules of thumb, the overenunciated words combined with common sense set out in formulated phrases. She assured the audience that teen suicides were terrible tragedies and, furthermore, that they were now epidemic. Terrible as Gordy's death was, however, it was important to recognize that it had been one of many such suicides all across the United States, each one of them tragically preventable. Saul noticed that the word "tragic" was cropping up repeatedly, compulsively, though no one really meant it or felt it. "I am sorry to report to you," she said, "that your community is only the latest to have suffered from this terrible plague. What can we do? We *can* do something. We can empower ourselves. We can watch for signs of trouble." She then listed, using a PowerPoint demonstration, the ten warning signs of a tragically troubled teen—including clothing signs, verbal signs, gestural signs, the closed doors, the sullenness, the touchiness in response to questions. Gordy had exhibited four and one-half of these signs. He could have been spotted and helped out; at the very least, he could have been given counseling and, perhaps, medication.

"You have to be alert," Jane Henderson said. "These events can precipitate into a contagion in a community like ours."

Saul sat with his head in his hands. You couldn't answer human disorder like Gordy's with PowerPoint demonstrations. He now wished he had never brought those baby pictures into his remedial-reading class.

. . .

Harold reported to Saul that Gordy's death was the biggest and some-times the only topic of conversation in the barbershop, and the talk often implicated Saul and Patsy, but ambiguously and circularly, and only because they had been standing nearby in the house when Gordy's gun went off in the front yard. What *had* he been doing on their lawn, in front of that tree? What had he been doing there, off and on, all that year? No one could explain. It was mystifying, and Saul knew that his and Patsy's proximity to Gordy's death would mark them as accessories to the mysti-fication.

The boy hadn't previously threatened to kill himself or anyone else. He had displayed the gun the way other boys displayed their baseball cards. There had been no desperate spoken ultimatums. He hadn't seemed particularly unhappy; he wasn't atypical, unless you counted his attention deficits. As the days went on, Saul thought that Gordy had fired a bullet into his brain on a whim. MAD IN AMERICA . . . that was Gordy all over, committing suicide as a weirdly unpromising practical joke. Or: he had performed an auto-jihad. Even Bob Pawlak had no explanation. "Total surprise to me," he said, shrugging. The autopsy turned up no drugs or alcohol in Gordy's bloodstream. The other possi-bility, of a genuine despair, was somehow unthinkable in Gordy's case. Certainly the gun itself wasn't to blame. Was it? In any case, after the medical examiner's autopsy, there was no funeral and no memorial service and no reminiscences about the boy. Gordy's family couldn't afford a funeral, his aunt had said (really, since no one except the aunt wanted to acknowledge him as kin, there was no family), and no one had much of anything to remark about Gordy's life, such as it had been. What could you say about him? Like God, he was who he was. He was close to invisible, and then he had erased the only visibility he had. She said she would just scatter his ashes out in back of the trailer where he had lived. When Saul began to inquire over the telephone about this economizing, Gordy's aunt asked him: *What* about Gordy, did he think, was worth remembering? He was better off held back in the past without anybody creating too much of a fuss over him now, she said. It occurred to Saul that Gordy's aunt thought that suicides were shameful and that she had to get rid of him in a hurry. When she used those school words, "held back," Saul felt himself shiver, as if someone's fingers soaked in ice water were traveling down his spine. "No use crying over that boy anymore, no earthly use that I can see," she said, in a call she made to Saul on a Saturday afternoon. "I've cried enough. Leave him be, resting in peace. Don't you want him to rest in peace?"

The child Cossack, he thought, my adversary, he deserved better than this.

"Yes," he said. "Only it makes me angry that he killed himself."

"Angry?"

"Sure. I get mad when I think about it."

"Oh, I wouldn't get *mad* about it," she said. "I wouldn't get riled up." Saul didn't have the impression that she really wanted to talk to him anymore; her voice had a smoky flaring-up and fading-back. She went on talking in her dazed way. "You aren't responsible or anything. I'm not going to sue you or anybody else, is what I'm saying," she said. "Despite what some people have been suggesting to me. Don't you worry about that. I'm not going after your money now. Besides, I already thanked you for your generosity."

Saul knew better than to respond, especially about money. After taking another breath, Brenda Bagley said that she *was* sorry that she hadn't hidden the gun any better than she had. Gordy had found it squirreled away in a shoe box in her closet, where she had thought he'd never find it.

On the afternoon following this conversation, he and Brenda Bagley drove to the Five Oaks Funeral Home and picked up Gordy's ashes in a plastic box. The funeral director, Lewis Binch, was an affable man in a pinstriped suit, perfectly tailored; his eyes were alert and searching in an Irish manner—the entire face displayed a resigned, comic intelligence as he sat behind his desk in his office, offering good-humored consolation. He seemed well acquainted with grief and was not frightened of it. Saul wondered how he hadn't met this funeral director before; he wanted him as a friend and took his business card, hoping for another occasion to meet prior to a death, especially his own.

The box of ashes was as big as a dictionary, and its contents rattled;

Saul estimated its weight at about twelve pounds. After driving Brenda Bagley back home, he carried the box into her trailer, following her. As soon as she was inside, she turned on the enormous television set and stood for a moment to see what programs were on. "You can put it over there," she said, pointing to a sofa on which a white cat slept, while she watched the TV screen, as an old sea captain would watch a lighthouse. Saul laid the box of ashes on the sofa opposite the cat. He left without saying goodbye, while she went on watching the TV screen, avoiding shipwreck, though she waved absentmindedly as he walked out the door.

After the summer storms and the articles about Gordy's death in the *Five Oaks News-Chronicle*, accompanied by a lengthy and hard-hitting editorial about troubled children and guns, and the terrible inexplicable epidemic of student violence in American schools, Patsy went to her OB-GYN and confirmed what she already knew, that she was newly pregnant. She did not say that Gordy's death had inspired the two of them to create this child; some things you *didn't* have to tell Saul.

When she informed Saul that night at dinner about her pregnancy, he stood up at the table and walked over to where she sat to kiss her and hug her. His joy was manufactured for her benefit—she could instantly tell—but manufactured joy was better than none at all, and she admired his efforts to be glad on her behalf. He himself would be glad spontaneously, in time. His feelings needed some duration to establish themselves on whatever solid ground Saul might find.

The stain of Gordy's blood on the linden wouldn't wash off: Saul had tried soapsuds and Clorox, sponging the bark of the tree, until it came to him that he was being just like Gordy's aunt, trying to wash all traces of him away, and he stopped.

For a week after that he watched television. It was like taking a bath in forgetfulness. Whatever they had on television wasn't good or bad: it was just television. If you put a Vermeer on television, it stopped being a Vermeer and turned into something else on television.

Sometimes he watched with Mary Esther perched in his lap. He combed her hair idly, shook her music-box teddy bear, bounced her, fed her, read *Pat the Bunny*, and sang "Little Red Caboose" to her when the mood struck him. He began to hope for certain commercials to reappear, the ones with happy tunes. Whenever she fussed, he carried her around the house and then outside. He did not sleep consistently at night. He wasn't unhappy, nor was he depressed; he just wasn't anything—this was how he explained it to himself. He was preoccupied by a certain variety of nothingness, full of colors and moods. It was a kingdom, and he had just made his respectful way through the front gate. Patsy stayed up with him as long as she could, holding his hand, and then she went to bed.

It made no sense to try to love one's enemy when the enemy was already dead. It was a stupid spiritual practice, and Christian, besides.

After enduring another week of this, Patsy came downstairs one morning and told Saul that he should take a trip somewhere, anywhere, just for a few days, to let the miles soak up in him. He needed to travel, to watch the telephone poles fly by in their sedative manner. It wasn't that she wanted him out of the house; she just thought that he needed to get away. He didn't hunt or fish—he didn't have any of those male outdoorsy escape valves—but he could at least go to one or two cities and visit the museums. That would be a nice Saul thing to do, she said, before school started again and he found himself extemporizing in one classroom or another. She could manage Mary Esther on her own for a few days.

Following her advice, he called ahead to a few friends and then packed several days' worth of clean clothes. He didn't like to fly because airport terminals and their long receding concourses reminded him of gigantic vacuum-cleaner hoses sucking him and everyone else into nullity. He preferred taking the train.

At the doors of the Detroit Amtrak station he leaned into the car and kissed Patsy and Mary Esther goodbye. He took the train to Washington on a coach ticket he had bought on the Web. He arrived at Union Station three hours late. For two nights he stayed with a couple he knew, Buzz Henselt and his girlfriend, Sarah. The two of them lived in a walkup near Cleveland Heights in the District and were doing moderately well— Sarah worked for a writers-in-the-schools project, and Buzz, who was good at budget analysis, had landed a job in the Department of Transportation—but Saul realized that he was in a fog and wasn't keeping up his end of the conversation, particularly when Buzz and Sarah asked him about himself and Patsy and Mary Esther. All he could say was, "Oh, we're fine," before lapsing into silence and staring at their Edward Hopper poster (the house, not the nighthawks) framed on the living-room wall, or the Ralston Crawford poster in the dining room. He realized that his presence there was a puzzle to them. He was an inexplicable and unsatisfying guest. He wasn't terribly interested in them anymore and answered their questions as if he were talking about someone else or taking a quiz, and, no, as it turned out, he *didn't* want to go to the National Gallery.

He slept on a cot in their study, close enough to the computer so that he could hear its internal fan whirring all night in sleep mode, almost covering the sounds of Buzz and Sarah's snoring and snorts and conversations in the next room. Still childless, they hadn't yet learned how to muffle themselves. In the corner, Buzz and Sarah's African gray parrot, Jack, muttered and scrabbled about in his cage. The bird had acquired a fiendish expertise for imitating ringing telephones and dripping faucets, and in moments of bravado would imitate Sarah's asthma wheeze, allergy-related coughing, and gasps during intercourse. "Shut up," Saul would say, and within hours the bird started to answer, "Shut up."

At breakfast, Buzz asked Saul whether there wasn't something he— Saul—wanted to talk about, and Saul shook his head. "I'm sort of in this *box,* and I can't exactly open it up, but I'm okay," he said. "That's all. It's not serious. Don't worry about me." He went back to his bagel and the sports page. He didn't mention Gordy Himmelman, feeling that it would be an imposition. Too long living in the Midwest had made him a practitioner of self-effacing obtuse cheerfulness, he realized.

Finally, after calling to make sure she'd be there, he borrowed Buzz and Sarah's car and drove over to Bethesda to his mother's house. He had grown up in this house and was happy to think of it as no longer *his*, or as *home*, or as a place where he would willingly stay for more than a few hours at a time. Standing on the sidewalk, Saul inspected the lawn and the front garden: they were carefully tended, the edges of the grass properly clipped, the lilac at the side of the house perfectly trimmed, the geranium in its pot on the front stoop well-watered. Pansies filled the flower bed. Somebody was indeed taking care of his mother, or of her lawn, lush and green as it was—prodigal and green and carnal, in its second adolescence, pubic, procreative. After he rang the doorbell, the door opened, and his mother presented herself. "Ah, the weary traveler. You like it?" his mother asked, glancing around at nothing in particular. That was Delia: she had always asked him questions that were too vague to answer.

Saul smiled at her and shrugged. "Very much." Carrying his overnight bag, he ambled up to her and hugged her.

On close inspection, he could see that something had indeed happened to her. Delia was not herself anymore. She had been divested of her affectations and stripped of her usual ornaments. He had prepared himself for more of her mustard-gas perfume, more girlishness, a bonanza of bracelets and amber necklaces, but she wasn't wearing any bracelets or necklaces, she had stopped dyeing her hair, and she had done away with the bloody-looking fingernail polish. She just stood there, wearing a new simplicity. She was almost elegant. "Sweetie," she said, patting him on the cheek. "It's good to see you. I'm *so* sorry about that boy. Put your suitcase inside in the foyer and let's go to the supermarket. We need some groceries for dinner."

Behind the wheel of his mother's Camry, negotiating traffic, his newly remodeled mother beside him, Saul suddenly remembered why he disliked the suburbs and had developed an affection for dusty, luckless midwestern cities tucked away inside the folds of the map. The drivers here in suburban Maryland were cunning and ruthless. They engaged in savage tailgating. They were overachieving supervisors in their professional lives and now they were doing their best to overachieve behind the wheel.

They wore their successes on their huge muscular sheet-metal fenders. Darwinian, emotionally Republican even if they were registered Democrats, they had acquired German sedans or American SUVs that looked like staff cars for Rommel, or they had huge spotless V-8 pickup trucks with nothing, ever, in the cargo bed—that would spoil the effect, like a suntan that ended at the shirt collar—and most of them drove with one hand, the other hand on their cell phones relaying news to the home-front on how the battle was going. Domestic life in the suburbs, simple trips to the mall, had shifted to a war footing, the drivers so high and mighty behind the wheel that they looked down on any sedan inhabited by civilians.

At the green light, when Saul failed to accelerate immediately, the woman behind him, driving a burgundy F-250, honked at him, and Saul flashed her the finger and began yelling helplessly and with great enraged enthusiasm. She zoomed past him in the left lane, lowered the passenger-side electric window, shouted "Dickhead!" at him, and raced forward. On her truck's bumper there was a diversity-rainbow sticker. She was very beautiful. He couldn't chase her: he was driving his mother, his ancient enemy, to the supermarket. Besides, they were underdefended in the Camry, the sort of car driven by worker bees.

"I wish you'd calm down, Saul," his mother said a few minutes later, after he had flipped the bird to another driver who had first tailgated him and then cut him off. They entered the parking lot for the supermarket, and Saul began the desperate search for a spot. "You're awfully tense this morning." She patted him on the knee. "Why don't you park over there?" She pointed to a space. Saul ignored her. He parked one row farther off, in an opening that he had found for himself. "I see you've acquired a bit of road rage," Delia said, after he stopped and put on the emergency brake with a furious gesture. "I don't remember that in you before. Don't go blaming me for that."

"Oh, I would never blame you for anything," Saul lied, dropping the keys into the pocket of his leather jacket. "It's the drivers here. And when did I ever have any equanimity? Well, come on."

He walked slightly behind her to the doors of the market and noticed how his mother's physical movements had taken on a pensiveness that

she'd never displayed before. It wasn't an effect of aging; it was the conse-
quence of seriousness, of something profound that had happened to her
and had taken root. She most likely couldn't discuss it with him. Having
secrets apparently gave people dignity. Watching her, he felt amazement:
his mother had acquired an inner life. She had warmed up. And all from
a boy lover. He took her arm as gently as he could, and she smiled at him.
"Hi, Saul," she said, stepping up to the curb, as if he had just arrived.
"How are you?"

He told her in his blandest voice that he was fine, and as he grabbed a
shopping cart inside the automatic doors, she said, "You know, I'm fine,
too," but her face occasionally displayed brief expressions of resignation
followed by inappropriate private smiles. Her head nodded, quick flicks.
Saul could see that she was carrying on a lengthy inner conversation. She
was lying to him; she wasn't fine at all, of course, but sprightliness had
once been in her nature, so she would try to maintain it.

"What?" he asked.

"What 'what'?" she answered. "Grab some of that romaine lettuce,
would you?" He did as he was asked. Music drifted down like plastic icicles from speakers in the ceiling: "Mona Lisa" in a string arrangement.
"Do you like green peppers in your salad? Tomatoes? I don't remember."
Still smiling, she added, "It's been such a long time. After all, I'm not
your mother anymore." Planted near the produce, she gazed at him,
examining him for one second too long. "Sometimes when you stand like
that you look like your father." She made an all-purpose gesture. "Too
bad you didn't inherit his sense of humor."

"We're having another child," he said, trying to forestall any discussion of what he had or had not inherited. "Patsy and I," he clarified.

"Oh, yes, Patsy told me." Saul dropped the peppers into the cart, as
his mother beamed. "That's so wonderful. They never arrive when you
expect them to, you know—children. By the way, have you talked to your
brother lately?" She straightened herself, cleared her throat with a noise
like a sheep, and pushed the cart ahead of him, toward the meat counter.
She picked up one of the T-bone steaks inside its shrink-wrap and examined it closely, as if, Saul thought, for an infection. "He makes all this
money and then he goes out on those extreme sports, or whatever they're

called. Rock climbing and such. So *aggressive*. At least he's not moody. When you get into these moods, Saul, I wish you'd go into therapy, or at least get a hobby the way your brother does."

"In Five Oaks? That's a good one. You've gotten kind of moody yourself, Ma."

"Me? You still eat meat, don't you? You haven't turned into one of these vegetarians?" She dropped two of the steaks into the cart and gazed down the grocery aisle toward the dairy products. She didn't seem to want to look at him. "*I'm* not sitting up watching television and sitting around all day, Saul. *I'm* not making trips all over the country."

"My seeing you doesn't have a purpose? Seeing my mother? That's a hell of a thing to say. It's summertime. Besides, I'm not in your way. You don't have a job or anything."

She banged the shopping cart into his hip, as a nudge. "Well, I know you do have a purpose, being here. And I certainly do have a job. I *work*. You just don't know what it is that I do. *Do* you? No, you don't. I go to an office four times a week, Saul, where I . . ." She nodded to herself. "Oh, never mind. It's nice, that I have a job, a *serious* job, and you don't know what it is. You don't keep yourself informed. Don't have a ghost of a clue, do you, honey? You don't ask." She turned around to look at him. "What do you mean, I've gotten moody?"

"I'm your son," Saul said. "I can tell." Shoppers passed them quickly. The two of them, mother and adult son, were becalmed in a sea of shoppers passing by them in waves. "So what's this job? What's going on with you, Ma?"

Delia had been looking straight ahead of her, and all at once she flinched. "What's going on with me? I'm hanging by a thread. Oh, look. Somebody fell."

"What? What are you talking about?"

"Up there." She pointed toward the dairy products and the case for frozen foods. "Somebody fell up there."

Saul looked in the direction where she was pointing and saw a man on the floor. He was reasonably well dressed, and Saul was quickly ashamed of himself for thinking that people who fell to the floor in public places were always shabby. Anyone could fall to the floor. Saul himself could do so; he was quite capable of it. The man had apparently slipped on some wet linoleum tiles—there was a standing yellow hazard marker just off to the left with a little silhouette figure of a falling person on it—and by the time Saul got there, being careful of his own footing, the man was already on his knees, and then, with Saul's help, on his feet. "My mistake," the man said, in apology. Next to where he had fallen there stood, in the center aisle, a pyramid display of canned tomatoes with their brightly dark red labels, and after the man thanked Saul, he brushed himself off and went on his way, carrying a frozen dinner he had picked up from the floor. Saul stayed where he was. He could not take his eyes off the display. The red of the labels was magnetic, visually fixating. Tomato cans! He was unable to look at anything else. People and things passed by him. More bland music of some sort drizzled down from the ceiling speakers—small, drabby, synthetic music—as Saul felt himself sucked wholly into the blood-red colors on the cans.

When he finally came to his senses, his mother was beside him. "A mitzvah," she said. "Good for you. What's with those cans, Saul?"

"I don't know," he muttered. "They look like . . . never mind. Let's go."

Ten minutes later, at the checkout line, his mother turned toward him and smiled again. "Oh, I know it's hard doing this with me. It's no fun, is it, all grown up and still going to the grocery store with your mother. I just thought it would give us something to do."

Saul unloaded the grocery cart, lost in thought, watching his mother take out her checkbook. She did it with a restrained bossiness. Down through the years, she had carried on her life without altering it very much for Saul's, or Howie's, benefit. Her feminism was personal and private and therefore eccentric, and she had formed the habit of resenting men as a class because her husband had died and left her alone with two sons. Solitude had made her flirty at first, and then impersonal. Getting anything personal out of her was like trying to open a tuna fish can with your thumbs. Saul and Howie had their worlds, she had hers. And the boys shared a guilt with their father, because, one by one, they would grow up and abandon her, which was what males did. Either they died or they took off. In Delia's version of things, male adulthood was disloyalty by its very nature. Even providing her with another grandchild wouldn't close that wound.

No wonder a sweet and devoted teenaged lover had knocked the stuffing out of her.

Watching her pay for her groceries, Saul thought of his mother's dutifulness. She had been good about taking Saul, and then Howie, to Little League practice after Saul's father had died, but her heart wasn't in it, in any of those male activities, those *sports*. Howie's sickliness had given her a cause to preoccupy her, but her sons didn't have anything to give her in return. But now, some shift had taken place in her. Her heart had been stripped bare. Sympathies had opened up. Suddenly she was out of character. In midlife she had become someone else. And she deserved everything she got, all the rewards of feeling, Saul thought, especially if she had lost her heart to this kid.

Carrying the groceries out to the car, feeling brave, Saul said, "How's your love life, Ma? Any prospects?"

"Why? Did Patsy say something to you?"

"No, in fact, she didn't."

Saul was putting the grocery bags in the trunk, but he could tell that his mother was checking his face for deceit. She had an internal psycho-galvanometer with Saul and could detect his polite lies a continent away. Her right eyebrow went up, like that of a food critic, and she ran her fingers through her hair. "Yes, there is somebody," she said. "But I can't talk about it."

She waited at the passenger-side door for Saul to unlock and open it for her, which he did, practicing his manners. Back behind the wheel, he asked her why not.

"Because some things you can't talk about," Delia said. She was getting grumpy. She harumphed and squirmed in the seat. "All your generation does is talk about sex all the time. Some things should be left to themselves."

"Oh, that's not true," Saul said.

"Listen to you! You quit your job, you come here, you drive me to the

Giant and stare at a display of tomato cans, and you tell me that you can talk about anything. Saul, you and I can't talk about the important things in life, because they're all secrets. Everything important is a secret. No one ever talks about anything. Deny it. I dare you. That student of yours died, and his death was his secret, and you don't have the words for it. Who would?"

"It's not that I wouldn't, but that I *can't*. It's beyond me. In your case, you *can*, but you *won't*."

"Well, as for 'can't,' I can't believe I'm having this conversation," Delia said. Saul turned the key to the ignition, and the car, in its puny way, roared to life. "All right. I'll tell you something. He's very . . . young. He's a very young man."

"What's his name?" Saul asked, driving out of the parking lot and pretending nonchalance.

"Jimmy," Delia told him, and when she said the word, Saul accidentally hit the brake, throwing both himself and his mother against their seatbelts. A car behind them screeched to a stop and the driver honked at them.

"Sorry," Saul said. "I'm not used to this car." He was blushing.

Delia stared straight ahead at the traffic. Saul could see that his mother's eyes were watering. "Patsy told you, didn't she? Patsy told you about Jimmy."

Saul nodded. "And it's not that he's married, right?"

"Well," she said, "no. Just that he's very young. Anyway, anyway. You keep driving. Drive home and I'll make you dinner, and then you can go back to your friends. Maybe I'll say something about him and maybe I won't. But first let me say this, honey. I'm really glad you came. And of course I *do* know why," she said, looking radiantly pleased all of a sudden. She tapped his right knee, like a chum.

"Why?"

"Don't be coy, Saul."

"I'm not being coy."

"Of course you are. It's so nice, your doing this."

"Doing what?"

"Coming to see me. *Today*."

"What about today?" Saul asked.

"Are you waiting for the right moment?" his mother asked. "Any moment is the right moment."

"To do what?"

"To wish me a happy birthday!" She smiled at him and put her hand on his leg.

Great Leaping Jesus. Jesus on His Throne in Ohio. He gasped for a breath. Saul calculated the date and realized that—yes—it was indeed his mother's birthday today. Maybe he really did need a therapist, one to accompany him everywhere he went from here to the grave, and possibly beyond. Another prank played by the unconscious, one of the many. Imagine the *planning*, the *care*, the *indecency*, the *deceit*. Where was dignity? Nowhere on this Earth. Perhaps in Israel. Maybe he would move there; his mother would never follow him—she had a thing about Palestinians—and his unconscious would band together with the other unconsciouses running amuck in Jerusalem and the Occupied Territories. Looking in the rearview mirror, as if he were being swallowed by what was behind him, Saul was horrified, as ever, by the terrible ironies of which life was so fond. But he was driving, and in Maryland traffic, so he could not express his horror safely and honorably. He would have to bottle it up and put it with all the other demented preserves in the basement and then wait for it to explode. He kept his hands on the wheel. The FBI would be here any minute now.

"Well, yes, exactly," he said with pretended calm. "Happy birthday, Mom!"

"Thank you. Don't pretend you *forgot*." She smiled and touched her hand to her hair. "Don't you dare pretend that your visit here was accidental. I'm so touched that you made the trip to see me on my birthday. Especially at this time in your life."

"Actually," Saul said, "I want to stop at a flower shop. Or somewhere. Right now."

"Oh, you don't have to get me anything, cupcake. It's enough that you were so thoughtful to come see me."

"Please don't call me that cupcake thing, Ma. No, I want to."

He turned the car into another strip mall with a flower shop. He quickly bought some cut roses and came running out to the car with them.

"Happy birthday," he said, shoving the flowers in her direction through the passenger-side window. She smiled, sat up, and put them into her lap.

"You're so thoughtful," his mother said, with sweet, dignified, middle-aged irony. "I'll be lucky if Howie even remembers to phone."

When they returned to the house, Saul spied a pickup truck two houses away, and, out in front, a scrawny young man mowing the lawn, an ordinary guy, Saul thought, wearing a T-shirt and a cap with the visor turned backward. When he glanced at his mother, she gave him an almost imperceptible nod. Saul thought that if this guy had appeared in one of his classes, he wouldn't have given him a second look.

After a quiet dinner with his mother, and his return to his friends the next morning, Saul took the train up to New York. The cheapest hotel he could find was close to Gramercy Park, and for his first day he walked around Manhattan. The wonderful ruined glorious old city. He particularly enjoyed getting lost in Chinatown and Little Italy, the tangle of ethnicity and streets in the lower part of Manhattan, where every place you turned from midmorning to the middle of the night you smelled food cooking, scalding cooking oil mixed with the overripe background odor of garbage, and he enjoyed the heat that rose from the pavement, the way it went through your body like an X-ray, the flesh porously absorbing it, how there was no stopping it and no cooling off. Everyone became hot, everyone became the heat. Particularly around West Broadway, the city streets felt abandoned by serious persons in the summer, nothing but human castoffs and scruffy kids filling up the sidewalk space and yelling all day and night. He felt right at home. In the East Village he sat on a park bench soiled with dried pigeon dung and ate an ice cream cone. He watched everyone pass by, and he was perfectly happy.

On the second afternoon, a Thursday, following a trip uptown, he had disembarked from the Lexington Avenue local at Grand Central and was headed down the underground tunnel in the direction of the shuttle to Times Square. He had an out-of-towner's pride in his mastery of the New York City subway system and never consulted a map. And he loved the subway itself: the noise, the electric-iron smell, the occasional glimpses of rats, the whackos riding the trains, the sweat of flushed bodies in proximity to one another, the ads in Spanish advocating safe sex. For him the subway was an urban ideal. On the subway, Saul felt very tall, and very blond, and very handsome, at least in comparison to everyone else. The most intricate stations—Times Square, Grand Central— were monuments of human ingenuity and engineering. Saul was more impressed by the ceiling of Grand Central Terminal than he had been by man's journey to the moon, and he suspected that the entire New York subway system was now beyond what human beings were capable of. Not the technology, but the willpower, the ideal of the public good.

Halfway through the tunnel he heard music. On the other side, close to where the shuttle trains were, stood a band, a typical subway assemblage of musicians, in this case of Peruvian Indians playing music from the Andes. The music reverberated through the narrow subterranean passage; he had heard the music before he had seen the five men performing on their charangos and mandolins and guitars and sikus. It sounded like high-altitude mountain music, harmonies and rhythms and chord changes conceived in the upper atmospheres and brought down to the metal and concrete below ground level. He approached the band. They had CDs for sale; the label said that their name was Ch'uwa Yacu. He even loved the sound of that, without having any idea of how to pronounce it. Saul felt himself drawn up into the music, absorbed by it, as he had been by the heat off the sidewalks. He tossed a five-dollar bill into the musicians' open guitar case.

When he looked up, on the other side of the small crowd, wedged in near the back, he saw Gordy Himmelman behind what seemed to be a slight curtain of gauze, his eyes wide open and staring. Gordy, a hayseed ghost out of his element, was looking first at the musicians and then back at Saul, full in the face, and his mouth was gaping dark with distracted amazement. But of course it wasn't Gordy. It was just anybody's boy.

He was offering himself to me for adoption, Saul thought. He was a stray dog. That's why he stood out there on the lawn. But I didn't want to. I couldn't take him.

Saul waited for a moment, and then it came: what he had been anticipating, the breaking-open, and, very quietly, so as not to disturb the other listeners, he unobtrusively boarded the shuttle to Times Square, his shoulders shaking. He didn't know how long he sat there, once he got on, though he did remember to put on his dark glasses. Tears streamed quietly from under the lenses down his cheeks and onto his shirt. The shuttle took him to its destination, and then took him back to Grand Central, and then returned to Times Square. Everyone ignored him. They came and left, came and left. He simply lost track of the time as he was ferried from one place to the other.

Part Three

Thirteen

A squirrel squatted in the birdbath. Another squirrel was hanging by its claws onto the birdfeeder. The girl, looking out her bedroom window at the backyard, cleaned her fingernails halfheartedly with the nail file and thought of the end of the world, and then she wondered why, if there was a word "ruthless" that was often applied to enemies of the U.S.A., then what happened to its opposite, its lost positive, "ruth," which would have to mean "kindness" but didn't mean anything because no one used it? We had ruthless enemies but no ruthful friends.

If some people were "unruly," then who was "ruly"? Nobody. When her room was messy, her mother said it was "unkempt," but when it was clean, it was never "kempt" because the word didn't exist. Disgruntled postal workers were everywhere. Where were the gruntled ones? Everybody had a word for the wrong thing, but silence prevailed for the right.

Early in the morning just after the sun was up, the squirrels looked like boys, somehow, she couldn't say why. Maybe because of the way they moved, skittering and chasing each other, twitching. Or maybe it was the fur. Something.

Her name was Gina, she was sixteen years old, and it was Sunday, Family Day. After staring at the squirrels, she remembered to feed her guinea pig his breakfast food pellets. Wilbur squeaked and squealed softly as she dropped the pellets down the cage bars into the red plastic tray. It didn't take much to make *him* happy.

On the other side of her room was a picture of Switzerland her mom had put up years ago. The picture had a lake in it, which was ruthlessly blue. Gina felt funny when she looked at this picture, so she didn't look at it very often. She couldn't take it down because her mom had given it to her.

Family Day. The plan was, her dad would show up and take them— her brother, her mom, herself—to the beach. Gina threw on a T-shirt and a pair of jeans. She grabbed her flute and went into the basement to practice for the school marching band, of which she was a member.

Ten minutes later she heard the thud of the morning newspaper flung against the front screen door. Gina put her flute on top of her dad's workbench (he had never bothered to move it to his apartment after he moved out) and went upstairs to read the headlines. The news consisted of Iraq (bombs), Cuba (jails), Ireland (more bombs), and then there was something about Gordy Himmelman.

Gordy Himmelman! He had shot himself. To death. It was permanent. Why hadn't anyone called her about it?

She had been in classes with Gordy Himmelman since kindergarten, but he was in a class by himself, and she hadn't seen much of him since he'd dropped out. He muttered and swore and blew his nose on notebook paper, and he talked to himself in long strings of garble and never had any friends you could show in public. You could feel sorry for him, but he would never notice how sorry you felt, and he wouldn't care. Pity was lost on him. It was a *total* waste of time. In third grade he had brought a penlight battery into school and, standing next to the monkey bars, he had swallowed it during recess to attract attention to himself. The battery was only a double-A, but even so. He had black-and-blue marks all over him most days. His breath smelled of dill pickles that had gone unfresh. You couldn't even talk to him about the weather because he never noticed it—it didn't make any difference to him what the sky was doing or how it was doing it. He had this human-junkyard-don't-mess-with-me look on his face and would kick anyone who got in his way, though he did have one comic routine: slugging himself in the face so hard that his head jerked backward. He had bicycled to that teacher, Mr. Bernstein's house, where he had blown his brains out in the yard, in front of a tree, in the morning, a matinee suicide. On the front page of the paper was a picture of the tree. It was a color picture, and you could sort of see the blood if you looked closely.

There hadn't been a suicide note. A suicide note would have been like a writing assignment. Way too hard. He would have had to get his aunt to write it for him.

Gina felt something stirring inside her. She was kind of interested in death. Gordy was the first person she'd ever known who had entered it. He had gone from being Mr. Nothing to being Mr. Something Else: a temporarily interesting person. She sat at the kitchen counter eating her strawberry Pop-Tart, wondering whether Gordy was lying on a bed sur-rounded by virgins, or eternal fire, or what.

It was sort of cool, him doing that. Maybe the smartest thing he'd ever done. Adventuresome and courageous.

If you didn't have a life, maybe you got one by being dead.

Her dad was late. Finally he showed up at eleven-thirty in his red Durango, saying, "Ha ha, I'm late." He and Gina's mom were divorced, but they were still "friends," and her dad had never really committed himself to the divorce, in Gina's opinion. He was halfhearted about it, a romantic sad sack. They had cooked up this Family Day scheme two years ago. Every weekend he'd come to pick up Gina and Bertie, her little brother, and their mom—Gina envied most divorced kids who went from their moms to their dads, without the cheesiness of Family Day—and then they'd do bowling-type activities for the sake of togetherness and friendliness, which of course was a total fraud, since they weren't together or friendly at all. Usually Saturday was Family Day but some-times Sunday was. Today they were going to the beach. Wild excitement. She had meant to bring a magazine.

. . .

In the car, Gina studied her father's face. She had wanted to drive, but no one trusted her behind the wheel. For once she had been allowed to sit up front: semi-adult, now that she had filled out, so they gave her front-seat privileges sometimes, occasional woman privileges. Her mom and Bertie were in the back, Bertie playing with his Game Boy, her mom with her earphones on, listening to music so she wouldn't have to hear the plinks and plunks of the Game Boy, or talk to her ex, Gina's dad, the driver, half-committed to his divorce, an undecided single man, driving the car. He would fully commit to the divorce when he found a girlfriend he really liked, which he hadn't, yet. Gina had met one of the girlfriends whom he had only half-liked, a woman who tried way too hard to be nice, and who looked like a minor character on a soap opera who would eventually be hit by a rampaging bus.

Gina had mentioned Gordy Himmelman to her dad, and her dad had said yeah, it was way too bad.

She was interested in her father's face. Because it was her father's, she didn't know if he was handsome or plain. You couldn't always tell when they were your parents, though with her friend Gretchen Mullen you sure could, since Gretchen's father looked like a hobgoblin. At first she thought her own father had a sort of no-brand, standard-issue father face; now she wasn't so sure.

He was possibly handsome. There was no way of knowing. Her dad was a master plumber. Therefore his hands often had cuts or grease under the fingernails. Very large hands, made big by genetic fate. His hair was short and brown, cut so it bristled, and near his temples you could see a change in color, salty. On his right cheek her dad had a crease, as if his skin had been cut by a knife or a sharp piece of paper, but it was only a wrinkle, a wrinkle getting started, the first canal in a network of creases-to-come, his face turning slowly but surely into Mars, the Red Planet. His teeth were very white and even, the most Rock Star thing about him. His eyes were brown and spaced wide apart, not narrow the way teenaged boys' eyes are usually narrow, and they drilled into you so that sometimes you had to turn away so you wouldn't be injured by the Father Look. Her father's beard line was so distinct and straight it looked

206

put in with a ruler, and was so heavy that even if he shaved in the morning, he usually needed another shave around dinnertime, an interestingly bearlike feature of the masculine father type. His nose was exciting. His breath had a latent smell of cigarettes, which he smoked in private. You couldn't find the boy in him anymore. It wasn't there. He was growing a belly from the beer he drank nights and weekends, and most of the time he seemed comfortable with it, though it seemed to tire him out also. He didn't smile much and only when he had to. He had once told Gina, "Life is serious."

On winter weekends he watched football on television speechlessly.

He looked like a plumber on a TV show who comes in halfway through the program and who someone, though not the main character, falls in love with, because he's so manly and can replace faucet washers. He would be the kind of plumber who wisecracks and makes the whole studio audience break up, but he would be charming, too, when he had to be. But then sometimes at a stoplight, or when he saw a car pull in front of him, her dad's face changed out of its TV sitcom expression: suddenly he grimaced like someone had started to do surgery on him right over his heart without anesthetic, and he was pretending that nothing was happening to him even though his chest was being cut open, bared to fresh air. And then that expression vanished like it had never been there. What was that about? His pain. His secret squirrel life, probably.

Still, there was no point in talking to him about Gordy Himmelman.

At the lake they settled in on their beach towels. Bertie, who was oblivious to everything, went on playing with his Game Boy. Gina's mom stretched out on her back in an effort to immerse herself in lethal tanning rays. Her dad carried the picnic basket into the shade and started to read his copy of *Car and Driver*, sitting on the picnic-table bench. Gina went to the concession stand to get herself an ice cream cone, which she would buy with her own money.

The stand itself had been constructed out of concrete blocks, painted white, covered overhead by a cheap corrugated roof. Under it, everything seemed to be sun-baking. Behind the counter was a popcorn machine with a high-intensity yellow heat lamp shining on the popped kernels in their little glass house, making them look radioactive. The sidewalk leading up to and away from the stand, stained with the residue of spilled pink ice cream and ketchup, felt sticky on the soles of Gina's feet. The kid who worked at the stand, selling snack food and renting canoes, was a boy she didn't recognize—about her age, maybe a year or two older, with short orange hair and an earring—and he stood behind the counter next to the candy display, staring, in pain and boredom, at the floor. He was experiencing summer-job agony. He had a rock station blaring from his battery-powered radio perched on top of the freezer, and his body twitched quietly to the beat. When Gina appeared, the boy looked at her with relief, relief followed by recognition and sympathy, recognition and sympathy followed by a leer as he checked out her tits, the leer followed by a friendly smirk. It all happened very fast. He was like other boys: they shifted gears so quickly you couldn't always follow them into those back roads and dense forests where they wanted to live with the other varmints and wolves.

Raspberry, please, single scoop. She smiled at him, to tease him, to test out her power, to give him an anguished memory tonight, when he was in bed and couldn't sleep, thinking of her, in the density of his empty, stupid life.

Walking back to the sand and holding her ice cream cone, she started to think about Gordy Himmelman, and when she did, the crummy lake and the public beach with the algae floating in it a hundred feet offshore in front of her, she felt weird and dizzy, as if: What was the point? She kept walking and taking an occasional, personal, lick at the ice cream. There weren't too many other people in the sand, but most of the men were fat, and their wives or girlfriends were fat, too, and already they had started to yell at each other, even though it was just barely lunchtime.

She kept walking. It was something to do. Nobody here was beautiful. It all sucked.

The lake gave her a funny feeling, just the fact that it was there. The sky was sky blue, and her mother had said it was a perfect day, but if this was a perfect day, if this was the best that God could manage with the available materials, then . . . well, no wonder Gordy Himmelman had shot himself, and no wonder her mother had put up that picture of Switzerland in her bedroom. Gina saw her whole life stretched out in front of her, just like that, the deck of fifty-two cards with Family Day printed on one side, like the picture of the lake in Switzerland that she could barely stand to glance at, vacuuming her up. Why couldn't anything ever be perfect? It just wasn't possible. This wasn't perfect. It was its opposite: fect. A totally fect day. Just to the side, off on another beach towel, somebody's mom was yelling at and then slapping a little boy. Slapping him, wham wham wham, out in public and in front of everybody, and of course the kid was screaming now, screaming screaming screaming screaming.

Everybody having their own version of Family Day.

Gina carried the ice cream cone to the water's edge.

Right there, she saw herself in the algaed water, walking upside down holding a raspberry ice cream cone, and, next to her own water-image, another water-image, the sun this time. Gina walked into the water, out to where the algae dispersed, staring first at her diminishing reflection and then at the sun. *It'd be interesting to go blind,* she thought, *people and seeing-eye dogs would take care of you and lead you through the rest of your life forever. You'd be on a leash. The dog would make all the big decisions.* Then she noticed that when she walked into the water her images were sucked into it. As the water got deeper, there was less of you above it, as if you had gone on an instant diet. Okay, now that her legs had disappeared, you didn't have to look at her legs, because they weren't there anymore. Well, they were underwater, but the water was so dirty she couldn't see them as well as she could see her reflection at the surface: of her waist, her head, her chest, the ice cream cone. She wished she were prettier, movie-pretty, but walking into the water was a kind of solution, watching your girl-image get all swallowed up, until there was no image left, just the water.

She held the ice cream cone above the water and then after another lick let it go as she went under.

Under the surface she held her breath as long as she could, and then she thought of Gordy Himmelman, and, sort of experimentally, she tried breathing in some water, just to see what it was like, and she choked. She felt herself panicking and going up to the surface but then she fought the panic when she imagined she *saw* somebody *like* Gordy Himmelman, though better-looking, more like her dad, under the water with her, holding her hand and telling her it was better down here, and all the problems were solved, so she tried to relax and breathe in a little more water. She registered thunderbolts of panic, then some peace, then panic. Then it was all right, and Family Day was finally over, and, because she wasn't a very good swimmer anyway, she began to sink to the bottom, though there *were* all those annoying voices. She would miss Wilbur, the guinea pig, but not much else, not even the boys who had tried to feel her up.

She drifted down and away.

Her father and the lifeguard had seen the cone of ice cream floating on the surface of the lake at the same time. They both rushed in, and Gina's dad reached her body first. He pulled her up, thrashed his way to the beach, where, without thinking, he gave his daughter the Heimlich maneuver. Water erupted out of her mouth. Gina's eyes opened, and her father laid her down on the sand, and she said, "Gordy?" but what she said was garbled by the water still coming out of her lungs into her mouth and out of her mouth into the sand. As she came around, her hair falling around her eyes, she seemed disarrayed somehow, but pleased by all the fuss, and then she smiled, because she had seen her father's face, smeary with love.

Fourteen

When she arrived back home, having survived her near-death experience, Gina was supposed to lie down, but she didn't want to be horizontalized. She couldn't see the point to it since she wasn't particularly tired and she certainly wasn't dead, either. Her throat hurt; that was about it. What she really wanted to do was to call a few people. She took her cell phone along with four cookies into her room, closed the door, and sat cross-legged on her bedspread with two of the cookies hidden beneath one knee and the other two cookies behind the other knee, and she wondered which of her friends she would call first to tell about her near-death. She was glad to see Wilbur again, scrabbling in his corner. He welcomed her back with a few quiet, loving little squeals.

She bit into the first cookie, leaving three and a half.

She decided to give her friend April the first call, but April wasn't at home—nobody was (and they didn't have an answering machine or voicemail over there, it was medieval)—so she tried Danni instead. Danni took it on the second ring. Danni did all the phone-answering at the Wiesiewski house. Danni was pretty and stuck-up like the rest of the Wiesiewskis, but she was a good listener when she had to be. When Danni asked Gina, "Whassup?" Gina told her that they'd been out at Copper Lake, and she'd been swimming, and—this was a secret, Danni absolutely could not tell anyone—she thought she saw this ghost-person under the water who looked exactly like Gordy Himmelman, and, no, she couldn't describe how it had happened, but it was like he had dragged her down under the water, and it was incredibly beautiful down there—it was *not* ugly—and she almost drowned, but her father or somebody had brought her back to life.

Gordy Himmelman? Danni asked. You're kidding. That freak? Besides, he's dead. Are you crazy? What are you saying?

No. Gina said that she was not kidding, swear to God, and not crazy. Did she *sound* crazy? No. This was weirder than being crazy. In fact, she said, it would be just exactly like Gordy Himmelman to be a ghost, because when he was alive, or semi-alive, or whatever it was he had been when he had been living, he had always wandered into places where he wasn't wanted, and it would therefore be like him now to show up here, there, and everywhere. She ate her cookie and bit into another one, which left two and a half. She touched her hair. It was still damp and probably dirty from the lake water. She would have to shampoo it soon.

It's like he's in charge of something real interesting, Gina said.

Danni asked Gina if she could tell anyone, and Gina said, well, no, not really, or: well, you can tell some people, but only as long as you get my permission first, and they have to promise not to tell. "I don't want *everybody* to know," Gina said. "It sounds too weird."

Danni said she understood perfectly.

Within four days Gina's telephone was ringing every half-hour from kids she knew who thought they had seen Gordy or someone like him: Ron Burr told Chrystal Chambers that he thought he had seen Gordy in the Elysian Fields Shopping Mall, walking as if he were battery-powered and under remote control from Mars, into one of the theaters at the multiplex, but when he followed him in, Gordy wasn't there. He had just vanished like shit in a shitstorm. Ron said he was a loser. Losers disappear on you, but now that he was dead maybe he wasn't such a total loser after all. Death could revise you. The day after that, April, Gina's friend April Cumming, claimed that she had seen Gordy Himmelman outside her window, looking in, like some creep stalker jackoff; then ugly little Georgette Novak, who wanted to be popular and who worked at McDonald's because people claimed that her parents wouldn't give her an allowance for clothes, said that she had served Gordy Himmelman a Coke and fries, and that he looked verifiably dead, which at least was convincing, and he paid her with money that totally disappeared after she put it into the cash drawer. He had paid her with bogey money. Rona Elliott said she had seen him out in the park, where she had been walking her dog, Buster, who barked hysterically at him. Gordy stood on the other side of the park, waving at her, as if he were signaling. She turned away, and when she turned back, he was gone.

Other reports put Gordy in a tree, way up where you couldn't reach him, Gordy moving around in the house at night, Gordy's image appearing suddenly on the computer screen, Gordy calling in the middle of the night and asking for the time, Gordy appearing on a three-A.M. infomercial—in the background in a kitchen, staring at the camera, while in the foreground they were selling a kitchen gadget.

They said he looked like himself. They said he was everywhere.

Danni told Gina that April had said that all these sightings were, like, mass hysteria, and that the Justice Department was looking into it, because it might be the work of terrorists. You had to be on a twenty-four-hour alert.

And it would have died down, too, Gina thought, if one of the nicest boys in her class, Sam Cole, who was sweet and a good athlete and really good-looking—he wasn't like most of the other boys, and the boys knew it, and because he was both tough and goodhearted, nobody ever said anything bad about him—hadn't been riding home from a dentist's appointment on his bicycle and hadn't been hit by a newspaper truck backing down a driveway. Because, after that, all the kids in Five Oaks who were even close to Sam's age knew that Gordy Himmelman had pushed him into the path of that truck. They didn't exactly tell their parents, but they told each other, and that was how they knew.

This is how it was: there were terrorists for their parents, and there was Gordy Himmelman for them.

Fifteen

The woman in front of Patsy at the VitaDrug prescription counter had been taking antipsychotics for so long that she had apparently lost control of her tongue. Patsy didn't even pretend to look away. While the woman waited for her credit-card number to go through, her tongue emerged from her mouth like a snake from its nest, angled left and right experimentally as if testing the air for bugs or oxygen density, then retreated back into her mouth before emerging again, this time staying out as it continued its ceaseless explorations. Her purchases were piled on the counter in a haphazard fashion. Along with the drugs nestled in their bar-coded, stapled bags with the "Ask the Pharmacist" cartoon on the front, showing a bald-headed man with a small-town smiley face (none of the pharmacists here looked like that: they were all East Indian), the woman had bought three cylindrical containers of potato chips, four cans of tuna, and two six-packs of diet cola. She made Patsy think of a lizard-lady preparing for a party with the other lizard-ladies, all of them sitting outside on the terrace, passing the tin cans from lap to lap, their tongues wagging, the fat of their ankles spilling out over the tops of their shoes.

All through October, when she was alone, or running errands after work like this, after having picked up Emmy from day care, Patsy somehow found herself at the end of her goodwill. This falling-away from sympathetic feelings for the helpless was new for her. Random compassion without any outlet now struck her as a Saul-like indulgence. Against strangers, she could feel her heart slowly hardening, developing a shellac. Her charity was failing her. If any woman deserved her pity, this woman did. But her pity seemed unavailable to her. Everything she had was directed toward her children these days: this one, and the one to come. And Saul, too, of course.

After picking up her prescription for Dorylaeum, a vitamin supplement and sleep aid for pregnant women whose occasional side effect was that it made time speed up, Patsy wheeled Emmy in her stroller down the aisles past the magazine rack, where two middle school girls were talking quietly to each other as they flipped through the new issue of *Gloor*. They appeared to be dressed for Halloween, and it was now late October, and their white hair, kohl-darkened eyes, bleached skin, and black raggedy clothes accessorized with pins displaying cryptic symbols gave them the aspect of ghosts. When Patsy passed them, they gazed at her with the fixedness of the dead. They were part of the growing number of middle schoolers and high school kids who were affecting the gothic mortuary look. In the space of several weeks, a small but significant cult of Gordy Himmelman had surfaced, and this style, Patsy had heard, was meant either to ward him off or to evoke him. They called themselves Himmels. All over town, out of the corner of your eye, you could see these neo-goths, these Himmels, with their staring-fish expressions. Saul and Patsy's paperboy, Darryl Anderson, was now a part-time Himmel. He was a nice kid and hadn't quite mastered the doom-laden frown yet. Some of the others talked in a kind of code, the way they imagined that the dead might.

The school superintendent, Floyd Vermilya, had sent home a notice to parents encouraging them to celebrate life, not death, at the level of family. He had threatened suspensions. Students who ghouled their way into school with Himmel-haircuts, Himmel-overcoats, or even Himmel-like expressions on their faces could just ghoul their way out again until they were ready to dress and act like normal young people. Unfortunately, the new restrictions were hard to enforce. Himmelism had spread to both of Five Oaks's high schools—though who would know? So many of those kids acted and dressed like that anyway. An underground goth cell had established itself there some time ago. Besides, adolescents could disguise themselves as ordinary, decent American kids and then, when school was out, turn into Himmels in the privacy of their homes. At that age, they all wore masks anyway. Masking was the pride of adolescence. Himmel-speak, the language of the dead that the Himmels had fabricated, was forbidden in the classroom or the athletic field, though none of the athletes were Himmels anyway. *Probably.* You could never tell. There was an unsubstantiated rumor of a Himmel sleeper-cell on the football team, the second-stringers and bench-warmers, though it strained credulity: What would a would-be dead football player *say*? And to whom? Himmel-athletes didn't bleach their hair, but many of them had the trademark blank look. And their cheers lacked conviction. The school guidance counselor had suggested to parents at the latest PTA meeting that they motivate their kids to participate in more upbeat sports activities. Playing a musical instrument, he said, might also overcome the recent community-wide tendency to morbid display.

Vermilya had told Saul, and Saul had told Patsy, that he feared national attention to this phenomenon. If that happened, if the networks showed up, there'd be no stopping it. He feared Himmel websites, Himmel chat rooms, docudramas on Himmelism . . .

Something has gone wrong with our children, he had told Saul. *Something is spreading, and I don't even know what it is.*

The door flipped open electronically, and Patsy walked out onto the sidewalk. She crossed the street into Governor John Engler Park, a square city block decorated with a few surviving petunias planted in an uneven row on the south border. To the north was a stage and a bandstand. Skateboarders leapt up and down the benches and roared across the proscenium. The air felt autumnal and cool. In the center of the park stood an eight-foot-high statue of the former governor, holding his hand out in welcome. On his face was a smile contaminated with a dubious affability. This statue was now permanently blocked off from the sun by the WaldChem building, under construction across the street, a bright yellow steel crane perched on the topmost beam, and by the AddiData building to the west, whose windows had the rectangular shape of the holes in IBM punch cards. The WaldChem building would be the highest structure in Five Oaks. Although the Chamber of Commerce had lobbied for its construction with the zoning board, both the mayor and the City Council had complained mildly about the architecture, which was in a downsized Black Rock style. It was considered by many to be dour and not suitable for the Midwest. It did not glorify the heartland.

In the park Patsy took Emmy out of the stroller and bounced her on her lap. She was being fussy today. "Down me," Emmy said. Patsy let her down. Emmy walked experimentally around the bench, singing her toothpaste song. With a mild shock, Patsy saw Anne McPhee sitting on the park bench opposite her, and Anne's son, Matt, running back and forth before her, as if he were searching for some interesting trouble to get into but hadn't yet found it. Anne was visibly pregnant and wore a besieged expression: she was still a beautiful young woman, Patsy thought, with great features that her pregnancy had not diminished, but she seemed distracted and solitary. Her blouse was stained with apple juice. She looked *used*. She had a rash on her wrist that she scratched absentmindedly. Something about her suggested helplessness and excessive brooding. She waved at Patsy without enthusiasm.

Five Oaks might boast of the new WaldChem building, but it was still a city where you kept running into the same people. You would have to move at least as far away as the Caspian Sea to avoid them.

Patsy had wanted to be Anne's friend ever since she and Saul had shown up, muddy and in shock, at the McPhees' door after their car turned over following the party at Mad Dog's, but the friendship couldn't last.

The day had arrived some months back when the McPhees announced themselves at Patsy's office at the bank, presenting their case for a home loan. Patsy couldn't tell if they had concocted a plan to trade on what they assumed to be her friendship. Maybe so. Emory had been holding Matt's hand, and the young father wore his baseball cap with the visor in back. He had just shaved, and he gave off a first-date odor of drugstore cologne. Very proudly, speaking in married-couple relays, first the husband, then the wife, they announced that they wanted to buy a house in a new development, Maple Meadows. They were tired of paying rent for their current house, they said. They wanted this as a *real* investment; it was time to build a *future*. They recited these sentences as if they had rehearsed them, fanfare, emphases, and all. But Patsy, as one of the bank's loan officers, had to refuse the loan almost on the spot. They had virtually nothing in savings or collateral, and Emory's employment as a housepainter was sporadic. He was a high school dropout. Their credit rating was dismal. When Patsy had told Anne and Emory the bad news, Anne cried. She began her sobbing slowly, then really worked up a storm of tears. It went on and on.

You tried to create a community, but money always got in the way, and finally lines were drawn. Friendship ended at the bank's front door, at least for working people.

Like some lovers who get romantically entangled young, in high school, both the McPhees, Emory and Anne, had an intense, greedy physicality. They always reminded Patsy of two healthy animals who had mated, almost without thinking. Their stories were always stories about the body; they never got past it.

Patsy took Emmy's hand and walked over to where Anne McPhee was sitting in the park. North of the women, on the block bordering the park in which they sat, the yellow construction crane turned slowly, lifting a steel beam. A man, small in the distance, standing on another beam and wearing a hardhat appeared to be watching them. He appeared to wave.

"Some of those construction workers get rich, if they live long enough," Anne said. She checked Patsy out, then smiled halfheartedly. "I see we both got ourselves knocked up again." There was a brief pause. "Congratulations."

"I didn't think I was showing that much yet," Patsy said.

"You aren't. Not in front," Anne pointed. "Only if a person is looking. A mom would know. It's the way you're walking."

"Do you mind if I sit down?" Patsy asked. She would be the soul of politeness.

"Go ahead." Anne patted the bench. "Please."

"Thanks, Anne." She sat down.

"Want a cookie?" Anne pulled an Oreo out of her purse. Matt grabbed it out of her hand before curling up at her feet. She smiled indulgently at her son. "Public space. It's free to everybody. Hey, I see Emmy's getting real big." Anne smiled at Mary Esther, who was folding herself for protection against strangers into her mother's lap.

"Matt, too. Good-looking boy." He was, of course. He looked like a three-year-old James Dean, a little pint-sized greaser heartthrob. His mouth was smeared with cookie crumbs, but he was beautiful anyway. "Where's Saska?"

"Saska? She's home with Emory. Yeah, well." Over to their right, the skateboarders made their racket, and when one of them fell, the others yelled encouragement. "I got another one coming. My *third*. Another hell on wheels, I guess."

"Boy?" Patsy asked.

"Yeah. I think so."

"When'd you find out?"

"What do you mean?"

"Well, the ultrasound . . . the amnio?"

"Oh, I haven't had any of that. I'm just guessing. You?"

"This one's a boy. For sure. I suppose I always knew it, but I did have my doctor do an ultrasound, and she asked me if I wanted the big news, and I said I did, and she said, 'It's a boy,' so that's how I know."

"Our medical insurance ran out," Anne McPhee said. "No ultrasound for me."

In front of them, a squirrel scurried up the pedestal of the governor's statue, stopped, then scurried down again. A whistle blew near the construction site's trailer. Quitting time. The construction worker seemed to wave at them again, two pregnant women sitting in the park.

"I'm sorry," Patsy said. The man on the steel beam continued to watch her.

"Oh, you don't have to be sorry for us. It's not your fault. And in case you're wondering, I've forgotten all about that business with the home loan."

"Really, Anne, it wasn't personal. My apologies."

"No need to be so sorry so much," Anne McPhee said, mirthlessly laughing. "Besides, it's not your fault, not giving us that loan. You work for a bank. We went to the other banks. Same thing. Besides, it's Emory. It's who Emory is, as a provider. Years ago we had the red-hots for each other and we got married and I got knocked up, and now here I am, sitting on this park bench with you." She shot Patsy a huge disarming smile. She had a quality of dishonest sincerity. "We kissed ourselves right out of school into having a family before we had prospects. Same old story. Story of the ages. Story of the sower and the seedbed. We couldn't help ourselves."

"You get married, you struggle for a while," Patsy sighed, scratching at her own arm in sympathy.

"It's different for you," Anne said. "You and Saul have two incomes. You at the bank, him at the school. No offense, Patsy. Emory and me, we had so much love so fast it just kept us ignorant about other things. The whole rest of the world."

Patsy nodded. This conversation was like an old cat that wouldn't get up from the carpet, that wouldn't move anywhere at all. Anne McPhee scratched and scratched and scratched at her rash. Finally Patsy said, struggling against the silence, "How *is* Emory?"

"Oh, he's okay. He's thinking of getting his equivalency, then going to the Community College, get a degree in commercial art. We're sort of fine. We're still happy, you could say. No problem with each other. We worry about money, though." She touched Patsy on the knee. "*All the time.* Which is more your department. You still ever ride that motorcycle you bought—what, two years ago?"

"No," Patsy said. "Not for months and months. Not since I became a mom. It's getting dusty in the garage."

There was a long pondering silence. The silence was about being able to buy a motorcycle that you then didn't use. It was about that luxury. "Sometimes I wonder," Anne said.

"Wonder about what?"

"How long it'll last."

"What?"

Anne said nothing. She wasn't talking about the motorcycle anymore.

Her voice now came out very quietly and slowly. "How long it can last without enough money."

"Depends, doesn't it, how strong it is?" Patsy asked.

"I don't think so. It's strange how I loved him without exactly wanting to. Because of him, I couldn't help myself back then, all that time when I didn't have a clue about anything. Sometimes I think he resents me. You ever think that the sex thing is like a trap, that it cages you? Well, considering the way it happened," she laughed, "you can't say we didn't have the grand passions. If love was dollars, we'd be millionaires, and us not even voting age yet. Before I got pregnant again, he was still lovin' me up so often and so strong I couldn't hardly sit down in the morning. We'd do it whenever Matt and Saska were sleeping. Pardon my language. Perpetual honeymoon, is what it is," she sighed. "I'm the envy of the county. How's that for weird? And me a Christian, too. Doesn't add up."

"Married life," Patsy said. "No one can tell you anything about it."

"That's for sure. Listen. I've gotta go." Anne stood, and her son raced in circles around her like a tiny courtier. She was like a princess rising, Venus out of the half-shell, a pregnant Persephone with apple juice stains. Patsy gaped at her. No wonder Emory had carried her off into the underworld of marriage and kept her there. "You and Saul, you sure are the center of attention right now, all these Himmel kids sprouting up everywhere."

"Oh," Patsy said. "That's not about us." The sun was setting with unexpected speed. Night was racing toward them on its chopper.

"Not what I heard. You should talk to that Brenda Bagley, Patsy. This thing'll keep growing if you don't do something. Somebody'll come along and do some real harm to Saul. I mean it. That kid, that Gordy, he must've loved Saul. Or you. Or something. I think it was Saul he loved, though. That's my theory. All his hatred, that was just love in disguise. I should know. But the other parents, they see this thing growing after Sam Cole got hit by that truck, and they think that you people are responsible. You know how people talk. You know what they say."

"Responsible? Wait a minute. What do they say?"

"Come on, Matt," Anne McPhee called out. "Hey, what's your baby boy's name gonna be?"

"Theo," Patsy said. "What do they say, Anne? Tell me."

"They say you're cursed. Outcasts of God. Now *that's* small-minded. No kidding, Patsy, I'd go talk to Brenda Bagley if I were you. You got some unfinished business over there."

Driving to Brenda Bagley's house, Patsy had the disagreeable sensation that Gordy Himmelman was sitting in the backseat, ruminating over his life and the stray impulse that had ended it—just there, slumped beside Emmy, making a minor ectoplasmic pest of himself, unseatbelted, more alive now that he was dead than he had been when he happened to be living. That was his way, his particular posthumous style. She thought she smelled for a fraction of a second the characteristic Gordy scent of pickles and wet dog. Okay, so he was back there. He *was* like a dog: he always enjoyed riding in cars, hanging around on the front lawn, waiting for a project.

Waiting for a head-pat. As a ghost he was probably harmless. Funny: weeks and weeks ago, after she and Saul had made love, Saul had abruptly said that he wanted to have a dog, but Patsy wasn't going to get one, not with Emmy around and a new baby coming. Maybe having Gordy would satisfy Saul. Maybe not.

Coming to an unfamiliar street corner, she recognized that she was lost. Because of the city's loose zoning laws, low property taxes, and the we-won't-enforce-anything environmental understandings, Five Oaks's industrial area had grown rapidly on the south side of the city in the early 1980s, and then, with the move to globalization, had declined just as rapidly. The streets were laid out in rosette and slipknot patterns. Boom and bust cycles happened so fast in the city these days that factories were closed months after they had opened; only the chemical plants were still holding their own down by the river, still profitable, still toxic. Now as Patsy tried to figure out where she was, she spotted the Hawkeye plant for school-bus frames to her right—the frames piled like steel skeletal remains near a loading dock. New as it was, the plant was about to close and move to Mexico. Or Honduras. Some damn place where they would work for ten cents an hour. Negotiations were still continuing. The clos-

ing of the factory had been major news in the papers, and as a bank officer, Patsy had to keep up with the latest statistics concerning the city's
economic infrastructure and indebtedness. Workers were losing their
pensions and their savings and were being advised to move to the South-
west. The whole neighborhood had a clammy out-of-work dinge to it.
Sooty warehouses that had gone from youth to old age without anything
in between were located here, next to parking lots and solitary clapboard-
exterior bars named The Wooden Keg and The Shipwreck, with their
quietly slumped clientele visible through the front windows.

The Chevy advanced under a sequence of darkened streetlights, and
Patsy found herself in a blind alley. As she backed up and turned around,
her headlights caught sight of three kids out on the sidewalk, three Himmel middle schoolers fooling around in the early dusk: bleached skin,
bleached faces. Just like albinos, Patsy thought, putting the car into drive
and accelerating. She shouldn't have brought Emmy along on this
errand, she thought, but after all, it was an emergency.

The street ahead of her extended and contracted in a kind of daze,
prolonging itself and then foreshortening in a visual pattern associated
with the vertigo that accompanies anxiety, but then, maybe what she was
seeing and feeling was just a side effect of the Dorylaeum she was taking,
those strange red-and-blue pills that came accompanied with the long
sheet of warnings. The car accelerated into a pool of buttery light.

She drove past a parked car with a cracked windshield and a wire
coat-hanger in place of the radio antenna. On the car's bumper was a
small sticker whose words had been printed with purple ink:

I'm so gothic
I'm already dead.

After she had found her way back to Strewwelpeter Street, she made
quick progress to Brenda Bagley's manufactured house. Saul had taken
her past here twice during one of his obsessive weeks following Gordy's
death, and the house had a strange unmistakable individualized dreari-
ness, easy to locate. You could spot it in a crowd of manufactured homes.

Most of them were cheerful and simple, but an air of indescribable gloom hung over Brenda Bagley's. It appeared to have been constructed out of stale, brittle candy left over from an unsuccessful birthday party: its exterior white vinyl siding looked like hardened cake frosting decorated with tiny highlighted splotches of chocolate mud. Moths threw themselves toward the exterior door light and then fell, burned and wounded, to the pavement. At the same time, the two front windows, facing the street, with their half-lowered windowshades, had the momentary appearance of hooded eyes examining her as she approached them. It was like the House of Usher in a trailer park.

She drew Emmy out of her child seat in the back, leaving Gordy Himmelman's spirit-remains still there—if he wanted to follow her in, he would, but she doubted it—and, a few moments later, with her daughter in her arms, Patsy rang the bell of Brenda Bagley's house. From inside she heard the happy cries of a singing television commercial. The doorbell tolled out in three tones, and its song was followed by a rumpus-like clatter of dishes and silverware. The door opened, and Brenda Bagley peered out through the gap.

"Brenda," Patsy said. "It's me. Patricia Bernstein. Patsy. You know, Saul's wife."

"Sure," Brenda muttered, exhaling cigarette smoke as she nodded. Her florid face examined Patsy and Mary Esther. Brenda's eyes were still red-rimmed. "Of course. What brings you here, Patsy?"

"May I come in for a minute? I have to talk to you. It'll only take a second. I just couldn't do it over the phone."

"Yeah, I guess so," Brenda Bagley said. "But it's kind of a mess in here. So it's not a good time for visiting impromptu like you're doing. Well, come in anyway."

She opened the door, and Patsy followed her, carrying Emmy inside her left arm. Her daughter seemed to be getting heavier by the minute and reactively cried out with grief or shock, once she was inside, from the effect of the stale cigarette smoke and the squalor. On the other side of the living area, a gigantic television set facing the doorway enjoyed a regal presence, except that a dinner plate with crusted food rested on its uppermost flat surface, reducing its dignity. The TV had a screen that was too large for the home's interior, and its volume had been set so high that it was hard to hear or even to see anything else in proximity to it. The chairs and side tables and lamps appeared to be dwarfed by the huge electronic apparatus. Patsy wondered how they had managed to get the TV in here. Its size seemed so gargantuan that it could not have been squeezed through the doorway—the enormous television set in the tiny living room had the visual effect of a clipper ship assembled piece by piece inside a glass bottle. Patsy had the momentary feeling that the smoky room was airless, or the air so thoroughly consumed that it would not sustain life. The television set had used up most of the oxygen, and the remaining air had acquired a blue smoky tint from Brenda Bagley's cigarettes. It was positively industrial. Bunched-up pieces of facial tissue littered the floor. Had the woman been crying, alone, in the evenings, with the TV set on, thinking of Gordy Himmelman?

Just to the left of the door was a sofa on whose cushion a white cat slept nestled against a plain plastic box.

"I'll turn that off," Brenda Bagley said, reaching for the remote. She pressed a button, and the screen at once went dark with an angry static crackling, as if the beast had been told to start hibernating or had been hit with a stun gun. "I can tell what you're thinking—you think it's a big TV. That's what everyone thinks. And you're right. It *is* big. I won it at the State Fair, is why."

"You won it?"

"I guessed at the number of marbles in a jar. They had this little booth for an appliance store, and I've always been good at guessing things like that ever since I was a girl. I've won staplers and telephones. This time, the prize was *that* thing. They couldn't downscale it, they said. That was the one they had to give away because they advertised that particular model. They had to take the door frame off my house to get it in here." She seemed to lose her train of thought. "I should've traded it for a smaller one. It's a mess in here," she said, glancing up in a vague manner. What appeared to be coffee stains dotted the ceiling tile. Perhaps the coffee had spilled upward. Perhaps the laws of gravity did not operate successfully here.

"It isn't a mess in here at all," Patsy said evasively, to be polite. She looked toward the television set and saw herself reflected in its dark, blank, sleeping screen.

"Nice of you to say," Brenda noted. "Please sit down, won't you? You must be tired out carrying that little one around."

Patsy lowered herself and the still-crying Emmy onto the sofa on the opposite side from the white cat and the box. The cat, annoyed by the child's noise, jumped off and away toward the kitchen. Emmy needed a diaper change and was being fussy. Patsy plugged her mouth with a pacifier.

Patsy could feel the words she wished to say making their way up her throat, but they seemed to stop before they could quite get out. While she waited, she studied a picture on the wall near the doorway to the kitchen where the cat had retreated, and she bounced Emmy in her lap. The photograph was a studio portrait of some man and Gordy: sitting in the man's lap, Gordy was much younger, just a toddler in the picture, not that much older than Emmy was now, and he smiled a toothy, dimwitted smile. Emmy continued to fuss and to reach for Patsy's breast, but Patsy had stopped breastfeeding and, in any case, wouldn't have opened her bra to Emmy's mouth in front of Brenda Bagley if the world had depended on it. Some free-floating malice in this room wouldn't permit that physical openness, some starveling bitterness that permeated the walls and the air.

"Brenda," Patsy said. "I just talked to somebody I know. *Knew.* Well, it doesn't matter when I knew her. She said that people—you know, parents—are starting to blame Saul and me for Gordy's death, and they're blaming us for Sam Cole's death, too, and now this Himmel craze that the middle schoolers have taken up."

"Oh, yeah. Everybody's trying to look like Gordy. Isn't that something? He's a star."

"That's right. And she said I should talk to you."

"Why?"

"She said people are blaming us. Saul and me."

"Oh, are they? For what?"

"I don't know. That's the thing. For Gordy? For Sam? Why would they blame us?"

"You're asking me? What would I have to do with it?'"

"Well," Patsy said, "she *said* I should ask you. She said we had unfinished business with you. She said I should come here right away."

"I just go to work, and then I come home, Patsy. I'm a waitress, you know, at the Fleetwood. It's not like I *circulate*."

"I know."

"All I do is sometimes talk to the customers. Look at him over there," Brenda Bagley said, aiming her face at the photograph. "There he is, Gordy, with his dad. Only picture the two of them ever took together."

"It must have been hard, trying to be his mother and dad, just you alone with him here."

"Yeah, well," Brenda Bagley said.

"What was his name?" Patsy asked. "The father?"

"Rufus. Rufus Himmelman. I thought you knew. People called him Rowdy for a while. Then they called him Ray. He had aliases. Names didn't stick to him. Ray, Rick, Rob—he went through a lot of the R names. He could have been anything, I guess." She waited. "But what he really was, was a con," she said quickly. "He needed different names in his lines of work."

"How come you took over the care of Gordy?" Patsy asked.

"It's a long story. With the mother dead in that fire, somebody had to do it."

"It doesn't make sense," Patsy said suddenly. "His father leaving and not coming back or asking about him. Disappearing like that. Then you, being Gordy's guardian."

"Oh, you think it doesn't make sense?" Brenda Bagley stubbed out her cigarette in the ashtray and promptly lit another one. She gave Patsy a broad and very angry smile. Patsy waited for the Big Speech that usually follows the angry smile in the movies. But often there is no Big Speech and no explanation, just the angry smile, which then subsides as the cigarette rises to the mouth, and smoke is inhaled and exhaled. Not everyone had the resources of instant articulation. Once again, Patsy saw herself and her daughter and Brenda Bagley reflected on the blank TV screen, though they didn't look like people on TV but like themselves: a toddler needing a diaper change, a frazzled woman with a cigarette, and an anxious and pregnant young mother. Then Brenda Bagley said, "Men leave their children all the time for parts unknown, you know, and they don't come back for years, *if* they come back. Well, I don't care. Maybe it don't make any sense, but I took over the boy's raising anyway. Nobody and nothing was offering to marry *me*. Didn't have a boyfriend back then, or now either, and no children of my own to attend to, so I thought: he's the only one I'll ever get. Gordy will be mine. You see this face?"

She meant her own. Of course Patsy saw it. It was right in front of her, staring at her like a peeled tangerine with eyes. She nodded.

"I know what you're thinking. You're thinking: With a face like that, no man would marry her. You know, nobody in my life ever called me 'pretty.' That's a word I only heard about. I heard it applied to the other girls and then to the women I knew, but I sure never heard it applied to me. Bad skin all my life, and nothing the doctors could do. *Dermatologists!* Everybody said, 'Oh, Brenda, she's so polite and kindly,' and then they'd go off behind my back and say that my face looked like the craters of the moon. Soon as somebody's down, they start kicking at her just for the fun of it. And now here you come around, asking this and that, as if you got the right."

Patsy sat silent while Emmy continued to squirm, arching her back. She was crying quietly. Gathering her wits, Patsy said, "That wasn't what I wanted to inquire about. It was all these children, trying to look like Gordy. And the blame for what happened to Sam Cole."

"What do you think I have to do with them?" Brenda asked. "You think I'm giving them orders? You can't give a child orders. Well, you can, but it's a joke."

"No. It's just . . . have you been saying things about Saul and me? Anne McPhee said we were outcasts of God."

"Are you? Didn't know that God cared that much. Well, that's just *her* opinion. I don't know as I've said that."

"People listen to you."

"People certainly *don't* listen to me."

"Oh, I'm sure they do."

"They never have. You think I have any influence with anybody? Where'd you get that idea?"

"Anne McPhee," Patsy repeated.

"What does she know about outcasts of God?"

"I don't know what she knows," Patsy said, feeling as if her time was up.

"I'm the expert on outcasts of God," Brenda Bagley said huffily, and with an odd touch of snobbery. "I've got everyone beat on that score."

"Would you do me a favor, then?" Patsy asked. "Would you please tell people that Saul and I had nothing to do with Gordy's death? We didn't do it, we didn't influence it, we're sorry it happened, we're miserable about it—can you say that, please, if people start asking?" She did not mention that Gordy's ghost was, at this very moment, sitting in the car, waiting. The time was not right for a revelation of that sort.

"I guess I could say that if you want me to," Brenda Bagley muttered, as if she was thinking about something else. "If anyone cares to know. I might mention it. But I want you to come see something first."

"What?"

"Gordy's bedroom." She stood up without warning, then clumped down the narrow hallway in the opposite direction from the kitchen. After a pause, she made a windmilling motion for Patsy to follow her. Patsy picked up Mary Esther, who seemed to be watching something floating invisibly in the air in front of her, and carried her into Gordy's bedroom.

The room smelled of boy-mildew and had one overhead light. On the north wall Gordy had cut out and pasted up, with adhesive tape, magazine photos of soldiers in camouflage clothing, holding their guns. They were walking through jungles. They were crawling through rice paddies and marshes. They had determined and brave killer expressions on their faces. In other pictures they were firing their guns or shouting the war shout as they plunged into battle. Movie stars dressed as soldiers were among them. It was standard stuff. So were the cartoons of superheroes cut out and pasted next to them. Near these pictures was a small poster of Wolverine, the superhero, the X-man, with his razor fingers, and another one of the same guy, in rage-against-the-world mode, beast mode. Patsy wondered why, if Gordy couldn't read, he had all these comic-book figures pasted onto his bedroom wall.

"He loved Wolverine," Brenda Bagley said.

Patsy felt herself indeliberately startle. In the midst of all this warfare and welter was a photo of Mary Esther as a small baby, the one with her leaning against the back of the sofa, her stuffed gnome in her lap. It was the picture that Saul had handed out in class. She rested there, an illustration of a baby, among the soldiers and superheroes and archvillains.

Patsy was finding it difficult to breathe.

"People said he couldn't read," Brenda Bagley was saying, "but he sat in here with those comic books of his, and the other magazines, X-men and so on, and I sure thought he was doing something, and if it wasn't reading, I don't know what it was."

Also on the wall above the headboard was a picture of a beehive. Good Christ, the sadness of things.

"He was a strange boy," Brenda Bagley said.

Patsy changed Mary Esther's diaper in the car, in the front seat, throwing the old diaper into a baggie and tying it closed. Then she put her daughter into the child seat in the back, and after starting the car, she turned on the radio and headed home. Because the radio was broken, no sounds came out of it.

How was it? You weren't in there for very long.

Well, Patsy thought, under her breath, you know how it was, you have your nerve, *you* lived there.

I was just kinda wondering what you thought of it.

It bothered me, Patsy thought. I couldn't breathe in there, the big TV and the cigarette smoke and everything.

I couldn't breathe in there, either. How'd you like the walls? Didja like the pictures I put up?

231

They were okay. You must've read a lot of comic books. But I was surprised: no computers. No computer games. I guess your aunt could never afford one. Gordy, why *did* you kill yourself with that gun? In *our* yard? While we were looking? Would you just please explain that to me? I really, really need to know the answers to those questions. If you're going to hang around with us, you could at least do me the favor of telling me why you did all that. To yourself. And to us.

But no new words descended into her brain, emerging from the backseat, where it was now very quiet, with Mary Esther sleeping. The car advanced through pool after pool of buttery light cast from the lamp posts, and Patsy took a route circling the downtown area. She felt a vague movement in her uterus and also noticed that she was feeling distinct emotions, as if they were hands slipping out of the gloves that usually held them. She passed by a green sign on the outskirts announcing Five Oaks as a sister city of Nikone, Japan, and of Tübingen, Germany. But those cities were ancient and historically identifiable, and this one had almost no history at all and very few identifying marks. It was on the map, but in no other respect was it on the map. Patsy tightened her hold on the steering wheel. The local pride in anonymity ate away at everything. It devoured lives and turned the inhabitants into ghosts both before and then after their deaths. Resignation was the great local spiritual specialty, resignation and a fleeting recklessness, a feverishly hypnotic and prideful death-in-life. All the Himmel kids were acute cultural critics, she decided. They had a point. If the city of Five Oaks had any true siblings, they wouldn't have names like Rheims or Pisa. They would be the close relatives with names like Terre Haute or Duluth or Flint or Grand Forks or Davenport or Burlington or Scranton or Kenosha—cities you had heard of but couldn't quite picture, cities that called nothing in particular to mind except for an eagerness to be larger and more prosperous than they were, and an all-consuming late-stage boosterism that was mostly insecurity and worry masked by bluster. The wolves were never far from the door in cities like these, and sometimes the wolves got in. The churches tried, with varying success, to keep people calm when the members of the congregation felt like screaming. Five Oaks would always be the sort of place you had to apologize for whenever visitors from out of town—from larger towns, real cities—arrived at the airport on their little turboprop commuter planes, shaken up and curious about what had brought them there.

Or else: you lived here for years and you found you liked it, and you stopped apologizing, and visitors noticed that, too.

They had to get out before they were destroyed. She would not let her son be born in a place like this. Plans were being hatched to turn Saul into a scapegoat. She would get Theo and Emmy out of here before desperation took hold of them, desperation and alligator malice, meanness and the liquefaction of the soul.

Sooner or later, wandering is done.

When she arrived at the house, she carried the sleeping Emmy over one shoulder and the diaper-bag over the other into the foyer. She noticed a black BMW parked in front. What was it doing here? Her arms and shoulders were getting muscular and her biceps in particular were swelling from the effort of carrying Emmy and the stroller around. The minute she came inside, she said, "Saul! The scapegoating has started! We have to move! We have to move out of this place!" She smiled at herself as she prepared herself to sing—what was it?—the Animals, a tragically hip band before it was tragically hip to be tragically hip, but softly, so as not to wake Emmy. *"We gotta get out of this place! If it's the last thing we ever do!"*

From the kitchen came Saul, accompanied by the most handsome man she had ever seen in real life, Saul's brother, Howie, who gave Patsy a raised-eyebrow greeting and an all-purpose wave that was more a shrug than a genuine wave. Being beautiful, he could be a minimalist in his gestures. Big hugs were too much trouble, too much strain on the equipment, and were uncool, besides, especially with a lady carrying a toddler. A surprise visit! Well, that was Howie's style, to appear without an invitation and to leave at about the time you had become used to him and felt a bit of warmth toward him. You fell for him, and he'd be out of there. He had had a ban on intimacy—well, maybe he had changed. But this was his way of enforcing the ban, these surprises, as if he lived across town and could drop in for coffee now and then.

Howie was wearing a perfectly tailored shirt and trousers, rather colorless, so that he appeared to mimic the monotextured heroes in 1940s films—the young John Garfield, only better-looking in the post-humanist style. He had left his shoes at the door, and for some reason Patsy noticed the high arch of his foot inside the sock.

The brothers walked together in a similar style of locomotion, and though Howie was the handsome one with jaw-dropping good looks, Saul was the more lovable, the man with whom you'd want to spend your life. For Howie's beauty you would pay the price of a lifetime of sorrow, and all the varieties of rage. Eventually you would have to go to church to get rid of him.

"Oh, Howie," she said, and kissed him. "So that was *your* BMW. What a nice surprise. Sorry you caught me singing."

"Patsy." He kissed her back. Cool professional lips. A slight, low-voltage tingling. "Love, you can sing anytime."

Sixteen

Saul had been working at his desk, correcting student assignments and watching the sky for signs of the four horsemen of the apocalypse when a black BMW pulled into the driveway. Its headlights went dark; the smooth, muffled engine quieted. Saul did not move, and the driver did not get out of the car. Observing the bug-spattered headlights and grille, and the stationary, immobilized driver, half-hidden behind the tinted windows in the gathering dusk, Saul made a mental checklist:

- The unannounced visitor was certainly Howie, his brother. In one of his previous phone calls, Howie had proudly mentioned his black BMW, which he called "The Avenger." No one around here had a car like that, and certainly not with (Saul now noticed) California plates.
- Howie hadn't called ahead, nor had he *in any way* intimated that he would be dropping in. He had always favored surprise visits. For this one, he would have had to drive about 1,700 miles, give or take a few hundred here or there, from Palo Alto to Five Oaks. Such a trip was a feat of determination and willpower in the service of a strange, perhaps insanely prolonged, spontaneity. The

distance and the effort involved in crossing it did not mean that Howie's stay would be a lengthy one. He might be gone by tomorrow afternoon.

- He would, no doubt, surprise in other ways as well. Howie always had multiple astonishments ready for whatever audience he could command. He liked lifting people up and then keeping them off balance, using his charm as a weapon, part of his latter-day Gatsbyish acrobat approach to things.
- How had he found Saul and Patsy's new residence? He just had. Bystanders tended to give information willingly, greedily, to Howie. The charm, the charisma, did the trick every time.
- First Gordy Himmelman's death this past summer, and now this.
- No, that was wrong: he loved his brother.
- Nevertheless.
- Saul still wasn't moving. He wouldn't budge. No budging, not a bit of it. He wasn't going to move until Howie did. As the guest, Howie was supposed to get out of the car and ring the doorbell before the noises of greeting fell on him like so much rain.

They hadn't said a word to each other, and already they had a standoff. Because Halloween was three nights away, Saul half-expected Howie to remove himself from the BMW dressed in a costume—that of an ordinary man, a role he had never successfully played. But no: he probably wouldn't get out of his trophy car until Saul came running downstairs, came charging out the front door, his arms wide, his face joyously radiant with the startled welcome, the glee, the sheer human *pleasure* of being in his brother's company again after so long an absence, now that Howie had deigned to visit without warning.

Maybe he, Saul, should dress up in a costume himself, the Gordy Himmelman clothes piled on the floor in his closet. That would surprise Howie.

But no. That, Saul thought, was what he—Saul—would not do. He would not rush downstairs. He would not dress up, or down. He wouldn't give his brother the satisfaction.

Half of any manipulative strategy had to do with how you arrived and how you departed.

The German motor ticked quietly as it cooled. This standoff was like several others the two brothers had had. Howie wasn't passive so much as immobile, a Don Juan of stillness: he liked everyone to come to him so that he might gain the advantage of not making the first move. This was the dubious legacy of a childhood marked by illness and indisposition and the death of a parent. He had been born one month premature, a blue baby—incubated—and as an infant he was jaundiced and scrawny and tearful. One of Saul's first memories was of his mother carrying the misbegotten Howie around the house on a pale-blue goosedown pillow, as if any sudden move might break him. Soon after his birth, Howie had proved to be allergic to breast milk—the metaphoric implications of this were not lost on him as an adult—and he continued to be lactose intolerant. He had suffered from anemia, earaches, uncommon food and substance allergies (carpeting made him sneeze, cats made him choke, he might die if he ate a peanut, and he could not mow a lawn), and repeated bouts of childhood flu and bronchial troubles had kept him in bed for weeks. He had had multiple strep infections and one incidence in middle school of rheumatic fever. In high school he came down with pneumonia and missed classes for a month.

"Be careful of Howie," his mother always used to say to Saul. "He's very fragile."

After their father's death—Howie said he could hardly remember him (Saul doubted this) and would never speak of him—Delia seemed to direct the few motherly concerns she had toward Howie in the furtherance of his well-being. Saul she left alone. With Saul, it was hands-off anarcho-laissez-faire parenting all the way. She treated Saul like a wonderful, charming guest or a performer in a rather dull show. But with Howie, the slightest sign of postnasal drip could mean another desperate search of *The Merck Manual* for symptoms, along with worried consulations with the long-suffering pediatrician, Dr. Greene. Howie had really made his illnesses *work*. Every time Howie got sick, he somehow came out, personally, in the profit column.

Sickly children with distant or absent parents have a tendency to become unattractive adolescents, Saul believed: bent-over, whining self-pitiers, autoerotic virtuosi of hypochondria. Unable to make conversation, they give themselves the attention and care they receive from no one else. But something had turned the other way with Howie. Saul watched with disbelief as his little brother gradually acquired a glow from some mysterious source, a light in his eyes that was somehow related to the animal kingdom. The growth hormones that in other boys produced acne, simian proportions, quick tempers, and cantaloupe-shaped heads, produced in Howie an eerie grace and beauty. From his years of illness he also acquired an inner quiet and watchfulness and a finely honed skill at manipulation.

He had large, liquid eyes—now like a doe, now like an owl.

In high school, Howie had led around a long trail of girlfriends, not to mention a host of bewildered guys who were friends of his but who also seemed to have fallen under his spell. Saul suspected that his brother would sleep with anything as long as it was beautiful. Howie had become a beauty snob, though he practiced secrecy about his love interests and never explained where he was going or whom he was seeing in his nocturnal prowlings. But he had also become rugged, given to endurance sports like rock climbing and marathon racing and soccer. He fought his sickliness with everything he had, and in the process had evolved into a man in whom contradictory male and female traits were mixed equally, producing a sleek, androgynous charm. He had a weakness for mirrors and stood before them for long periods when he thought no one else was observing him, studying the tough, beautiful mystery of himself.

Watching Howie grow into manhood was like reading two biographies, one of Teddy Roosevelt and the other of Greta Garbo, going back and forth between the two, getting the personalities mixed up.

Their father had died of a heart attack while driving to work the year when Howie was eight years old and Saul ten. In the Baltimore funeral home, following the memorial service, there transpired a scene that Saul would always remember whenever he thought of Howie. Howie had been seated on a metal folding chair in the corner, behind a table where the two Bunn-o-Matic coffeemakers were positioned, along with the cream, the sugar, and the Styrofoam cups. Friends and acquaintances of their father milled around the room, bending down to Delia and Saul to offer consolation. Howie refused to talk to anyone. With a manly and stoical expression on his face, Howie sat quietly there in the corner, the tears streaming down his cheeks, unsociable in his grief. He had loved his father, whose death was, Saul thought, a permanent injury for which Howie would never have words. The luster had simply gone out of everything. Later, in the house, when more friends of their parents dropped by, Howie found another corner to sit in, where he would cry inconsolably, then wipe his eyes and stand up and make brave conversation and eat cookies, before sitting down in his corner to cry, inconsolably, again.

Delia never remarried—out of loyalty, Saul thought, not to her late husband but to Howie.

Saul and Howie had tried some brother-to-brother male bonding once a few years ago on a long-distance bicycle trip. They had set off from Baltimore and had made it as far as Chicago. They did not speak much about personal matters during their evenings together: each had brought several books to ward off that possibility. They discussed the route, their provisions, the locations where they would camp or the motels where they would stay. Or they would confer about the bicycles, the condition of the gears and the tires.

Saul had been in charge of the maps, because he claimed he was good at maps. Howie was apathetic about their route. They stayed on back roads day after day and, after three weeks had passed, made their way carefully past the tangle of outlying Chicago neighborhoods toward Lake Michigan, which Howie had never seen. They had been bicycling in the northwest side of the city, avoiding traffic in the early morning, weaving their way through Greektown and heading for Lincoln Park, when Howie braked too suddenly, swerved, and hit the curb in front of a Greek restaurant, the Acropolis. He went flying over the handlebars and landed on the sidewalk, his belongings—which had broken loose from his pack—scattered around him.

Saul was horrified. *Be careful of Howie. He's very fragile.*

Howie stood up quickly, seemingly unhurt, and out of relief at seeing that his brother was still in one piece, Saul began to laugh. His laughter provoked Howie to fury. Enraged, he danced a little dance of humiliation and wrath on the sidewalk before he stomped a plastic water container, his baseball cap, his Robocop wraparound sunglasses, and his uncapped tube of sunblock, which squirted orgasmically over the pavement. Saul only laughed harder, knowing he shouldn't but unable to stop. As he did, Howie walked over to Saul and waited for him to control himself. Howie's face was bright red.

"Someday in the future we can laugh about this," Howie said, "but right now I swear to God that if you keep laughing, I'm going to fucking kill you."

Saul composed himself, wiped the tears off his face, and helped Howie collect his things. From the experience he learned two facts about his brother and himself: first, that Howie feared being the object of ridicule—lethally—especially in moments of vulnerability; and, second, that he himself feared Howie's ire at such moments, not for himself but for his brother's sake. He had seen a pool of bitter sediment in Howie's eyes, which spoke of old grievances and all the memories of illnesses that had brought forth both welcome and unwelcome responses.

They found an old hotel near Lincoln Park to stay in—they would be flying home in two days and would ship the bicycles back—and after taking showers they walked around the Loop, making their way down to the Art Institute to see the Seurats. That evening, when the weather was still humid and unsettled, they strolled through Lincoln Park. There were crowds of other young people like themselves, walking and talking and eyeing one another. Within sight of the lake, they were standing near a water fountain when an attractive young woman wearing jeans and a Chicago Cubs T-shirt and holding a sketch pad began speaking to Howie. Howie carried with him a wounded look that women apparently found irresistible. Addressing the sky in a tone of cool, hip indifference, she remarked on the weather, and Saul's brother said something in return, equally cool and hip, speaking of the clouds in a way that suggested that he, too, was indifferent to the weather, being from out of town and not subject to these particular clouds. She asked where he lived and he told her. *Baltimore!* she said, with admiration, touching Howie's arm. He had *bicycled* here? Amazing. She had never been to Baltimore. No? Well, the row houses, he said, came right down to the water in the harbor. Where are you staying? she asked. Howie named the hotel. They introduced themselves: Howie, Voltaine. Yes, the name: her parents had been hippies in Vancouver; she herself was a Canadian citizen, and when she was a girl her mother had sung "Mellow Yellow" to her and her sister Saffron night after night, year after year, as a lullaby. Now she was a student here in Chicago at the Art Institute. Howie didn't say anything about *his* occupations or *his* age; it didn't seem necessary. Nor did he bother to introduce his brother. Saul was standing a few feet away, lost in bemusement and pride in his brother's social skills, though feeling like an encumbrance himself. In disbelief, from his safe distance, Saul detected Chanel No. 5 emanating from Voltaine, an expensive scent his mother sometimes wore when she hadn't applied the mustard gas. Voltaine, for some reason, hadn't noticed him. Girls didn't turn their heads when Saul walked past. Howie was the one who got them riled up and confused. Instead of introducing himself, Saul just watched his brother and this woman, and he took deep breaths of Voltaine's perfume. Howie had given Saul a semidetached look, as if something was on the tip of his tongue that he would not say. Voltaine and Howie proceeded to sit down on a bench quite close to each other, and as the light faded, she removed the cover of her sketch pad and outlined his face on paper using pencil and charcoal, including in her drawing the scrapes on his forehead from his bicycle accident. After ten minutes of small talk between the two, Howie finally got around to pointing toward Saul, who smiled, nodded, and belatedly shook hands with Voltaine. He hadn't been able to decide whether he should return to the hotel or lurk in the middle distance. Voltaine continued to pencil in details of Howie on her sketch pad, but by then it was getting so dark that Saul couldn't make out what his brother looked like in Voltaine's version of him.

Out of politeness, she asked Saul if he would like her to sketch him, and, out of politeness, he said no.

When she finished the portrait of Howie, she showed him what she had done, kissed him on the cheek, and wished them both good night.

The brothers asked her if she would like to go somewhere for a beer, but she said she couldn't, she had to get back home. Saul was relieved that he would be seeing no more of this scented hippies' child.

At two in the morning, the phone in the hotel room rang. Saul answered. Voltaine, of course, and she wanted to speak to Howie, she said, just a small matter of business, nothing important. Saul passed the receiver over to his brother in the other bed. Howie sat up, alert. He then turned off the light and crawled under his sheet and blanket to talk. His voice, from under the covers, was muffled and laughing and flirtatious and thickly sexual. Well, they were kids, after all, though Howie was only two years younger than Saul himself, the designated adult. Saul went into the bathroom to piss, and when he returned, Howie was still on the phone there under the covers, very quietly attending to business. "Do you want me to leave the room?" Saul asked his brother. Receiving no answer, and knowing he had been heard, he tucked himself back into bed and tried to sleep. He counted sheep in the dark to the background of his brother's unintelligible rumbling, and he imagined long, dull historical accounts of the Treaty of Versailles to help himself doze off. None of it worked. He went down the names of the states alphabetically, trying to remember each state capital. That didn't work either, though he did get as far as Helena. His brother talked for what seemed like an hour. In the dark, after hanging up, Howie said only six words: "This sure is a friendly town."

The next day, no mention was made of the phone call. As far as Saul knew, his brother never saw or heard from Voltaine again.

Where was Patsy? She had been delayed getting her refill of Dorylaeum, it seemed, and now Saul would have to start their dinner. He clomped downstairs, feeling muddy and doomstruck as he always did whenever Patsy arrived home late.

He peered in the refrigerator. Baby food—ground lamb, sweet potatoes, mashed peas, and leftover oatmeal (leftover oatmeal? whose idea was *that*? perhaps Patsy would eat it herself, late at night, watching the paid commercial programming)—resided in recesses of the refrigerator close to a package of hamburger, salad fixings, and a jar of nameless forgotten food cobwebbed with mold. Saul and Patsy were busy parents and sometimes for days or even weeks forgot certain sectors of the refrigerator. Terrible neglected substances, green and gray and almost alive again inside their Tupperware containers, were visible in the back of the lower shelf. He threw the jar, unopened, into the garbage.

Howie still waiting, waiting, waiting in the car . . .

Saul removed the fresh greens and made a salad for Patsy and himself. He contemplated what ingredients they had on hand and decided to make an omelette. Therefore: he opened a bottle of white wine ("the white whine" Patsy sometimes called it, and sometimes called *him* under its influence), helped himself to a glass, and pulled out a mixing bowl from the cupboard and a cutting board for the vegetables. After chopping the onions and the mushrooms and the tomatoes, he dropped them into the bowl, and he—

He couldn't stand it any longer. Howie's furious apathy was larger than his own. Saul's love for his brother couldn't be much clearer if it were out of the water in the well.

Take care of Howie. He's very fragile.

Saul washed his hands and put on his shoes before strolling out to Howie's car. The suspense was killing him. Actually, he adored his brother for no particular reason. His brother being his brother was reason enough. Why should he pretend otherwise? Why should he feign this indifference? If Howie wanted to be indifferent to *him*, to Saul, fine. Howie was his little brother, always had been, even now, multimillionaire though Howie might be, the money couldn't protect him from everything. Howie required looking after. Everyone did. Of course, Howie liked suspense—a seducer's trait—and could handle much more of it than Saul could. By the time he had reached the Avenger, Saul was almost running, desperate to hug his brother, desperate to love him again in person.

There, behind the wheel, was Howie, fast asleep, a tiny trail of drool declining from his mouth. Slumbering though he was, Howie had the appearance of a bleary, worn-out man, a former hobbyist-seducer whose charm, through overuse, had faded on him. He had a piteous gray streak in his beard. Saul knocked on the driver's-side window, and when Howie awoke, he stared at Saul for a moment in nonrecognition, as if in his sleep he had been inoculated with amnesia.

"Howie," Saul called to his brother through the glass. "Wake up."

Howie continued to look blankly at Saul.

"Howie!" Saul cried out. "Buddy. *Pal.* It's Saul. Your brother. What's going on? Get out of the car! Come inside."

Howie rolled down the window. Speaking like a man coming back to consciousness after general anesthetic, Howie said, "Hey, Saul. I've been driving for seventeen hours straight. I got here, and I thought no one was home." He smiled wanly. "I guess I fell asleep."

"Come inside," Saul repeated. "Please."

Howie opened the car door. When he tried to stand, his knees appeared to give way before Saul grabbed his elbow, and then his arm, helping him back up. Saul hugged his brother fiercely. Howie gave off a smell of exhaustion and breath mints and fast food. Saul supported him by holding him around the shoulders in a brotherly clasp as they proceeded up the front walkway, through the front door, past the foyer, into the kitchen, where he sat his brother down at the dinette table.

"New house," Howie said, looking around and shaking his head. "New baby, new furniture, new house. New everything."

"Yeah," Saul said. "I guess so. Though Emmy isn't *that* new. She's over a year old. And Patsy is pregnant again. You knew that, right?"

"Could I have a glass of water?" Howie asked. "I'm beat."

"Sure." After placing the water down in front of Howie, Saul sat beside him and waited while his brother drank. Slowly, his face began to take on its customary qualities, and Howie's character reappeared in his eyes. "So. Howard. To what do we owe the honor of this visit?" Saul asked.

"I wanted to give you and Patsy and Mary Esther . . . do you call her Mary Esther or Emmy? I've heard you say both."

"Well, Emmy, usually," Saul said.

"I have an announcement. And I wanted to see my little niece, and you, and Patsy, and the new house, and actually the truth is that I wanted to give you some money."

"*Give* us? Money? For what? We don't need any money." He waited. Perhaps he was being ungracious. "How much money?"

"I'll tell you later. It's sort of a bundle. I need to get rid of it. You'd be doing me a favor. By the way, where *is* Patsy?"

"Getting a prescription filled. She'll be back anytime." Saul touched his brother's arm. "It's so good to see you, Howie."

"Well, yeah." Howie twisted his head back and forth, loosening the neck muscles. "You, too." He gazed toward the ceiling. "That was one long drive. I did like Colorado, the Rocky Mountains, but of course everyone does, though I think those mountains are too *big*, somehow. I like smaller mountains, softer ones, more on the human scale. When I got to Five Oaks, I wasn't sure I'd find your house, but then I saw some white-haired kids, palely loitering in their front yards, and I thought, 'This must be where Saul and Patsy live, somewhere around here,' and I asked, and they directed me to you. Hey. Could you give me some towels? For a shower?"

"Oh, sure," Saul said. "By the way, how did you like what you saw of our very wonderful city?"

"Five Oaks?" Howie appeared to consider this question, then gave his head a shake. "Five Oaks is the Tübingen of the Midwest, wouldn't you say?" Saul had forgotten Howie's habit of rhetorical traps, delivered with a thin smile.

"I might, or I might not." Saul felt dismayed by how quickly the two of them became quarrelsome. They had skipped the stage when they would both be pleasant and agreeable.

"Those towels, Saul? I've got to take a shower."

"Okay, okay. I'll go get them."

Waiting in the kitchen, while the hot water ran in the shower upstairs, Saul thrummed his fingers on the table. He stood up and gazed out the window to see if there were any signs of Patsy. Far in the distance down the subdivision's main street, out in the semidark, were two bleached-haired kids, two Himmels, yes, palely loitering (that *was* the phrase), bent over a bag of some kind, conferring. Then they straightened up and stared at his house.

During the past few months, the middle school and high school outsiders and losers and dropouts and freaks and disaffiliated and disinclined and unmotivated and semi-destroyed and embittered kids—it was quite a sizable group—had all turned their hair a sickly blond or white and created a semi-secret cult of the undead with Gordy at its center as inspiration and centerpiece, and Sam Cole associated with him for the beauty part. Saul had heard that they considered Gordy to be still among them, apparitional, and all these albino-haired, blank-eyed kids had taken a particular interest in Saul himself as a focus of their undead attention.

There was, Saul had heard, a dispute among the Himmels about himself. Some considered him an enabler, someone who had made Gordy possible. For others, he was the one who had hastened Gordy's end. In any case, whether as John the Baptist or as Judas, Saul was on their minds.

When Howie finally came downstairs, wearing a clean shirt and fresh trousers and clean socks, Saul hugged him again and in the living room poured him a glass of wine. They clicked glasses, and out of nowhere, Howie said, "I'm going to get married, Saul. I wanted to tell you in person."

Saul tried not to act surprised. This was, after all, standard practice for Howie, to say nothing about the person or persons he had been seeing or what he had been doing and then to announce big decisions as done deals. He avoided advice, consultations, and unwanted intimacies this way. He loved to ambush with surprise news, then watch the reaction. Or maybe he just didn't want to deliver big news over the phone. "Hey, congratulations," Saul said, trying to think of an alternative way of saying what he was about to say in a non-clichéd form. But the cliché was there in front of him like a roadblock. "So. Who's," he asked, "the lucky girl?"

"Her name?" Howie seemed briefly taken aback, stunned by the question. He shut his eyes twice, as if he had been plunged into profound thought. "Her name is Phyllis."

"Phyllis?" Saul asked, his voice carrying a small current of disbelief. "That's a name for old people. Nobody is named Phyllis. Not anymore."

"Well, *she* is. I guess nobody told her parents. She goes by 'Lis.'"

"Lis," Saul repeated.

"Yeah. Or 'Phyl'—whatever." Howie glanced at Saul, then glanced around the living room. "You'll be my best man?"

"Of course. Where'd you meet her? What's she like? Do you have a picture? When's the wedding?"

"Naturally I have a picture." Howie took a sip of his wine. He gave Saul his trickster smile.

"Well, *may I see it?*"

"Oh. Okay." Howie reached for his wallet and pulled out a photograph, which he handed to Saul. It showed a pretty young woman standing on the seashore in the Bay Area—Ocean Beach, Saul guessed—whose auburn-colored hair was shoulder length, and with a display of short bangs and delicate hands raised in a double wave. She wore a thin blue jacket. In the photograph the wind was apparently blowing from left to right, causing several strands of her hair to press themselves against her cheek. The hair against her cheek attracted Saul to her. He was moved by how she stood in the wind. Her smile was lovely and warm. She had the appearance of amiability and sweetness and strength, though her eyes were slightly recessed and did not quite participate in the smile she was smiling. *She looked like Patsy. She looked like Patsy's sister, if Patsy actually had a sister. She looked like Patsy. She looked like Patsy. She looked like Patsy's sister.* Saul felt a mild shock before he recovered himself.

Howie might have said, "So. What d'you think?" but then he wouldn't have been Howie.

"She's very pretty," Saul told his brother. "Is she Jewish?"

"Yes," Howie said noncommittally. He glanced straight up at the ceiling. "Why do you ask?"

"Just thinking about Mom. Not that she cares one way or another.

Well, that's another story. She's very pretty," Saul repeated, suddenly and unpleasantly aware that he had accidentally left his pronoun referent vague—the unconscious at work, always busy, always looking for opportunities to make Saul slip up.

"Thanks," Howie said, as if he were responsible for his fiancée's good looks. "You know, I can't wait to see Emmy." He said this without enthusiasm, the phrase oiled with politeness.

"She and Patsy will be home any minute now," Saul said. "Any minute." Then he blurted out, "You know, this Phyllis of yours looks a lot like Patsy."

Howie coughed angrily. Then he said, "That's a strange thing to observe. She doesn't look *at all* like Patsy. They're completely different. You're hallucinating."

"Of course she looks like Patsy. They could be sisters."

"Saul, what makes you say that?"

"Look at her *hair*. Look at her *smile*. That expression on her face." *Look at her benevolence,* he wanted to say, but didn't, because no one ever said things like that, except sentimentalists.

"Are you telling me that I searched around until I found someone like your wife?"

"No," Saul backpedaled, "I'm not telling you that."

"Because she doesn't look like Patsy at all." Howie sat up like a guard who has heard an alarm go off. "She looks completely like herself."

"Sure. Of course."

"*I* know," Howie said, "we'll ask Patsy, once she gets home." He stood up and stretched, as if he had reached the inevitable crossroad and had made the correct turn. "Let Patsy decide whether Lis looks like her." He leaned backward. "You asked what she's like."

"Yes," Saul said. "I did."

"She works with me . . . with us. At eFlea." In one of his phone calls, Howie had informed Saul that he currently was one of the partners in an online flea market, positioned to compete with eBay. "She's smart and beautiful." Then, after a long beat, Howie said, "She reads the encyclopedia to relax. On New Year's Eve we both made resolutions, and I made her resolve to go on exactly as she had been in the past. And she did. She resolved to go on being the way she was. We met when . . . well, she came to me when I was coking up and drinking too much and screwing everything in sight, and she sort of fixed me up with herself. I was a mess, all glue and shards." Howie waited. "The Great Chain of Misbehavior, with me at the bottom, buried in all that cash I had made and was losing. There are a lot of *me*'s out there," he said, apparently meaning the West Coast. "You know," Howie said, warming to the subject, "my character doesn't exactly fill me up. My character only goes out partway to my edges. But Lis's character goes out all the way to her fingertips. Do you understand what I'm saying?"

"Yes," Saul said, because he himself could have said it about Patsy.

"Anyway," Howie said, "I had to come out here and ask you to be my best man, and also, before Lis and I are married, to give you what I want to give you."

"What's that?"

"About two million dollars," Howie said.

"That's a lot of money," Saul said, in a blank, not registering at all what his brother had said.

"Well, it's in equities from various companies out there I've bought into, and you can't sell them, as I'll explain to you tomorrow, because that would be illegal. It's all paper wealth. Is there any more wine in there, in the kitchen?"

"Yes," Saul said, so numb that he felt that he might have had a stroke. "Come with me."

When they were in the kitchen, the front door opened, and Patsy came in the house with a noisy bustle, and she sang out, "Saul! The scapegoating has started! We have to move! We have to move out of this place." Then she began singing. *"We gotta get out of this place! If it's the last thing we ever do!"*

He and Howie came out of the kitchen, and when Patsy saw Saul's brother, she said, "Oh, Howie." She kissed him. "So that was *your* BMW. What a nice surprise. Sorry you caught me singing." They gave each other brotherly-sisterly kisses—Saul watched them do it.

"Love," Howie said, unwrapping his charm before her, smiling. "You can sing anytime."

Howie picked up Emmy, and he made kissing noises as he looked in her brown eyes. He kissed his niece on the cheek, and in return she smiled at him broadly, which she had never done so rapidly with a stranger before.

"She's very solid," said Howie, once so fragile himself.

Seventeen

"What a beautiful woman," Patsy said, holding Howie's photograph of his fiancée. She and Saul, tag-teaming, had taken Emmy upstairs, changed her into a fresh diaper and her pink pajamas, sung to her, and watched her fall asleep. Now they were together in the living room, the three of them drinking white wine and examining the picture of Howie's Lis.

"Saul thinks she looks like you," Howie said, glancing at Patsy. He was slurring his words a bit. "I said she didn't."

"She doesn't look at all like me. Her hair is different from mine, for one thing."

"She certainly *does* look like you," Saul muttered crossly, staring at his wife, as if he were the final authority on all questions of resemblance.

"You guys. No, she's not a bit like me. The only female in the world who looks a lot like me," Patsy said, "is my daughter. Howie, you're a lucky man. When's the wedding date?"

"Next summer." He then lowered himself from his chair onto the floor. There, on the floor, he continued his side of the conversation as he performed stretch exercises. He said he was stiff from the day's drive. "We're going to be married in Golden Gate Park. Lis wants to honeymoon in Hawaii, and she's found a place on Maui where you can walk and go on excursions if you want to, or you can just stay right there, and it's still Paradise. There are plans, and more plans, and more plans after that, about this wedding. You don't even want to know about all these plans. *I* can't keep track of them all. I never knew getting married was so complicated. It's like managing a merger. Strategy and paperwork."

Patsy and Saul glanced at each other.

"But the main thing is, Saul, you have to be my best man, and the other main thing is how beautiful Emmy is." As if under silent orders for a fixed routine, he then sat down and did a runner's stretch on the other side of the coffee table, with one leg behind him and one in front. "What a beautiful daughter. You two are so lucky. Except for living in Five Oaks."

"Well, there's another one coming," Patsy said, patting herself, ignoring his remark about their very wonderful city. She explained to Howie that this one was a boy and that the due date was May thirteenth.

Howie stood up, holding his arms entangled with each other in front and then behind him, wrenching them from side to side for flexibility.

"Hey, congratulations. Or do you withhold congratulations until the baby is born? Patsy," he said, "there's one thing I have to ask about. When you came home, you said the scapegoating had started. What did you mean?"

He lowered himself to the floor. While he did several push-ups, Patsy told him about Gordy Himmelman's suicide. Saul sat in his chair, watching his brother's exercises without commenting on them or on the Gordy Himmelman story that Patsy was telling. Public calesthenics had seemingly turned into acceptable social behavior. The only time Saul allowed himself a reaction occurred when Patsy reported that she had talked to Anne McPhee and then had driven over to Brenda Bagley's house. Saul's face took on a raised-eyebrow attentiveness. Howie's reaction was minimal, though he had a peevish expression as he listened and exercised, as if the story were a mind pollutant.

"You do have to get out of this place," Howie told them tonelessly, finishing his last push-up and taking a breather in a sitting position, his hands on his hips.

"Nothing doing," Saul said. "I'm staying. I have to. I'm on a mission. *We* are."

"And what would that mission be?" He took on an expression of petulance.

"I don't know," Saul explained. "In due time, the mission will reveal itself."

"Your mission is to get out of the Midwest, Saul, before something here balls up its fist and hits you. Come out to the Bay Area. We'll go into business together."

"Well," Saul said, "I'm going to bed. See you in the morning, maybe."

"I made up the guest room," Patsy told Howie, yawning. "Uh, Howie, could you tell me one thing, before you go to bed?"

"What's that?"

"Well, Saul told me when we were upstairs that you were going to give us some money."

"I already *have* given you some money. Well, not money, but equities. That is, I've bought some stocks and put them in Saul's name. You're my family, you see. Anyone would do this. And I thought it was time to spread the wealth around. There's money to spare. I won't miss it."

"How much is this?"

"About two million dollars," Howie said. "But it's not in blue chips. They're kind of risky little companies, what I bought you. Lots of *marginal enterprises*. Techno stocks, things like that, e-commerce stuff. That's how I . . . well, never mind. The thing is, you shouldn't sell them. You should hold on to them for years. If you sell them, you'll be sorry. You can just go on right here with your lit——your life now as it is. Pretend all this money doesn't exist."

"You're kidding! We can't take this!" Patsy said. "You have to be joking! You can't give us two million dollars! You can't. That's crazy. We'll be ruined."

"Yes, I can," he said, heading toward the stairs, his hand already on the newel post.

"I'm not taking any of this . . . *largesse*," Patsy said. "I'm giving it all back to you."

"Actually," Howie said, just before he turned around, "the stocks are already in Saul's name. If you want to give them away, it's his decision, to tell you the honest truth."

"What would we do with two million dollars?" Patsy cried out in agony.

"Anything you want."

In the middle of the sleepless night (to her surprise and dismay, Saul had fallen asleep immediately—a very aggressive thing for him to have done), on one of her several trips to the bathroom to pee, Patsy heard a spattering sound like that of a bird flying into a window, and then another: two impacts. Whack—pause—wham. They came from downstairs, and Patsy could feel the hair on the back of her neck stand up. One blow was an accident; but two were deliberate. Two meant intention and human volition. Two meant harm.

The floor, as she ran down to the living room, felt unclean and unwelcoming to her bare feet, no longer hers, provisional: the carpeting was gritty and the wood slats squeaked. In the living room Patsy stood in darkness, studying the front window, where two egg yolks and the raw white of the egg surrounding them dribbled down the glass windowpane. Far in the distance she saw the white bleached albino hairs as the Himmel-perpetrators disappeared into the night.

So it had started. Somewhere, out there in the dark, someone had thrown two raw eggs at the house, and then, in all probability, had run off, sick with laughter or righteousness. Gordy, with his visits, was gone physically but now his substitutes were doing their methodical retributive work. Perhaps there would be escalation: rotten tomatoes, toilet paper, followed by firecrackers, then arson, then, finally, gunshots. Or painted swastikas. Of the punishing of good deeds there would be no discernible end. All at once the idea of owning a handgun made perfect sense to her. Staring out through the window, she crossed her arms over her chest. But she didn't feel like herself; her body was always surprising her nowadays. Her breasts were so big, she still wasn't used to them. Her feet were swollen, and her arms were getting thick and muscular.

Her mouth had gone instantly dry and she could hear what remained of her saliva as she swallowed.

It wasn't her own safety she worried about so much as that of her children. Emmy and Theo didn't deserve encirclement, to be brought up as the stigmatized children of God's outcasts, or, even worse, as the children of millionaires.

When she returned to the upstairs hallway, Howie was standing there in his pajamas. Even in the dark he had an aura about him, attractive at the surface level but not quite to her taste at any particular depth. Getting up from bed, he would still be perfectly groomed, forever unmussed, his hair in order, his odors still concealed by soap and cologne. The stink of humanity was absent from him.

"What happened?" he whispered. He was studying her nightgown gnomishly, but in the dark there was precious little to see. "I heard something."

"Weren't you sleeping?"

"I never sleep," he said, with a trace of pride. His face in the near-dark had a perfect symmetry, the eyes like gentle X-rays. Patsy noticed his chest and thought: *Hmm, family resemblance.*

"Well, we got egged."

Mary Esther muttered quietly in her sleep from one room, and Saul groaned in his sleep from another. They were alike in that respect: they both vocalized in their dreams.

"You got what? *Egged?*" He leaned forward toward her.

"It's complicated. The kids around here think we're responsible for that boy, Gordy's, suicide. They've formed a Gordy cult. It's called Himmelism. Goth stuff. Come down and see for yourself," she said. She took his hand and led him across the hallway toward the stairs, where she let go of him and reached out for the sticky bannister, grubby from child-and-baby productions.

On the first floor, she led him to the front room and showed him the egg yolks on the window.

"Ah," Howie said, crossing his arms on his chest. "Golems."

"What?"

"Golems. Jewish mythology from three or four centuries ago. They're automatons made out of clay by rabbis. They're created to be servants—but they always run amuck and the rabbi has to destroy them." He gazed at the window. "So now I guess they're running amuck. Did Saul make them in his spare time?"

"Nice theory," Patsy said. "But I think these kids are all-Americans. How come you know about golems? That's not Delia's line. Or yours either."

Howie shrugged. "Mom took Saul and me to the Jewish Cultural Center when we were kids. That's about the only Jewish thing we ever did. And all I remember from those sessions were the myths and stories. The first time I saw the marching broomsticks in *Fantasia*, I thought: Yeah, golems." He smiled at her in the dark.

"Hey," she said, "let's go into the kitchen. If you can't sleep, and I can't sleep, we might as well sit up together. Come on." She inclined her head. "We'll wait for the sun to come up if we have to."

After they had arranged themselves in the lightless kitchen, Patsy on a chair near the refrigerator and Howie close enough to the counter so that he could lean his head against it, they sat drinking tap water from glasses Patsy had purchased, years ago, at the hardware store. They had no elegance; she liked the sense of commonality, of plain making-do, when she served drinks in these glasses to guests like Howie. If you were going to be elegant, the true note would have to come from somewhere else. The digital clocks on the stove and the microwave gave off sufficient illumination so that she could see where Howie was sitting, but she could not quite tell what expression was on his face, which suited her. There was an aspect to Howie that was not quite domesticated, that was unsafe, and dangerous to look upon. He could be oddly arousing.

"Tell me more about Emmy," Howie asked, and Patsy was touched that he would ask about Emmy even if he might not be interested in children generally—single men usually weren't—a curiosity evoked for the sake of the appearances that Howie spent so much of his time trying to keep up. "Tell me what she's like," he suggested companionably, though the request contained a hint of his business side, his wish to issue commands.

"Oh," Patsy said, "she's already an individual. They're individuals the minute they come out of the womb. Emmy's very sensitive to sounds. She first turned her head in the crib when she heard the singing of a bird outside the window. She's demanding, you know, like most kids—she likes to have the same things happen in the same way all the time—and she's still learning that she can't always get what she wants, but that's a stage. That's how infants turn into children. She's going to have a good sense of humor as a little girl and as a woman, I can tell. She's very curious about everything. Her first word was 'Wzzat?'"

"I was wondering," Howie said from his dark corner, "if you like her. I mean, I know you're her mother, of course, so you love her, but I was wondering if you liked her, too."

"What a question!" She waited, trying to unpack Howie's subtext. Failing at it, she said, "Of course I like her. Mothers always like their children."

"No," Howie said. "I don't think so. Nice to say so, but no. I don't think my mother ever liked me very much. She protected me because I was sickly, but that's different. *Loved*—sure, of course. But it's a weird scene when your parents don't like you, don't feel that friendly affinity, and I don't think my mother ever did. We were sort of peripheral to her concerns."

"You know, she had an affair with her yard boy last summer."

"Yes. She finally told me." He sounded bored by the subject.

"What did you think of that?"

"I didn't care for it," Howie said. "I think she should act her age. She's a predator."

"Well, I kind of liked it, myself," Patsy said, careful not to reveal that Howie's mother had also told her that she had loved the kid, at least a little. "I give her credit. I take off my hat to her."

"For what?" Howie asked.

"For guts. For nerve. For being an older woman who can still take steps."

"Steps. Ha. She's not *your* mother," Howie observed. "When it's your mother, it gets . . . strange."

"Howie," Patsy said in the dark, using her flattest voice, "we can't take your charity. We just can't."

"It's not charity. It's an investment in you two. Did you talk to Saul?"

"No," Patsy said, "I didn't. I just can't stand the idea of being a millionaire. It would turn Saul and me into . . . I don't know—*villains*."

"Then give it away to someone else," Howie said with equanimity. "Give it to charity. Give it to your children."

"It'll turn *them* into villains." She shifted in her chair. She had an odd, fugitive idea that Howie liked talking to women in total darkness, that it answered some early-childhood need of his.

At that moment another flying egg hit the outside of the kitchen window. Patsy glanced at it, decided to ignore it, and because she ignored it, so did Howie. What the hell. They were being egged. It wasn't the end of the world. You could always clean it up.

"Give it to *them*," Howie said.

"Who?"

"The Himmels. The golems. The kids who're throwing those eggs at your house."

"That's impossible," Patsy said.

"Why?"

They looked at each other in the dark, but Patsy couldn't quite see him—his eyes, the entryway into his soul, were masked and invisible to her.

Another egg hit the house.

"Tell me more about Lis," Patsy said. She needed to keep asking questions. If she didn't, he might try to kiss her. She felt his anarchic erotic charges bombarding her. He seemed to be leaning forward in her direction.

"Who?"

"Lis—your fiancée. The girl in the picture."

"Oh, Lis." And for the next half-hour, until they both felt sleepy again and went upstairs, Howie told Patsy about the woman he loved: her hobbies (tennis and photography and cooking), her favorite reading (the encyclopedia, and British novels, mostly Murdoch and Winterson), and her work at eFlea, where her training as a lawyer had helped them establish the business and keep it running, free of litigation. Patsy leaned back in the dark and felt relaxed and happy over her brother-in-law's happiness. His voice went on, rhapsodic, washing over her. She could not remember another time when a man had felt so trusting in her company that he could describe in full-throated detail a woman he loved, both the inner and outer qualities that had attracted him to her.

"May you live in joy forever," Patsy said finally, and Howie thanked her for the blessing.

Eighteen

The next morning, after his brother and sister-in-law and niece had costumed themselves for the day, had had their meager cereal breakfasts and then were utterly gone, leaving him alone in the silent breathing despoiled storybook house, Howie found a bucket and a clean sponge in the basement under the laundry tubs. He located a spray bottle of glass cleaner and a roll of paper towels in the kitchen pantry, and after mixing soap and a household cleanser in warm water, he took a scrubbing brush and scoured off the disfigurements on the north side of the exterior wall facing the driveway. Vinyl siding! His brother lived in a house with white vinyl siding! Very poisonous, very up-to-date. Human beings would go far to disguise themselves so that they were invisible to other human beings. Using the glass cleaner and the paper towels, he wiped off the windows, making sure that the sticky raw eggs left no residual trace. By the time he was finished, the glass was perfect, immaculate, and he himself had worked up a small sweat. But no smell. His sweat had no smell and never had had one. His perspiration was as pure as distilled water. This feature he shared with the gods.

Having finished with the windows, he extended the ladder, climbed up to the roof line, and emptied the gutters of their leaves. October, days until Halloween, autumn days, the days of the harvest and of uncurable sadness. Before going up the ladder's rungs, he'd been unable to find a pair of work gloves in the garage or the basement or the pantry. Perhaps no one here really worked. Therefore, he would have to do the job bare-handed. The leaves gave to the flesh of his hands a smell of vegetative mold—Madagascar. His hands smelled the way Madagascar would certainly smell when you arrived on the cruise ship into the harbor of Madagascar's seaport . . . Toamasina. He made fists of both hands and brought them to his nostrils and inhaled the smell of that harbor, of the men and women working there, beads of their sweat falling onto the docks of that island kingdom. He felt transported. He would stay in Toamasina as long as he wished.

At the bottom of the ladder were the used paper towels scattered here and there. He gathered them up one by one and went inside, wiping his shoes first, before he dropped the towels into the garbage bag in the kitchen, the little perfect garbage can in the little perfect kitchen.

He washed the dishes in the kitchen sink. The light seemed to be everywhere.

His brother and sister-in-law had no idea how the world worked. They had *no idea* what people could do to you. And *did* do to you. One small misstep, one stumble, and the jackals were upon you. Protected and insular in their storybook house, his brother and sister-in-law eased themselves from day to day with no glimmer at all of the steady-state diminishments of everyday life—until the jackals had picked the body down to the bone and you were no longer able to cry out.

He found the vacuum cleaner in a closet off the laundry room and did a quick once-over of the living-room carpet. Then he went upstairs. In the guest room, he stripped the bed. He took off his clothes and masturbated into a wad of Kleenex. The relief lasted for ten seconds, fifteen at the most. He clothed himself again. After folding the sheets and pillow-cases into perfect squares, he bent down to where his suitcase was. He took out his wallet and stared at the picture of the woman—Lis—he had said he was engaged to.

He didn't know who this woman was. He could *imagine*, but that wasn't quite the same thing. He had found the photograph in a camera store in San Francisco, just off the J Church line, which he would ride when

he got tired of riding on BART. It had been inside a frame on sale for
$17.99. The cost of the frame wasn't too much to pay for a woman to be
engaged to, even if you were broke. Standing there in the store, Howie
had conjured up for himself the pleasantly surprised expressions that
would appear on Saul and Patsy's faces when he told them that he would
be married within a matter of months. He had thought the pictured
woman pretty, so he bought the frame, with her inside it. In this way, he
had captured her. The clerk said that if he wished, he could keep the
photograph, which was of a former employee of the shop.

Howie looked around for a piece of paper. A pencil, a pen, the neces-
sities.

Dear Saul & Patsy,

*I made a call back home this morning and it turns out that I must return
immediately. I know this seems terribly strange but it's just the way things have
developed. At least you now know about my engagement, and at least I got to see
the beautiful Emmy. I'll talk to you about the $2 mil later.*

Love, Howie
ps: I did the dishes and cleaned your gutters and the windows.

Howie put the note on Saul and Patsy's bed. Outside he noticed that
the sun had not moved for a couple of hours, nailed to its quadrant. A
violent stillness inhabited the air, punctuated by an occasional striking
sound of jug corks popping. He had had the strangest feeling last night
that Saul and Patsy and Emmy were shadows on the wall, their shadow-
voices echoing inside his own voices. Their shadows somehow exceeded
his own and were stronger than his. They knew so little about what the
world was coming to that they had become stronger than he was, thriv-
ing, as it were, on their own ignorance, the powerful bullying force of
their innocence.

He touched the quilt on his brother and sister-in-law's bed and
shouted quickly.

The sound of his shouting roiled through the empty upstairs rooms.
What you did alone, what you did by yourself when no one was looking

or listening, was acceptable, because whatever you did unobserved . . . well, it hadn't really happened, except to you, and was consequently unimaginable and meaningless to others, and would never be spoken of.

He returned to the bedroom in which he had slept, closed up his suitcase, and started down the stairs. The lie about the two million dollars was harmless and *beautiful,* in its way, as some lies could be, fragrant and radiant: he had wanted to see their reactions—to be in charge of their reactions—and to make his brother and sister-in-law happy for a few days. What was the harm in that? Saul and Patsy, innocent and happy, like a married couple in a sentimental MGM Technicolor musical from the late 1940s directed by Vincente Minnelli, echoing his happiness for a few months, for a year or two, before all the money flew away again, like a great flock of migratory birds, and the happiness dispersed with it too, and the euphoria, as ephemeral in their departures as they had been in their arrivals. The money, utterly magical, half-imaginary, until you no longer had it, first congealed and then evaporated.

There are a lot of me's out there, he had said, and meant it.

Strange, that Patsy hadn't wanted what he had offered her. The money. Well, now she wouldn't get it.

He took his car keys from a table in the front hallway, put them into his right hand, holding his suitcase handle in his left hand. He thought of going through Saul and Patsy's things—their drawers, their secret places—then thought better of it. They wouldn't have any secret places, no corners, no crimes, no disfigurements, no open wounds, no abscesses. Secret places and open wounds—well, that was what he himself had. Secret places were his stock-in-trade, the living stash. He lived in them. But here, in Five Oaks, everything was out in the open under the admonitory glare of the sun.

He carried the suitcase to the car and loaded it into the trunk. After getting in behind the wheel, he started the engine, which roared satisfyingly to life. He wondered where he would drive, how long his available money would hold out, and then the credit, how long the credit would hold out, how long people would believe him. Perhaps he would go back home, to bankruptcy court and the dates they had set, the settlements, the agreements, etc., etc., etc., etc., etc., etc. He tightened his hand on the steering wheel and thought of how he would call his brother in a month or so to announce, ever so sadly, the cancellation of his engagement to the beautiful Phyllis. *Phyllis!* Jesus, people were easy to fool, at least in the short term. Phyllis! It was a name like "Petunia" or "Esmeralda." It stank of the whimsical-imaginary. Maybe Saul would ask about the two million, and then again maybe he wouldn't. The subject just wouldn't come up. Perhaps, instead, he would see the trees leafing out, see the flowers blooming and wilting in his front yard, and the grass growing and mowed down, growing and mowed down in his plot of ground, his little patch of American real estate. The great pageant of life here in the Midwest in its cycles of growth leading to the harvest, waxing and waning just like the moon, would present themselves to Saul and to his storybook family, and Saul would read those cycles as students of the classics might read an epic. In the distance Saul's family might see Howie himself on the horizon waxing and waning like the moon. They might see the colossal mysteries of success and failure, and they would observe human beings, in passing, squashed by the marketplace, like bugs. More likely, however, they would see none of that. They would just trudge to work, to school, to day care, to the job, to retirement, to the cemetery, like little imaginary people on a little imaginary stage.

Howie pulled out of the driveway, looked at himself in the rearview mirror, nodded, snapped on the radio, and turned onto the first available road heading west.

Nineteen

Gina had been thinking for weeks of what her costume would be on Halloween, even if she didn't wear it from door to door, even if she was too old for trick-or-treating per se. As you got older, Halloween night was for other, more complicated, mischief. After sneaking out the back, she would walk over the railroad tracks to the mall in full regalia and meet her friends. They would go out prowling together, kick-ass their way to a party somewhere, get wasted, have fun. Having almost drowned this past summer when Gordy Himmelman, the ghoul, had wanted to pull her under with him, the first of many such local sightings by sharp-eyed Five Oaks youth, she wasn't going to dress up as Madonna or Britney Spears or the good fairy or Vampyra or Cinderella or Tinker Bell or Marilyn Monroe or any such girl-shit as that. That scene was all over with. She had her hair cut short a week ago (her mother had a total fit—rage and tears—but: the hair was *her own* hair, not her mom's), had found a pair of cool dark glasses, a baseball cap that she wore with the visor in back, a FEAR THIS T-shirt, a pair of Doc Martens, raggedy blue jeans without a belt, and over the T-shirt a black leather jacket she had borrowed from Eddie Loquasto, her on-again boyfriend, who this week had a thing for her, and who had gotten it, the jacket, from somewhere else. It fit Eddie Loquasto and it fit her, too, since she and Eddie were about the same size,

Charles Baxter

though he was way stronger, a muscular little dude. She had promised
promised promised to give it back the next day.

As she was dressing, Eddie called her to say that he had obtained his
dad's car and would pick her up in thirty minutes. He'd be wearing something, too, but wouldn't tell her what. She wouldn't recognize him. Cool.
They would go somewhere. Maybe they would find weapons of minor
destruction. They would be dangerous. If they were *too* dangerous, they
would end up in the dungeon together. Which wouldn't be so bad, being
dungeon-mates.

She looked down at her fingernails, bitten to the quick.

Unsatisfied by the appearance of her fingernails, she gazed into the
mirror through her dark glasses. A totally fucked-up boy looked back at
her. That was so perfect that it was scary. The boy kind of turned her on.
Gina could feel her motor humming.

On this earth nothing was scarier than boys. And, as long as she could
sneak out of the house, evading the unwatchful eyes of her exhausted,
half-asleep, sorrow-drowned-in-beer mom and her little brother, Bertie,
the original game boy who never paid attention, anyway, to the world,
tonight she would be that creature she had always wanted to be—a boygirl, on a rampage.

Twenty

All day, the thirty-first of October, Saul remained preoccupied with his brother's appearance and disappearance two days before, but more than that, more than his brother or his imminent wedding to Lis, the beautiful woman with the strange photographic resemblance to Patsy, he was preoccupied with the promissory two million dollars. All right: it hadn't actually appeared. All right: once he did have it, he still couldn't spend it. All right: the money was invested in techno stocks, Howie claimed, and even now might be worthless. All right: maybe this wealth didn't exist at all and had disappeared as quickly and as inexplicably as Howie had— called back to its origin, on business.

Still, real or not, whatever its status, the sum of two million dollars was an intoxicant. During homeroom period, talking to his sophomore students about Halloween safety, he mentally bought a boat (and a trailer, and, for good measure, a lake to put it in). During second-period American history—they were studying Federalism—he sold the boat and bought real estate, a place in the mountains. What mountains? The Rockies? No, in Vermont, near a ski resort of some sort close to Stowe. He had rarely been so distracted or had taught so absentmindedly, not even after Emmy was born. Saul forgot Ben Weber's name, and he *liked* Ben Weber.

The trouble was, he didn't ski, and neither did Patsy, so that particular fantasy was in the trash can by third period.

During third period, in the teacher's lounge, he drank coffee and corrected quizzes and devoted the money to better causes, to altruism, which led to the construction of a teen recreational center in Five Oaks, the Bernstein Center for Youth, which would help stamp out Himmelism. Ten minutes later, he gave all the money to the Environmental Defense Fund. He was about to go into his next class, a modern European history AP class for seniors, when the cell phone in his sportcoat pocket rang. Saul *thought* he had turned off the ringer. He disapproved of cell phones but had one anyway, for emergencies.

"It's me," Patsy said. "I'm at the office. There's something I have to tell you."

"What?"

"Well, it's your brother. Something about him gave me the willies this time. More than usual, I mean. So I called your mother this morning. Delia was home—it's not one of her workdays."

Saul waited. "Yes?"

"Saul, she never heard about this fiancée. She'd like to, but she hasn't. She has her doubts."

"Oh, Howie's always been shy and secretive about his girlfriends."

"Girlfriends. Yeah, right. There's something else."

"What?"

"It's about the money."

"What about the money?"

"Delia didn't want to tell me. She put it off. She hemmed and she hawed."

"Patsy, just say it."

"Howie's been borrowing money from her. From your mother."

"*Borrowing?* From my mother? How much?"

"It took a long time for me to squeeze that one out of her," Patsy said. "But she finally admitted it—and, after all, I *do* work for a bank. This is my bread and butter. She was sniffling as she told me. He borrowed about twenty thousand dollars from her, Saul. Delia's been trying to keep all this news from us, of course, because she doesn't want to seem to be playing favorites with her cash reserves. But, as I say, she's been lending him money because he's in such trouble."

"Why?"

Her voice came out thickened with exasperation. "Well, obviously he didn't tell us what's going on with him. Obviously he *couldn't* tell us. He declared bankruptcy four weeks ago. Hellhounds are on his trail."

"Aw, jeez," Saul said. "Aw, jeez."

"Your brother has gone a little crazy, Saul."

Saul made a noise, of outrage, and surprise, and sadness.

"I know," she agreed. "Well, at least he didn't ask *us* for money. Listen, on your way home, would you pick up a pumpkin? We need to carve up one of those babies for tonight. I'll buy some candy after I've gotten Emmy. This is her first real Halloween, darling. And I have a feeling the trick-or-treaters are going to mainly be trickers this time, with us. If we got egged last night, they'll have more in mind for tonight. Watch your step. We're going to have every single damn light on in that house, to keep the monstrosities away."

The last working farm that Saul knew about on the outskirts of Five Oaks, a place where they actually sold pumpkins, was on County Highway 6—the Czarnieckis' place, north of the river on a hill overlooking the WaldChem plant in the distance, and though Saul would have preferred to get a pumpkin at the supermarket, the only ones they had left at the SuperSaver were small and rotten and mean, the size of coffee cups and bowling balls. He craved ownership over something larger, a gargoyle object, a monument that would scare the hobgoblins and hexies away. When he drove up to the Czarnieckis' roadside stand, no one was in attendance. Underneath a coffee can with a plastic lid and a slot for money, someone had left a small handmade sign:

Take the one you want and
put the money in the can.
Cleerance: $5.00 or best offer

Saul dutifully put a five-dollar bill in the coffee can (it was the only money there) and carried away the biggest pumpkin he could find from the pile of misshapen castoffs behind the stand. The one he chose was so large he could barely lift it, and when he tried to load it into the Chevy's trunk, he was unable to turn the key in the keyhole and hold the pumpkin at the same time. After unlocking the trunk, he picked up his pumpkin from the gravel driveway and hoisted it inside. When he did, he heard an unpleasant sound from his back—he had lifted the huge pumpkin incorrectly, throwing out his spine somehow. The lid of the trunk would just barely close over the gigantic thing, and he was able to get the pumpkin in snugly only by flattening the stem down under the trunk lid.

Driving home, he listened to the Fifth Symphony of Joachim Raff on the NPR station—in the last movement, the devil-horses took the protagonist clip-clopping down into hellfire—and tried to pretend that Halloween, *this* Halloween, was a night like all other nights. The Czarniecki pumpkin muttered and rumbled from in back.

At home, he first removed his texts and classroom materials from the car to the house and deposited them on the floor of the upstairs study. Then he returned to the car and opened the trunk. The pumpkin looked at him and Saul looked back at the pumpkin. Once again he bent over, once again he heard popping noises from the region of his back, and with groans and grunts Saul wrested the outsized squash from its resting place into his arms, whereupon he staggered across the garage through the back door (he had remembered to leave the door open and the storm door propped), and, still holding the pumpkin in his embrace, he weaved his unsteady way through the mud room, past the hanging jackets and overshoes, into the kitchen. He was sweating now, his arms and his back ached, but he was not about to be defeated. He left the yellow-orange beast on the floor, retrieved some newspapers from the back hallway, and spread them around underneath it to catch the glop and the seeds.

He would need trash clothes for the next job. Saul went upstairs to his closet.

Gordy Himmelman's shirts and trousers were there on the floor where he had left them. They were his physical, material legacy from the boy, and he had been unable to decide what to do with them. They didn't seem to be the right size, and he didn't imagine that they would fit him. Or that they could *ever* have fit him. Nevertheless, he took off the shirt that he had worn to school and tried on one of Gordy's, a dingy red flannel imprinted with stinks and stains that fit Saul rather well, even though his arms went far past the cuffs. At least this shirt wasn't the particular one Gordy had been wearing when he shot himself—that shirt went into the fire with Gordy at the crematory. Saul loosened his belt, took off his pants, and put on a pair of Gordy's jeans. They were much too snug, but with some strategic breathing-in and struggles with the zipper, and with his shirts—his undershirt and the flannel shirt—hanging out, Gordy-style, rather than tucked in, Saul could manage it.

Saul looked at himself in the full-length mirror attached to the inside of Patsy's closet door. There he was, his bearded affable face attempting to smile above the clothes smelling of dog and defeat (what dog? Gordy didn't have a dog). As he was looking at him, he felt his mind cloud over, and Saul closed his eyes, lowered his head, and said a prayer for his brother. *Whoever You are, preserve my little brother from his demons. Save him from himself and from this world. Save him, please. What can I give You in trade? What do I have that You want? Tell me.*

Saul heard no answer coming back. Just then his wife and daughter pulled up in the driveway, and he had the abrupt impression that he had somehow found himself on the wrong side of the mirror.

He ran downstairs to greet them and managed to get into the kitchen before Patsy and Emmy entered. He heard Patsy call out, "Saaaauuul! We're home!" as she carried Emmy to the front hallway and took off her daughter's jacket and then took off her own. Saul could hear the noise of the coat hangers.

"In here!" Saul shouted, standing next to his pumpkin. "Ladies, we're in here!"

Patsy had taken hold of Emmy's hand. Emmy wanted to walk, apparently, and was doing so next to her mother when they both came into the
kitchen. Saul stood proudly next to his pumpkin.

"Hi, honey. How d'you like it? We're ready to carve," he said, and they
both screamed, his wife and daughter, together. Emmy was staring at the
pumpkin and Patsy was staring at Saul.

"What is this?" she finally managed to say, above her daughter's sobs.

"Carving clothes," Saul told her.

"But those are *his* clothes," Patsy said, approaching Saul, the way she
usually did every evening after they came home from work and saw each
other, for a kiss, but then she seemed to think better of it and drew away
from him. "That boy's. I thought you had gotten rid of them. What that
Bagley woman gave you."

"No, I didn't. They were in my closet. On the floor. Where I put
them," he added.

"I should go into your closet sometimes," Patsy said. "Hush, sweetie,"
she crooned, leaning over to pick up Emmy, who had been clutching her
mother's legs. Now Patsy kissed her on the cheeks, tranquilizing kisses.
Calming in slow stages, Emmy then looked up at her father and began
screaming again, truly hysterical, very much unlike herself.

"Maybe you should take her," Patsy said.

"Okay."

But Emmy squirmed out of Saul's grasp, retreating back into her
mother's arms. She screamed louder when Saul put the knife into the top
of the pumpkin, continued screaming as he carved around the stem, her
screams growing shrill, all-purpose screams, until finally Patsy carried
Emmy into the living room, where she sat down in the rocking chair
with Emmy in her lap. Saul could hear Patsy talking quietly, singing to
Mary Esther, calming her. After a few minutes, he heard Patsy carrying
Mary Esther upstairs, not for a diaper change—Patsy would have
changed her by now anyway—but to get her her music bear, a wind-up
music box inside a teddy bear whose head swayed back and forth as the
music played. Saul knew Patsy's moves, as she knew his. He didn't have to
ask. Someone should start dinner, he thought. Someone should heat up
food for Emmy.

Alone in the kitchen, Saul went to work on the pumpkin, clearing out its innards, dropping them on the sheets of newspaper he had spread around himself on the floor, before beginning on the face. He carved the eye holes, the nose, the mouth. How simple. He lit a candle and positioned it inside on a dish. He closed the lid back over the jack-o-lantern and carried it to the front door and out onto the front stoop. From inside, the flame continued to burn.

He switched on the front light.

Let them come.

Twenty-one

From her upstairs room, Gina heard the distant sound of a car honking, so far away that if your ears weren't perfectly tuned to it, you wouldn't have heard it, but she did, *she* heard it, the way a bird hears the cry of its mate from clear across the bright green rainforest, its bright cry, its shrill distant mating call. Her mother was in the back den watching TV. She hadn't put the front porch light on: no treat-or-tricksters for her, she didn't do that scene anymore. Her little brother was somewhere in the house, not eligible for Halloween this year, thanks to his misbehavior.

"I'm going out for a while," Gina called from the front door in her lowest voice, her boygirl voice, and her mother called back, "Going where?" but Gina was gone, was out, by the time an answer would have been expressed or implied, and both of them, her mother and her brother, would be into their after-dinner thing by now, anyway, her mother parental but glazed and half-asleep and not meaning to be indifferent but indifferent nevertheless, and smoking dazedly, and watching whatever show was on now, in the company of Bertie, their four eyes glued to the screen, unless Bertie was lost in the Game Boy. What could her mother do if Gina was going to go out? Gina's mother was helpless against Gina, age against feckless youth, especially after dinner, when her mother was exhausted from work and from making dinner and from the full menu of life. That's what she sometimes said when she was grim. *I'm helpless against the full menu of life.* Maybe if Gina's dad still lived over here instead of over there he would be laying down the law, but he wasn't here, this wasn't his day for custody. Her mother, half-asleep and single-parenting tonight, was glued to the TV, attached to it bodily. Gina felt a trace of love for her hapless mother. How she tried! She just wasn't up to it. Where were the mothers with hap? Nowhere. They were all hapless. Closing the front door behind her, Gina saw a TV screen in her mind's eye with eyeballs glued to it.

Eddie Loquasto's father's Plymouth pulled up in front of the house. Another vehicle trailed it. Gina ran over to the passenger-side door of the first vehicle and climbed in. The driver kept the engine running. A crow was behind the wheel.

"Hey," the crow said. The crow had Eddie Loquasto's voice, but that was about it.

"Hey," Gina said.

"You look sort of extremely weird," the crow said, shaking its head.

"Thanks. You, too." Gina twisted around. There was a garbage can with legs sitting in the backseat. The garbage can had two eye holes but no arms. Its lid was attached to the can with duct tape. "Who're you?" Gina asked.

"I'm garbage," the garbage can informed her. She couldn't tell who it was: the can did strange things to the voice of who or whatever was inside. "Who're *you*?" the garbage can asked irritably.

"I'm a boy. I'm fucked up," Gina told it.

"You said it," the garbage can muttered. It was very ill-tempered. "That's the royal truth."

Gina was not liking the garbage can, but she said, "Cool," to mollify it. She wanted to say, "You're just a goddamn garbage can, who're you to be telling me anything?" but it was one of those nights when you didn't want to insult anybody or anything too quickly. You could be hurt in strange ways. Curses and shit could fall like rain over you. Soon your life would be worth nothing. It would enter the zero column and stay there. She settled into the front seat and put her hands in the pockets of the leather jacket. Little demons ran around on the sidewalk, holding their bags of worthless candy. Her nail-bitten boygirl fingers touched some gum inside the jacket pocket, fresh bubble gum, and she unwrapped it and put it into her mouth and started chewing. "Where're we goin'?"

"Hey, that's my gum. We're going to that Mr. Bernstein's house," the crow said. "Us and that truck behind us." The crow nodded at the rear-view mirror to indicate a Ford pickup behind them. "We've got something for him."

"What?"

"Wait and see. Tricks instead of treats."

"Yeah," the garbage can said, affirming the crow's position. "Fucking A."

Gina saw that next to the garbage can on the backseat were some rolls of toilet paper, firecrackers, a paint can and a paintbrush, a few rocks, a box of matches, a can of gasoline, and an odd assortment of rotting vegetables. She wondered if somebody had also brought a gun.

"Are we going to use those?" the boygirl asked.

"If we have to," the crow informed her. "Are you in? Or not?"

"Blow me," the boygirl said belligerently, as if she ever wasn't, because, after all, she was on a rampage and would do rampage-things.

"You wish," said the garbage can.

Twenty-two

Saul discovered, as he dispensed candy to the goblins and fairies and Jedi knights and Osama bin Ladens and little ghosts in their white-sheet out-fits, that he really *had* done something to his back picking up that damnable oversized pumpkin: he could not straighten himself but instead stood half bent over in a crouching position, his face in a clouded grimace. He groaned inwardly. Everyone who came to his door seemed to assume that the bent-over posture and the facial expression were part of his costume, and if he only would stuff a loaf of bread inside his shirt, right behind the shoulders, he would be doing a fair Quasimodo.

"An ogre!" one precocious little girl said, catching her first glimpse of Saul. She was dressed up as a pizza, with sponges glued to cardboard to look like cheese. "Where's your teeth?"

Saul exposed his teeth, and the pizza screamed and retreated.

But the posture, and the huge glowering jack-o-lantern on the stoop, and the music—Saul had put Bernard Herrmann's soundtrack for *The Day the Earth Stood Still* on the audio system and was pumping it out onto the street—had, so far, kept away the worst trouble that the night might offer. Herrmann's theremins were charms against violence, Saul fig-ured—Eine kleine Walpurgisnachtmusik. While Patsy had calmed Mary Esther with songs and *her* music, an opposing sort of nocturne—nursery rhymes—Saul had made them dinner, a quick spaghetti and a salad. They had all eaten in haste, Mary Esther calmer now but still wary of her father. Then Patsy and Emmy had gone upstairs and shut the bedroom door.

Standing just inside the foyer, Saul was counting the candy bars left in the bowl when an old Plymouth pulled up in front of his house, followed by a truck that parked directly behind it. The motors in both vehicles were kept running as the drivers'-side doors opened at the curb. The truck's radio was playing AC/DC, full blast. From the car came, first, a crow, who had been behind the wheel, and then, after the crow, an androgynous boy blowing bubble gum, and, from the backseat rear door, and with some apparent difficulty in movement, a garbage can on legs. From their height, Saul guessed that they were high schoolers. He saw that inside the car they had packed tools of destruction, including a gasoline can. The truck disgorged a wolf, a hanged woman with a noose around her neck, and a girl or a boy—it was sometimes impossible to discern genders here—dressed up as a caterpillar. A Himmel, looking like Kurt Cobain, jumped down from the truck bed and sauntered across the lawn. Saul did a quick count: seven in all. So this was it. He brought the bowl of candy bars out front and closed the front door of his house behind him.

"Good evening," Saul said, holding out the bowl. He knew candy was no good with these characters, or good manners either. A hanged woman with a broken neck does not want a candy bar. Anyone knows that.

"Yeah," the crow said, nodding its head. From the bed of the truck another character appeared—it jumped out and joined the group. It walked like a man. This one was particularly unsettling: he was the size of a football player, with wide shoulders and thick muscles, and was wearing a football helmet with a plastic shield over the eyes so that you couldn't see the face. The words LITTLE HANS were written with Magic Marker on the helmet just above the shielded eyes. The same words were written in amateurish gothic script in back. Eight of them in all. Little Hans was probably the enforcer. His large, meaty hands were in fists.

"Want some candy?" Saul asked.

"Shut up," the crow said. "Just shut the fuck up." He walked away from Saul, and the others followed him like soldiers, regimented some-how, all of them directed toward the front door of the house. The largest one, Little Hans, served as the rear guard. Saul began to run, hoping to reach the door before they did—he couldn't remember whether the lock had snapped when he'd shut it—but before he had passed the wolf and the Himmel, something tripped him, and he fell to the lawn, and the bowl of candy fell with him, scattering its contents across the grass.

He heard several of them laughing, a scratching infernal sound. They were probably drunk, these creatures. They were keeping one another company, and that gave them courage, the courage of the mob—that, and the alcohol. And now they had had their first success.

Saul had fallen so that his nose bumped into the ground; he would have been able to break the fall better if he hadn't been holding the bowl of treats. His hands had freed themselves too late; he felt suddenly that his accidents tonight would not be lucky ones. Lifting himself up quickly, he made an effort to run toward the front of his house again, but hands, or paws, held him back. The exterior light to his house seemed suddenly a fragile and ineffective guard against these adolescents. It was more like a lighthouse that invited the storm. Saul, struggling against what he could see now was the caterpillar, and who, judging from his strength, was a young man, had forgotten how strong high schoolers could some-times be, how implacable. In a fury to match his own, their sweat had a rancid animal odor, and their sounds of struggle emerged from them in bestial grunts. At the same time, he heard, from behind him, two of the party of creatures scuttling around in the truck bed, and he turned in time to see them—it was Little Hans and the hanged woman—pulling out another can of gasoline, along with a box of kitchen matches.

With all the strength he had, Saul fought off the caterpillar arms hold-ing him. The wolf and the crow picked up the pumpkin easily, and then, as if all this had been rehearsed, carried it around to the side of the house.

Saul continued to fight, jabbing and kicking, as he watched the wolf and the crow swing the pumpkin to get some momentum before throw-ing it at a window. The arc of the pumpkin's flight reached the glass and broke it, but the pumpkin was too large, too sizable, too generous, to make its way inside the house. The window was just too small. But the sound of glass breaking would at least alert Patsy. The pumpkin fell back to the ground but did not shatter. Behind him, he heard the characteristic glug of gasoline being poured from a fuel container. He turned, desperately, in time to see Little Hans setting fire to the rosebush that he and Patsy had planted. The gasoline caught with a satisfied whooshing sound, a broken in-suck of breath.

Now, in front of him, he saw the wolf and the crow picking up the pumpkin again and moving toward another window. Little bush-league terrorists in training: all they wanted to do was break the damn windows. Or maybe that was for starters. The sound of breaking glass pleased them, gave them a rush. They were from that timeless sector of the disadvantaged that broke windows wherever they found them. This was all that was left of the revolutions of 1848. Hapless, still Saul fought, and he had almost freed himself when he felt himself being taken in hand by Little Hans, whose giant arms pinned Saul's arms behind his back and who put a thick pillar of a leg in front of him; it was as if, physically, there would be no more argumentation. The wolf and the crow were about to heave the pumpkin at the second window when Saul shouted. "Stop. *He's here.*"

The crow turned its beak toward him, and the pumpkin dropped to the ground.

"Who's here?" he asked.

Saul heard the bush burning behind him. Little Hans smelled of gasoline, as the god Vulcan probably did. He himself had the characteristic Gordy-odor, of dog.

"Gordy," Saul said. "Isn't he what you came for?" There would be no fighting them off physically; they were too strong, and they were legion. He would have to try something else. He looked up quickly and saw Patsy pulling the curtains and then lowering the shades. He didn't think the other creatures had seen her.

"The fucker's dead," the crow said, apparently the spokesperson for the group. "You killed him."

"He shot himself," Saul yelled. "Let go of me, Henry," Saul said, guessing that the kid inside the Little Hans suit was probably Henry Olschanski, a guard on the football team. As if by magic, the arms released him. No—tonight's accidents might in fact be lucky ones.

The wolf turned in Saul's direction. "Where is he h-h-h-h-here?"

"You want Gordy?" Saul asked. "I'll go get him."

The creatures appeared to be stunned.

"But you have to promise," Saul said, gathering his wits, "to stay where you are. Otherwise you get nothing."

"He's just going inside to hide," the garbage can said. "He's afraid."

"Who the hell are you?" Saul asked the garbage can. Some of these beings had to have been his students. Perhaps he would recognize their voices.

"I'm garbage!" the garbage can announced angrily.

"Well, listen, garbage," Saul said. "One thing I'm not, is afraid. And if you wait right there, I'll go get what you want."

"He'll call the police," the boygirl said. "That's what he's going to do."

Still, behind him, the bush continued to burn. When he turned to see it momentarily, it looked like someone's backside, with a crease down the middle.

"If I did that," Saul said, "all of you would come back here, and do this again. *I know you*," he said, gaining his advantage. *"I know all of you."*

"W-w-w-w-what do you know?" the wolf asked.

"I know what you want," Saul said. "I know everything you want. I know your thoughts before you have them. You want to see him again. Don't you want to see him?" His nose felt as if it had been broken in his fall—it was screaming with pain, but Saul felt suddenly calm. He recognized that, indeed, he was not afraid of them, and that his hatred of them was tempered, illogically, with curiosity. He had made up his mind that they were all children, and, within limits, he was going to give them what they wanted. Or needed, maybe without knowing. So far, they were amateurs at destruction and terror. Looking at them, he decided to adopt them as his own, such as they were, monsters of neglect and loneliness. It made more sense than being afraid of them. Somebody had to be a parent around here; someone had to have some feeling for what was hidden under the disguises. He, too, was disguised: he was wearing Gordy's clothes. The creatures walked toward Saul, surrounding him. All their movements seemed ironical.

"How come you're bent over like that?" the Himmel asked, evading Saul's question.

"Threw my back out picking up that pumpkin," Saul said, nodding toward his jack-o-lantern, now on the lawn. All of them—bubble gum, the crow, Little Hans, the caterpillar, the wolf, the Himmel, and the garbage can—turned to look.

"That's a r-r-r-r-righteous pumpkin," the wolf said. He had a stammer that involved swallowing and spitting up both vowels and consonants.

The wolf's stammer appeared to silence the crowd of creatures. Bubble gum looked through his/her dark glasses at the night sky. It was cold enough so that you could see everyone's breath, but no one was shivering yet, though they would be shivering soon. The hanged woman moaned. How odd it was, that he should find himself in the company of these castoffs!

"Everyone talks about you," the crow said. "Everyone says you're the one. They say it all the time."

"The one what?" Saul asked.

"The one who started all this," the hanged woman said. The garbage can nodded by shaking back and forth. Saul could not see through the eye holes to who or whatever was inside—he was more curious about the garbage can than he was about any of the others. "All this trouble with Gordy Himmelman and Sam Cole and things going wrong all the time!" The bush was mostly burnt by now, cracking down to ash, making sounds of expiration. "Everything going to shit. It's your fault."

"It wouldn't have happened if that kid hadn't shot himself on your front lawn," the Himmel said. "We need some payback." The last phrase sounded like a sentence an adult would say, and the Himmel said it without enthusiasm or conviction.

"And the sightings," the crow said. "There wouldn't be sightings if it wasn't for you."

"Sightings?" Saul asked. "You kids have your nerve to talk about sightings."

"*You* know," the crow said. He was not going to pronounce Gordy Himmelman's name, either. The mothball-stinking crow obviously thought it brought on bad luck. God, what a hotbed of superstition, and gossip, and malice, and Dark Age reasoning these kids were—these middle schoolers and high schoolers, at least the outcasts among them. Magical thinking was all they had. The other kind had failed them.

"So I bet you came here to throw things at the house, and scare us, and do all that, the pranks and troublemaking with the toilet paper and the eggs and the rocks and the slogans and the fire. Is that because I'm Jewish?" There was a long silence, and none of the creatures moved. "I bet it is."

"People say that you know th-th-th-th-things," the wolf finally managed to say.

"What do you want me to do?" Saul said. "With the things I know?"

"Bring him back," the crow announced to the crowd. He was a tough little crow. But he was improvising and not very clever. "Like you said you could."

"All right," Saul said. "I'll go get him."

The creatures stared at him. Saul had made of himself a master of resurrection. *That* was what Jews could do. All of them, including Little Hans, stepped away from him.

"You can do that?" the Himmel asked.

"Just watch," Saul said.

Five minutes later Saul came back, still bent over, with a small cardboard box. Inside the cardboard box was a cloisonné jar, and inside the jar— Saul showed the creatures this in the dark—were some ashes. The creatures drew back.

"That's him?" one of them asked.

"That's him," Saul said. In his other hand, he held a shovel. "All of you, come on," he said. He led them around the side of the house to the backyard, and then through the yard to a terrain of undergrowth and scrub and weeds beyond the lawn. Finally, reaching a small patch of ground between two bushes, he stopped. The trees and the night gave to the area a thick, profound darkness in which details—and the passage of time—were not discernible.

"Have we got everybody?" he asked. Quickly he counted the small pillars of darkness. There were seven. "Where's the bubble-gum boy?" Saul asked. Of course she was a girl, but he would call her a "boy" tonight.

"She got cold," the crow said. "I think she went back to the car."

"She was *scared,* man," the garbage can said. "That's all it was."

"She was crying, too," the caterpillar told them. "I'm pretty sure. What a wuss."

"Well, anyway," Saul said. He held out the shovel. "All right. Here's the deal. These are Gordy's ashes. We have to bury him. He's been undead. When the ashes aren't buried, you get the undead thing happening. You get the hauntings. So who among you wants to dig?"

"*I* can't," the garbage can said. "I don't have arms."

"Give me that." Little Hans had finally spoken up. He didn't sound like a high school student, but maybe he was; maybe he was really Henry Olschanski. He might have been anything. Saul handed him the shovel, and Little Hans began digging with it, his motions reflecting strength and fury. He was obviously practiced with shovels and knew how to use them. He was wearing heavy black leather boots, and he pitched the sharp blade of the shovel into the topsoil, which he lifted and cast off into the distance—the creatures were standing behind him—before arriving at the dirt beneath it, and then the clay. He hit a rock, and he scraped the shovel head around it, then threw the shovel onto the ground and dropped down on his hands and knees and scrabbled with his fingers around until he had a grasp of it, whereupon he lifted it out and heaved it on the dirt pile in front of him.

"I'm glad we brought him along," the Himmel said. "He's a force."

Little Hans picked up the shovel again and resumed digging. "Anyone else want to do this?" he asked in a deep bass voice, between breaths, while he dug, but none of the creatures replied.

"Mr. Bernstein," the crow asked. "It's your turn."

"It's okay," Saul told him. "Little Hans is doing a fine job." Standing there, amid the creatures, Saul reached up and touched his nose, confirming that it was, in fact, broken.

Working in what still seemed to be a total, life-defining rage, Little Hans continued to shovel until the hole was large enough for the jar, and then spacious enough for the box, and then, five minutes later, much larger than it needed to be for their purposes, as if he had been unable to stop, as if the shoveling was a kind of maniacal nightmare gravedigger assignment, tunneling down to the dark he met up with every night, not just this one. Finally, with the smell of sweat in the cold air drifting off of him, he rested.

"Is that deep enough?" he asked. He glanced around.

"Deeper than it needs to be," Saul said. "Deep enough for everybody."

"This is creepy," the crow said with distinct pleasure in his voice.

"Who wants to lower him in?" Saul asked, glancing around at where the group appeared to be, all of them half-unseeable, obscure. He held the box out. None of the creatures took it.

"*You* need to do it," the caterpillar said. "Where's your wife? Maybe she should, too."

"She's not here," Saul said. "She's not here." He waited. "Anyone want to touch the box before I put it into the ground?" The caterpillar reached out, and then the crow raised a wing, and the Himmel touched it, but the rest drew back. It was just too much for them.

"How come you didn't bury it sooner?" the wolf asked.

"You don't always bury the ashes," Saul said. "Sometimes you keep them around. That was my mistake. That's how come we had zombies around town." With as much tenderness as he could summon, Saul, still bent over, carried the box to the hole that Little Hans had dug, and he lowered it until it rested there, on its deep layer of clay. He stood up again, as straight as he could make himself go with his back out, and he waited, looking at the pitch-black assembly. There was an expressive air pocket of silence. Off in the distance, very faintly, he could hear a jet in the night sky, and, also in the background, freeway noise. The music from *The Day the Earth Stood Still* was no longer audible, but the truck was still playing AC/DC.

"We need a blessing," Saul said.

"What the fuck. What blessing?" the crow asked. "What kinda shit is *that*? He was a total loser. An asshole. Besides, he's dead."

"He won't leave you alone unless you give him a blessing," Saul said. "That's why you're here."

The creatures were silent.

"This isn't going to work unless someone says a blessing over him. That's how it's done. Either bless him or leave. That's how it's done." His back was causing him excruciating pain now.

"This is America," the garbage can said. "We don't do that here."

"Bullshit," Saul said, and the creatures seemed surprised that he knew the word.

"*You* have to do it," the wolf said. "*You* were his teacher."

"I can't," Saul said. "I never went to services. My mother never took me to a temple or a synagogue. She didn't believe in that. She still doesn't. Nobody taught me blessings. And I don't do them either, except for this, this time, now." Saul tried to look at them all, but it was so dark he couldn't quite see them. They had to do it; he could not. "Doesn't *any-one* here know a blessing? Doesn't anyone here know how to be human? Somebody here must. Doesn't anyone here go to church? Or a temple? Or to an *anything* where they do blessings?"

"We do," the wolf said. "Me and my sister and our parents." The other creatures nodded. "I just wish we had a flashlight."

"Well, say something," Saul told him. "Say what they say. We don't need a flashlight for that. This is what you all came for. I swear to you, if the wolf comes up with something . . ." He left the sentence unfinished, and the darkness around him seemed to shift inwardly.

"L-l-l-l-l-l-lord, help help help helllllp," the wolf said, before giving up.

"That's okay," Saul told him. "Try some more."

"Amen amen amen amen," the wolf stuttered. "Please thou please thou let-t-t-t-t us depart in please. Peas." There was a long silence. "I c-c-c-c-c-can't do it," the wolf admitted.

"Yes, you can," Saul said.

"A-a-a-a-awake and mourn, ye heirs of h-h-h-hell," the wolf said.

"No, that's a curse," Saul said. "Try again."

The wolf began again tentatively, as if by rote, and then seemed to find his voice. "Many many many many. M-m-m-may the Lord may the Lord may the Lord may the Lord bless you and k-k-k-k-keep you," he said, giving the foreign-sounding words a hallucinated, studied attention, as if he were dredging them up from his memory, and then, because he was half-singing, his voice rose in conviction, its pitch deepening with intensity. "May the Lord be g-g-g-g-g-gracious unto you," he said, no longer intimidated by the words, since he wasn't stumbling over them so badly now. "May the Lord lift up the light of his countenance upon you and give you peace both this day and forevermore," the wolf concluded, reciting the final phrase in a high, steady, clear voice, as if the meaning of the words had come home to him and he was now their bearer. The hanged woman started to say "Amen," then stopped herself. The crow appeared to be angrily agitated and shifted his weight from one claw to another. A fragment of the moon appeared from behind a cloud, and Saul saw the crow more clearly, saw how agitated he had become, how he hated the blessing: he was nearly in a fighter's stance.

"There," Saul said, keeping his voice authoritative and steady. "That was good." He handed the shovel to the caterpillar. "Here," he said. "You have to drop some dirt down there."

Slowly and reluctantly, the caterpillar took the shovel and flung dirt into the hole. The shovel went around the group, all except for the malign, armless garbage can, until the hole was nearly covered up. At last the shovel returned to Saul, and he filled in the rest of the dirt. He tried to straighten up, could not, but at least knew what he wanted to say.

"Go home, children," he instructed them. "Go home."

The group of creatures trudged back across his backyard, around the house, into the front yard, one of them, the Himmel, picking up the gasoline can and the matches, and then they made their way toward the truck and the car. Among them, only Little Hans stood up perfectly straight. The others walked with the errant slouch of defeat.

"See ya," the crow said, making the words sound like a threat. The garbage can had already positioned itself in the backseat. The crow got in behind the wheel of the Plymouth, next to the bubble-gum boygirl, put the car into gear, and with a spinning of wheels and a screeching, drove away, followed by the truck, whose radio was now playing Rush.

Carrying his shovel, with a last glance at the burning rosebush, now sputtering out, Saul, his own face burning with pain, limped toward the house, with its one broken window, its wife and child still safe inside, upstairs, for the moment, this one night.

Twenty-three

"You thought you were so tough," the crow said to the boygirl. "You just *chickened* out. Just like a little girl." He cackled. "The girl came out all over you. You have to have balls to be a boy, didn't anyone tell you? Maybe you should have dressed yourself up as a chicken." The crow was thinking that the evening was now totally and completely whacked: he had been planning on doing some serious hilarious damage and asking the boygirl to give him a blowjob later, when the fun was almost over, when the house was burning. Not that she'd do it, but it would be worth asking her just to see the look on her face lit by the flames. Now he didn't feel like drinking, or fucking, or fighting—he didn't feel like doing *anything* enjoyable. He was completely bummed out, and the feeling was conclusive.

"The air was cold," the boygirl said. "Besides, *I* chickened out? What's all that stuff in the backseat? Rocks, paint, paintbrushes, gasoline, dynamite? *You* could've, like, just set fire to his house if you had the nerve, like you were planning to."

"Oh, right. Like *you* weren't scared. Anyway, I didn't go running and crying back to the car when he brought those ashes outside," the crow said.

"Okay, then what *are* you going to do with all that?" The boygirl pointed to the paraphernalia of pranksterism and terror on the backseat next to the garbage can.

"I don't know," the crow muttered. "Keep it for later."

"What later? This is later. To use on who?"

"There's *always* people to use it on." The crow laughed and reached under the seat and opened another can of beer. "Innocent bystanders and people like that."

"That's not very nice," the boygirl said. "Opening a beer and not offering me any. Where'd you steal it from?"

"Sorrrrry, bitch," the crow said. "You want a beer?"

"Don't you call me that. Don't you call me a bitch."

"Oh yeah?" the crow asked. He shook the beer can with his finger plugged over the opening and then aimed the spray at the passenger side, wetting down her face and her shirt and the leather jacket. Then he laughed. "There's your beer."

"You *dickhead,*" the boygirl said. "Take me home, you piece of shit. At least it's *your* leather jacket you're ruining." The boygirl put her hands on the wheel to turn it. The car weaved unsteadily down the residential street, narrowly missing a parked car.

"Children, children," the garbage can said, laughing.

The crow's mood had changed. Now he would have to clean the car, thanks to what she had made him do. He would have to deodorize the Plymouth's interior. His jacket could smell of beer just fine. Thinking about all this work in store for him, the crow recognized that his rage was her fault. Now he *did* feel like doing something: taking the boygirl by force if he had to, the bitch, with the garbage can watching—and the image of how he would do it settled down on him the way the robin settles down on the worm. He would take her out there into the dirt and the dark and pull her apart if he had to, just open her up and brute-fuck her to death. And when he was finished with her, he would leave her out in the middle of nowhere to find her own way home, that is, if she could still walk, bloody and seeping. He drank down the rest of the beer. At last: here it was: some serious damage.

The car accelerated, and the night, kept at bay till now by the neighborhood streetlights, gradually enveloped them as they hurried on toward the outskirts of the city and the fields of farmland beyond it.

Twenty-four

"It won't work," Patsy said. "You can't import religion and ritual like that, not as a local anesthetic. It only works when the whole community believes in it. A ritual engaged in by part of the community is just schmaltz, just window dressing. If they're going to make us outcasts of God, Saul, that's it. We're going to be outcasts of God *forever*."

"Hmmm." He was falling asleep. "I love you, Patsy," he said. "It *did* work."

"You're going to have to go see a doctor tomorrow about your nose and your back, Saul."

"Hmm." He was lying in bed in a fetal position.

"Not that I don't admire you, Saul, for trying to help those kids out."

"Hmmm. Love you."

"The baby's been moving a little tonight. Guess I can't blame him," Patsy said.

"Hmm." He was almost asleep by now.

"As for you, I love you more than you will *ever* know. By the way, Saul, what did you bury back there? What did you use for those ashes? The ones you said were Gordy's? What were they?"

Part Four

Twenty-five

At certain times, particularly on the days when she was working at the Baltimore food bank—it didn't take much more than a certain cast of light in the office or the connected warehouse to cause her to be plunged into these moments of thoughtfulness—Delia would involuntarily remember her late husband, Saul and Howie's father, and a picture of him would rise up in her mind, usually a random mental snapshot in which her husband was getting dressed for work, knotting his tie or making an effort to get the lint off his suit before he kissed her goodbye and left the house for the firm where he labored as a patent lawyer, and at such moments it occurred to her that now, twenty years after his death, she thought of him more than she ever had when they were married, a marriage that at the time had felt more like a business arrangement than a real marriage, lacking as it did much of any real passion on either side, or so she thought. They were both ready to get married when they had met as seniors at the university and a year later had married each other out of convenience more than anything else, though she had pretended to be crazy about him with her friends and family for the sake of appearances, and because she thought she should.

With many women she knew, especially the divorcées, the memory of the husband just faded out through an act of will. Men left behind their objects; women left behind the memory of their looks.

But with Delia the process had been different. You could sometimes love someone, as it turned out, *after* that person was gone, though not before. One of life's larger ironies, its habit of making what was absent, visible. That was what had happened to her, and this odd recognition had followed lately from the fling she had had with that boy, the young man who had worked on her yard. Perhaps this paradox was commonplace, but she doubted it. The death, the absence of her husband, sweetened the memory of the life. Sweetened it almost intolerably. In life her husband might have been, well, exasperating and bound by habit and, on occasion, repulsive: now and then he would rub his scalp, for example, then examine his fingertips for dandruff, and, if there happened to be any dandruff there near the fingernails, he would, if he thought no one was watching, slyly slip the fingertips close to his nose, for a smell. Awful. In life, it was a disgusting habit. But now, long after his death, picturing it, Delia felt tender toward it, and him. It pierced her. The gesture made her see the child in him, which, all day long, he was at pains to conceal.

Another odd feature of her long-dead husband's remnants, her memory of him, was that whenever she thought of him, her thoughts were accompanied by no name. In death he had seemingly lost the name he had had in life. He had turned into a man, into *him*, into the images she possessed of him, and his smells, and his gestures, his curiosities as a human being and as her companion, and the ways—pokey and tentative—he had touched her as a lover and husband who, truth be told, did not linger much over the niceties but who sometimes cooked for her and brought her breakfast in bed on Sunday mornings, all these images and smells added up to the memory of the man she had married and had known. She recognized that he had been utterly faithful to her because women as a gender and group and class simply did not occupy his thoughts very much. Somehow, you could detect his obliviousness to other women just by looking at him—he did not have a roving eye. As an adult man, his thoughts had turned completely to the schematics of providing for her and their two children, without, really, much conversation at the dinner table except for expediencies and plans, and then, one day, he was gone, before the conversations might really have started. He wanted, more than anything else, to be a utility-husband and a professional at business, and then he was professionally dead, slumped over the steering wheel, blocking traffic. His life had appeared to have had no purpose except as a husband and father and a lawyer. Nevertheless, he had helped to ease Delia through this life by being her companion and being, in his way, considerate and thoughtful. Now, in death, he had lost his name, though she said it from time to time when she was by herself, mostly in order to preserve it, so that someone here on Earth would still say it: Norman. A plain old name. But he wasn't Norman anymore. He was those images he had left behind, and their accompanying gestures, and the associated scents, and he was also the father of the two children he had, with her, helped to bring into the world. He had become real once he became imaginary.

Working in the food bank, she wondered sometimes what it felt like to have a coronary thrombosis, whether you even knew what had hit you before you were out of this life, gone.

She had loved, in a very different manner, having an adolescent boy lover because now she knew what that experience was like to go through, once you were a full-grown adult. She had gotten it out of her system (again). Really, the whole experience had been an exercise in nostalgia, at being in high school one more time, and being desired. And loved, a little. It was a wonder to her that the boy had wanted her at all, even for a few weeks. The experience had left a few traces for which she was grateful—it was as if life had arranged something like a cookout for her at the top of a mountain—but now, back to her normal routines, working during the day and going back to the house at night and fixing dinner for herself and pouring her nightly glass of Merlot, she was newly reconciled, first, to herself, and, second, to the idea that she might meet someone else, someone more her age, or she might not, ever, and anyway the meeting or not-meeting would not make much of a difference, one way or another. She was through with the belief that having a relationship, or relationships generally, would in any way validate her life. She liked living alone.

. . .

She had wanted to convey this truth to her son Saul. She didn't feel jealous of Patsy, but she just didn't appreciate the way they had been married to each other and still were married to each other. He was—for this behavior of his there was an old word that no one used anymore—uxorious. They were always touching each other and telling each other how much they loved each other, and they did this routine in public, and it got tiresome after a while. Delia especially didn't like to see her son doting over his wife. She would have liked it better if they had been able to take their love for each other for granted, as if it were permanent and assured, and, similarly, she would have liked it if he could keep some of his emotions to himself. He should make certain adult assumptions, as everyone did, and then get on with things.

Delia had never heard a man say "I love you" as often as Saul said it to his wife, in front of her, Delia—in front of everybody. Delia supposed that some women liked that. They became used to the sweet talk and expected it as if it were their birthright. But you didn't cast out that phrase in public where everyone could hear it.

Saul doted on his wife, he doted on their children, he had doted over that boy who shot himself, and he was a sentimentalist, but that was how he was, how he always had been, ever since his father had died. He was a doter. He doted. How close this was to "dotage"! The etymology of the words—Delia as a Scrabble player took pride in her knowledge of words—must be related. She would look it up. She blamed herself for the way Saul had turned out. She had told him to be careful of his baby brother, to take care of him, noting his fragility; and some element had changed in Saul thereafter. He had become, in a sense that was difficult to pinpoint, a caretaker. He took care of things. A person shouldn't live like that. Caretakers were servants.

Well, Delia thought, laughing inwardly as she did an inventory of cartons of soup, she should talk. He came by it honestly. If only he would leave that dreadful little city snuggled away in Michigan! But he seemed to like it. Still, it was no place for a Jew; big cities had all the advantages. The doctors were more expert, the concerts had more adventurous programs, the friends conversed more freely, and you could get a few of the amenities, including the *New York Times* delivered to your doorstep every morning—you didn't go around in a cloud of unknowing.

And then Delia let her thoughts drift to her other son, to Howie, who had moved, first to Oakland and then to Moraga and then to Berkeley and then back to Oakland, and who seemed, just now, to have a steady job, working, as he said, "in retail," though he still occasionally called her and asked for a bit of money (he called these loans "investments"), the scamp, and because Delia liked having a purpose in Howie's life, she could never refuse him. He had grown used to having money around and missed it terribly when it was no longer there. It wouldn't end well, Delia feared, it wouldn't end well at all, but once they had emerged into their own lives, your children's fragility was theirs and not yours. Handsome Howie, her bankrupt baby. Who was so attractive that his looks had been his fate in life but who seemed to love . . . well, anyone? Who knew?

The thought of her younger son disturbed her, so she called up images of her grandchildren, Mary Esther, and the baby, Theo, who had been born with a handsome face but also a birthmark on his arm, an odd disfigurement in the shape of the state of Vermont. But it was tucked away where no one could see, thank God, and he'd been born with ten fingers and ten toes, and Delia had been there two weeks after he was born, and, my goodness, he was such a quiet and intelligent-looking child. His sister was already developing a mouth on her. She said, when she saw her little brother, that she wanted to throw him into the wastebasket.

She had watched Saul dressing Emmy in her snowsuit. As a father, he exhibited great tenderness, which had a touch of vanity in it, but even so . . .

Delia realized that she had lost count, by virtue of her daydreaming, and returned to her work. As she did, she heard the sound of two cars colliding out on the street. Immediately she looked up and saw through the doorway a man in a threadbare suit getting out of his car dazedly. In front of him, a teenager, a girl, sat behind the wheel of her car, on her face a broad staring smile, of shock. Her car's windshield had cracked in a spiderweb pattern where her head had struck it, and blood was beginning to ooze down from her forehead toward her self-sustaining grin. In slow motion, her hands lifted themselves to her face, to feel it, to detect if it was still there. Delia dropped what she was doing to rush out to the street, to try to help, to murmur some consolation to the threadbare man and the smiling bleeding girl.

Twenty-six

The strands of toilet paper—were they like a set of icicles? or delicate traceries on a canvas? or thin cirrus clouds? or the white strings of misaligned protein molecules collecting in the wasting brain hemispheres of an Alzheimer patient?—the white strands of toilet paper hung down from the branches of Saul and Patsy's tree in the front yard: ugly, and malice-begotten, and, finally, defeating all comparison. It was just toilet paper thrown into the tree. Patsy, seeing it there while stepping outside to get the morning paper, called out, "Saul! Goddamn it, Saul. Get out of bed and come see what they've done to us this time!"

After a few moments, during which Patsy watched a robin's attempt to fly between the tree's branches and the dangling toilet paper, Saul came shuffling onto the front stoop, rubbing his face violently with both hands. He put his palm on Patsy's shoulder for balance as he lifted his left foot to scratch his right leg near the knee. Gazing at the tree, he said, with what seemed to be a tremendous effort at remaining calm, "Blue sky today. You know, I've really *got* to quit my job. Yeah," he said, agreeing with himself, and nodding, "today is the perfect day for it, a blue-sky quitting day." He breathed his stale dream-breath on her. "Today I quit." Another pause. "I am no longer an educator. Today I am an uneducator."

Patsy glanced at her husband, sizing him up. Hard to think of what else he would do with himself if he wasn't in a classroom. Nor could she imagine what the world would welcome from him. Unemployment, maybe: the world would be happy to have Saul in no occupation whatsoever.

"Look," he said, pointing. "They've painted the lawn blue." She followed his pointing finger as directed. Yes, indeed, the little troop of local thugs had found some blue house paint and had poured it over their grass in no particular pattern. Vandal action painting alfresco. A blue lawn—she had never wanted such a thing or heard of it, except in a book she had once read. "He had come a long way to this blue lawn"—it was the only phrase she could remember from whatever book it was. Well, *she* had come a long way to *this* blue lawn, but this time the blue lawn wasn't a metaphor but an object of the adolescent devils of the community, still excitable boys and girls, still intent on destruction.

Saul shuffled back into the house, fingering his nose. In the early morning he sometimes reminded her of a grumpy old man, coughing, as spiky as a pincushion, plagued with odd odors, opinionated and rather unclean.

You didn't get rid of a contagion by blessing and burying its unquiet spirit, Patsy thought, as she went back inside to help Emmy get up and get dressed, and Theo diapered and fed. She had told him so and she was right. The unquiet spirits once stirred to action stayed stirred until they could manage some blood-spilling mayhem. Then they cooled down. Or else: they never would cool down. In the myths people lived by, devils stayed hot forever, perpetually fevered and licked by flames.

He wasn't about to go to medical school or law school—Patsy understood *that*, at least. He had an abiding distaste for doctors as a class, and an equal distrust of lawyers—like bottleflies at the scene of illness and trouble. He didn't want to turn himself into either one and had said so. In any case, his family on both sides was overpopulated with dermatologists and radiologists and litigators and patent attorneys and estate plan-

ners. They were all formidably short-tempered and quite well-off;
Howie, of course, was the exception. Their topics of conversation often
seemed to be limited to their golf games and their investment portfolios.
A few waxed eloquent about their remodeled kitchens and their trips to
Cancún. Saul had one uncle who could talk learnedly for an hour about
his Sub-Zero refrigerator and his Vulcan gas stove. This mania for appli-
ances was attached to both the men and the women. Their professions
had addled them and reduced their sympathetic imaginations to small
vestigial stumps.

No, Patsy thought, as she roused Emmy and helped her into her day-
care outfit, whatever Saul decided to do with his adulthood, he would not
go into one of those professions.

Soon after he had showered and shaved, taken Theo out of his crib
and into his high chair in the kitchen, Saul called the superintendent of
schools and then the principal, to let them know he wouldn't be coming
in today, or, for that matter, ever. He was resigning. Vermilya and
Kabeláč both tried to argue with Saul, to persuade him to return to his
job. He genially refused. They assumed, they both said, that this resignation was a joke of some sort, a grandstanding gesture, a "stunt" (Vermilya), an "opening move from Mr. Don Quixote" (Kabeláč), because if
it was meant seriously, it was unprofessional and, Vermilya said—probably by accident—grounds for dismissal. Besides, schoolteachers never
resigned voluntarily, Kabeláč informed him in his nasal voice. Saul was
sitting on the living-room sofa listening to Kabeláč, the telephone cradled on his shoulder. In the kitchen, Patsy was spooning baby food into
Theo while Emmy ate her cereal. Kabeláč continued with his theories
about schoolteachers. *They didn't have the nerve for actual unemployment. Nor
could they exist in the real world, with authentic jobs. This was why they taught: to
evade both employment and unemployment.* This was exactly the sort of person
Saul was, Kabeláč continued: a teacher, unfit for the rigors of competi-
tion out there in the dog-eat-dog American business scene. Saul wasn't
doing, therefore, what he said he was doing.

"Zoltan, you knucklehead," Saul said, "this is counterproductive argumentation you're engaged in."

"Come on, Saul," Kabeláč pleaded. "As a friend, I'm advising you: stop with the quitting. We need you down here. We can all understand why you would want to do this, but—"

"No," he said. "I can't do it anymore. My heart wouldn't be in it. I've got that kid's blood to think about, and besides, I need to do something else. When I've thought about it, I'll let you know what I'm going to do. Goodbye, Zoltan. You're a good guy—and I know this'll inconvenience you and everything, and I'm sorry about that."

"I won't ever write you a recommendation," Zoltan said. "You'll be unrecommended."

"Okay," Saul said happily, before he hung up. He liked the idea of being unrecommendable.

That day, on her way home from work—the newly unemployed Saul had taken Theo and picked up Emmy in their recently purchased used car—Patsy found herself at the Valu-Rite checkout line, with a pile of Bartlett pears, three grapefruit, a small bag of apples, and a bottle of cheap domestic champagne from the U.S.A., penny-pinching budget bubbles. She planned to celebrate Saul's unemployment that evening with the booze and fresh fruit. Going unemployed was one of the braver actions he had ever taken. It was as if he had borrowed a leaf from Howie's book; perhaps there was a correspondence in the two brothers' genetic infrastructure that gave them a tropism toward indolence, lassitude, laziness, apathy, lusterlessness, acedia, disinterest. Then again, perhaps not.

"Uh, miss?" the checkout clerk said. "Your credit card?"

"Yes?" Patsy asked.

The clerk was a short, mostly pretty young woman with blond hair, a hard, narrow, birdlike face, and turquoise fingernail polish. She had, however, minimum-wage bags under her eyes, the result of working long hours for low pay and few benefits. She was, Patsy guessed, gradually going to fat: frustration-eating would soon be having its effects on her. She probably had a boyfriend who sometimes hit her where it didn't show.

"Your credit card didn't go through," the clerk said.

"What?" Patsy stood up straighter, to give herself more stature. She was, after all, a loan officer at the Five Oaks National Bank and Trust. "That's impossible."

The clerk shrugged. "We can try it again." Patsy ran the card through the reading-strip once more. Again the message came back: *Credit Refused*.

"I don't know what the matter is," Patsy said. "This never happens."

The clerk gazed at her, the smallest ghost of a smile appearing on her face. "Well," she said, "you could always pay in cash."

Patsy took her wallet from her purse and opened it. There was no cash inside. Patsy felt herself suddenly reddening. Behind her, three people stood in the checkout line, watching her, shifting their weight from one foot to the other. Patsy seldom bothered with cash anymore except for small purchases like candy and breath mints and gum. But she thought she had stashed a few dollars in there. And where was the two-dollar bill she kept in her wallet permanently, for luck? Also missing, and anyway insufficient for pears and sparkling wine.

"I don't know what's gone wrong with the card," Patsy said.

"Maybe you hit your limit and your credit ran out," the blond girl said before reddening and putting her hand up in front of her mouth. "I'm sorry," she said. "I didn't mean to say that."

Patsy looked up at the ceiling and then at the floor. She felt nervous sweat on her back and under her arms, as this strange public humiliation continued. "I don't suppose you offer credit," she joked. She reached into the wallet and pulled out a quarter.

"No," the clerk said, her ghost-smile now, just under the surface of things, turning to visible annoyance, her teeth beginning to show, an animal grimace.

"Do you have a public phone?" Patsy asked.

"Over there," the clerk said, without gesturing. "Over there, by the doors."

"Is it okay if I leave my groceries here?"

"Yeah, well—I'll put them off to the side," the clerk said. "But I can't leave them there for long."

"You won't have to," Patsy said. "I'm calling my husband."

. . .

Waiting at the automatic doors for Saul and Emmy, Patsy thought of the enchanted carnal moments she and Saul had had when they first met and first made love as two sensual animals on fire with each other. That ended with the onset of marriage and routine and childbirth and child care and fatigue and day-to-day indifference. But, after all, *this* was what their marriage had come to: they depended almost blindly upon each other to get each other out of trouble; they were easing each other through this life. About Saul you could always say, *He's dependable.* If he said that he'd be at Emmy's day-care center at three in the afternoon, he would be there. He wouldn't forget about Theo for a minute. If he said that he would pick up a friend at the airport, he would not forget the date. If you were in trouble, he would drop everything and get you out of trouble if he could; if you were itchy, he would make love to you, and if your back ached, he would rub it. He had once been an educator, until someone died. Now he was in search of an occupation. He was comfortably self-centered, though the caretaker side of him would never go away, and he was probably no woman's fantasy of a mate, but, sitting near the automatic doors of the Valu-Rite, Patsy waited for him, and at the moment when he walked in, carrying Theo in a front-pack and Emmy on his shoulders, he smiled and waved at his wife, and she almost wept.

In the woods behind their house, a shrine had developed on the site where the ashes of Gordy Himmelman were said to be buried. An underclass of mourners skittered into the woods during the day and early evening and left behind their remembrances: packets of chewing gum, and a standing red-and-silver pinwheel that twirled when the wind caught it, and a carved yellow dog, and a few flowers here and there, and gold and blue ribbons; and a glass piggy bank with pennies inside it halfway up, as far as the pig's tail, and more toys, including a battery-powered electric car, and several plastic figures of X-men, though the figures were mostly Wolverine, with his fingernails out, ready for combat; and more little flowers pasted onto the nearby trees, and a wooden cross

with GORDY, WE MISS YOU written on it. It looked like a Mexican cemetery plot for a child, or a roadside shrine where someone had died in an
accident, and day by day, week by week, the toys and decorations and
flowers accumulated, and when Patsy walked out to visit it, as she did
from time to time, she was at first horrified, then surprised, and then,
finally, accustomed to the sudden involuntary appearance of her own
tears. The tears had once belonged to Saul, but now they were hers, too.

After first thinking that he would make a good funeral director, a first-
class assistant to Binch, a man he had instantly taken a shine to, Saul told
Patsy that the profession was, in fact, too much like being a doctor,
though he suspected that the daily sight of corpses going in and out of
the funeral home would calm his nerves and bring him spiritual qui-
etude. There was something peaceful about a dead body, Saul informed
Patsy. She listened to these opinions without comment.

Finally, at last, he had a good idea: he drove over to the *Five Oaks News-
Chronicle* and offered his services as a columnist, three or four columns a
week, to be titled "The Bloviator." The features editor to whom he
applied had never heard of the word and said that they certainly weren't
going to hire Saul as that, or as anything else.

Saul offered to write a sample column, full of excellent opinion. He
would bloviate.

On the day Saul brought back his first column, the features editor was
short on copy and ran the piece on spec, close to the editorial page,
where he thought it wouldn't attract much attention. The column that
day was titled "Why Quit? A Manifesto," and it caused a great deal of
furor in Five Oaks, resulting in an increase in circulation and several
angry letters.

The angry letters continued and peppered the editorial page—the
anti-Semitic ones were discreetly screened—but the bloviator had apparently managed to help keep the newspaper's circulation on the rise, and
Saul was made a permanent fixture of Five Oaks discourse.

Behind the house the pinwheels and toys and flowers and signs began
to fade and to grow sodden.

. . .

Saul is currently on a campaign to rid the city of WaldChem and its toxic chemical plant, and he has begun to write about factory-farms just out-side of town with their relentless pollution of the groundwater.

Patsy sometimes is approached in the bank by people who ask if she is married to that jerk—one person used the word "scum"—who writes for the paper. She usually smiles and points to a laminated letter to the editor she has put up on the wall behind her desk. The print is so small that no one can read it without walking behind her desk, and no one ever does that unless she invites them to do so. When they do read it, they often find it puzzling that she would be proud of her husband's having inspired such a letter.

To the editor:

I have been a resident of Five Oaks for forty-six years and have had to suffer a great deal of nonsense in my day but "Saul Bernstein's" recent column on his own so-called "personal" view of zoning in the southeast corner of the city just about beats anything. Whatever gives this blowhard the confidence to criticize the fine businesspeople in the city who are all for growth and prosperity? You can't have an omelet without a few eggs. This bloviator fellow—I believe his name as printed in the paper is a pseudonym—is an enemy to employment, to business, to profit, to life liberty and the persuit of happiness and I happen to believe that the oldstyle tar-and-feathers is too good for him. If he was in charge we would all be on welfare in a welfare state taking orders from Mr. Big, who would be him. He writes like he owns the secrets to the universe and I for one am fed up and am cancelling my subscription to the newspaper. I encourage other likeminded folks to do the same. No good society was ever made from the likes of him.

Yours sincerely,
Floyd Muscat

Patsy's heart is gladdened every time she reads Floyd Muscat's letter. It is always pleasing when a man finds his true vocation, as Saul has, and can inspire fervor in others.

Twenty-seven

One summer day, on his way home from his new job, Saul passed through a recently constructed residential neighborhood close to his own new home on Kingfisher Road. He and Patsy had moved again, for a bit more space. This particular location he was driving by now was where, years ago, he and Patsy had first lived in the rented house with loose brown aluminum siding. All the farmland surrounding it had been leveled and developed into a subdivision. He decided to motor around and snoop. He had about twenty minutes before he needed to get home, but he was curious about housing developments where no trees had yet been planted, how people lived in such places, without shadows, exposed to everything, saturated with sunlight and wide open to the elements.

About three blocks in, on the sidewalk, close to the curb, he saw a girl who seemed to be about ten years old sitting behind a card table, reading a book. Behind her, shadeless, on its narrow lot, the vinyl-sided, two-story house stood, stark with optimism and sanitation. The girl had light red hair in pigtails and a white dress cinched by a red patent-leather belt, and she wore patent-leather black shoes. She sat with her arms crossed, the book flattened on the table in front of her. Her face was not cute but defiant. On the table, along with the book, was a small cardboard box for cash, a lemonade pitcher, a few Dixie Cups, and some oddly shaped objects Saul couldn't make out from his car. Next to the table, facing the street, was a large cardboard sign with block letters written in thick green ink.

LEMONADE
AND OTHER THINGS
BUY SOME

It had been a long day; Saul was thirsty and desired lemonade. It had always been his habit to stop for curbside children selling their wares. After parking the car and wiping his forehead with his sleeve, he approached the little girl's stand while fingering the change in his pocket. He had several quarters. It would be enough, he thought.

"Good afternoon. I'd like some lemonade, please," he said. As he advanced upon the table, he saw that the oddly shaped objects that he hadn't been able to make out before were stones, plain stones from the ground.

The little girl glanced up from her book and examined him. "Okay. That'll be one dollar fifty," she said.

Saul reached into his wallet. "Well," he said, "that's a bit more than I expected. I only have three quarters. I do have a five-dollar bill, if you have change."

"No," the little girl said. "I don't have change." She seemed bored or obscurely dissatisfied with Saul. "I don't have any change at all." She lifted up the small cardboard box and then quickly dropped it. No coins clinked.

"Well, what else do you have for sale? I could buy five dollars' worth of stuff."

"These stones," the little girl said. "I have some stones you can buy." She pointed at the stones on the table. "I picked them out myself."

"I don't get it," Saul said. "Why should I buy stones from you? I can get stones anywhere."

"These stones," the little girl said, "are magic." She glanced up at him to see if he believed her. She had strange azure eyes. The eyes didn't go with the hair, or with anything else about her.

"What do the stones do?"

"What do you want them to do?" she asked. She was a clever little girl.

"Oh, I don't know," Saul said. "Make me rich. Cure the common cold."

"Well," she said, "they can't do that." She pretended to go back to reading her book. She peered at the words and turned a page after slowly and rather sensually rubbing it between her thumb and index finger.

"If they can't do that, then what *can* they do?"

"What do you want them to do?" she repeated.

"I just told you," Saul said. He twisted around to see the title of the book she was reading. She had lifted it up as if for inspection. There was a horse on the cover. It was something called *Heaven Is a Wind Swept Hill.*

"No, I mean, what *else* do you want them to do?" she asked, without looking up.

"Help me find objects around the house that I've lost."

"They can't do that, either."

"Name one thing that these stones can do, then," Saul told her, irritated by the privileges the girl had assumed were hers just because she was a child. "Or I won't buy any of your damn lemonade."

"Don't be so mean," the girl said, glaring at him. "All right." She sat up. "These stones can mend a broken heart."

"Oh, right," Saul said. "What do you know about broken hearts?"

"You think I'm just a little girl, don't you?"

"Well, that's the way it looks right now."

"Actually," the little girl said, "I'm actually a very old woman. I'm actually a witch. I'm *ancient.* I only look like a girl."

"Have it your way," Saul said. "So, how much are the stones? Their price, I mean."

"I could sell you this one for four dollars." She pointed at a gray, nondescript rock.

"That's a lot of money for a rock. Do you have anything else for sale?"

"Yes," the little girl said. "The number five."

"Excuse me?"

The girl's face had settled down into dailiness, and she looked bored again. She turned a page of her book with a self-satisfied flick of her hand. "I own all the rights to the number five," she said smugly. "You can buy the rights from me if you want to use the number five this afternoon and tomorrow morning."

"You're crazy," Saul said. The adjective just slipped out before he remembered that he shouldn't say things like that to children.

"That's what you think," the girl said. "You're the crazy one. I'm as sane as a sunbird."

"My apologies. What happens if I use the number five without getting your permission? What then, little girl?" When he saw her expression of contempt, he added, "I'm just asking."

"It won't work," she said. "You can *try* to use the number five, but it won't work. It'll be wrong. All your arithmetic will be false, and you'll be mistaken, and you will fail."

"That's a new one. Where'd you get the rights to the number five?" Saul asked.

"They gave it to me," she told him.

"Who's this 'they'?"

"Oh, I can't tell you. That would be telling. They're pretty scary."

"I bet they are. Okay," Saul said. "I think I see what's going on here. So, I guess I'll have one cup of your lemonade, please, and that rock, the one that mends broken hearts, and the use of the number five for this evening and tomorrow morning."

"That'll be seven dollars," the little girl said.

"Seven dollars! Too much, I say," said Saul. "Five dollars. Take it or leave it." Maybe he would get a column out of this, an exposé of lemonade stands.

"Oh, all right," the girl grumbled. She slapped her neck, as if a mosquito had bitten her there. She poured Saul his lemonade, handed him his rock, and dropped his five-dollar bill into the cardboard box. Saul took his first sip of the lemonade. It was wonderful, just the right combination of sweetness and sourness, the best lemonade he had had in a long time.

"Do you live around here?" he asked. "Here? In River Pines Estates?"

"Yeah." She waited, as if in thought. "But I won't tell you where."

"Did you make this lemonade?" He took another sip. "It's wonderful."

"Thank you. My mom and I made it out of lemons," she said, "plus the secret ingredient. Do you have children?" She was gazing at the Chevy.

"I have a daughter," Saul said, "four years old, and a son. Theodore. He's a year old."

"Who's that in the car?"

Saul didn't turn around to look. "Nobody. There's nobody there."

The little girl made a face at the car, a disagreeable and taunting expression, the way she'd look at any boy she didn't know.

"Okay," she said, shrugging her shoulders. She leaned back and closed her eyes in a deliberately languorous manner seemingly imitated from the paintings of Balthus. Saul, alarmed by this preadolescent display, put the little girl's stone in his pocket, finished his lemonade, gave her the Dixie Cup, and returned to the Chevy. Then he drove home, having turned the rearview mirror upward so that he wouldn't be distracted by whatever might have been back there.

At home, later that evening, after singing to Theo and reading Emmy a story, he put the stone—surrounded by bubble wrap—into a mailing box, which he addressed to his mother, together with a note telling her to keep the enclosed on her dresser. Maybe he should return and buy one for his brother and another for Brenda Bagley. Yes, he would do that. Secretly he had admired the little girl, who had found her vocation— salesmanship that thrived on indifference, peddling worthless commodities, infused with auras, to strangers—and, gazing down the hallway to where Patsy was sitting with Theo asleep in her lap, he thought with gratitude of his own skills and gifts, such as they were.

About the Author

Charles Baxter lives in Minneapolis and teaches at the University of Minnesota. He is the author of seven previous works of fiction, including the 2000 National Book Award finalist *The Feast of Love*.